THE
WATCHMEN

THE
WATCHMEN

Brian Freemantle

THOMAS DUNNE BOOKS

ST. MARTIN'S PRESS

NEW YORK

THOMAS DUNNE BOOKS.
An imprint of St. Martin's Press.

www.stmartins.com

Library of Congress Cataloging-in-Publication Data

Freemantle, Brian.
    The watchmen / Brian Freemantle.—1st ed.
      p. cm.
    ISBN 0-312-24274-3
    1. Government investigators—Fiction. 2. Biological warfare—Fiction. 3. New York (N.Y.)—Fiction. 4. Organized crime—Fiction. 5. Terrorism—Fiction. 6. Russia—Fiction. I. Title.
PR6056.R43 W38 2002
823'.914—dc21

2001051305

First Edition: March 2002

10 9 8 7 6 5 4 3 2 1

To Lizzie and Denis Riley, with love

Author's Note

The Watchmen, a work of total fiction, was conceived and completed several months before the terrorist attack of September 11, 2001, upon the New York World Trade Center and the Pentagon and the anthrax-outbreak aftermath. While I felt it logically necessary to make minimal reference to those events at the proof stage, this book is in no way predicated upon the atrocities of September 11, nor did I in any way draw upon them.

Winchester, 2001

The watchmen that went about the city found me, they smote me, they wounded me; the keeper of the walls took away my veil from me.

—Song of Solomon

THE
WATCHMEN

1

There is never a moment of the day or night when the United Nations' buildings between New York's East River and First Avenue are completely unoccupied, but just after dawn, when the missile hit, the green-glassed, skyscraper Secretariat Tower, is one of the emptiest periods, which was fortunate. What was later to be described as a miracle was not immediately recognized.

Five people—three night-duty clerks and two cleaners—died instantly when the missile smashed into that level of the tower at which China has its secretariat.

By the diplomatic treaty under which the United Nations complex came into being in 1947, the land upon which its three buildings are constructed is international, not American. And does not, therefore, come under American jurisdiction or legal authority. Initially the Chinese refused any New York emergency service access to what was technically Chinese territory, not even to confirm the deaths or remove the bodies. The impasse was broken when the incumbent secretary-general, an Egyptian, pointed out to China's UN ambassador in an outside corridor confrontation that the deaths and damage so far had apparently been caused only by the impact of the device, not by the detonation of its warhead, which could presumably occur at any moment. The ambassador still insisted that two totally unprotected members of his staff accompany an armor-suited NYPD bomb disposal team into the wrecked area.

It is standard operating procedure for such teams to work with live television and audio equipment, for their every action and movement to be permanently recorded for analysis in the event of a devastating mistake, which was how the image of the missile came to be instantly relayed beyond the shattered offices even before the unit assembled itself and its other paraphernalia. The main television monitor was in the control truck far below in the flag-bedecked forecourt fronting First Avenue. The intermediary link in the outside corridor, being watched by both the secretary-general and the ambassador, was operated by a nervous police technician named Ivan Bykov, who could read and speak the Russian language of his immigrant grandparents and whose potential catastrophe-limiting contribution was never recognized.

The virtually intact missile had come to rest against the wall of the fourth office in from the East River with the lettering on it toward the approaching camera. Bykov's lips moved as he read the Cyrillic script, which he did twice before experiencing the first panicked awareness that he could already be dying. The words wouldn't come at his first effort but then he managed: "Stop!" although too weak for it to register through the headsets of the disposal team. Then the panic took hold and the warning came out as a scream. "Stop! For fuck's sake stop! Get back out of there!"

The camera—and the squad—stopped. The unit commander said, "What?"

Bykov said, "The third word in, on the top line. It says *poison*, in Russian. The next word is *agent*. It's a biological or chemical warhead. If it's fractured, it's leaking already."

The unit commander said, "Fuck. We're dead," and when the recording was replayed later, he couldn't believe he'd sounded as calm as he did. He couldn't remember, either, leaving the camera focused on the broken-necked missile, although he later publicly claimed it had been a positive decision.

The secretary-general realized at once that if microbiological agents were already leaking from the warhead, his life couldn't be saved and reacted with a selfless bravery that was later to be internationally acknowledged. He issued instant although probably futile orders for the Secretariat Tower to be totally evacuated for the first time in its history, remaining himself on the possibly infected floor because it was quicker to use the telephones there than go to his own suite. From an office that had functioned as the Chinese delegation mailroom, he spoke, in carefully considered order of priority, to New York's mayor, for Manhattan first to be closed to early-morning commuter traffic; then its residents and already arrived workers had to be cleared off the island. Having done that, he spoke directly to the American secretary of state and the president. The Russian ambassador to the UN was the second representative of the five permanent UN members nations to whom he spoke: China's earlier obstructive envoy was by then urging his driver to go faster to the already backed-up Hudson River tunnel to reach New Jersey.

On the direct instructions of the FBI director, the helicopter carrying the microbiological scientists from Fort Detrick, Maryland, detoured to Andrews Air Force Base to pick up William Cowley, head of the bureau's Russian Desk. As Cowley hurried aboard, head bent, James Schnecker, the leader of the scientific unit, said, "You think it's happening all over again?"

"At the moment I don't know what to think," said Cowley. For once there wouldn't have been any guilt in taking a drink. He wished he had one.

Patrick Hollis gazed in numbed disbelief at the scenes being relayed on the breakfast nook television, his stomach in turmoil. It should have been only a game—*was* a game—the sort he played on the war sites most nights. Not this. Not real. The General had tricked him. Told him that's what a quartermaster's function was, to guarantee supplies, and persuaded him to disclose how a campaign could be financed. Not a problem, Hollis decided, in relieved self-assurance. That's what his pseudonym was, anonymously to roam and hack wherever he chose, unknown and unsuspected by anyone else. The Quartermaster. A soldier. Not Patrick Hollis, manager of loans and securities. He could never be caught. Found out.

"It couldn't reach us here at Rensselaer, could it?"

Hollis physically jumped at his mother's voice, from the stove.

"No," he said. "We're safe." Where had the General gotten it? How? People didn't actually die in war games. Not a game, not anymore.

"There's more waffles."

"I'm not hungry."

"You've got to keep your strength up; you're not strong."

"No more, thank you."

"You sure we've safe?"

"Quite sure."

"I really wouldn't know what to do without you, Patrick."

"You're never going to need to find out, are you?"

2

The protective suits had been developed from those designed by
NASA for space and moon walks, completely isolating and insulating
the wearer from all outside environment. There was internal temperature control, with oxygen provided by built-in backpacks. The
head domes had a dual relay voice system, for every conversation
between them to be simultaneously recorded and monitored.

Schnecker ordered his three-man team to suit up very soon after
the helicopter's liftoff from Andrews, predominantly to acclimatize
Cowley. Schnecker took the FBI man through the operating procedure, repeatedly insisting that the protection was total, providing
the suit skin was not punctured.

"And from the look of it there's a lot of sharp-edged crap to
avoid," warned the bearded scientist, indicating the uneven, sometimes broken pictures from the abandoned bomb squad television
camera that were being patched into the helicopter during the flight.
"How's it feel?"

Cowley was a big man, six foot two and with neglected college
football muscle taking him just over 200 pounds. He shrugged the
suit around him, tensing his shoulders, and said, "OK, I guess."

Schnecker said, "Make sure you see where you're going before
you move. And when you do, do it slowly."

Neil Hamish, the team's ballistic expert, looked up from the manual he had been comparing with the TV pictures and said, "Nothing
like it here. Looks like a double delivery. Binary principle, maybe."
He looked sideways at Cowley and in a molasses-thick Tennessee
accent said, "You make out the writing on the side?"

"The word's definitely *poison*. And *agent*," replied Cowley.

"Like to know what I'm asking the meters to detect," complained the third scientist, Richard Pointdexter. He had two devices with calibrated dials tethered by individual straps to his wrist.

"Me, too," said the fourth man, Hank Burgess, attaching a matching detector to his arm.

"All we can do is play the field for the obvious," judged Schnecker.

"Jesus George Christ!"

The pilot's voice brought them away from their protective preparations and the picture-split television monitor. New York was on the absolute horizon. Between them and the faraway view was a surreal, tidal-wave imagery of vehicles of every type and description surging along every road and highway but all in the same direction, away from the jagged-toothed Manhattan skyline. In too many places to count, as they flew over and against the one-way movement, there were jams and bulged blocks of collided cars and trucks, the obstructions swollen by the frantic but failed efforts of following drivers to detour through adjoining fields and properties.

Hamish said, "Like Orson Welles and *War of the Worlds* all over again."

Schnecker asked, "What's the current wind direction?"

The pilot said, "Southeast, tending northerly. Slow."

Schnecker said, "None of them down there are in the slightest danger. If it's been released, it's going over Brooklyn."

"What about Brooklyn?" Cowley asked.

"Until we identify what it is, we won't know how containable it is," the leader of the microbiological team replied.

"The only man in the bomb disposal team to be showing any respiratory affect is asthmatic," Burgess, a qualified doctor, reminded them. "They were in the proximity of the warhead for precisely three minutes and forty seconds; that's long enough to have picked up something,"

"We don't know the warhead: how it's programmed to operate," Hamish pointed out.

"Or who launched it," said Cowley.

"Your problem, buddy, not ours," said Schnecker.

"We get the easy part," said Pointdexter.

"Will you look at that!" demanded the pilot, who had flown far to the west of New Jersey to skirt any airborne contamination, finally approaching Manhattan from the north, from upstate New York to keep the wind behind them.

Cowley decided he was perfectly dressed for the sterile moonscape that was his immediate impression of the city below them. There *was* movement—there were emergency units at the island side of the Triboro and the Brooklyn bridges and a swarm of media helicopters infesting the sky overhead—but the gridlocked streets below appeared as eerily deserted but as haphazardly traffic-blocked by panic-abandoned vehicles as any Hollywood depiction that Cowley had ever seen of a nuclear attack. And then as Cowley gazed down more intently—continuing the Hollywood script—he picked out more isolated pockets of people, presumably playing out the end of their world.

A group were dancing in what appeared to be a street party by Columbus Circle, and there was another partying gathering outside the Tavern on the Green in Central Park. Tables had been pulled out from a restaurant or café and set up in a gap of abandoned traffic on Broadway. Cowley counted twelve people sitting around bottles of looted wine, apparently determined to die drunk. One man was already lying full length and motionless in the gutter. As they passed overhead, two women looked up and waved. One inexplicably lifted her sweater to expose her braless breasts. Some still-burning movie and theater lights added to the party atmosphere. A lot more looting was visible as they finally turned to cross town, although most of the loot—from Macy's in Times Square and along 42nd Street—seemed quickly to have been discarded outside the stores from which it had been stolen. One man was determinedly pushing a cart loaded with television sets and microwave ovens up Lexington Avenue, whirling his free hand in dismissal to the fluttering machines overhead.

Schnecker checked William Cowley's suit and said, "Everything OK?"

Cowley nodded without replying, conscious of other helicopters coming in on them as their own slowly descended. He was surprised there was sufficient space to land directly in front of the UN complex.

Looking at the other camera-sprouting helicopters swarmed above them, Hamish said, "Here's our fifteen minutes of fame."

Schnecker said, "Let's keep the conversation to its regulated essentials. Count-off time. Cowley?"

"Ready."

"Hamish?"

"Ready."

"Pointdexter?"

"OK."

"Burgess?"

"Let's see what we've got."

Although also protectively suited, the pilot didn't turn off the rotors, so they left the machine bent forward and in single file, Schnecker leading. Everyone except Cowley carried various pieces of equipment, some unseen in oddly shaped containers. Directly out of the downdraft they stopped, at Schnecker's gesture. Pointdexter and Burgess stared down at the dials of the calibrated meters held in front of them, like temple offerings. Pointdexter said, formally, "The time is nine of ten. There is negative register at ground level."

Burgess said, "I confirm."

Cowley hadn't expected to be able to move so easily. His sweat, he supposed, was nervousness, not a malfunction of the suit's temperature control. He didn't consciously feel nervous. Neil Hamish moved slightly to one side, operating their own shoulder-held television camera to track their every movement. Cowley acknowledged that their film, as well as their every verbal comment—like the earlier footage and remarks of the NYPD bomb disposal unit—was for corrective assessment if the five of them were overcome and died. He wished he could think of something profound to contribute; so far his only sound had been noisy breathing of his oxygen. He wondered if Pauline was watching a television relay from one of the overhead helicopters. The voices of the others were distorted, with a metallic echo, and he didn't expect she'd recognize his if he spoke. He certainly wouldn't be identifiable encompassed in his moon suit and didn't expect the bureau to name him. They would, if he died.

They huddled around Pointdexter and Burgess directly inside the Secretariat Tower vestibule. Maintaining formality, Pointdexter said, "Nine-fifteen. Still negative register."

"Confirm," said Burgess, bent over his meter.

"Let's take our time," coaxed Schnecker. "Repeat the full check."

Both monitoring scientists did so without protest. Pointdexter said, "I repeat, nothing."

There was a moment of uncertainty before Schnecker said, "Electricity's still on, so let's use the elevators," and then at once raised a warning hand. "Too many for one car in these suits and with all this equipment. Me, Hamish, and Pointdexter in one, Burgess and Cowley in the other."

Cowley didn't feel himself sweating anymore. Hamish filmed their exit from the second elevator. The first three men weren't waiting as a courtesy gesture, Cowley guessed; procedure probably required confirmation of no chemical or biological agent from Burgess's meter, which the man gave at once.

Schnecker said, "I'm beginning to think everyone's been lucky."

"I don't know the type of warhead," reminded the ballistics expert. "Maybe what's inside it is new to us, too."

They didn't need the floor plan, which was Cowley's FBI contribution. Through a gaping hole that spread from a distorted window frame, the East River was clearly visible to their right, where the corridor that bands the skyscraper at every level curled away. The wrecked offices were ripped open for examination on their left. Two internal walls were collapsed, their remains barely supporting the falling-in ceiling, which looked to have burst an outside wall. An internal door was bowed but unbroken by the pressure of debris from above. Another door had disappeared, leaving only its buckled frame. The wind, which hadn't seemed strong at ground level, whined through the gaps in the outer wall, constantly swirling papers and documents, many of which were slowly leaking out to drift over the river. All five men jumped at the sound of a telephone from one of the open-doored offices behind them.

Burgess said, "Damned double-glazing salesman!" and Hamish laughed.

Schnecker said, "Let's pass on the comedy," and led the way

forward until they reached the fourth office. The door had crumpled inwards and faced them with jagged splinters, like a medieval animal or man trap. None of the intervening walls remained, and a domino fall of cabinets, all their drawers burst open, seemed to mark the passage of the disjointed missile that lay in front of the hurriedly discarded police camera. To their right there was virtually cleared space to the gaping hole through which the rocket had entered.

The five bodies were in the farthest office, although that of one of the cleaners wasn't to be discovered beneath the collapsed roof for another week. The rocket had totally decapitated the two clerks. The body of the other cleaner appeared to have suffered no visible injury. Neither had that of the fourth clerk, who still remained upright on a chair.

"Poor bastards," said Hamish. "It would have been instantaneous, though."

Cowley realized that, incredibly, the missile had entered perfectly through an actual window, the glass of which would have presented no obstacle and probably accounted for the warhead remaining intact. All the other damage would have been caused by the peripheral shock waves. He said so and Schnecker agreed. Cowley was glad an astutely intelligent observation would go on record. He was at once embarrassed at the reflection in the close proximity of the dead people.

There were creaks of further settling masonry and a slight fall of dust and grit from what had once been an adjoining office. Schnecker said, "Don't touch anything that might be a support. It wouldn't take much to bring the roof in on us."

Hamish edged in first with his camera, keeping as far away as possible from the needle points of the shattered door. He turned off the police camera and said, "It *is* a first. Nothing like it in any of our manuals. Double-aligned canister warhead, estimated meter in length, estimated fifteen millimeters in circumference—"

"Damaged," Schnecker broke in. "Indentation to the left nose cone. We'll test before moving them. We can record the specifics from the pictures."

Burgess and Pointdexter stooped side by side, clicking their meter controls through test sequences. It was Pointdexter who said, "At nine thirty-two the warhead appears to be intact, with no evidence of leaking."

"Affirmative," confirmed Burgess.

Slowly, spacing the words, Schnecker said, "I am now going to move the warhead for the lettering to be deciphered. From the visual appearance, it looks as if it has snapped from the mountings of its delivery system, the fins and body of which are badly crushed and distorted. Hank . . . ?"

"Providing it is structurally safe to do so, I intend examining what could be the entry trajectory," took up Burgess. "I agree from what external examination is possible that at the soft point of impact, through the window, the device spun into reverse and that the inert delivery section of the missile and residual shock caused the damage."

"Which had the effect of shielding the nose cones and preventing the warhead from exploding to release whatever the contents are," completed Schnecker. "Ready with the detectors?"

"Affirmative," replied Pointdexter and Burgess in unison. They set their meters side by side, against the nearest canister edge.

From a bag he shrugged from his shoulder, Schnecker took matching, rubber-encased long-nosed pliers the mouths of which were adjustable by a shaft-mounted control knob to fit the diameter of an object. The team leader connected each grip individually to the top and bottom of the warhead, locking the jaws in place. He said, "Ten-oh-five. I am starting to lift. There appears to be no triggering attachment linking the warhead to its delivery rocket . . . no resistance from anything not externally visible . . . no register on any of the three detectors. . . . I am now turning the head, for the lettering to be visible . . ."

"Gorki," read Cowley, at once. "Plant 35. Numerals in spaced groups: 19 gap 38 gap 22 gap 22 gap zero. And sarin. The word is sarin, on the head nearest to me. Then comes the words poison, highly toxic. And an emergency telephone number: 8765323. The date is January 1974." He strained, as Schnecker slowly rotated the warhead now totally removed from its pod. "It says Gorki on the second arm. Plant 35. Different numeral markings: 20 gap 49 gap 88 gap zero gap six . . . and anthrax. The word is anthrax. The same date as on the first. And the same poison and toxicity warning. The same emergency telephone number. Definitely sarin on one, anthrax on the other."

In front of him, Pointdexter and Burgess finally calibrated their detectors to the chemical and biological agents. Pointdexter said, "There is no leak."

"Affirmative," said Burgess.

For the benefit of the relayed recording, Schnecker said, "We have recovered intact a dual-headed missile of a design unrecognizable to us. Manufacturing designation is Gorki, Russia, Plant 35. With the missile separated from its delivery rocket, it is possible to see at the base to which the head was originally fixed what appears to have been intended puncturing detonator pins." The team leader moved slightly for Hamish to bring his camera in closer. "Both are bent, one snapped completely off and lying on the floor below . . . I am now removing the warhead, separate from its delivery mechanism, from where it might be crushed by the further collapse of ceiling or room debris. . . . Technician Burgess will independently remove the delivery system."

Hamish said, "We don't have a neutralizing container it'll fit."

"We'll have to take it as it is—" began Schnecker, jerking to a stop at a rasping, tearing noise and then a burst of dust from the most badly damaged, river-fronting office as more ceiling fell in. "All out, slowly," he started again. "You really need that trajectory trace, Neil?"

"I'll be careful," the ballistics expert replied.

Everyone except Hamish walked back to the safety of the area immediately outside the elevator bank. Once there, Schnecker and Pointdexter transferred the warhead to a rubber-meshed carrying sling.

Schnecker said, "I'd like to get this back and safely locked away without any Washington detours."

"There'll be a lot for me to do here in New York, so I'll stay," said Cowley. Where should I begin? he wondered.

Everyone turned at Hamish's exit from the shattered offices farther along the corridor. At the empty door of the room in which the bodies lay, the man briefly crossed himself before coming toward them, patting the camera in satisfaction.

To the FBI division chief Schnecker said, "We'll have to stay suited up all the way back to Fort Meade, just in case this starts to leak, so you'll be safer here in New York anyway."

"How's that?" demanded Cowley.

It was Burgess who reached out, touching the tear in the left sleeve of Cowley's protective suit. Burgess said, "We probably could have saved you if only one had detonated, knowing what we were dealing with. But you'd have felt like hell for a very long time. Not so sure how you'd have been if both had gone off, like they were obviously intended to."

Furnishing his Ulitza Petrovka office with the latest available flat-screen television was one of several indulgences Dimitri Ivanovich Danilov allowed himself after his confirmation as operational director of Moscow's Organized Crime Bureau. Another was ensuring it received American CNN newscasts, which enabled him to watch live the unfolding events in New York. He'd wondered if Cowley had been the unnamed FBI official to whom the helicopter-borne reporters had referred, long before the familiar, overpowering figure, space suit discarded over his arm, walked from the UN tower slightly behind the rest of the group still in protective clothing. With Cowley was a slightly built, immaculately dressed Mediterranean featured man whom the CNN reporter immediately identified as the UN secretary-general. The cameraman held the shot as Cowley tossed his suit and helmet into the helicopter before retreating under the entrance canopy with the diplomat.

Danilov watched the running newscast for another hour before the summons came from the Interior Ministry. By then the death toll from traffic accidents and stress-related causes—mostly asthma seizures and heart attacks—had been established at fifty-four. One victim was the asthmatic member of the original NYPD bomb disposal squad. The Russian source of the missile had also been confirmed.

For once there was no shuffled expansion to prevent his joining a crowded table, and Patrick Hollis slid gratefully into the sort of group from which he was normally excluded in the bank's cafeteria. He let the discussion swirl around him, holding back from any opinion: Having gotten to the table, he didn't want to be ridiculed.

"Madmen!" declared Robert Standing, one of the senior clerks in the mortgage department and Hollis's chief tormentor. "Deserve the chair when they're caught."

"They'll demand money," anticipated Carole Parker, the blond counter clerk who was the latest focus of Hollis's fantasies.

"That's how they'll get the bastards," agreed Standing. "Set a trap with the money."

It would have been wonderful to contradict the man: show Standing up for the boastful, know-nothing fool that he was, with his hand up every willing skirt. Just as it would have been wonderful to let everyone around the table—Carole most of all—know how he'd amassed the fortune of nearly $2,000,000 that no one knew—or could ever know—he had.

3

Although slightly built, Ibrahim Saads, the secretary-general, was a tall man whose prematurely graying hair added to the ambiance of easily worn authority. At the moment of re-entry, however, both he and Cowley remained slightly uncertain. Saads said, "I'm glad there wasn't an accident."

"Yes," agreed Cowley. They hadn't expected to find Saads when they emerged into the vestibule, the unguarded warhead still tentatively suspended in its sling between Schnecker and Hamish. The diplomat hadn't known they were in the building, either, although it had been the noise of their arriving helicopter that brought him to the ground level. Cowley didn't think the surprise would have been sufficient to startle Schnecker and Hamish into dropping the

device but was still glad it had been Pointdexter who'd first confronted the UN chief, who clearly realized there had been a danger.
It was his third reference to an accident being avoided.

"There's no contamination whatsoever?" asked Saads, another
repetition.

"None," confirmed Cowley.

"I've got calls to make," said the diplomat.

"So have I," said Cowley. "I'd appreciate a phone."

This time Saads did use his own suite, gesturing for Cowley to
take his pick from the immediately adjoining office and leaving the
linking door open in invitation.

The FBI director's demand was immediate. "No doubt it's Russian?"

"The lettering certainly is," Cowley said cautiously. "It was a
design no one's seen before."

"You know anything about a chemical or biological weapon facility at a Plant 35 at or near Gorki?"

"I'll start a records check when we've finished talking. We
also—"

"Need to check the CIA," anticipated Ross. "I'll speak to the
director personally. And State and the White House."

"The secretary-general's here. He's making calls, too."

"Which have to be duplicated," insisted Ross. There had been a
period when he'd regretted leaving the New York bench, where he'd
been the senior judge, for the FBI directorship, but he had become
more comfortable after mastering what he considered all the necessary internal and external political footwork. "There'll be meetings
I'll need you back here for."

"The city's in chaos but the trains should work sometime later
today. I'll get the Metroliner."

"You got any thoughts so far?" asked Ross, knowing it was a
question he was going to be asked as he climbed the political ladder.

"Terrorist," Cowley said shortly. "If it is there should be a claim
for responsibility soon. Or a demand."

There was another momentary silence. "We're going to need a
task force," decided the director. "Antiterrorism, scientific, you and
your division . . . liaison, too, maybe, with the Agency and Customs.

And diplomatically it's going to be a bitch, so I guess State will be involved. . . ."

Through the open door Cowley saw the secretary-general talking animatedly on the telephone, gesturing with his free hand, and thought they'd need the General Assembly chamber to accommodate the sort of task force Leonard Ross was imagining. Who, Cowley wondered, would be left to conduct the actual investigation while everyone else publicly made meaningful statements and promises? He said, "I need to start things here."

"Be back by tomorrow."

It would not have been politically correct to ask his director to transfer him. Cowley disconnected and immediately redialed his own department to research a Plant 35 anywhere in the Gorki area. He also asked for an independent bureau comparison of the warhead from TV freeze-frame pictures against anything similar in their files and for checks to be extended to all Washington-based technical publications and sources. He insisted the inquiry be spelled out in the greatest possible detail to their office at the Moscow embassy. There was no reply from the New York FBI office on Third Avenue, and the answering machine hadn't been switched on.

Ibrahim Saads saw Cowley hovering at the door and beckoned him in to the river-view suite. The Egyptian switched on a television preset to a scheduled NBC program, with Tom Brokaw promising a live telecast from the White House.

The anchorman continued a voice-over commentary on earlier footage, initially of the car-abandoned, still-deserted Manhattan streets and then of the Secretariat Tower viewed from the river. Papers continued to flow in a slow stream from the hole torn into the side of the building. From the outside the hole looked far bigger than Cowley had imagined from the inside. It was more a horizontal, three- or four-meter tear than a direct hole, as if the initial shattering of the outer glass and fabric had rippled sideways in some seismic aftershock, buckling and distorting the metal and reinforced concrete frame. There were what appeared to be hundreds of fissured splits, a giant spider's web, emanating from the main damage to the floors above and below.

"No one can be allowed back in until engineers confirm it's safe," decided the international diplomat. "If it gives way at that level, the entire tower could collapse into the river. Which means the river will have to be closed, too, I suppose. Until we're sure."

The picture abruptly switched to a boat and seaplane marina identified in the caption as Asharoken, on Long Island. The caption also named the fair-haired seaplane commuter pilot as Arnold Payne. He'd been coming in to land at the downtown terminal, bringing in his regular four Wall Street traders, when he'd been attracted by a flash. It appeared to have come from a cruiser, and his initial thought was that there had been an explosion on board. At once the side of the United Nations' building had exploded. By the time he'd circled, it had been possible to see how much had been ripped from the side of the Secretariat Tower, although there was no sign of the fire or smoke that he'd expected. There had been at least seven vessels— three of them cruisers—in the East River vicinity, all heading toward Long Island Sound. None, certainly not any of the cruisers, showed any smoke or was firing distress signals, which he thought they would have done if there'd been an explosion to account for the flash he'd seen. He realized now, of course, what he'd seen had been the ignition of a missile he hadn't seen in flight.

Cowley made a note of the man's name and seaplane base and added a reminder to himself to check with the New York Port Authority and however many other official bodies existed for the identification of as much river traffic as possible. He also made a note to discover what other seaplane taxis might have witnessed something.

Watching at Cowley's shoulder, Saads said, "I wouldn't be surprised if you'd like a drink."

"Scotch would be good," accepted Cowley, as the other man went to an expansive cabinet on the other side of the room. Just one, Cowley told himself. Maybe two, if a second was offered. It wasn't a problem anymore. Never had been. Stopped it before it became one. Too late to prevent some difficulties, but the job had never been endangered. Not true. Endangered but he'd gotten away with it, with a lot of help from a special friend.

The diplomat was walking back across the room, glass in hand, when Brokaw announced the presidential address.

There had, that day, been committed another outrage against the city of New York that only a miracle had prevented becoming a catastrophic disaster, declared the president. Had the missile, fitted with a combined chemical and biological warhead, detonated, hundreds, maybe thousands, of lives would have been lost. The missile had been recovered intact and was already safe in a specialized U.S. government installation. The emergency, although not the disruption, was over. The United States of America regarded what had occurred as an attack upon the international community represented by the United Nations and was inviting international cooperation. Already, in these first few hours, there were important investigatory lines of inquiry, the most important being Russian markings on the warhead. The State Department was already in contact with Moscow. His thoughts and sympathy were with the relatives of those who had died as a result of the incident. The president personally praised Secretary-General Ibrahim Saads, who knowingly accepted the risk of agonizing and certain death to remain at his post, first to clear the UN buildings themselves and then to alert all emergency services to evacuate Manhattan and the surrounding New York boroughs. He acknowledged the bravery of the specialist American unit that, together with a senior FBI official, went into the Secretariat Tower to retrieve the warhead and render it harmless.

At that point in the live transmission the picture briefly split to show Saads and Cowley walking from the building with the Fort Meade scientists carrying the warhead to the waiting helicopter.

The president's face filled the screen again. "No one, no group, should imagine they will go unpunished for mounting the attack that was attempted today. No matter how long it takes, wherever they try to hide, they will be sought out and brought to justice. Of that, my fellow Americans, you have my solemn pledge."

Saads said, "They would have intended the warhead to detonate. To kill as many people as they could."

"Yes," agreed Cowley.

"So if they've got another warhead—or access to one—they'll try again."

"And succeed the next time," predicted Cowley. "Miracles don't happen twice."

Although a general in title, Dimitri Danilov was outranked in authority by everyone else in the baroque office of Interior Minister Nikolai Gregorovich Belik. Even the place accorded him was the lowest, close to the separate secretarial bank. It was a passing acceptance. The more important awareness was that he was physically between men representing the new Russia and those of the old, still-resistant regime. As the president's chief of staff, Georgi Stepanovich Chelyag was the spearhead of the new in the sanctum of the old. The deputy defense minister, General Sergei Gromov, and Viktor Kedrov, chairman of the Federal Security Bureau, the intelligence service that replaced the KGB, were publicly known to be Belik disciples. Only Deputy Foreign Minister Yuri Kisayev was a reformist.

Where did that place him? wondered Danilov. Possibly between a rock and a hard place, he decided, calling upon an American axiom he liked. Once, when his career had been important, it would have been a worrying realization. Since the personal disaster, little mattered anymore. As he usually did these days, he felt an uninvolved observer, a one-man audience to a performance of others.

"This is a crisis for the country, not of ideology," opened Chelyag, at once moving to establish Russian White House control. "Our decision must be totally bipartisan." Chelyag was a squat man of few facial expressions, least of all approval or condemnation.

There were nods and mutterings of agreement around the table.

"Let's establish facts," Chelyag continued briskly. "Is there a Plant 35 at Gorki?"

"Yes," said the already prepared deputy defense minister. He was a bull-chested, mottle-faced man who'd worn his uniform as a reminder of the importance of military support to a Russian government.

"What's its function?" persisted the presidential aide.

"It's a defense research establishment," defended Gromov. "Against biological or chemical weapon attack."

There was a silence, which Yuri Kisayev hurried to fill to distance the Foreign Ministry. "If it is still operating, Russia has abrogated an international nonproliferation treaty to which it is a signatory."

Danilov glanced at the industrious note-takers, recognizing how effectively the outnumbered reformist faction was bureaucratically establishing potential responsibility.

"*Is* it still operating?" demanded Chelyag.

"I have no information about that," the army general said uncomfortably.

"The Defense Ministry is well aware of the terms of the biological and chemical weapons treaty, though?" pressed the blank-faced presidential chief of staff.

"My understanding is that stockpiles were in the process of being destroyed, under the terms of the agreement," said Gromov, in another prepared response.

"We need that positively and provably confirmed," declared Chelyag. "If necessary to open the facility to American inspection."

The announcement caused the second silence, longer this time. Viktor Kedrov said, "From which I presume there is to be every cooperation with America?"

It was a protective qualification, but Chelyag threw it back at the intelligence chief, a sallow-featured man whose receding hair and round-rimmed glasses gave him a remarkable resemblance to Lavrenti Beria, Stalin's reviled pogrom-organizing security head. Chelyag said, "Do you know of any reason why we shouldn't?"

"Absolutely not." Kedrov flushed. "I'm simply trying to avoid misunderstandings."

"There is also to be total cooperation and liaison between the departments assembled here," ordered the chief of staff. "I want that completely understood and accepted."

As if in answer, maintaining the every-word-recorded formality, Kedrov said, "Which department or ministry—and who, from that department or ministry—is going to lead the inquiries here in Russia?"

"If it did indeed come from Gorki, the warhead was stolen," said Chelyag. "Which is a criminal act. And crime is the responsibility of the militia, which is why this meeting was convened here in the Interior Ministry." The man looked for the first time directly at

Danilov. "And you, Dimitri Ivanovich, have worked with American agencies, especially the Federal Bureau of Investigation, on previous occasions?"

At last everyone's attention concentrated upon Danilov. He said, "Twice."

"Which uniquely qualifies you to do so again," decided Chelyag. "More particularly because such a theft would not have been committed by amateurs and you head the Organized Crime Bureau—"

"Here in Moscow," broke in Danilov.

"You will operate directly and specifically with the authority of the White House," Chelyag set out. "Everyone in Gorki—and anywhere else it's necessary for you to go—will be made aware of that." He paused, looking around the table again. "General Danilov is to get total and unimpeded cooperation."

"I don't think there's any doubt about the degree or extent of support that is being made available," said Belik, speaking at last.

Or whom the sacrifice would be in the event of a mistake or failure, Danilov realized. Once more he thought how irrelevant that seemed. On his way home he'd change the flowers on Larissa's grave. He hadn't been there for four days.

"I think the bank imposes upon you too much," complained Elizabeth Hollis. She was a tall, stiffly upright woman, close to being gaunt, her iron-gray hair in tightly permed ridges.

"Nothing I can't handle," said Hollis.

"You know how you've got to be careful."

Hollis winced at the reminder. Physically he was a complete contrast to his mother, a round-faced, bespectacled man overweight by at least twenty pounds, which he had been from grade school. As he felt about a lot of things in life, Hollis considered his size unfair. Because of it—and for what doctors labeled a weak chest, because it stopped just short of asthma—he'd been judged unfit for the army cadets and later for the National Guard and had long ago abandoned diets, none of which worked. He was still careful about what he ate, though, as he was careful about everything.

"Dinner will be about half an hour. Steak," said the woman.

"Broiled," Hollis insisted at once. "Trim the fat."

"I know how you like it!" said the woman in mock irritation. "What are you going to do?"

"Work on my computer for a while."

"I don't understand why you want to spend the time you do on a computer here when it's all you do at work."

"It's like magic, mother," said the man in the awed voice of a committed cyber nerd. "There's nothing I can't do—nowhere I can't go." But some places he wouldn't go again. He could go on playing the war games—retain his rank as the Quartermaster if he chose— but he wouldn't maintain the telephone contact code worked out with the General through the personal columns of *Soldier* magazine. It had been a mistake but one easily rectified. Tonight he wouldn't even go to war. Easily Hollis began cracking into unaware host systems, for them to be charged his usage time, burrowing through three before dialing up the porn channel. He took his time with his selection, too, and when he found the movie he wanted charged it against the credit card number he'd gotten from the issuing bank in Buffalo. The woman was blonde, and it was very easy for Hollis to imagine it was Carole Parker, not an actress.

Clarence Snelling wasn't enamoured of computers. He didn't understand them and didn't want to and thought of them as an enemy, technology that had made him redundant as a clerk, throwing him on the scrap heap on a pension so inadequate he had to scrabble around as a part-time bookkeeper for businesses too small to afford a screen and a keyboard. And those businesses seemed to be decreasing by the day.

To Clarence Snelling a handwritten page of figures was a thing of beauty, art almost. It was nothing at all like the sterile electronically printed sheet he was studying at that moment, comparing it to the ledger into which he was carefully transferring it. He threw the bank statement impatiently aside and called: "Martha! They've done it again!"

4

William Cowley was discomfited by so many still and television cameras, particularly when he was recognized as the man who had gone into the UN building with the germ warfare scientists and became the filmed and question-shouted focus of the gathering. He tolerated the cameras but studiously ignored the questions. Most of the other public figures around him were self-consciously posing to appear unposed, irritated that Cowley's sudden fame was deflecting attention—and the cameras—away from them.

For the benefit of daytime newscasts and evening newspapers, Henry Hartz, the guttural-voiced, German-born secretary of state, stressed to the assembled journalists that the official status of everyone present showed the importance America was giving to what he referred to as "this appalling near atrocity." He held up what he claimed to be a personal assurance from the Russian president of complete cooperation, which in fact it wasn't. It was notification from the Moscow ambassador that such a guarantee had been promised by the Russian Foreign Ministry. Hartz concluded with the promise of a longer statement at the end of the meeting.

Cowley didn't think, from an earlier breakfast discussion, that Leonard Ross had fully absorbed the horror of what might have been postponed only by a fluke. Even more certainly Cowley didn't believe the bureau's twitchingly eager, nervously laughing antiterrorist chief had, either. Burt Bradley was the first director of the bureau's specially dedicated unit. There'd been the New York World Trade Center attacks and Oklahoma and before that the Beirut U.S. Embassy bombing, but the unit's primary function had otherwise been liaising with other more frequently attacked European countries. Cowley's impression wasn't that Bradley was overawed, as he initially had been. He thought Bradley was positively frightened. And from his just completed personal analysis, he couldn't condemn the man for it. Any more than he criticized anyone else in the room for what he regarded as performance warmup time, practicing posterity phrases and photo-shoot postures.

"I want a complete update," opened Hartz, without introducing people he expected already to know each other. His German birth precluded Hartz from ever running for the presidency, which he coveted, but he considered being secretary of state the next best political role and ran his Foggy Bottom fiefdom as he would have run a White House administration, with unquestioned, unchallenged autocracy. He knew—and didn't mind—that he was referred to within the department as the Führer. Looking between Cowley and Schnecker he said, "Let's have the scientific thinking first."

Unencumbered by his protective suit and domed helmet, James Schnecker was a surprisingly small man with an even more surprising tendency to squint, as if suffering unexpected pain twinges. He coughed, clearing his throat, and said professorially, "One warhead contained sarin, a known nerve agent produced in either liquid or vapor form. As liquid it's absorbed through the skin or mucous membranes; as vapor it's inhaled, obviously. In both states it attacks the respiratory and nervous systems. You'll remember it was released on the Tokyo Underground in 1998 by a fanatical religious group. It's a well known and long-standing weapon, first produced in Germany in 1937. The other warhead contained anthrax which you're all familiar with after the events of September, 2001. Bacillus anthracio is again a pulmonary complaint. Biologically it's most commonly found in cattle—although to a much lesser extent in sheep—and in Africa, where it is endemic, humans contract it from tics. It's produced as a biological weapon as a plasma-encoded toxin by combining three bacillus proteins. Separately none of the proteins has a biologically harmful effect. Combined they create edema, the pathological accumulation of fluid in the body tissues and pulmonary collapse. There's acute and agonizing swelling and hemorrhaging from all body openings. It attacks the spleen and causes splenetic fever. In weapon form, as it was in this warhead, it infects through inhalation. It's almost invariably fatal to humans after an incubation period of between one to five days."

"So it was both a chemical *and* biological attack?" broke in Frank Norton. The president's chief of staff was a former Pentagon general on the short list for when the present White House incumbent completed his second term of office. He'd already decided that the outcome of what had been thrust upon him now could determine whether there needed to be anyone else in the race. It had been Norton, who cultivated for its political appeal the appearance of the rawboned marine officer he'd once been, who'd proposed the media invitation. The concentration on the goddamned FBI man had been unexpected and annoying.

"Absolutely." Schnecker frowned, surprised at the question. "We'd never encountered a delivery system like it before at Fort Detrick. It seems to be a modification of a Russian missile known as the Grail or SA-7: two warheads attached to the body of a rocket intended to carry just one. Which probably prevented the catastrophe. It's top-heavy, quite out of balance. All the forensic examinations we've carried out so far point to it spinning, top over bottom, instead of traveling in a proper trajectory. And to it, incredibly, striking glass through which it passed virtually unobstructed. The fins and the body sustained all the impact damage and in doing so snapped the detonation mechanism, which was extremely crude: percussion pins intended to shatter the containers to release their contents."

"Thank God for a bad design," said Hartz.

"An almost too obvious bad design," Burt Bradley broke in quickly. "Bad enough to have been realized from its first test firing. Accepting that it's Russian, what's the chances of the warhead being put together here, by unqualified people?"

"All our ferroalloy tests haven't been completed yet," the scientist said doubtfully. "So far all the metal is provably Russian. If it was a hybrid cobbled together here, there'd be some American components. I don't think we should overlook the possibility that we've never seen anything like it before because it was a design that *didn't* work and was abandoned after preliminary or failed tests. The date on the casing was 1974."

Cowley saw the overly ambitious antiterrorist chief wince at the rejection in front of the FBI director, a carelessly fat, carelessly dressed man. If Ross saw it as a rebuff he gave no indication.

"Guide us here," demanded the CIA director, John Butterworth, a retired navy admiral anxious to counteract criticism of naive amateurism from intelligence professionals at his Langley appointment. "What would have happened if the missile had *missed* the tower? Flown on?"

Schnecker frowned at the hypothesis. "I can't itemize every one, but there are quite a few skyscrapers after the UN building it could have hit. Had it done so, there probably wouldn't have been the miracle of it going through window glass. Or tailfirst. If it missed all the high buildings, I guess it would have gone on into New Jersey. The single payload of the SA-7 is fifteen kilograms, with a range of ten kilometers, or 6.2 miles. This double warhead weighed twenty-two kilograms. That would have shortened the range, which would also have been affected by the top-over-bottom instability. And there was the crosswind. You want a ballpark guess, draw a line down from Newark to Trenton."

"And how likely would it have been that the warhead would have burst simply by impact against the ground, whether it hit nosefirst or not?" asked Butterworth, a bald, angularly featured man.

Schnecker continued frowning. "It's another hypothesis, but I would say a rupture of some sort, if not an actual detonation, would have been inevitable."

"What about the combined effect of both warheads, if they'd exploded?" asked Norton.

"I'm not aware of any research that's mixed the two. Scientifically it's not possible to combine them. I think the idea was a double delivery of two separate agents."

"Are there antidotes, treatment?" said Ross.

"There's treatment for isolated cases, if it's immediate. The casualty rate yesterday, if they'd activated, would have been overwhelming."

"How many?" demanded Norton, seizing the headline question. "The president guessed at a thousand dying."

Schnecker hesitated. "It could have been more than *a* thousand."

"How many more?" demanded the man. "Tens or hundreds?"

"It could have gone as high as five, conceivably higher still," estimated the scientist. "It wouldn't have simply been the sarin or anthrax. It would have accelerated existing medical conditions from which people were already suffering. The vapor could have gotten into hospitals through the air conditioning."

"Jesus!" said Norton, the only sound in a long silence.

Breaking it—and remembering his conversation with the UN secretary-general the previous day—Cowley said, "They meant to kill. Dramatically and hugely. Next time they will. And people this determined *will* do it again, if they have a missile. Or a way to get another one."

"How's an SA-7 fired?"

"Shoulder-held portable launcher," replied Schnecker.

"All the statements aren't in yet, but it's obvious it was fired from a moving boat," said Cowley. "Assuming that the UN tower *was* the target, which I think we must, the fact that it was hit at all from a shoulder-held rocket launcher fired from a moving boat—to some extent against the wind—surely indicates whoever did it has some military experience of missiles."

"I would say so, yes," agreed Schnecker. "From which a working knowledge of missiles naturally follows."

Looking to the antiterrorist chief, Cowley said, "There *are* files on known or suspected terrorists, right?"

"Yes?" Bradley frowned.

"Anyone specifically listed with a knowledge of missiles would be worth publicly posting."

"The check's already being made," the younger man said impatiently.

Then it would have helped if you'd mentioned it at the breakfast meeting, thought Cowley. To Schnecker he said, "What about something as practical as fingerprints on the missile?"

Schnecker shook his head. "Clean."

"Knowingly to set out, as these people did, to kill thousands of people is fanaticism. Zealotry. Or total homicidal madness," said the terrorist chief, who had a degree in forensic psychology. "Zealous fanaticism fits Islamic fundamentalism, which we're all familiar with from the past."

Bradley had shared the breakfast meeting with the FBI director but hadn't offered any opinion about anything, remembered Cowley. Now Bradley seemed to be trying too hard. Leonard Ross appeared to have the same impression, looking curiously sideways at the man. Cowley said, "Don't we have the same problem if we're dealing with a bunch of homicidal maniacs?"

Bradley shook his head. "They wanted to hit and run. So they'll want to boast, claim responsibility."

"Why haven't they, after more than twenty-four hours?" asked Cowley.

"What's your point?" the younger man demanded belligerently.

"Simply that at this stage, this early, we don't know enough to speculate about anything and certainly not to exclude any group," said Cowley.

"The obvious essential is to prevent a repetition," declared the CIA director. "I suggest we make it immediately public that the missile is a flawed design that won't work. If the terrorists have another, it might prevent them from trying to use it."

There were frowns at Butterworth from around the table.

"Sir," said Schnecker. "The missile that hit the UN building didn't detonate because it went in backward and through practically unresisting glass. A fluke. If it had hit the concrete of the building, it would have gone off. As would another—bad design or not—if it hit a hard and solid object."

"How many eyewitnesses do we have?" Hartz broke in quickly, to spare the agency chief.

"Three who seem reliable," Cowley responded at once. "Another seaplane commuter pilot in addition to the one from Asharoken. And the captain of a trash barge that was going downriver. All were attracted by the firing flash but none was looking directly at the cruiser. They all agree it was motor, not sail, but we've got three different descriptions of size, color, and potential make. None of them saw the missile or the launcher, and when there wasn't any obvious fire or distress signal all three dismissed it."

"We've got nothing, in fact?" demanded Butterworth, too eager again.

"I've moved thirty agents up to the New York office," said Ross. "There *does* seem to be agreement that the cruiser had a flying bridge. The uncertainty is the color: whether it was totally white or had some blue at the waterline. Quite obviously we're tracing the owners of every flying-bridged cruiser in every marina, yacht basin, and mooring between New York and Boston as well as Long Island. We're not, in fact, imposing a territorial limit: I've gone south as far as the Chesapeake. But we're talking *thousands* of boats. We're also, again obviously, checking any cruiser thefts or cruiser hire." He looked invitingly back to Cowley.

"None of the three we've traced so far talk of anyone on the cruiser dressed unusually for a boat."

"What did they see?" broke in Butterworth.

"Two people—the second commuter pilot thought one was slim enough to have been a woman—both in unmarked bill caps and boat anoraks, again unmarked, no distinguishing color: dark blue or black maybe."

"I can't understand if they looked in the direction of the flash why they didn't see one of the two still with the rocket launcher," protested Hartz.

"The missile hitting the UN tower appeared practically simultaneous with the flash," said Cowley. "All three witnesses say they thought that was what caused the flash. They virtually ignored the cruiser after the initial seconds."

"How many more potential witnesses could there be?" demanded the CIA director.

"We've got from the New York Port Authority the names of three cargo barges that were on the river at the time." Cowley paused, looking at Peter Samuels, the Customs and Excise director who had been silent so far. "And Customs is checking reported yacht and cruiser arrivals in the East River back five hours from the time of the attack."

"But our records would only be of incoming boats *reporting* their arrival," qualified Samuels. "There's no legal requirement for a yacht or cruiser to do that if it merely came down from an upriver mooring and turned back before exiting the river. At least half the craft that leave the river to go up and down the coast don't report their return anyway."

"The missile *is* Russian, whether it had one or two warheads," said Bradley. "And by sea is the likeliest way of smuggling it into the country."

"There's something like four thousand miles of U.S. coastline, and that's a straight measurement, not including about a million creeks and inlets and navigable rivers," said the Customs director. "Of course I've issued watch orders at every major port, but the reality is that's about as practical as trying to check every yacht and cruiser between Boston and Washington. It's being done, because it's got to be done, but no one should expect a quick result. No one should expect a result at all, unless the miracles continue."

Once again there was silence. This time it was the CIA director who broke it. Butterworth said, "We don't have enough to make a row of beans."

"Everything that can be done has been done to initiate the most comprehensive investigation in the bureau's history," Ross said defensively.

Hartz concentrated on the CIA chief. "What about Plant 35, at Gorki?"

The bald man shifted uncomfortably. "Throughout the Cold War Gorki was a closed city. We know there were extensive armament and weapon facilities there but we have nothing specific about a Plant 35."

"*We* have," announced Ross, to an immediate stir around the table. "Our files have it as a conventional weapons facility at which production began to be wound down in 1994."

Butterworth's face blazed at what he regarded as territorial intrusion. "I was under the impression that this was a totally shared investigation."

"It is," said the disheveled Bureau director. "I've just shared."

There was a ripple of forced laughter. Flushed because of it and trying to recover, Butterworth said, "If the Russians still possess the sort of warheads fired yesterday—which they clearly do—they are in provable breach of the Chemical Weapons Convention that was internationally concluded, with them as signatories, in 1993." He answered Hartz's look. "Are we making diplomatic representation about that?"

"I don't think our two countries need to get into that sort of exchange at this stage," the presidential chief of staff warned sharply.

"I agree," said Hartz just as quickly and as diplomatically rehearsed. "I spent an hour with the Russian ambassador last night and spoke to him again on the phone before this meeting. They're as concerned—as frightened—about this as we are. We need to cooperate, not confront."

"As we've done before," reminded Ross, indicating Cowley by his side. "And as we need more than ever to do again now."

The connection an hour later between the FBI headquarters on Washington's Pennsylvania Avenue and the Moscow Militia building on Ulitza Petrovka was immediate. Dimitri Danilov said, "On television it looked as if you'd put on weight."

"I'm already losing it," said William Cowley.

"I'm glad it's you," said the Russian. He was, genuinely. It made a change for him to have anything like a personal feeling about anything.

"And I'm glad it's you." Having been in Moscow when Larissa had been killed and knowing the other man's devastation, Cowley said, "How've you been?"

"So-so. You?"

"So-so. You in operational charge?"

"Officially appointed by the White House, with a remit as wide as the Volga itself," confirmed Danilov.

"The assurance here is total cooperation?"

"Here, too," said the Russian. From his just-concluded conversation with the Gorki Militia detective chief, Danilov suspected the working relationship was going to be more difficult there than with Washington. He said, "What have you got?"

"Two intact warheads, one containing sarin, the other anthrax. And a smashed up SA-7 delivery system."

"I'll need the details."

"I'll fax it all now. And wire photographs. What about Plant 35?"

"Includes a facility for defensive chemical and biological weapon research," Danilov admitted at once.

Normal voices, conversational voices, Cowley thought: How's the weather with you, raining here, good to hear everything's all right with you. Except that *nothing* was all right. At this very moment, while they were talking, two other cans of topsy-turvey shit capable of killing thousands of people might already be slotted into a delivery system aimed at a building anywhere. . . . Cowley stopped the drift. Not *anywhere*. The United Nations complex had been chosen for exactly what it was, the one—the most—internationally attention-attracting target in the world. The next, inevitable attack would be on a similarly focused site. Which could only be Washington itself. Security alerts had gone out throughout the country, but Cowley was suddenly convinced they needed to be concentrated in D.C. "You coming here or am I coming there?"

"Let's decide the order of priority first," said Danilov.

"The priority is the priority," said Cowley, and immediately wished he hadn't. It echoed like a soap opera sound byte just before the credits ran, to bring viewers back for the next episode. Hurriedly he added, "Whoever, wherever, gets the first break."

"Let's hope one of us recognize it," warned Danilov.

Someone had stolen Larissa's flowers, which didn't surprise Danilov. The daffodils he'd brought now would probably go within a day. He cleared the fallen leaves and twigs from the Novodevichy Cemetery grave, unashamedly talking to her as he always did, imagining her replies in his mind.

Remember Bill, the American . . . big man? That's right . . . good to go to America again . . . get away. Olga's Olga, just the same. . . . Of course I miss you—ache for you. Don't feel like being careful. . . . All right, of course I will be. . . . Why couldn't you have been. . . . I know, I'm sorry. Not your fault. Yevgennie's fault—your cheating, bastard militia colonel husband, failing his Mafia masters. Why did you have to be in the car, though? Leave me? I won't be long. . . . Wish I could bring you something . . . see you . . . be with you. No, I'm all right. No, not all right: able to handle it. Sorry about the flowers. It's Moscow— Russia. Good night. I love you.

Danilov rose, just as unashamedly staring back at another mourner looking curiously at him. He drove without hurry or interest to Ulitza Kirovskaya, knowing the sound was from his apartment as he stepped out of the elevator. His wife sat in front of the new, blaring set that had been her latest insistence, initially oblivious to his entry. She became aware of it when he went in front of her to reduce the volume.

"It's too loud!" It was a Russian subtitled Australian series that had been running for weeks. There was a kangaroo that did tricks.

"I like trying to hear the English words."

"You don't speak English."

"Irena says this is a way to learn."

"She's wrong." Irena, who worked in the same ministry office as Olga, claimed to have learned her English from American movies. Danilov, who'd studied languages at the university, reckoned she knew about a dozen words, most of which she mispronounced.

The kitchen sink still had the stalagmite of unwashed dishes that had been there that morning, and on his way to the bathroom to wash Danilov saw the bed was in the upheaval in which she'd left it when she'd gotten up. The Australian soap had ended when he returned.

He said: "What words did you learn?"

"You interrupted me. I couldn't concentrate."

"I'm going away."

"Where!" she demanded, suddenly attentive, turning to him.

"Gorki. What happened to your hair?"

"Igor said I needed this color, while the other tints grew out. What's in Gorki?"

"That's what I'm going to find out."

"Any point in my making a present list?"

"None."

"That American you worked with was on television before my program. Something about a missile."

"I spoke to him today."

Olga's interest returned. "You're going to America!"

"Maybe."

"So I *can* write a present list!"

Danilov realized for the first time she was wearing a shirt he'd brought back for her the last time. Two buttons were missing and the stain over her left breast looked old and ingrained. Larissa had been wearing the bracelet he'd given her from the same trip. It had been one of the few things that had been identifiable after the bombing of the car.

"It's the fifth time it's happened in the last six months!" protested Clarence Snelling.

"The bank's extremely sorry," apologized the desk assistant, who'd dealt with the man's previous complaints. "Computers do make mistakes."

"No, they don't!" Snelling replied. "It's the people who handle them who make the mistakes."

"It's twenty-two cents," the bank official pointed out. "It's never been more than fifty. And as before, I'll see that the amount is immediately restored."

"I want an assurance that it won't happen again!" insisted Snelling. "And this time I want it kept, which so far you haven't done."

"Sir," said the man, "I promise you we'll do our very best."

5

Dimitri Danilov's plane came in directly over the joining of the Volga with the river Oka. Briefly it was impossible to see both banks of the waterway that flows for more than two thousand miles from the frozen north to the subtropical Caspian Sea, to separate European from Asiatic Russia. It narrowed nearer to Gorki itself, but there were so many boats and ships—two cruisers large enough to be considered liners—that they looked from the air like discarded debris, without any regulated direction. He tried to locate the canal from the Volga to Moscow that Stalin forced his gulag prisoners to scoop from the earth with their bare hands but couldn't and decided it must be farther downstream. The vast, flat hinterland of taiga forests was black, not conifer green, pockmarked in a lot of places into total baldness by clear-cutting without replanting. There were also the huge interruptions of uniform, regimented weapons and military materiel manufacturing buildings, each visibly divided from its matching neighbor by watch-towered, fenced perimeters. Two actually on the riverbank were on either side of an enormous man-made canal he could see humped with the pens in which the submarines now hemorrhaging their nuclear core into Murmansk harbor were originally housed, ready to fight America into mutual atomic annihilation. Which factory below was known simply by the number 35 and specialized in another sort of annihilation? Danilov wondered.

The aircraft, surprisingly, arrived exactly according to the schedule he'd given Colonel Oleg Reztsov, head of Gorki's serious crime division, but there was no greeting officer. There was no waiting militia car outside, either, and Danilov accepted both, sadly, as an augury.

The smell of stale tobacco competed with the even staler stink of body odor in the rattling, sag-seated taxi festooned with dangling trolls and head-nodding toy animals. One had a broken neck. Danilov had forgotten the horizon-to-horizon taiga-covered mosquito bog and marsh. Flying things feasted off him, despite his lowering the window as far as it would go. The incoming breeze didn't disperse the smell, either. When he told the inquiring driver, who'd smiled expectantly at Danilov's American-bought suit bag, that he wasn't going to pay in dollars, the man said having luggage inside the car would cost an extra fifty rubles. Danilov told the driver who he was, and the man said there wasn't an extra charge for carrying a militia general.

Danilov's room at the National Hotel overlooked a trash-strewn square at the rear, next to an air-conditioning or heater unit the throbbing of which reverberated into his room. Cockroaches killed by whatever was in an upturned cardboard container in the closet lay atrophied, legs stiffly in the air. There was no soap or sink or bath plug, which Danilov knew he should have anticipated and was annoyed that he hadn't.

Colonel Reztsov wasn't available when Danilov called. The woman who answered the telephone said she didn't know where he was or when he would be back. Danilov suggested she find out to tell the president's chief of staff when he called from the White House in Moscow in fifteen minutes, and in ten Reztsov came thick-voiced on the line.

"I didn't think you were arriving until tomorrow."

"I sent a fax."

"It must have been mislaid."

"You do understand how seriously it's being treated?"

"I've got a squad on it already."

"I'd like whoever's in charge waiting when I get to your office. Which I will do in thirty minutes."

"That—" the man began but stopped.

"What?" demanded Danilov.

"Nothing. I'll send a car."

Danilov parted with another ten dollars to get his room changed to one with soap and a bath plug and without mummified cockroaches. The mystery throbbing was less intrusive, too. The promised driver waiting in the lobby was a woman and blonde, and the car was a blue BMW. Danilov stopped momentarily—stupidly, he recognized at once—halted by the unneeded and unwelcome déjà vu: The vehicle in which his mafia paymasters had blown up Yevgennie Kosov had been a BMW, blue like this one, and Larissa, who'd died with him, had been blonde, although slim and poised and beautiful, not at all like this woman, who was plump and round-faced and waddled. The obvious comparison made his reaction even more stupid. It had to stop, as the one-sided graveside conversations had to stop. He was hovering, Danilov supposed, on the edge of a nervous breakdown—close to some sort of breakdown. Time—long past time—to take hold of himself. Learn to live with the grief, as sensibly mature adult people adjusted to loss, no matter how traumatizing or unbearable it first appeared.

The driver took Danilov's hesitation to be admiration and said it was Colonel Reztsov's personal car. Danilov decided Reztsov was either a fool or very arrogant to show off a vehicle that would have cost the man a lifetime's salary if he'd bought it honestly. And then Danilov accepted that Reztsov was probably neither. What the police chief was, in fact, was a typical senior Russian militia officer, living more than comfortably on a mafia payroll, and eager to show a visiting senior Moscow militia officer he imagined similarly cared for that life was as sweet in the provinces as it was in the capital.

What about his own foolishness? Danilov demanded of himself, settling into the squeaking leather upholstery and initially savoring the aroma from an unseen, perfumed deodorizer after the gagging journey from the airport. Danilov wasn't a rarity in Moscow policing. He was now an arm's-length, ostracized oddity, as unknown in modern Russia as the Neolithic long-haired mammoths occasionally found frozen in perfection in Siberian glaciers. So why had he come—alone—expecting honest, find-the-truth cooperation from a major provincial militia? He should, at least, have brought Yuri Pavin, whose apparent elephantine slowness belied a mind of jaguar speed. On something as high profile as this he should have risked the very real and constant backstabbing danger of an unsupervised department to bring his trusted deputy with him. Although Pavin *was* his deputy, now with the rank of senior colonel, he was still a street-level, gutter-thinking policeman who could smell a lead, like a bloodhound scenting a trail. It was the sort of expertise Danilov suspected he was going to need.

If Reztsov's car hadn't been a sufficient pointer, the police chief's appearance would have been. Danilov wondered if it was an institutionalized psychology for men whose supposed function required uniforms to dress like the mobsters with whom they exchanged money-filled, back-alley handshakes. Reztsov's single-breasted Western-style suit was blue, practically a match with the car, and had a silky sheen. The watch and its band was gold, balanced by the gold identity bracelet on his right wrist. On the man's right hand the diamond shone with lighthouse brightness from a knuckle-reaching gold band. Major Gennardi Averin, the other man in Reztsov's opulent office—which smelled of the same perfume as the car—was a clone of his superior, although the shiny suit was gray and Averin didn't have a gold identity bracelet.

Both men were as sleek as their clothes, smooth-faced, well barbered, confident of their surroundings and their domination in it. The handshakes were effusive, Reztsov actually retaining Danilov's hand to lead him away from the officialese of the grandiose desk to a lounge-chaired, plant-dotted informal area close to a book-lined cabinet. There was Chivas Regal as well as vodka already set out. The glasses were cut crystal. Danilov accepted vodka, going along with the charade. Reztsov and the major both had whiskey.

Danilov said at once, "How can you help me?"

"We've come up with something from records," announced Reztsov. "An arms smuggler."

"What sort of arms?"

"Conventional," said Averin. "Not something either of us have personally dealt with."

"What have you done?"

"Waited for you."

"Was any loss reported from Plant 35?"

"No," Reztsov said immediately.

"Have you spoken to Plant 35 directly?"

"Decided to wait until you got here," parroted Averin. "Got an appointment for us with the director tomorrow, at ten."

"But you *have* spoken to him?"

"By telephone," said Averin. "Just to make the appointment."

"You didn't ask him if there was anything missing?"

"He said he'd check. Tell us tomorrow."

It was difficult for Danilov to curb the anger. He wasn't sure if he should bother, confronted by this almost smirking contempt. "How much conventional weaponry disappears from the establishments here?"

Reztsov made an uncertain movement. "Can't remember the last time we were called in. Security's very good."

"How many official crime families do you have in Gorki?"

Reztsov made another shrug. "Hardly families. Just one or two loose-knit groups."

"As well as the last case of known thefts from factories here, I'd like all your intelligence on organized crime groups," set out Danilov. "Particularly those with known links to families in Moscow. I'm having checks carried out there, for connections here. Most particularly—and obviously—I want any known association with America . . . any supposedly genuine America joint venture businesses here. You'll put that in hand right away, will you?" The condescension began to go, and Danilov was glad he'd kept his temper.

"That could be quite an undertaking—" Reztsov began to protest but Danilov overrode him.

"If it's too much for your department, I'll move militia personnel from Moscow," he said. "Normal local authority and jurisdiction doesn't apply. I want an office to work from, and I'd like to start on the organized crime material right away."

"Yes, of course," said the now-subdued local police colonel.

Dimitri Ivanovich Danilov read the intelligence dossiers on organized crime in Gorki with the expertise of a detective who had once been on the take and could learn as much from what was not recorded as he could from what was. The slimmest and most inadequate file was on a group headed by Mikhail Sidak, the thickest— and the most actively investigated—on the family led by Aleksai Zotin, which told Danilov they were the biggest two in the city, in turf competition with each other and that Reztsov had most probably earned the sweet-smelling BMW from Sidak for harassing the opposition. There had been prosecutions against four low-level members of a third family headed by Gusein Isayev for importing drugs along the Volga from the opium-producing south. Danilov surmised it was a business in which Sidak was eager to expand.

Both trials of the already identified conventional weapons trafficker, Viktor Nikolaevich Nikov, had failed through lack of evidence. Nikov was described as a bull—the Russian underworld term for a hit man—predictably in the family, or brigade, of Aleksai Zotin. The cases had involved a consignment of Kalashnikov rifles and antipersonnel mines. The chief prosecution witness had been the storeman at Plant 20, a conventional weapons factory, who'd retracted a sworn statement that Nikov had been the man to whom he'd sold the guns and mines. Three defense witnesses had testified that Nikov had been with them in Moscow, buying imported foreign cars for his garages, when the prosecution claimed he had been in Gorki. None of the Moscow defense witness names meant anything to Danilov, but that was hardly surprising, considering the number of brigades in the capital. The only names he knew—ingrained in his memory—were the crews of the Chechen and Ostinkono families whose territorial war had led to Larissa being killed. Some—too many—had escaped, were still alive.

"There's the sort of Moscow connection you were asking about. I'd momentarily forgotten about it," said Reztsov. Apologizing that it might take several days to find an available office, the local police chief had insisted that a desk, chair, and filing cabinet be moved into his own suite and remained attentively close to Danilov, even selecting and offering the folders.

"Considering how big the arms industry is here, I'm surprised there's been so very little crime—leakage—involving it, particularly now that so much is superfluous with the end of the Cold War," said Danilov.

"I told you, security's good," reminded Reztsov. "It's directed from Moscow."

"There's no more than this?" pressed Danilov. Their attitude wasn't patronizing but their selection was. It had taken less than an hour to produce.

"This is what I understood you wanted," said Major Averin. "How else can I help?"

"Zotin is the foremost family?"

"We've moved against them a lot," Averin pointed out.

"You got any feedback from informants that they might be connected with what happened in New York?"

"Not yet," said the major. "My task force was only formed two days ago. We've spread the word."

"We should talk to Nikov," said the local police chief, as if it were a decision no one else would have reached.

"Does he still run the garages referred to in his file?" asked Danilov. They'd sell cars stolen in Western Europe and smuggled in largely through Poland.

"When we last heard," Averin said carelessly.

"You haven't checked the whereabouts of someone who twice escaped arms-dealing prosecution?" Danilov demanded sharply.

"We always know where he is," assured Reztsov, the condescension edging back. "We always know where all our major players are."

"Let's bring him in then; see what he's got to say," agreed Danilov.

The dinner that Danilov decided he had to accept and to which they drove in Reztsov's perfumed car showed how fully the police chief's preparation—and his misunderstanding—had been. The genuinely French owner greeted Reztsov at the door of the restaurant overlooking the oil-smooth river. It took a long time for Danilov's disinterest to register with both Reztsov and Averin before they stopped recommending several girls smiling invitingly from the bar and an outer lounge.

There was a message from Yuri Pavin asking Danilov to call him at home, at any time, when he got back to the National Hotel. Pavin answered on the first ring. Two of the defense witnesses at Viktor Nikolaevich Nikov's second trial were logged on Moscow's criminal records as being associates of a family operating under the aegis of the Dolgopruadnanskaya, the city's largest mafia grouping. The third had been shot dead in a territory war with a Chechen gang soon after testifying for Nikov.

"What Chechen gang?" Danilov demanded at once.

"Not the one that would interest you," said Pavin, equally quickly, accustomed to the question. "Perhaps Nikov's your man?"

"We'll soon find out," said Danilov. "He's being brought in for questioning." Danilov supposed his religiously minded deputy actually believed in miracles. He certainly didn't.

William Cowley and Burt Bradley moved up to the more centrally convenient Manhattan FBI office and split equally between them the interviews with what in the end turned out to be six claimed eyewitnesses, three commuter plane pilots, a second trash barge captain, and a yacht charter skipper. They dismissed completely the account of the yacht skipper, whom they decided was seeking business publicity—and who later asked payment for media interviews—and at the end of a long day distilled down to just one page anything remotely of value from the remaining five. The consensus was that there had been two people—one possibly a woman—on the cruiser from which the missile had been fired. None of the witnesses had actually seen the ignition or anyone holding the launcher because the hitting of the Secretariat Tower had been more obvious. Four insisted the cruiser was blue and white, one that it had been entirely white. Two thought a blue canvas canopy had been erected over the flying bridge, three weren't sure it had a flying bridge at all. None could suggest a make, and the estimates of its length varied from between thirty feet and fifty-five feet. Only two chose the same photograph of one of the eight cruisers reported stolen in the previous week. One of the commuter pilots was so unsure he said it could have been any one of three.

By the end of that third full day no terrorist group had claimed responsibility, and the special task force Bradley created at Pennsylvania Avenue to computer analyze and cross-reference every known and potential faction—with an emphasis on missile or military technical expertise—had processed eight, with four breakaway associations, covering the spectrum from the Ku Klux Klan to the Black Brotherhood. Islamic fundamentalism was definitely slammed. It was Cowley's suggestion to ask Interpol to provide all likely international organizations in their files and to extend beyond known Islamic fundamentalist movements by asking the Mossad, Israel's intelligence service, for what information they possessed on the state terror structures of Iraq, Iran, Algeria, and the Sudan. The personal authority of Leonard Ross had been invoked for all three branches of the military to research their files for people with specialized weapons knowledge—particularly missiles—who had recently left or been discharged from their service.

Bradley said, "We're building ourselves a paper mountain and we ain't got Jack squat. We're just waiting for the next outrage."

"I know," accepted Cowley. He'd expected the FBI director to have more readily accepted his assessment that Washington was the most likely target. It had been bridge building to suggest it to Burt Bradley, too: The resentment from the other man at Cowley being officially designated case officer was obvious. For that reason Cowley had urged Bradley to include the warning in one of his early assessments, as if it had been his idea.

"You think your guy in Moscow's going to get anything?"

"Not on what we've been able to give him so far."

Bradley looked at his watch. "We're too late for happy hour, but I'm ready to pay full price."

If Bradley hadn't suggested it, Cowley knew he would have done so. Continuing the bridge building, to the benefit of the investigation, he told himself.

Cowley was struggling into his coat, so Bradley took the telephone call. At once he shouted, "Leave it! Don't touch a thing! Rope everything off until we get scientists up there." He looked across at Cowley with the telephone still in his hand. "Highway Patrol took until this afternoon to check out a report of a fire in a creek near New Rochelle. And found the *Eschevaux*, one of our missing boats."

"This is wonderful!" enthused Elizabeth Hollis.

"It's foreign. A Jaguar," said her son. "I can go 120 miles an hour at least."

"You haven't driven that fast?" the woman demanded, swiveling in her seat to look at him.

"Of course I haven't, mother! That would be illegal."

"You promise me?"

"I promise you."

"I couldn't live without you, Patrick. Without knowing you're always going to be close to me, looking after me now that your father's passed on."

"You're never going to have to. I keep telling you that."

She patted the leather seat. "I love the new smell!"

"It's nice, isn't it?"

"Only what you deserve, working so hard for the bank as you do."

"I don't want you to tell anyone how grateful they are," warned the man. "You know how jealous people get." He still used the three-year-old Volkswagen to drive to Albany. Would Carole— would *any* of the girls—go out with him if they knew about the Jaguar?

"I'd like people to know how important you are."

"No, mother. It's better this way—the way the bank wants it."

"I like going out for rides like this."

"Then we'll do it a lot," Hollis said.

Ironically the exit Hollis took off the interstate to get back to Rensselaer was very close to the mobile home park in which Clarence Snelling lived.

Snelling said, "They're not going to do anything about it, you know? They don't understand the technology they're relying on."

"What are *you* going to do about it?" demanded his wife.

"Go to the police," decided Snelling.

"What can they do?"

"Maybe they can frighten the bank into taking more action than they are so far."

6

The helicopter flight gave Cowley the chance to review everything he'd ordered put into place, as case officer in total charge with absolute authority and responsibility. He felt quite confident about it, with none of the first-day unreality.

He might have misunderstood, but he hadn't detected any of the usual resentment at federal authority interference from the local police chief, sheriff, or Highway Patrol commander to whom he'd spoken in turn, not even when he'd insisted the sealed-off area remain clear until the helicopter arrival of the forensic scientists and technicians from Washington, whom he'd alerted first because they had the farthest to travel. He had, though, accepted the police chief's offer of scene-of-crime forensic and communication vehicles and the suggestion that a sports field on the outskirts of New Rochelle, reasonably close to the coast, would be the best place for their helicopters to land. And there hadn't been any argument against his asking for an initial media blackout, although the police commander, Steven Barr, had warned that with so many agencies involved, it might already be too late. If it was they'd ensure no one got anywhere near the boat.

"The *Eschevaux* was one of eight cruisers reported stolen," reminded Bradley, beside Cowley. "What if this isn't the right one— just burned out by joy riders when they'd finished with it?"

"Better overkill than underkill," said Cowley. "Joy riders are more likely simply to have abandoned it."

Bradley nodded, persuaded. "So how much forensic will be left for the scientists to find?"

"Pray to whoever your God is," suggested Cowley, who didn't have one.

Steven Barr's distorted voice came on to their headsets from the already in-place communications van, promising to ferry them from the sports field to the boat. Then came the voice of Terry Osnan, the FBI agent in charge at Albany, who'd actually been working the area and reached New Rochelle by road, asking what he should do. Cowley repeated that he wanted no one anywhere near the cruiser until it had been scientifically checked for tire tracks or footprints "or for anything that might be there." He said, "Absolutely no contamination. If there's anything left at all it'll be forensic."

"Will do," assured the man, in a Southern accent.

"How many more of our guys are coming in by road?"

"Maybe five or six. And I'm told the owner's on his way down from Norwalk. A lawyer named Bonwitt. Harry Bonwitt. Bringing an insurance assessor with him."

"Who the hell told him?" Their information was that the *Eschevaux* was a fifty-two-foot Sea Ray that had disappeared from the biggest marina at the Norwalk inlet on Sunday night, after Bonwitt had returned from that day's sailing.

"Marina people, I guess. When the check was made on the boat's name."

"If Bonwitt gets there before I do, tell him the boat has been seized as a federal exhibit. Same rules for them as everyone else. Nowhere near it."

"He won't," intruded the pilot, linked to the conversation. "We'll be there in five minutes."

All the sports field nighttime lights were on, perfectly illuminating it as a landing area. There didn't seem to be a lot of light from nearby houses. There was one helicopter, marked Highway Patrol, already droop-rotored like a sleeping insect. There were a lot of cars and three vans, mostly marked police vehicles, parked in perfect pattern on the perimeter. As they began to descend, the pilot of the inbound Washington machine patched into their circuit with an estimate of ten minutes from landing. A new voice came on insisting the area remain totally untrampled. Cowley said he knew and so did everyone within a hundred miles, and the voice said he hoped so.

The three local force commanders were waiting by an unmarked but antenna-haired communications van. All were in uniform. Steven Barr was tall, bespectacled, and spoke in a slow New England accent. John Sharpe, the sheriff, made a stark comparison, short and overweight, his belt sagging. Alan Petrich, the Highway Patrol chief, was overweight, too, and clearly asthmatic, wheezing his way through the introductions performed by Osnan, a sports-jacketed, angular-faced man.

To the three men Cowley said, "Thank you for what you've done."

"Let's hope it produces something," said Barr, flat-voiced. "Bastards hit New York again and it goes off this time—and the wind's in the right direction—we could be right in line."

"You're the one who went into the tower with the secretary-general, aren't you?" said Sharpe admiringly. "What was it like?"

If there was a media leak he'd know who it came from, Cowley decided. "A mess. How many people walked around after the boat was found?"

"My patrolman, Wayne Mitchell," said Petrich.

"No one else?" pressed Cowley hopefully.

"No."

"What about the person who found it?" Bradley asked.

"Wasn't found," wheezed the man. "It was a phone in. Woman said she'd seen a flash fire and gave a location that didn't check out. That's why it took so long for us to find it."

"We got a name for who phoned in?"

Petrich and the sheriff exchanged looks. "Phone got put down. Gal cheating on her husband, maybe."

"Lot of that goes on in these woods," said Sharpe.

"You run a numbers check!" demanded Cowley.

"Doing it," said the man.

"The message recorded?"

The man extended his hand, cupping the cassette. "Every word that went between the caller and my dispatcher." He smiled.

"The original?" Cowley demanded again.

"Didn't think you'd want the rest."

"A copy won't be admissable in a federal court!" said Cowley, the anger burning through him. He kept his voice even. "I need the original. Can you arrange that now? I don't want it overrecorded." He didn't respond to Bradley's sideways look.

As the Highway Patrol commander disappeared inside the communications truck, Cowley told Osnan he wanted the man to become communications and evidence officer, handing him the copied cassette. The end of the conversation was almost drowned out by the noise of the descending Washington helicopter, a huge fore- and aft-rotored Chinook. The baggage-laden scientists and technicians filed off with military precision, led by a tall and heavy black man who imperiously demanded Cowley by name, said his was Jefferson Jones and that he hoped to Christ everything had been left as is. Cowley decided that if the man had brought spare scene-of-crime coveralls, he wouldn't be as constricted as he'd been going into the UN building in the protective space suit.

Most of the Washington group fit into a commandeered bus Cowley hadn't seen until it approached the control center. He traveled with Jones, Bradley, and the three local men in a backup carrier, which in turn was followed by marked and unmarked police cars. It was abruptly dark out of the sports field illumination, with only isolated house lights along the streets. Cowley guessed it was a comparatively high-priced residential area. Jones said they intended to carry out the most detailed search possible on the immediate surrounding area and what was left of the boat itself but would probably bring in a Tarhe Sky Crane the following day to fly the wreck for laboratory stripping and examination in Washington.

"We know how much *is* left?" he asked.

"My patrolman says it's burned down mostly to the waterline but that there's some cabin and superstructure in places," said the Highway Patrol chief.

"Then we're in business." Jones grinned. "If the bad guys really knew how much we can recover, there wouldn't be any crime—they'd know we'll catch them in the end."

Cowley thought the black man looked too old still to be influenced by the confidence of the bureau training videos. They left all house lights behind very quickly, and from the widely interspersed streetlamps and heavy jolting Cowley guessed they had turned on to country side roads. Steven Barr seemed to know where they were, warning they were only about two miles away. Almost at once they came to the first road block, jointly manned by Highway Patrol and local police. They had to stop for spiked, tire-puncturing strips to be moved out of their way. Cowley was impressed. There were two more blocks—although no puncturing strips—before Cowley became aware of a growing brightness. His initial, frightened thought was that somehow the fire had again taken hold of the cruiser.

Barr said, "We've got every available floodlight there—ours, the patrol's, and fire department—each with separate generator trucks."

Cowley was about to speak when Jones said, "Seems to me you've done one hell of a good job. If all local forces were as efficient, we'd all spend more time at home with our wives and families."

When he got out Cowley realized what passed for a road had narrowed to little more than a track, which the generator trucks totally blocked ahead of the arriving vehicles. To the left a sparse forest was whitened by artificial light right to the track edge, where the yellow scene-of-crime sectioning tape began. Although the line of light indicated the direction of the burned-out cruiser, it wasn't possible to see it or the creek. There was no path leading toward it, either, although about twenty yards back in the direction from which they'd come, their lane widened into a turnoff. In it, already parked, were several vans, one another communications vehicle. Another was Wayne Mitchell's Highway Patrol car. He stood waiting beside it, a young, fresh-faced blond whom Cowley put no older than twenty-five. He saluted his commander as they approached. Cowley led but it was Jones who again spoke first. "You wanna tell me what we got in there?"

"Top part of the boat's mostly gone, just odd bits still there and some deck railing," said Mitchell. "What's left is full of water, so I guess it's holed somewhere although I didn't see where. The moment I saw the name I recognized it as one of the boats reported missing so I came straight back to the car and called in."

"How come you stopped and walked into the forest at this precise point?" asked Cowley.

"Didn't," said the man. "The report that was phoned in put the fire about a mile down the creek, toward the bigger inlet where there's quite a few boats. So that's where I started. When I didn't find anything I walked along the bank until I came to it. It's not in the creek itself. Looks like a long time ago someone dug out a space to leave a boat: a kind of a canal. That's where it is—kinda pulled out of the channel and left in its own space."

"So did you walk out that way?" pressed Jones, indicating the lighted area.

"No sir," said Mitchell. "Took myself some markers toward the road here—those three trees over there, taller than the rest—and went back along the creek to my car. And drove up here."

"Did you go in to check once you got here?" pressed the scientist.

"Just once. Straight in, straight out."

"What's the ground like, underfoot?"

"Soft. I can show you my tracks."

"This is getting better." Jones beamed.

"What about the creek bank and the canal itself?" asked Cowley.

"Mud."

"But the creek is navigable for something fifty-two feet long?" queried Bradley. "That's a big boat."

"Hardly," said the officer. "I didn't spend any time looking closely and the current's washed out any marks there might be on the bottom, but you can *see* the bottom. And where the water doesn't reach there's a lot of score marks on the bank, where it obviously hit."

Jones looked in the direction of the light again and said, "Don't know how we're going to get the goddamned thing out through those trees."

"There's some open ground by the canal itself," offered Mitchell.

"Sufficient to get it clear of the water for the first examination?"

"I'd say so," guessed the patrolman.

Turning to Steven Barr, the forensic leader said, "You think you could get me one of those dinky garden tractors, small enough to maneuver through those trees? I'll want to haul the boat out of the water. Drain it and then go over it tonight and tomorrow. Depending on how we find the creek, after that I might raft it back to where there's enough hard standing to bring in the lifting helicopter."

"I got one of my own in the backyard," Sheriff Sharpe said proudly. "Happy to make it available."

"Then let's go to work," urged Jones to the scientific team assembled loosely behind them.

Jones did have a spare plastic anticontamination coverall, which he loaned to Cowley with the injunction not to enter the forest until there was a signal. Bradley borrowed one from another scientist approximately his size. The technical squad suited up and moved off with the military precision with which they'd disembarked from their helicopter, Wayne Mitchell going to the tree line with them to point out his route. One of the squad, another black man, immediately took a plaster cast of Mitchell's indentation and one of the patrolman's foot. From the way they worked Cowley guessed they were a permanent professional team. There was hardly any conversation, everyone seeming to know what to do without any instruction from Jefferson Jones. The group divided into three-man squads, each to a section that they subdivided by tape, stirring and lifting the forest debris with slim, rubber-encased sticks. Twice more footprint casts were taken. From the line, Cowley guessed they were again those of the Highway Patrol officer. Behind the main body a still photographer and a television operator maintained a constant record.

One of the turnoff trucks turned out to be a refreshment truck—which further impressed Cowley, although the coffee didn't. He welcomed the excuse to abandon it when he was summoned, by name, to the communications van. From his communication truck back at the sports field, Osnan said Harry Bonwitt had arrived with his marine insurance assessor. He was refusing to accept the legality of what remained of the *Eschevaux* being a federal exhibit and was insisting on coming down to the scene to examine his property.

"Put him on." Cowley sighed.

"You hear what I'm telling you, sir," rasped a voice without any greeting.

"And I'd like you to hear what I'm telling you, Mr. Bonwitt," Cowley said politely, knowing the exchange was being recorded. "This area is sealed, on my authority as a federal officer. And by that same authority I have declared what's left of the *Eschevaux* to be a federal exhibit in any future prosecution. Neither you nor your assessor will be allowed to examine it until all our forensic tests are completed, which isn't likely to be for at least another twenty-four hours. Probably longer. If you attempt to do so, you will be arrested for attempting to impede a federal investigation. If you want the appropriate statute for that, I'll be happy to direct you toward it. Is all that clear to you, Mr. Bonwitt?"

The silence was broken only by the hiss of static. At last the man said, in a quivering voice, "Are you familiar, sir, with the law of habeas corpus?"

"Perfectly familiar," assured Cowley. "But I don't want this to escalate into your arrest or your need to invoke it. There is no cause for either. I'm extremely sorry what's happened to your boat and I am not in any way trying to be obstructive. I am, in fact, asking for your cooperation. Your boat will be extensively photographed in situ and at all stages during its examination. And as soon as it's possible I'll make photographs available to your and your insurance examiner."

"I shall sue," threatened the lawyer. "I'll sue you personally. And your director. And the bureau. For illegal detention of property."

"Perhaps we shouldn't imperil your action or my defense by talking about it anymore?" said Cowley, depressing the cut-off switch.

Terry Osnan answered when Cowley called back almost immediately.

Osnan said, "He's stormed off. I think he's coming your way."

"Any more of our guys turned up?"

"Three."

"Send them after him. He'll be stopped at the first roadblock. They're to arrest him."

"For what?"

"Willfully obstructing a federal investigation."

Cowley got back to the refreshment truck in time to see the plastic-suited Burt Bradley moving into the forest toward the unseen boat. Some of the arc lights had been moved farther in, too. Barr said, "You've been given the go-ahead. Mind if Alan and I tag along?"

"Not if Jones doesn't. But do me a favor first. Speak to your guys at the first roadblock. The owner's probably on his way here. Tell them not to let him pass until some bureau guys catch up to arrest him. Might be an idea to leave those blowout strips down."

The borrowed protection was slightly too large but it was still more comfortable than the space suit. The soft ground sucked underfoot as Cowley walked side by side with the Highway Patrol chief. Cowley said, "Patrolman Mitchell did well. I'll see there's a commendation from the bureau."

"I wish we'd done so well at headquarters," apologized Petrich. "I'm not sure but I think the original tape might have been overlaid."

"When *will* you be sure?"

"Couple of hours."

The forest floor shelved nearer the creek into a low, sloping bank.

What Mitchell had described as a canal was, in fact, the shape of a boat long ago dug out and abandoned. The burned hulk of the *Eschevaux* fit snugly into it. What remained was almost completely submerged, just some fire-twisted bow and portside rail and a small section of the cockpit protruding above the water. A lot of blackened debris had collapsed below it, but Cowley didn't think there was enough for there to have been a flying bridge. He didn't actually know what a Sea Ray looked like. Four forensic technicians were already in the water attaching hawsers so malleable Cowley guessed they were specially manufactured for a purpose like this. Two were standing in the creek itself. As the water only came up to their thighs, Cowley decided it would be difficult to raft the cruiser down to deeper water. The two cameramen were also in the water, taking pictures. Everyone else stood around, waiting for the hulk to be pulled clear of the water. Metal mesh matting had been laid out to receive it.

Jefferson Jones saw Cowley and the Highway Patrol commander arrive at the forest lip and immediately raised a stopping hand, walking back toward them with Burt Bradley.

To Petrich the scientist said, "Here's fine, but I don't want you any closer without a suit, OK?"

"OK," agreed the man.

"Although it's probably an unnecessary precaution," Jones added, to Cowley. "You know what we found? The bastards raked after themselves as they walked away. Didn't leave a thing, not a goddamned thing! They won't have left anything in the boat, either."

"And look at the creek," prompted Bradley. "Getting a boat that size this far would have been like Humphrey Bogart and the *African Queen* all over again."

"They certainly knew what they were doing," said Jones. "I'd have said it would have been impossible to leave ground this soft without a single impression, but that's what they did. We get them I personally want to ask them how they did it. These guys had jungle training, for sure."

"How'd they sink what's left?" asked Cowley.

"Holed it twice in the bow, as far as I can make out while it's still in the water," said Jones. "We'll have to be careful how we rig those hawsers so the damn thing doesn't fall apart as we haul it out."

They turned at an approaching noise. Sheriff Sharpe sat commandingly on his garden tractor, maneuvering it through the tree line, smiling at the flash of the official camera. "All gassed up and ready to go," he announced.

From this direction it was easier to make out the track at which the forest stopped. Steven Barr was there, beckoning, although Cowley couldn't hear what he was shouting. He set off back toward the policeman as Barr started toward him. Cowley walked, mentally trying to assess what he had, but perhaps more worryingly what he didn't have. Even if the Highway Patrol's copy tape wasn't admissible in court and the original was lost, a voice print would still be possible if indeed the call had been made by whoever was involved and not some woman cheating on her husband. The total lack so far of a single piece of forensic evidence was the overwhelming disappointment. Jefferson Jones was right. The bastards had known *exactly* what they were doing, how and where they were doing it, right down to choosing the place to burn the boat and that they'd need rakes to cover their tracks. *These guys had jungle training for sure* echoed in Cowley's head. And if . . .

Cowley stopped, numbed by the awareness, and turned. Bradley and the uniformed sheriff and Highway Patrol chief were the only people he could see, the others all hidden at the bottom of the slope where the boat lay. He heard the roar of the tractor engine being gunned and screamed, "No! Stop! No!" but the accelerating noise was too loud for them to hear. Cowley started to run back but there was a deafening, ear-blocking explosion and the three men Cowley could see were visibly lifted off the ground. He saw pieces of other bodies—certainly one unattached head—in the air before he was stopped by some invisible force that hit him so hard all the breath was driven from his body and he couldn't suck it in again. He felt himself lifted off his feet, too, and there was total, spinning blackness. Cowley's last conscious thought was that there wasn't any pain and that maybe it didn't hurt to die after all.

As they drove north, leaving the Gorki outskirts behind, Dimitri Danilov recognized that his impression from the air was confirmed on the ground. The military manufacturing plants were carefully created individual parts of an entire and composite whole, each factory separated by its perimeter fence and barriered—sometimes tower-dominated—private approach road.

It was one of several realizations, ranging from the fact that even this close the taiga through which they were driving still appeared black, not green, to the complete reversal in how he was being treated. From the one extreme of his dismissively ignored arrival there hadn't been a waking moment when he hadn't been in the watchful presence of either Oleg Reztsov or Gennardi Averin or both, like now. And the plainclothed presence of two men at an adjoining breakfast table that morning had been almost embarrassingly obvious. He wondered if they'd already reported his slipping the side plate knife into his pocket before asking for envelopes at the reception desk.

Identifying another of Danilov's already reached awarenesses, Reztsov indicated a service road controlled by both barriers and a tower and said, "See what I mean about the degree of security? Nothing left of these plants that wasn't intended to."

"Exactly," Danilov replied.

"I meant officially," said the stiff-faced police chief.

"We're already getting street rumors," said Averin from the front seat, trying to come to his superior's rescue. "The gangs are worried about the sudden interest we're taking in them."

Danilov didn't bother to challenge the ridiculously premature claim or ask why the interest had been so sudden. "What about Viktor Nikov?"

"The most interesting of all," said the major. "Not at his home or any of his garages. Hasn't been seen for several days, apparently."

"Why not, do you think?" questioned Danilov. He hadn't told them of Pavin's discoveries in Moscow about Nikov's defense witnesses.

"Who knows?" Reztsov shrugged.

"The question we've got to answer, along with all the rest," suggested Danilov.

According to Danilov's separate parts-of-a-whole assessment, Plant 35 was at the very edge of the straggling installation. Beyond the barrier and tower checkpoint there were two more manned control points before they reached the gates themselves, where their identities were confirmed for a fourth time.

Professor Sergei Alexandrovich Ivanov, the director of Plant 35, was a hugely bearded, limp-haired man with the distracted demeanor of an academic and the physical appearance of a Mongol wrestler. The office was a box, like all the boxes—some empty and without lights, most of the others seemingly inactive, despite their being occupied by white-coated or protectively dressed staff—that had preceded it. Ivanov's white coat was not newly stained but dirtily ingrained by wear. There was so little room that Averin had to remain standing. There was no hospitality prepared for the visit, which Danilov believed the scientist, whom he guessed to be well beyond seventy, had genuinely forgotten. Danilov said, "You know what happened in New York?"

There was a hesitation before the bearded man said, "Yes. Of course."

Danilov offered the FBI photographs of the missile and said, "You recognize it?"

The frowned hesitation was longer this time, before the director said almost wistfully, "These were a very long time ago. I'd almost forgotten."

"But they were produced here!" demanded Danilov, impatient with nostalgia.

"Before my appointment," said the man, instantly defensive. "It was a ridiculous idea, trying to improvise a hybrid. The rocket wasn't designed to deliver it. But in the sixties everything and everybody was paranoid: Everyone's finger on the red button, no one thinking beyond the official line." He frowned toward the two policemen, and Danilov identified the never-lost communist legacy of fear of informants and provocateurs.

"As long ago as that?" queried Danilov.

"The prototype was developed here in 1961. I stopped the program myself when I got here in 1975," said Ivanov. "Absurd. Could never properly have worked without its own delivery systems."

"How many such warheads were built?" pressed Danilov.

Ivanov gave a shrug of uncertainty. "Who knows throughout the Soviet Union?"

The disappointed Danilov said, "They weren't *only* made here?"

"Of course not," said Ivanov, as if the question were naive. "Inconceivable though it seems now—as it was then, scientifically or ballistically—this thing"—he swept a disparaging hand toward the photographs, still laid out on his desk—"this thing was to be our recovery for Khrushchev being faced down by Kennedy over Cuba. It didn't matter that it never flew properly, or that the rockets Khrushchev put on Cuba didn't have a guidance system that would have gotten them to Florida. Central Planning decreed they had to be produced and so they were, by the hundreds—"

"Hundreds!" broke in Danilov, in stomach-dropping despair.

Ivanov gave another empty shrug. "At least. The prototype was produced here; it proved to be totally ineffective. But what did that matter at that time? Moscow always knew better. They demanded a stockpile—set a norm which we initially met but couldn't sustain so the production was extended."

"To where?" Reztsov broke in.

Ivanov's shoulders rose and fell again in what Danilov guessed to be a habitual responsibility-avoidance gesture. "Moscow, I believe. Two definitely just outside Leningrad, as it was then. And in the republics that were then part of the Union. Kiev, certainly. There was a great concentration of weaponry—nuclear, too—in the Ukraine because of its geographic position, so close to the West."

"What about these numbers?" demanded Danilov, pointing to the print that specifically showed them on the side of each canister. "What do they signify?"

"Stock designation," identified Ivanov.

"So they identify the manufacturing plant?" seized Danilov, suspecting an admission.

"No," said Ivanov. "They were issued from Moscow, for Moscow's records, not ours. The zero in both lines of numerals: That's Moscow."

"What about the emergency phone number?" persisted Danilov.

"Seven numerals," the professor pointed out. "That's Moscow again."

"There's a treaty. Signed in 1993. Everything should have been destroyed," reminded Danilov.

"You can't just pour these things down a sink, flush it away. There's been a start."

"This warhead didn't work and was developed more than thirty years ago!" protested Danilov.

"*Because* it didn't work it was considered the least important. We still work to Moscow's instructions: Follow ministry guidance."

Danilov knew he shouldn't have been surprised at the inference of a treaty being abrogated—Washington was probably only making token gestures, as well—but he was. How many people at the emergency meeting—Sergei Gromov, from the Defense Ministry, in particular—had known about the extent of the program and Moscow's control of it? "How many of these do you still have here at this plant?"

Ivanov groped in a desk drawer. Papers erupted at once, and he disturbed more shuffling through the lucky dip tub, finally emerging triumphantly with a three-ring binder it took him several more minutes to pick through. Still triumphant, he announced, "Fifty-six!"

"When was that count taken?"

The shrug came again. "There's no date. It's a program that ended a long time ago, as I said."

"So it's an old figure?"

"Yes," conceded the man.

"It wasn't verified, before our coming today?"

"No."

"So you wouldn't know if one—or more than one—was missing?"

"No. I don't see how there could be, though."

"Can I see them?"

"What!"

The question came from Reztsov, not the director. Danilov didn't respond to the police chief. Instead he repeated to Ivanov, "Can I see them? They're inert—harmless—in storage, aren't they?"

"Yes," Ivanov said doubtfully.

"So we could look at them?" persisted Danilov, not knowing to what question the older man had been responding.

"I suppose so," said Ivanov, still doubtful.

"Then I'd like to. Now." As Danilov rose, intending to carry out his breakfast knife idea, another occurred to him. He decided to wait. The other three men followed hesitantly. They went along a different corridor from the one along which they'd approached. Some of the protectively suited and helmeted scientists in the now-occupied offices were working with their arms and hands encased in sleeves and gloves forming permanent parts of the sealed chambers at which they stood.

Danilov said, "The process of destruction?"

"There is always a defensive need," said Ivanov. "Parts of our country are far closer to those known to possess chemical and biological capability than we ever were to the United States of America."

So the 1993 agreement wasn't just being abrogated, it was being positively ignored, Danilov realized. He watched the elevator's indicator light blink down to the fourth basement level, which he calculated from the time it took to pass the preceding three basement tiers to be at least half a mile underground. Danilov wondered how many hundreds—thousands—of germ warfare weapons were stored above and below him; there had been a fifth and sixth level on the indicator panel. There'd been no security check on their entering the elevator—Ivanov had not even used an electronically operating pass key—and there wasn't on the level at which they emerged. The basement was simply an enormous, gouged-out cavern, the central corridor disappearing into a joined, arrowhead point of infinity at its unseen end. It remained closed despite their walking for at least five minutes toward it, to get to a numbered door, and Danilov judged that underground the chemical and biological facility of Plant 35 extended at least three times the building's size above ground. He adjusted that estimate to five times the size when he followed

Ivanov into the side chamber the far end of which he still couldn't see.

It was stark and simple, row after row of floor-to-ceiling metal framing, each double warhead in its special, clamped pod about a meter from the one next to it. Danilov didn't need to multiply row number by row content to know this one storage chamber alone contained at least four times Ivanov's estimate of surviving warheads.

Obviously aware of it himself—but seeming genuinely confused—the huge, bearded man said, "Our records must be wrong. It was always difficult to be accurate, maintaining norms."

Danilov knew it had been. But the falsification had invariably been to exaggerate the insisted-upon production figures to appear to comply with the demand, not to *under*estimate it. The fresh wash of frustration was wiped away almost immediately by anger. He was being treated like a fool by the local militia on one hand and suffering the chaos of norm-fulfilling, responsibility-avoiding centralized bureaucracy on the other. Just as quickly he curbed the fury, sure there was still a way he could beat both: certainly to prove whether what smashed into the UN building had come from here.

Every module in orderly lines before him was printed with the same stenciled lettering as in the American photograph, and there was similar batch numbering. None of those he saw as he passed, however, matched those in the photograph, but the designation of Plant 35 appeared to be in identical stenciling. None was dated after 1975. He continued slowly down the corridor, between the racks, isolating the break halfway down, to his left. There was a gap of three empty frames before the storage continued. None of these warheads was dated. Pointing to those beyond the separation, Danilov said, "Why the division?"

"They haven't been filled," said Ivanov. "That's why they're undated. Must mark my arrival, when I stopped the program."

"Good!" Danilov said briskly. "I'm impounding one now under presidential authority. Have it removed from the frame for me to take it with me."

"What . . . ?" said Reztsov, his voice trailing. "I don't—"

"A comparable exhibit," said Danilov. He wasn't looking at the other three men. Instead he went back to the lettered canisters, taking from one pocket the envelope and from another the table knife he'd picked up that morning from the hotel.

"Now what are you doing?" Reztsov demanded impatiently, as Danilov began carefully scraping both the letter and numerical paint and undercoating into an envelope.

"Forensic exhibit," Danilov said shortly.

"For what?" asked Reztsov.

"Proof," answered Danilov, although still concentrating on the facility director. "To whom do you report the loss or theft of materiel?"

"It doesn't happen," insisted Ivanov.

"It has now," said Danilov.

"Yes," agreed Ivanov. "I suppose it has. Moscow. That's who has to be told. That's who I thought you were, someone from the Defense or Science ministries."

"I don't envy you this investigation," said Reztsov, on their way back into the city. "Don't envy you at all."

Yuri Pavin's third anxious call came as Danilov entered the National Hotel, the canvas-wrapped missile casing under his arm. He took the call in the lobby booth.

"Is he dead?" Danilov demanded at once.

"That's not clear," said the colonel. "Television reports are naming him as being there; he was in charge. And they're saying at least sixteen people died. But the bureau is refusing to name them until all the next of kin have been informed."

The woman who answered Cowley's extension when Danilov called Washington direct said she wasn't authorized to give out any information but that she'd pass Danilov's name and inquiry on and suggested that he call later. Danilov telephoned Moscow again, for Pavin to initiate the inquiries he wanted.

And then, alone in his room, Danilov spent some time on the empty warhead and the paint scrapings to complete the idea that came to him in the missile basement, pleased bad Russian workmanship and material made it comparatively easy. He'd feared he might have needed a tool, pincers or pliers, for the warhead, but he didn't. Finally satisfied, he put the empty containers in the clothes closet.

When he located CNN on his room television, a reporter was talking to the camera from a forest track about a scene of total devastation where no devastation was visible. But then the picture changed to a helicopter shot of a crater already turned into a lake from the flowing creek, with every tree snapped or totally flattened for what the reporter said was a radius of a hundred yards. Unnecessarily, because it could be seen, the man added that although it had been extinguished, the underbrush was still smoldering from the fire that followed the explosion. The death toll had risen. It now stood at seventeen.

"Hi! Can I sit with you?"

Hollis looked up, startled, at Carole Parker standing by his otherwise empty table. "Yes . . . please. Of course." He tried to get politely to his feet but she'd sat before he was able.

"Whatever was on your mind certainly wasn't here!" she said.

"Thinking about a lot of things," said Hollis. His determination not to receive the next contact call from the General was wavering. He knew he shouldn't—that to do so was ridiculous—but part of him, a bit part, wanted to take it.

"Must have a lot to think about, being the manager."

"It's a lot of responsibility." Why was Carole Parker, pursued by every man in the branch, choosing to sit with him?

"Surprised you haven't been head-hunted yet by one of the bigger groups."

"I'm happy here." He hoped he wasn't sweating. He had the same sort of empty-stomached feeling he'd felt on the day of the UN attack.

"You mean you wouldn't go to somewhere like New York or Chicago if you got an offer!"

Hollis laughed, hoping his chest wouldn't tighten up as it did sometimes when he was excited. "I'll decide that when I get the offer."

"I wouldn't mind transferring to a department like yours."

"Why don't we talk about it sometime?"

"I'd like that." She smiled.

7

Dying—being dead—did hurt: It was the worst pain Cowley had ever known. His head was being crushed and he wanted to stop, to push away, whatever or whoever was doing it, but he couldn't move his hands or his arms—any part of him. Nothing would move or do what he wanted. Paralyzed. He tried to call out for it to stop, and his throat felt as if there were words but he couldn't hear himself speak, although someone was saying something a long way away. When he tried to open his eyes it was too bright, searing light burning directly at him. It hurt even more and got worse, if it was possible to get worse, when he jerked his head to one side to avoid the glare. There were a lot of hands on him, pushing and feeling, and his name, his name being said over and over again, but still it was a long way off. He tried to say yes, that he could hear whoever it was, but there was no sound of his saying it. The faraway voice said they'd try to stop the pain but to keep his eyes closed, which he didn't need to be told. There were more voices, the noise of talking, but he couldn't separate the words, not enough to make any sense of them. The pain did start to go—not go, not completely, but lessened so that it didn't feel as if his head were being crushed to the point of bursting, making him scream. He wondered if he had actually screamed because there was this feeling, like a vibration in his throat that there was when you talked.

"Bill?" The voice was louder, to his right, not his left. It said, not quite so distinctly, "The perforation is in the left, not the right," and then more directly, "Yes, Bill. You're talking. We can hear you. You're all right. You're fine. You're going to sleep now and it'll be a lot better in a while."

The blackness wasn't the blackness of dying. The pain stayed in his head, although not so bad—bearable even—and there was a dream that he knew wasn't really a dream. Of people being in the air, as if they were flying: Burt Bradley and the sheriff with the tractor whose name he couldn't remember and the Highway Patrol commander whose name he couldn't remember, either, but then he could—Petrich, Alan Petrich—and an explosion although he couldn't hear any noise this time. But there were voices he could hear, real voices that he could hear much more clearly.

One said, "You feeling better this time, Bill?" and Cowley felt himself—distantly heard himself—say, "Yes," because he did, compared to how it had been before. He could endure the pain in his head now. He hadn't been aware of the ache in his chest the first time but that was bearable, too, as long as he didn't breathe too deeply.

"My name's Pepper. Joe Pepper. You're in the George Washington University Hospital in Washington, and I'm your neurologist. You understand what I'm telling you, Bill?"

"Yes."

"That's good!" Pepper said enthusiastically. "That's very good indeed. I've taken away all the harsh light and I want you to open your eyes. I'll tell you when we're going to shine a beam directly in, OK?"

"OK."

"Open now."

There were several people—the movement of several people—around the bed, but he couldn't distinguish anything about them. Everyone had more than one face and body, each superimposing on the other, although they didn't quite fit, each outline slightly off center. He said, "I can't see. Not properly. It's blurred . . . like. . . ."

"Here comes the light," warned Pepper. "We're going to hold your eye open."

It hurt but not so much as before, and a different voice said, "No corneal or retinal damage. I'm pleased with that. Looks like it's all down to you, Joe."

Pepper said, "There had to be some good news."

"I thought I'd been killed," said Cowley. The blur wouldn't go but it didn't hurt any longer to keep his eyes open.

The neurologist said, "You've got a pretty severe concussion. You were against a tree so you were either blown into it or something hit you. You've got twelve stitches in the side of your head but there's no skull fracture. You've got a busted rib, on the right. And your left eardrum is perforated . . ."

"My eyes . . . ?"

"Temporary," assured the other voice. "You've jarred, maybe even bruised, the optic nerve. It'll go, very quickly."

Pepper said, "And the hearing in your left ear will get better, although it won't ever be quite like it was before. Considering, you're one hell of a lucky guy."

"What about everyone else?" asked Cowley. He already had the impression that his hearing was clearer.

"No need to talk about that now," Pepper said at once.

A woman's voice, pleasantly soft but urgent, said, "We need the debrief. He turned back. We need whatever it was—"

"Who's that?" demanded Cowley.

"My name's Darnley, Bill. Pamela Darnley. I'm from the bureau. You feel able to talk to me?"

"What unit?"

"Terrorism. You OK to talk to me?"

"Of course I'm—" began Cowley, impatiently loud, but he had to stop because of the quick burst of pain at his own noise. More quietly he said, "How many dead?"

The woman said, "A lot. Seventeen."

Cowley squinted at the blur of faces at the bottom of his bed, wishing he could see her. "Burt Bradley dead?"

"Lost his right arm completely. And his right leg, below the knee. And he's blind.

"Jesus Christ! The rest?"

"Every one."

"I saw—" started Cowley, but she came in too quickly.

"That's what I need to know! What did you see?"

"—bits of bodies," Cowley finished.

There was a silence around the bed. She said, "It was a hell of a mess. You sure you can go on with this?"

"I'm your case officer! Sharpe. What happened to Sharpe?" That was the sheriff's name, John Sharpe. His chest throbbed from the fresh outburst: the broken rib, he supposed.

"Dead," she said.

"Petrich?"

"Dead. The only local guy to survive was Steven Barr. He was farther away than you; didn't get touched. But he saw you turn and start to go back. Say something?"

Cowley carefully moved his head toward where he imagined the neurologist to be. "What day is it? I mean, how long have I been here since it happened?"

"It's the day after. The afternoon. Less than twenty-four hours."

"How long before my eyes clear?"

"Forget it," said Pepper. "You're not doing anything for a long time."

"Neither are seventeen others guys, are they?"

He'd slept again, although he hadn't wanted to, but when he opened his eyes once more there was a definite improvement in his vision. The ophthalmic surgeon who'd examined him before said the nerve was obviously only jarred, which was good, and Pepper, who turned out to be a young but completely bald man, decided it was OK for Pamela Darnley to go on with the debriefing.

Even close up he couldn't properly discern her features, although he could see she was dark-haired, worn short, and had large glasses, which were black framed. She smelled good. She told him she'd set up the tape recorder on the edge of his bed and that the moment he felt like stopping he had to—Dr. Pepper was sitting in on the interview with them—but the bureau wanted everything he could remember, particularly why he'd turned and started to shout at the moment of the explosion.

"The video and still camera?" demanded Cowley. "They survive?"

"The video was relayed automatically. So we've got it all. The still camera was badly smashed, but they're working on that now to see what they can salvage."

"What about the video commentary?"

"That's with the video. That's OK."

"Anything on it about jungle training? Raking their tracks?"

She didn't reply at once. "There's something about raking the ground. I don't remember anything about jungle training: I need to check."

"While they were waiting for the tractor, to pull the boat out, I talked with Jefferson Jones. He told me that they'd literally cleared their tracks. He said, "These guys got jungle training, for sure." Soldiers—particularly special unit guys who might also know how to fire a missile from a moving boat—get jungle training. And special unit training always involves booby-trapping abandoned materiel. That cruiser was very specifically abandoned and the trap set to get the maximum number of people—bureau personnel—around it by initially giving the wrong location."

"That all?" She sounded disappointed.

"If I'd worked it out five minutes earlier seventeen people wouldn't now be dead and Burt Bradley would still have his arms and legs and eyes."

"I'm sorry," said Pamela.

"The wrong-location call to the Highway Patrol been traced?" he asked.

"A public booth in a mall at New Rochelle."

"The cassette we've got is a copy."

"The original's gone. Wiped."

"Shit! Any claimed responsibility yet?"

"No."

"How'd the bomb work?" he demanded.

"Bombs," corrected Pamela. "From the amount of recovered metal, there were at least three."

"How'd they work?"

"Again it's preliminary thinking, but it looks like antipersonnel stuff with a slack wire connected to the detonator or pin. When the boat started to move the wire tightened, activating the detonator or pulling out the pin." She hesitated. "And they *were* antipersonnel. Shrapnel-packed, for maximum physical damage after detonation."

"Russian manufacture?" pressed Cowley.

"Nothing on that yet. The metal's being analyzed, obviously."

On the helicopter flight from New York he'd said overkill was better than underkill, Cowley remembered. He remembered, too, the forensic team leader's praise of the local organization and the remark about spending more time with wives and families. "Jefferson Jones have any kids?"

"Six," the woman said shortly.

"You told me you were with the terrorism unit?"

"I've taken Burt's place. Temporarily at the moment."

"Tell Ross I'm not off the case."

"I think I should have some input here," intruded Pepper but Cowley spoke over him.

"I'm not off the case! We *are* looking for people—*some* people at least—with special military experience and training. The whole thing was planned like a military operation: the attack on the UN, everything that happened afterward. I want every militant or crazy in the New Rochelle area—everywhere in New York State, Connecticut, and New Hampshire—checked out. If it wasn't local knowledge, they reconnoitered, certainly the creek. Patrolman Mitchell talked of a marina farther downriver. Check every single boat owner and marina—and I mean *every single one*—for strangers seen moving about, as if they had a special interest: taking notes, photographs, stuff like that. And go hard on the military. They're ducking. I want the names of every guy—and girl—whose records show a connection with any militant group that got them recognized or into trouble. Especially if it got as far as a court-martial. OK?"

"Bill," said the woman upon whom he couldn't properly focus. And paused. "Bill," she started again. "A few hours ago you thought you were dead. So did a lot of other people, me included. We've got to get these bastards before they kill anyone else, which means everyone's got to be thinking straight, seeing straight." She stopped. "I'm sorry, I wasn't trying to be smart about seeing straight. The director's asked me to report back, how you are. And I don't think and the hospital doesn't think—Dr. Pepper here doesn't think—that you're in any fit state to go on heading this investigation. That if you tried you'd endanger it. We're not talking feelings or attitudes here. We're talking operational practicality." And my future, Pamela Darnley thought. My big chance, once-in-a-lifetime fast-track future opportunity.

"You got any problem with the way I've been thinking, analyzing?"

There was a pause. "No." Who the fuck did this guy thing he was, Superman?

"You believe you can organize the manpower—switch it from the concentration upon finding the boat, which we don't need to do anymore—to pursue the special services' check?"

"Yes."

"You got any other line of inquiry to follow at this precise moment?"

"No." She wished she had.

"I'll judge my own capability. And if something comes up before I think I *am* capable, I'll back off. Not for one moment, for any half-assed personal reason, will I endanger a successful investigation. You do me a favor and tell Ross that? Say that's how I feel and ask him to go with me."

"I'll tell him," promised the woman. She wouldn't have had to—could have used different words and expressions without actually lying—if the damned neurologist hadn't been there as a witness.

"Tell him that although the Hoover Building isn't a line office, that's where I think the incident room should be, where he has instant access. Bring Terry Osnan in as controller and evidence officer."

Pamela nodded, hating what she considered the subsidiary, gofer role.

"Anything else?"

"There was a call from Russia. Dimitri Danilov. Just to find out about you."

"You take it personally?"

"No. But he's calling back."

"Get all the Russian calls put through to you personally. Tell him you're in temporary charge; that he should tell you all he gets. He's a good guy. Straight as an arrow. Anything else?"

"A Pauline called. Your ex-wife?" She sounded doubtful.

"Pauline *is* my ex-wife."

"Needed to check: Director's imposed personal security regulations and you're getting a lot of media coverage at the moment. You want me to call Pauline back?"

"I'll do it."

A nurse had to dial the number, because Cowley couldn't see to do it, and it was difficult for him to listen with the phone to his right ear because he normally held it against his left. The ringing tone hurt. Pauline wasn't in her apartment so he left a message on the machine that he was fine and would call again.

The overpoweringly perfumed smell in the BMW was beginning to nauseate Dimitri Danilov, along with all the other things he was sickened by.

It was impossible to calculate how many thousands more biological and chemical weapons had been stored all around him in Plant 35. Or equate the total, disregarding cynicism with which international pronouncements were made about peace and stability. Portentious reflection. What about personal attitudes? Although, since Larissa, he'd imagined he'd had no interest in his career or his future or in anything—content to operate virtually as a nonfeeling, nonreactive automaton—there was an unexpected, even surprising, uncertainty at the extent to which he was going to challenge the highest level of government without the slightest degree of personal insurance.

There was a very real physical distaste now, this very moment, enclosed in a sick-making car with two policemen epitomizing in suit-shining flamboyance the core of what was wrong with Russian justice. Despite their knowing he was not one of them, they still believed themselves capable of manipulating him. And above all, in the very forefront of his mind, was the distraction of not knowing if William Cowley—with whom the thought of working again had penetrated the self-pitying lassitude—was alive or dead. Thinking back to his earlier impression of several separate but connected parts making up a whole, Danilov recognized all the different aspects and emotions—his concern about Cowley most of all—had made him start thinking like the detective he was supposed to be.

"We should have obtained an official search warrant," complained Colonel Oleg Reztsov.

Danilov actually sniggered at the mere thought of this man being eager to observe the law. He said, "I'm the ranking officer. It's being done upon my authority and I accept all and every liability." He'd actually delayed telling them what he wanted to do—search without warning the apartment of Viktor Nikolaevich Nikov—until he'd gotten into the car.

"An illegal search will make illegal anything we find," persisted Reztsov.

Or which could have been planted *for* them to find, if there'd been time, thought Danilov. Enjoying the question before he asked it, Danilov said: "You always so particular about legality, Oleg Vasilevich? And you, major? Haven't either of you ever moved first and bothered about procedure later?"

Averin made no attempt to answer. It was some moments before Reztsov said: "It was you who stressed from the beginning the need for nothing whatsoever to go wrong."

"Viktor Nikolaevich Nikov has disappeared, according to your information. Entering his home will not be an illegal search for evidence. It will be a search to satisfy ourselves that he has come to no physical harm. Have you any problem or objection with that explanation, Oleg Vasilevich?"

"None," said Reztsov, tightly.

Viktor Nikov occupied what was clearly the newest apartment block in the city, most levels of which had a startling and unobstructed view of the confluence of the Volga and Oka rivers that Danilov had first seen from the air. By Russian standards—American even—the lobby was clean to the point of being sterile and the elevator, in which they ascended with the smiling, bribe-expectant janitor with his master key, rose without any normal stop-start uncertainty. There wasn't any graffiti, either. By the time they reached Nikov's level, the ninth floor, the disappointed janitor's smile had gone, he'd acknowledged Danilov's authority and insisted he hadn't seen Nikov for a week, maybe longer.

The apartment was immaculate. The beds in the master and second bedroom were made, everything in the bathroom was arranged or in cabinets, the towels edge to edge on their rail. There were no unwashed pots or pan in the kitchen or trash in the undersink bin. There were some American-imported pornographic videos in the living room, and in a locked desk drawer, which Danilov forced, there was $900 in American currency. He had to force two more locked drawers completely to search the desk. There were some two-year-old American travel brochures, to Florida and California, and a receipt for $1,300, made out in dollars from Moscow's Metropole Hotel and marked "paid in cash." The bottom drawer held a Russian-made Makarov, with a clip of 9mm shells, and an American Smith & Wesson, with two clips of ammunition. Danilov fully extracted each drawer and on the undersides of two found stuck two separate envelopes, one containing $3,200 and another $2,000. He returned to the bedroom, checking closets and drawers as neatly arranged as everywhere else. On a closet shelf there were three empty suitcases and at its bottom five side-by-side pairs of shoes, all Italian made. Danilov looked hopefully for a telephone answering machine but there wasn't one.

Either Reztsov or Averin moved from room to room with him. On the second bedroom search the militia colonel said, "He's run, obviously."

"Why?" challenged Danilov.

Averin snorted a laugh. "Because he knows we're looking for him, of course."

To the hovering janitor Danilov said, "Be more precise. One week or two since you last saw him?"

"More like two," said the subdued man.

"Before I got here. Unannounced and unpublicized. And even longer before you began asking at his garages," Danilov pointed out. "And I would have thought he would have taken more of his clothes and certainly all the money that was in the desk, wouldn't you?"

"There's been enough publicity from America. An investigation here was obvious," insisted Averin. "He was in too much of a hurry to get out. And there's no passport. He's obviously taken that."

"Doesn't something about the desk surprise you?" asked Danilov.

"What?" Averin frowned.

"There's nothing personal there whatsoever. No letters, no photographs, nothing. This doesn't look to me like a hurried departure. To me this looks like an apartment that's been thoroughly sanitized, cleaned of anything that might have helped this investigation. Or that might have told us where to find him."

"Either way he's running," insisted Reztsov.

Seeing the direction in which the janitor was looking, Danilov said, "We'll take the money for safekeeping. Log it in an evidence file."

On their way back to the hotel Danilov declined the invitation to dinner for the second night, insisting he had too many calls to make. As he passed through the lobby he identified one of his breakfast companions still engrossed in the newspaper the man had been frowning over that morning.

The same voice as before answered Cowley's extension and asked him to hold to be transferred. Another woman who identified herself as Pamela Darnley said she'd actually seen Cowley that day and that the injuries weren't life-threatening, although it was still too early to say when—or even if—he'd be returning to the investigation.

"I'm acting case officer," continued the woman. "He told me to tell you to share everything with you—that everything's two way."

"So what happened?"

The speed with which she talked betrayed Pamela Darnley's impatience to hear whatever Danilov had to share.

"Do you know where the bombs came from?" Danilov asked when she finished.

"Still under analysis. Anything from your end?"

Danilov hesitated, at once accepting the stupidity of not wanting to work with anyone but Cowley whose integrity and ability he knew so well. "I haven't been to the plant yet," he lied easily. "I'll keep in touch, either direct like this or through Moscow."

There was a matching hesitation from the other end before the woman said, her disappointed suspicion obvious, "OK. Look forward to hearing from you."

The connection to Yuri Pavin was just as quick. Danilov said, "Who or what does the Moscow telephone number on the warhead belong to?"

"It doesn't exist," said Pavin. "At least not any longer. I've asked the telephone authorities to check their records, but they say they don't keep any for discontinued numbers."

"Shit!" said Danilov. It fit, he supposed, with Ivanov's assertion that the program had been abandoned twenty-five years earlier. "We can't find Viktor Nikov."

"He's dead," replied the deputy in Moscow. "Found in the Moskva, jammed under one of the Smolenskaja Bridge supports. Shot mafia style, with a bullet through the mouth. Another one in the head."

"How long . . . ?" started Danilov, but the other man continued talking.

"He wasn't alone," said Pavin. "He was handcuffed and roped to another man, Valeri Alexandrovich Karpov, who'd been killed the same way. Not listed in records. According to what we found on him, he lived at Pereulok Samokatnaja 54, here in Moscow. I'm just on my way."

"Wait until tomorrow," ordered Danilov. "I'm coming back."

Neither Reztsov nor Averin looked like proper detectives even when they were doing what was supposed to be their proper jobs. It was the major who escorted Aleksai Zotin, whom they identified as Nikov's brigade leader, into the interview room at Gorki militia headquarters, but he did so subserviently, standing back almost politely for the gang leader to enter ahead of him.

Zotin was an immensely fat, damp man preceded by the odor of his own perspiration. He waddled to the desk that divided the room and had to splay his legs to sit down. He said to Danilov, "You're new. This a shakedown?"

"Haven't you heard that Viktor Nikov's been murdered in Moscow?"

"Who?"

Danilov sighed. "Viktor Nikov, one of your bulls."

"Don't know what a bull is. Had a driver of that name a long time ago. Haven't heard from him for a long time."

Danilov realized that it didn't appear as if he could perform properly as a detective, either. "You think your memory might improve in a cell?"

Zotin laughed at him openly, nodding toward Reztsov. "Even he does better than that, and he's paid a lot of money to put me out of business."

"That's not true, of course," said the militia colonel. Like everything else about the man, it was a token gesture.

It had been a stupid threat, acknowledged Danilov. There was absolutely no evidence upon which to hold Zotin, and to do so—and then be forced to free him—would make him look even more ridiculous than he already did.

"The murder's a major investigation in Moscow. If we can make a connection between Nikov and you, I'll charge you with complicity to steal microbiological weaponry from Plant 35. That's a life sentence, no remission."

Zotin yawned exaggeratedly. "I don't know anything about Viktor Nikov or what he was doing in Moscow. I haven't seen him for months. You're wasting your time."

He was, admitted Danilov. He hoped the other things he was doing would not be so frustrating.

Patrick Hollis hadn't anticipated his mother demanding to ride with him when he'd announced he was going out in the new car. He hated upsetting her, and the dispute had delayed him. Now he was having to drive faster than he should have to keep strictly to the time schedule. He wasn't sure what he would do if the booth was occupied. If it was, then it would be an omen, a sign that he wasn't intended to take the call, so he'd drive away—keep to his original intention and sever the link.

But the booth wasn't occupied, although the telephone was ringing when he pulled up outside.

"Where were you?" demanded the voice when Hollis picked up the receiver.

"Traffic," said Hollis. He was short of breath from hurrying and apprehension.

"Build in time for delays."

"You did it, didn't you? The missile in New York?"

"You knew we were going to. You're part of it."

Hollis hesitated, trying to calm his breathing. "A lot of people got killed."

"We're fighting a war, aren't we?"

"I don't want any part of it."

"You *are* part of it."

"Not anymore." It had been right to take the call. Proved himself to be a man, confronting a situation and refusing to go on.

"Listen to me! The war's ongoing and we need more money. You've got to help us get it. Give us more account numbers—a lot more than you have already."

The man was frightened he was going to pull out. It was a strange feeling—a feeling he'd never had before—knowing another man was frightened of him. "No."

The sensation he'd never known before—power? authority?—stayed with Hollis as he drove away. It was going to be easy asking Carole Parker out, too. He'd have to make up a story for his mother. He didn't want another scene like the one tonight.

The duty complaint detective didn't hide the sigh, knowing everyone else in the squad room was laughing and finding it difficult not to laugh himself. He said, "Sir, you're telling me that in six months you've been shortchanged a total of seven bucks!"

"Seven dollars and sixty cents," corrected Clarence Snelling.

"What does the bank say?"

"That they're sorry."

"They make it up to you?"

"Yes."

"So there's no actual loss?"

"No. But it's the principle."

"What exactly would you have me do?"

"Investigate it, what else?"

"Sure," said the man. "You'd better let me have the details." He'd be able to turn it into that day's funny story in the bar later.

8

There were a lot of officers and detectives who became distressed, vomited even, when confronted with the victim of violent death. Dimitri Danilov never had been, apart from Larissa, whom he'd had to identify from her belongings and which hadn't been an un-involved professional duty.

A dead body mattered to him only for the clues it might scientifically provide to catch its killer. Beyond that it was a lifeless thing, of no interest or emotion. He felt absolutely none as he stood beside Pavin in the police mortuary, staring down at the naked gray flesh, following the pathologist through the external medical findings. The testes of both victims were ballooned from torture before they died. There were also whip marks across their backs and the round marks of cigarette burns on both faces, which no longer had eyes. There was severe restraint bruising to the ankles and wrists, which the pathologist guessed to have been caused by metal handcuffs, not softer rope, and the doctor also thought from the testicle damage that they had been tortured over a period of several hours—as much, even, as an entire day. The head shots had been what killed them, the teeth-shattering mouth wounds following, for symbolism. Medically Nikov had been suffering gonorrhea and Karpov ulcers, for which antacid medication was among the man's effects.

Pavin had met Danilov in at the airport that morning and brought with him the recovered pocket contents of each victim, but they'd spent the journey to the mortuary discussing Gorki.

Pavin identified ownership by placing the appropriate plastic evidence sacks at the foot of each body on its adjacent gurney. As Danilov picked up the bag marked with Nikov's name, his deputy said, "The other one's more intriguing."

Danilov said, "I want to keep my head in sequence. All I've heard about for the past three days is this man."

Viktor Nikolaevich Nikov had come to Moscow to be murdered carrying $1,470 in American currency, a gold cigarette case containing ten now-soaked Marlboro cigarettes, and a gold Zippo lighter. The watch was gold, too, a Cartier, and the gold signet ring had an onyx setting. The only other jewelry was a gold, unengraved identity bracelet. There was a passport, showing two American visa entries and two driver's licenses, one in his own name, the other in that of Eduard Babkendovich Kulik. They reminded Danilov that he'd forgotten the previous day to check for a vehicle or a garage that might have belonged to the man's apartment. Carelessness was obviously contagious in Gorki.

Danilov said, "Like they always say, crime pays."

"Until you get shot in the head and mouth," said Pavin. "Now try the other one."

Valeri Alexandrovich Karpov had been carrying $420, again in American currency. There was a gold, Swiss-made watch, which had stopped at 12:40, and a wedding ring. All the contents had been removed to dry from a new leather wallet. There were curling photographs of a blond woman, from the background standing on the bank of the river into which Karpov had been thrown untold years later, one of a much younger Karpov with the same woman, and two more of the man with smiling children, both girls. There was only one driver's license. As Danilov put it aside for the next item Pavin, beside him, said, "And finally the interesting part."

It was an official pass, on yellow cardboard kept dry by its laminated plastic case, and contained a photograph of the dead man, whose job description was given as stores supervisor. Reading the cover page imprint, Danilov said, "Do I need to ask what's manufactured at Plant 43, Moscow provincial area?"

"Chemical as well as biological," confirmed Pavin. "It's some way out of Moscow, to the northwest. Actually on the Skhodaya River, in the Tushino region."

"Which connects with the canal and the Khimkinskoy Reservoir," recognized Danilov. "I wonder if anyone ever worries what would happen to Moscow if there were to be a leak, like there was at Chernobyl?"

"Of course they don't," said Pavin, responding seriously to Danilov's cynicism. "Our appointment there is for three this afternoon."

"Did you tell them why?"

"I didn't need to. Did you see the television coverage of what happened in America?"

"Some. What did the factory say?"

"That we needed authority from the Ministry of Science as well as the Ministry of Defense. So I called Chelyag's secretariat at the White House. We got permission an hour before you landed."

"Thank you," said Danilov. It hadn't been a mistake at all to leave Pavin in Moscow.

"We've got time to check out Pereulok Samokatnaja," Pavin pointed out.

"The wife been informed yet?"

"You told me to wait," reminded Pavin.

Which might have been a mistake, thought Danilov—not putting any family there under protection at least. "I think we should."

Karpov's apartment block was comparatively new and therefore, by that definition, prematurely old and decaying. It had been one of the last developments under the Brezhnev diktat promising a home of their own for every Russian family. The limited success of the program had been secondary to the million-plus kickbacks Brezhnev and his immediate family received from prefabricated material suppliers, incompetent architects, and cowboy builders. Some of the average-size rooms were smaller than the alloted space, and chicken coops at the rear of each apartment allowed the occupants some self-sufficiency in meat and vegetables they'd never been able to buy because Brezhnev and his ministers had run the country's food supply and distribution as a private enterprise, too.

Karpov's apartment was a surprising exception when Naina Karpov admitted them. In the living room there was a matching suite of two chairs and a sofa and a glass-fronted cabinet displaying a set of matching goblets. As they passed the open-doored kitchen, Danilov had seen an impressively large refrigerator/freezer, and the television looked new and had a very good picture: It was a cartoon program for the girl of about ten who whined in protest at being told to turn it off and go and read in another room. It was only when Danilov turned to see the child open a linking door that he realized that it was not, in fact, one apartment but two, connected by what must have been a later, additional door.

"What's happened?" she demanded at once as the door closed behind the girl.

"It's serious," said Danilov. Naina Karpov, the woman in the photographs the man had been carrying, was neatly dressed in uncreased skirt and sweater. She wore no makeup or jewelry, and she had about her an uncaring resignation that reminded him of Olga, which was scarcely fitting because if she had been made up and dressed differently Naina Karpov still might have been an attractive woman. The incongruous reflection reminded Danilov that he hadn't bothered to call Olga from Gorki the previous night or telephoned today to tell her he was back. He didn't imagine she'd be interested. There was still plenty of time.

"What?" said the woman.

"I'm afraid your husband has been killed," said Pavin.

"He didn't come home last night," declared the wife, as if it was a contributory fact.

"It happened yesterday," said Pavin.

"How?"

Pavin looked at Danilov, who nodded, watching the woman curiously. Pavin said, "He was shot. With another man."

Naina Karpov nodded without any obvious emotion. "I told him."

"Told him what!" demanded Danilov.

"That it had to be wrong, what he was doing."

Danilov suppressed the sigh. "What, exactly, *was* he doing?"

"Selling stuff from the factory," she declared bluntly.

"What sort of stuff?" coaxed the more patient Pavin.

She frowned. "Metal, of course. That was his job, ordering a lot of the metal they use there: making sure there was always a supply. Keeping a proper account of it. Which made it easy. He ordered more than they needed and sold the surplus. Said it was easy. That he'd never be caught." She made a vague gesture around the connected apartments. "That's how . . ."

"Who'd he sell metal to?" queried Danilov.

She shrugged. "I don't know. He said other factories who didn't have their supplies organized like he did. And garages. Places like that who always needed metal."

"He told you all about it then?" said Pavin.

The shrug came again. "Not really. Not like I'm telling you. It just came out, in bits and pieces."

"So he's been doing it for a long time?"

"I suppose so."

"How long would you say?"

"Two or three years."

"Which?"

"Three, I suppose."

"And you warned him to stop?"

"I told him I was frightened."

"Why—and of what—were you frightened?"

"I didn't like the friends he was making."

"So you met them?" seized Danilov.

"No. That was the problem. I never met any of them. He said it was business—*his* business—but there wasn't any socializing. He said the men he dealt with only liked dealing with other men."

"You weren't surprised when he didn't come home last night?" challenged Danilov.

"He said he might be late."

"Late?" qualified Pavin. "Not that he wouldn't be coming home at all?"

"No."

Danilov said, "Were there many nights he didn't come home at all, Mrs. Karpov?"

The woman didn't answer for several moments. "A few times."

"Once or twice a week?"

"About that."

Danilov said, "You're sure you never met any of Valeri's friends?"

"I asked, in the beginning. Wondered why we didn't go out together. That's when he told me it was business, but I didn't believe him. Not that it was entirely business."

Despite the denial, Danilov took the Gorki police file picture of

Nikov from his briefcase and offered it to her. "Do you know this man?"

She dutifully studied it. "No."

"Did he ever speak about any of his friends by name?"

"No, never."

"Does the name Viktor Nikolaevich Nikov mean anything to you?"

"No, nothing at all."

"Did he ever talk about Gorki?"

"No."

"Go there?"

"Never, as far as I know."

Pavin looked to Danilov for guidance. Danilov said, "Is there a desk anywhere where Valeri kept his papers? Bills, official letters, things like that?"

"A box in the bedroom." Without being asked she led the way into a room off the entry hall of the apartment that they were in. Again the suite matched and there was a fitted, silklike cover over the bed. The box was at the bottom of the closet. When she opened the closet Danilov saw there were three good-quality suits—one with the familiar sheen—with a separate pair of shoes neatly arranged beneath each. The box wasn't locked. There was the couple's marriage certificate and birth certificates of both girls and some photographs. The leases for the two apartments were pinned together, and at the very bottom there were photographs of an elderly couple—the man in uniform—and old, tattered food allowance books.

The woman said, "They're Valeri's parents. His father fought in the Patriotic War. He said he kept the ration books as a reminder: that he'd never let himself be as poor as they were."

"There's no bank statements?" said Pavin.

"Who trusts banks in this country!" she said almost indignantly. "Valeri certainly didn't."

"Or letters?"

She shrugged. "Who's there to write to us? Both our parents are dead. Valeri always dealt personally, face to face, with anything official. There's no point in writing."

"Have you got a car?" asked Pavin.

"Foreign. An Audi. He was very proud of it."

"They're not easy to get in Moscow. And they're expensive," said Danilov.

"Valeri said they were easy to get when you had friends like he did. I told you, he sold metal to garages."

"Did he drive it last night?"

She shook her head. "He didn't like using it at night. Leaving it. Too easy to get it stripped." She pointed toward the dressing table. "There are the keys."

Danilov led the way back into the main room. As they reached it, Naina Karpov blurted suddenly, "Was it a fight over a woman?"

"No," said Danilov. "It was a gang murder. Mafia."

For the first time she reacted, eyes widening. "Mafia! How could it be mafia?"

"That's what we're trying to find out," said Pavin. "And we're going to have to ask you formally to identify the body. Not today. Possibly tomorrow or the day after." It would take at least until then for the postmortem to be completed.

"All right," the woman agreed, retreating into resignation again. Then she said, "I know there was a woman. That there had to be. But"—she looked around the room—"I don't have anywhere else. Any*one* else. And now I don't have him, do I?"

"I'm sorry," said Pavin.

"Can you find out who did it? Have . . ." She stopped, groping. "People who saw it . . . witnesses . . . ?"

"No," admitted Danilov. "But we're going to try very hard. It's very important that we do. We'd like to look inside the car. Can you take us down to the garage?"

At the apartment door Naina called out to her daughter that she would only be a few minutes, and they rode in silence to the ground floor. The garage, like the car, was immaculate. Danilov sniffed apprehensively, but there was no overperfumed deodorizer, just the smell of newness. The tachometer registered just over 1,500 kilometers. There was nothing in the glove box or side pockets—not even the car's documentation—and only a forgotten doll, which the woman retrieved, on the backseat. The trunk was empty, apart from a quilted jacket.

She said, "He kept it very tidy."

"I can see he did," said Danilov. He handed her a card. "If you remember anything you think might help, will you call this number? Ask for me or Colonel Pavin?"

"Yes," she said emptily. "Yes, of course." She paused. "If you find who the other woman was, will you tell me?"

Neither man replied.

"No," she accepted. "No, there wouldn't be any purpose in that, would there? It's all over."

As he picked up the first of the two highways to take them back to Moscow Pavin said, "He told her he sold metal to garages. And Nikov had three garages in Gorki, from what you've told me. What better place to get a foreign car than a mafia garage?"

"I made the connection," said Danilov. "Not actually distraught, was she?"

"She'd accepted the marriage was over. A lot of people—husbands and wives—go on doing that when they've nowhere else to go. Which she said she didn't."

"There is—or had been—a lot of money," judged Danilov. "I've never seen two apartments connected like that before. And nothing in it was cheap."

"Why torture them?" demanded Pavin. "I can fit everything else together, but I can't see the reason for doing what they did to them before killing them. No one was coming to us with information. We don't know anything more now than when we started."

"There's one thing I'm anxious to establish from the Tushino plant," said Danilov. As the new question came to him he said, "More than one, in fact. Several."

Plant 43 was almost—but not quite—a clone of its Gorki progenitor, which Danilov acknowledged to be hardly surprising in view of the centrally controlled, centrally designed, centrally dictated, early 1960s, Cold War fridgidity of communist collectivism. The Tushino installation was smaller than the enclaves at Gorki, and each of its three divided factories were connected by an internal road, which by security-separating standards was a waste of time in the first place. They took the publicly designated turnoff to the centrally located Plant 43 itself. There was still the combination of control tower and private road checkpoint, but the tower appeared unmanned and there was only one yawning man at the gatehouse who waved away their offered proof of official authority because their names were already on his approved entrants' list.

They were early by fifteen minutes and kept waiting a further thirty minutes by the plant director. Vladimir Leonidovich Oskavinsky was an emaciated, imperiously mannered man who was so obviously surprised by their authorized visit that he insisted upon telephoning the Science and Defense ministries extension to reaffirm the permission and still seemed to disbelieve the confirmation. He coughed a lot, and Danilov wondered if his earlier cynicism about a leak had been as rhetorical as he'd intended.

"Of course I know why you're here," said the man, ahead of any explanation. "I've seen the pictures from America. It's Gorki, not here. How do you imagine I can help you?"

Instead of answering Danilov, just as impatient, offered the mortuary photograph of Valeri Karpov. The plant director's face twisted in disgust. He came back up to them and said, "What's this! Why are you showing me this?"

Pavin said, "Don't you recognize him?"

"Why should I?"

"He worked here. As a stores supervisor. Valeri Karpov." Pavin put Karpov's official pass beside the photograph.

Oskavinsky frowned down again at both. "Over two hundred people are employed here."

"Don't you recognize him?" asked Pavin.

"I think so. Vaguely. What happened to him?"

"I would have thought that was rather obvious," said Danilov. He offered a second photograph, of the dead man's balloon-size genitalia, and said, "He was working with organized crime: selling materiel from here."

"That's absurd! I refute that absolutely."

"I hope you're right," said Danilov, allowing his annoyance at official condescension to return. "You know—because you've just checked—the authority with which we are here. If you're wrong you'll be dismissed. As it is, I could have you suspended. I don't want—won't have—your arrogance. I want your total cooperation."

Momentarily Oskavinsky, king of his own tiny castle, was dumbstruck by the ramparts being breached. The coughing became more pronounced. Humbly he said, "How can I help?"

"By not trying to avoid—or lie to—a single question," bullied Danilov. Who didn't think from then on that the cadaverous man did.

After checking with his operational manager, Oskavinsky stated that there were 102 ineffectually designed double warheads at Tushino, conceding at the same time that while Valeri Karpov had no authority to go anywhere near the biological or chemical facility, it was conceivable that he knew the way to enter every facility.

The director's collapse continued when Danilov pedantically counted the racks of the identically stored weapons in their identically uniform racks in an identical subterranean cavern—at the fourth basement level once more—and only got up to ninety-eight. The side stenciling matched the size and print of Gorki but none of the numbering—for which Oskavinsky gave the same explanation—had the same sequence as the UN missile. Danilov didn't even ask permission to scrape the lettering and base paint from a warhead into one of the unused envelopes he still had from the Gorki hotel. Oskavinsky insisted on again calling the Science Ministry before allowing Danilov to take possession of an empty warhead.

Back in the director's office, Danilov said, "I want to talk about the metal that is used to make both the warhead and the delivery systems. Is it specially forged—made—whatever the technical expression is?"

"Yes," Oskavinsky replied at once.

"One metal? Or an alloy?"

"Alloys, for both," said the man, eager now to help. "There has to be a tensility to the missile base, to allow for the brief but extreme launch heat. If there weren't it would melt, exploding the contents at source. The launch mechanism is basically nothing more than a disposable frame. Because the one we're talking about was intended to be shoulder-mounted, it was made of lighter alloy—mostly aluminium, bronze, and copper. The faceplate, to protect the operator from the initial intense blast-back, was a laminate of heat-rejecting plastics with a bauxite infusion."

"As a stores supervisor, would Valeri Karpov's job have been to order such metals?"

"Various department requisitions would have been passed on to him, yes."

"Would the amounts he ordered have been cross-checked against the requisitions passed down after delivery?"

Oskavinsky shifted uncomfortably. "That's the system. Cost control."

"Was it observed?" persisted Danilov.

"To the best of my knowledge, yes."

"By regular, specific audit."

"No, not by specific audit," conceded the man. "By comparing the department request against the suppliers' delivery figure."

"Which effectively put Karpov in total control of what he ordered?"

"I suppose so, yes," the scientist admitted. There was a sheen of perspiration on his forehead.

"Is any of the metal alloyed here?"

"No. It's a precise process, needing specific expertise and a controlled environment quite different from anything we have here."

"These specifically produced, controlled environment alloys?" said Danilov. "Could they be used for anything else? Cannibalized for use in body repair work in garages, for instance?"

Oskavinsky looked at him incredulously. "Of course not! It would be like"—he waved his arms, seeking a comparison—"like trying to attach soft curd to hard cheese. They wouldn't mix. In laymen's terms, they wouldn't stick together."

"What do your other connected plants manufacture?" persisted Danilov.

"Basic high-explosive artillery shells."

"Mines?"

"Yes."

"Land? Or water?"

"Both."

"What about the metal used in those? Could they be utilized in other industries? Car repairs particularly?"

"No!" said Oskavinsky, exasperated.

"I didn't think so," said Danilov. "I want empty mine casings—land and water—as well."

"I didn't think so, either," said Pavin, as they drove back along the M11 toward Moscow. "I also don't think any of that takes us very far."

"Parts of a picture," said Danilov. "A picture we can't yet see. Which isn't what worries me the most at the moment. What worries me is that we've no way of knowing just how many of these things—how many warheads or bombs or whatever else—have disappeared from these plants. Or where they are now."

It was a worry that increased an hour later when Pamela Darnley told him the metal of what was now estimated to be the four anti-personnel mines from New Rochelle had tested positive to be Russian.

The conversation with Pamela Darnley lasted for more than an hour. This time Danilov was more forthcoming than he'd been from Gorki. He said he was wiring details and photographs of the two Moscow murders as well as summaries of his inquiries in Gorki and Moscow. There was some forensic evidence he wanted analyzed under superior FBI techniques that might confirm a source for the UN missile, one sample in particular he intended personally bringing to America.

"What's keeping you?" demanded the acting head of the bureau's terrorism unit.

"The need to get it right," said Danilov. "I've more to do here first." With the authority he had from the White House, he scarcely had to worry about legality. Which wasn't a consideration anyway. The need was to make people feel complacent.

"We're under a hell of a lot of pressure here," admitted the woman. She was sure the chauvinistic bastard was holding out on her.

Danilov remembered that he had to report to the presidential committee the following day. "How's Bill?"

"Pretending to be getting better faster than he really is, according to the doctor."

"He is going to get back, though?"

"Is our cooperation dependent on that?" Pamela demanded outright. She needed to get this man in her pocket if she stood any chance of properly using the opportunity she had.

"You've got all I've got. Which doesn't give us anything except my feeling that a lot more stuff could be missing."

"That's what we're terrified of here," said the woman.

"That's what we're terrified of here, too," said Danilov.

It was only when he pulled up outside their Kirovskaya apartment that Danilov realized he still hadn't told Olga he was back. Wednesday, he remembered. Wednesday was Olga's night at the movies with Irena. It was a fleeting thought, washed away by another, more personally surprising awareness. It hadn't occurred to him to go to Larissa's grave. He turned back to the car and then away again. Enough. It had to stop and now was as good a time—the right time—as any. It was maudlin. Ridiculous, actually talking to her by the graveside: a pretense for no purpose. Larissa was dead and he was alive, and he had to learn—*was* learning—to live with the emptiness. He wouldn't stop going completely—that would be a pretense in reverse—but he'd mourn properly.

There probably wouldn't be any food in the apartment. There often wasn't even when Olga knew he was coming home. He didn't feel particularly hungry; could always go out later. At that precise moment he wanted to think through the uncertainties of Gorki and those of today, here, back in Moscow. Which is what they were—uncertainties, nothing more. It would be wrong, a mistake, to misconstrue Gorki and because of it misconstrue—or wrongly read—the two Moscow murders. The stenciling today had appeared identical to that at Gorki, so it would only have been necessary to switch the name if the missile had come from the Tushino installation. And he could be making the cardinal error of allowing personal feelings and attitudes at his being patronized by the Gorki militia chief to influence his thinking. Which was what he had to do tonight: Think, analyze, and be totally objective.

The vestibule and the living room beyond were as Danilov expected, neglected chaos. He dropped his case and coat in the hall and went into the kitchen: He kept the vodka in the refrigerator. That was all there was in it, apart from two slices of curled-edged bread and an unopened can of fish eggs. The stalagmite of dishes had grown in the sink.

It was as Danilov was leaving that he heard the noise. He stopped at once, listening, and heard it again. Nothing positive, identifiable. Just the sound of movement. Carefully Danilov stooped, placing his glass on the floor, and eased the restraining strap off the Makarov on its waistband holster. Why hadn't he seen the marks of a forced entry—had difficulty with the key—as he entered? The noise came again, twice, louder the second time. The safety came soundlessly off the gun. He tested each step before making it, pausing, weapon ready, at what had appeared the empty main room. It was still empty. There was movement as he got to the bedroom door. He went in low, following his training, gun barrel upward but ready, back immediately and protectively to the wall.

There was no one there. Just the jumbled, unmade disorder there always was. And then the disorder moved and a tousled head—Olga's head—appeared from beneath the tangled bedding.

She said, "It's you! But you're in Gorki!"

Danilov slid the catch back on the Makarov and restrapped it. As he did so another head, a man's head, eyes staring, appeared beside Olga's. For a brief moment Danilov's mind went totally blank, refusing any thought. His first realization, absurdly, was that he must be staring wide-eyed, too. Then he wanted to laugh, which was laughable in itself, but it was the only feeling that came to him and he only just prevented himself doing it.

It became even more difficult when Olga said, almost formally, "This is Igor."

The man said, "Hello."

Then Danilov did laugh, unable to stop himself.

Olga said, "Don't laugh. Igor. My hairdresser."

Danilov became aware that despite what they'd obviously been doing, the man's perfectly blond hair, although now disarrayed, would have been a close-fitting coif.

Igor said, "I'm sorry. Don't hurt me."

Danilov said, "Get up."

"We haven't got any clothes on," said Olga.

"I know," said Danilov.

"Bastard!"

"Get up and get out."

"You fucked Larissa!" she shouted. "Why shouldn't I fuck who I want?"

Danilov hadn't known that Olga knew. Inexplicably—ridiculously—he felt embarrassed. He said, "You can fuck who you like, which you always have. With my blessing. But not in my home, in my bed. Get up and get out."

"I've got nowhere to go!" said Olga, quieter now.

Into Danilov's mind came the memory of Naina Karpov gazing around an apartment far more luxurious than this, protesting she had nowhere else. "Why not go home with Igor?"

"I'm married," said the man.

Abruptly it no longer seemed absurd or laughable. It was sad and miserable—a fitting part in the mess of his life. Their lives. "Call Irena."

Danilov went out of the room and picked up his carefully placed drink on his way into the living room. He had to clear a space on the couch, sweeping papers and magazines and discarded clothes on to the floor. Almost at once there was movement and the slamming of the door as the man left.

Olga appeared at the doorway and said, "I'm sorry."

"Of course you're not," Danilov said impatiently. "You made a hobby of being unfaithful from the moment we got married. I'll sleep here, on the couch."

"Thank you."

Danilov didn't say anything.

"Good night. And thank you again," said Olga.

Danilov didn't reply. If Olga's lover was a hairdresser, why did he let her hair look like it did?

———

Patrick Hollis had so much wanted to take the Jaguar—so much wanted to impress Carole in each and every way he could—but he changed his mind literally at the last moment. Not yet. Not until he knew her better. A lot of his penny-stolen fortune was deposited in ways to sustain a story of it being an inheritance, but it was still better to be careful. He told his mother it was a major conference of all the bank branches and went to the Italian restaurant Carole had suggested—*the* place in Albany, she'd said—in his lunch hour personally to reserve and choose the window table and talk through the menu so he wouldn't be caught out if Carole asked for guidance. On his way back he bought an orchid corsage.

The afternoon heat wilted it by the time he gave it to her, and the purple clashed against her yellow sweater so she didn't put it on. She named the bar for a drink, and Robert Standing and three others—a man and two girls—from the mortgage department were already there. Hollis was immediately frightened that Carole would expect to join them, but she didn't. Hollis was sure his casual wave had just the right degree of nonchalance. He wished his breathing was easier, conscious of wheezing. Carole had chardonnay. Hollis chose a martini, for its sophistication. He'd only tried it once before, and it burned his throat as it had the first time, but he resisted anything ridiculous like coughing. Carole asked for another, so he had to have a second and hoped the light-headedness wouldn't last. He managed another nonchalant wave to Standing as they left.

Carole made him taste her marinated calamari, and he was sure that was what made him feel sick, rather than the chianti. He left most of his veal, which he'd forgotten came in a cream sauce. He didn't think she saw him swallow back the belch that brought something up to the back of his throat.

Because she'd shown an interest he talked a lot about loans and securities, exaggerating some of the contracts he'd negotiated, and said his influence was sufficient if she wanted a transfer the moment a vacancy arose. Toward the end of the wine he had to grope for words that escaped him.

Carole's apartment was actually in Albany. As soon as they drew up outside, she got out of the car without saying anything, stopping some way away in apparent surprise that he wasn't with her.

"Aren't you coming up?"

He got hurriedly out of the car, fervently wishing he didn't feel so sick. It was a walkup, on the third floor, and he was wheezing badly by the time he got to her door.

"I have whiskey as well as vodka or gin. But I guess you'd like another martini. You want to mix?"

"I'd better stick with coffee. I've got to drive back to Rensselaer."

Carole frowned. "You're not staying over?"

"I didn't . . . I mean . . ."

"No reason why you shouldn't, is there?"

She wanted to sleep with him! Go to bed with him where he could do all the things he'd seen on the porn channels: things that made them groan and cry out. He couldn't! His mother. She'd stay up—awake, certainly—until he got back. It was already past eleven. She would have already started to worry. "Maybe not tonight. Left some work back at home that I'll need tomorrow."

"You want to skip the drink then—end the evening properly?" She smiled.

"Please," he said, not thinking what he was saying and tried to cough, to cover it, but knew he hadn't. Her smile was broader when she turned toward the bedroom.

He followed her in and she turned, holding out her arms. "Want to help a girl?"

He didn't undo the neck buttons of her sweater and had to pull it back on to unfasten them before it would go over her head. When he saw her breasts he said, "Oh my God, you're so beautiful."

She was helping him undress and their hands got in the way and the zipper of her skirt jammed and in the end she wriggled out with it only half undone. She kept her panties on and got into bed ahead of him, frowning back at his flaccid nakedness.

"A girl's feelings could be hurt."

Hollis got in beside her and reached with a single finger to touch her nipple. She said, "If you're counting, there's two."

Why wasn't he hard! He'd thought about this so much—fantasized about what it would be like really to do it and not just watch—and now he couldn't. He said, "I don't know . . . I'm so sorry."

"I've changed my mind anyway."

"No, please. Wait."

"I'm tired of waiting, darling. Let's skip it. Maybe you'd better get home."

On his way back to Rensselaer he had to stop once, because his crying blurred his glasses. His mother was up and said she had been about to call the police. Hollis said he'd had a flat.

"I hope you called out a repair truck. You're not supposed to do things like that."

"I couldn't," he said.

Virtually everyone in the FBI's Albany office was permanently seconded to the New Rochelle massacre and the UN attack. Only Anne Stovey was on duty when Clarence Snelling walked in.

The balding, stooped man said, "Bank robbery's a federal offense, right?"

"Right," agreed Anne.

"Good," said Snelling.

9

Six of the families whose husbands and fathers died in the massacre went to the same Baptist church just across the Potomac in Alexandria, and the funerals were combined. One was that of Jefferson Jones. There had been no children from Cowley's marriage to Pauline, and he had difficulty gauging the ages of the six Jones children. He guessed they tiered down from a boy of ten to a bewildered girl of four. Each—three boys, three girls—were in their Sunday church clothes, stiff-faced with determination to be brave. Grief only very slightly chipped away the beauty of their mother. All the other families were white, maybe ten more children between them. They moved through the ceremony—the churchyard entry from a cavalcade of matching funeral limousines and then the service itself—as a group, some linking hands, all needing the contact of shared sorrow. The Jones family refused to cry.

The priest talked of pointless and savage terror and of the mysteries of God's ways, and the White House chief of staff included a message from the president in an address in which there was again the personal pledge to track down the perpetrators. It echoed as emptily as it sounded, and Cowley thought, irritated, that the speechwriters should have done a hell of a sight better than virtually repeat what they'd written for the president for his televised address to the nation.

Cowley supposed the official representation justified what one commentator claimed to be the tightest security cordon, this time against an unknown enemy, since the interment of John F. Kennedy. But Cowley wasn't impressed by the political cynicism of turning the funerals into an even bigger media event than their initial State Department crisis meeting, although the reasoning now was simpler to understand. Acknowledging his own cynicism, Cowley thought that probably for the first time ever the near-hysterical media criticism genuinely reflected the fear—and outrage—of the general public. The television and newspaper attacks had culminated that morning in suggestions that the failure of the president to attend—after it had been officially leaked that he would—was because his safety couldn't be guaranteed.

As Cowley watched, Frank Norton left the lectern and paused by each family—kissing the women who weren't crying too bitterly—to rejoin Henry Hartz on the first pew. Next to the secretary of state was Leonard Ross and then the CIA's John Butterworth. All around them were senators and congressmen. Two rows behind Cowley identified the men, headed by James Schnecker, with whom he'd entered the UN building.

Cowley was glad he hadn't gone, even though there had been at least three references—one when his bureau-issued picture had been flashed on the screen—to his being too ill to be there. He'd seriously considered attending. From the previous night's telephone conversation with Pamela Darnley, who'd openly asked if he felt he could make it, he knew the bureau's public affairs unit would have judged his being there a criticism-deflecting coup. Which was the major reason—and the one he'd given Pamela Darnley—for deciding against it. He *would* have been the focus of every camera, making it even more of a circus, detracting from—denigrating even—the mostly sincere, nonpolitical mourning.

There was another reason, though: a personal, determined reason. The turban bandaging had gone but there was still a large dressing on the right side of his head. And the double vision had virtually gone: Certainly it wasn't a problem getting around the hospital room or walking to the bathroom, and he didn't have any difficulty identifying everyone on the screen before him. And that morning he'd managed to decipher enough from the *Washington Post*—certainly the attack on the bureau for its total lack of progress in the investigation and the doubt about the president's safety—to understand what the stories were about.

His problem was the broken rib, particularly if he tried to walk in anything like a proper manner at his usual pace. If he'd gone today, he would have needed a wheelchair to get from a car into the church and would have sat there in front of dozens of cameras like a physically destroyed man who might never recover. And the last impression Cowley wanted to create or allow was that he couldn't walk or stand, would never be able to get back to work. The total and absolute opposite, in fact. He was sure the chest pain wouldn't be so bad if he took the prescribed painkillers, but he was refusing them—actually agonizing himself walking too fast in front of the neurologist and hospital staff—and insisting there was scarcely any discomfort. He didn't believe Joe Pepper was impressed or convinced, but others were.

There were more public displays of condolence from the assembled dignitaries outside the church following the burials, before each hurried away encircled by his personal security, the sight of which immediately prompted a repetition of the presidential safety doubt from the commentators. As soon as the last of the mourners got into their cars—every member of the Jones family still refusing to cry—the program switched to a studio discussion among White House and State Department political correspondents and two men—one Arab looking—introduced as experts on international terrorism.

The State Department correspondent disclosed that before leaving Foggy Bottom for the funeral that morning, Henry Hartz had summoned the Russian ambassador for the third time to demand faster and more substantial responses from Moscow. The White House journalist insisted that relations between Washington and Moscow were strained to the breaking point by an apparent lack of cooperation. Which brought Cowley's mind back to the previous day's telephone conversation with Pamela Darnley about Dimitri Danilov's apparent reticence. Despite trying for most of the evening afterward to balance the woman's complaints against their possible personal advantage to himself when he resumed control, Cowley was still undecided about manipulating his special relationship with the Russian. The unpredictable was the necessary working relationship between himself and a possibly hostile Pamela Darnley. Secondary, he immediately told himself. Maybe, even, less important than that by the official edict of bureau director Leonard Ross. So why, he asked himself, was there reason for any hesitation?

Into Cowley's reflection broke the voice of one of the terrorism experts on television suggesting that within the FBI there was a growing belief that so badly had the New Rochelle bombers misjudged public outrage that they would never claim responsibility or commit another atrocity.

It wasn't until he heard the phone ringing in his ear that Cowley realized he hadn't had any problem picking out the numbers to dial the FBI director's direct line at the J. Edgar Hoover Building on Pennsylvania Avenue.

Danilov didn't think Olga had been asleep when he went into the bedroom that morning for a fresh shirt and underwear, but he'd gone along with the pretense as if believing she were, treading lightly and making as little noise as possible opening and closing closets and gently pulling the door shut when he left the apartment.

He did it knowing full well he was only postponing an inevitable confrontation, but he simply didn't know what to say to Olga. How to react at all. Long ago—long before he fell in love with Larissa—Olga's affairs had reduced their marriage to beyond lack of affection to their scarcely being even friends, so there was no feeling of bitter betrayal or outrage. Nothing, in fact, to be sorry for or about. So it didn't make sense—he didn't want for them to go on sharing the same apartment. It hadn't for years. It had just been convenient: too much trouble to find somewhere else. He didn't have any attachment to Kirovskaya, so he supposed it would be easier for him to move out. But before he did that he had to find another apartment and agree to some financial support for Olga. Which wouldn't be easy. His official income as a general was adequate, but it would be stretched maintaining two homes. Olga would be demanding when she realized he was serious about their finally divorcing, even though she was the guilty party. Of one thing Danilov was absolutely determined: He didn't want—wouldn't have—a court fight, dragging Larissa's name and memory through the mud. He'd simply pay, within reason. Get it over with. It wouldn't have been so difficult if he'd still had the additional income from the favors-for-friends understanding endemic in the Russian militia in general and in the Moscow force in particular. Danilov grew angry at himself—particularly with the reflection of how things had been years before. It was distracting from what should have been his sole concentration, more so because of the impressions that were hardening after Gorki and since his arrival back in Moscow.

He *had* been treated contemptuously in Gorki, which didn't make sense in view of the international enormity of what he was investigating. Even as accustomed as they obviously were to unchallenged corruption, Oleg Reztsov and Gennardi Averin had been far too confident. And there was something that didn't fit—because, in fact, it fit too easily—about the roped-together drowning of the mobster and the germ factory stores supervisor.

Despite the unexpected delay on the inner beltway, there was still enough time before the scheduled Interior Ministry appointment for Danilov to detour to Petrovka. Yuri Pavin was already there. The autopsy report on the two dead men had been promised that afternoon, and he'd arranged for Naina Karpov to be taken formally to identify her husband's body. Although the woman insisted she'd never met any of Karpov's friends, Pavin had taken from their criminal record files photographs of the two men who'd provided the arms-trading alibi for Viktor Nikov to be shown to her. The two were Anatoli Sergeevich Lasin and Igor Ivanovich Baratov. Their files—with other photographs—were on Danilov's desk. Their last known addresses were being checked for them to be brought in for questioning.

"We know the brigade they are with?" asked Danilov.

"Osipov," responded Pavin. "Mikhail Vasilevich Osipov. The biggest and best-organized gang centered around Vnukovo Airport. Fought quite a lot of turf wars a few years ago."

With the pointless Gorki encounter with Aleksai Zotin fresh in his mind, Danilov decided it would be another waste of time interviewing Mikhail Osipov, at least until there was something positive with which to confront the gang leader. "Where are the warheads and the mine casings?"

"Still in the trunk of my car. I thought they were safer there than in here."

"I think so, too."

"What do you want done with them?"

"Leave them where they are," decided Danilov. Would he be able to turn their possession to another, protective advantage? He was going to need something and couldn't at that moment—that far too impending moment—think what it was.

"This is becoming—might even have become—*precisely* the situation I made clear should *not* be allowed to arise!" declared Georgi Chelyag.

The Russian president's chief of staff spoke looking directly at Danilov, focusing everyone else's attention. Each man sat in his same assigned seat. So did the stenographers, faithfully recording the eagerness to avoid blame. Danilov accepted that the risk in exceeding his rank or authority was awesome, but he couldn't think of another way. He was, he realized, the only man in the room whose political allegiance wasn't known. He was supposed to be apolitical, concerned only in the crime he was investigating, but then the Russian militia was supposed to be made up of honest men. He wished he could decide which faction to back.

Yuri Kisayev said, "The relationship between us and Washington *is* at a very crucial stage. Our UN ambassador expects China to initiate a formal protest debate about the attack in the General Assembly. And that America is privately going along with the idea, because of the extra pressure it would put on us."

"Let's retain some objectivity," said Danilov's immediate superior, Nikolai Belik. "America's made absolutely no progress whatsoever. It's politically expedient—politically obvious—to try to divert criticism on to us."

"Tell us, Dimitri Ivanovich," demanded Viktor Kedrov, personally identifying Danilov for the note-takers, "exactly how far forward is our investigation?"

Easily, prepared, Danilov recounted the previous day's murders that linked the assassination of an accused weapons smuggler to a man who worked for a chemical and biological weapons establishment on the Moscow outskirts.

General Sergei Gromov said, "From which plant did the warhead come? Surely you've been able to determined that!"

"No," Danilov replied, a decision forming in his mind.

"The lettering—and where it was manufactured—was on the side of the damned thing!" attacked Gromov, with forced impatience. "That's identification."

"No, it's not," replied Danilov. "The only *apparent* proof is the name of Gorki itself." He pause. "Which is why I'm hoping you can help us, General."

The soldier's face clouded at the sudden switch of attention. "Me! How!"

"Control and distribution of these warheads was centralized. The letter and numbered designation was strictly controlled from your ministry here in Moscow. So it's from here that the source will be positively established for the missile used in the UN attack."

The older man's face blazed. Chelyag smiled very slightly.

Gromov said, "What evidence—authority—do you have for saying that?"

"The principal of the Gorki factory, confirmed yesterday by the professor in charge of Plant 43 here in Moscow," Danilov stated flatly.

"What's the importance?" demanded Gromov.

"From what I understand from both plants, this particular

weapon—despite not working—was manufactured in their thousands, not just in Russia but in several of the republics that were part of the Soviet Union. Knowing that the canisters would survive, it would make every sense to mislead by stenciling the name of a Russian city from which it did *not* come, wouldn't it?"

The presidential chief of staff looked directly at Gromov. "But with everything being centralized, under military control, you should easily be able to find out from the numerical markings where it came from, shouldn't you?"

Gromov started to speak, changed his mind, and said on the second attempt, "From what Dimitri Ivanovich says, it was a long time ago."

"But the White House expects you to do it," insisted Chelyag.

"Perhaps there is something else your central records could help with?" pressed Danilov. "That emergency number, 876532. It's Moscow. But the telephone authorities say it's out of service and they can't trace to whom or to what it was originally allocated. But your records should tell us that, too, shouldn't they?" He was appearing almost too obviously to align himself with the new against the old.

Gromov's face was white now, not red, in his fury at virtually being questioning by someone he considered a subordinate. "I'll make it part of the inquiry," he said, recognizing that he had no alternative.

"And I'll raise it from the White House with the telephone authorities," Chelyag said.

Danilov had a professional detective's ear for false notes in a rehearsed performance and located an undertone among the anti–White House group. To test the impression he had to appear to be opposing them, a chance he had to take because it was directly relevant to his ability to do his job properly. Confident he couldn't be caught out with the lie, Danilov said, "The Americans have asked for an undamaged warhead, if one exists. I brought one back with me from Gorki . . . obtained another from Plant 43 yesterday—"

"No!" interrupted Gromov, before Danilov finished. "That's admitting we've breached the chemical weapons agreement."

Too quick, too defensive, judged Danilov. "With respect, I don't believe it is. Everyone in this room knows we *have* breached it. I saw hundreds still stored both here and in Gorki. But the ones I am talking about are *empty*. We could relieve the diplomatic and political pressure by publicly announcing that by responding to the American request, we're proving our compliance with the disposal treaty: that this is a museum example of a weapon created too long ago for the current government to be held in any way responsible and just as long ago abandoned."

"I like that argument!" Chelyag declared, at once.

"What possible reason could they want them for?" demanded Kedrov.

"Metal and size comparison," responded Danilov, the improvised reasoning becoming clearer in his mind. "So we're giving nothing away: There can't be any dispute that the UN missile *was* ours."

"I think it's a good idea, a gesture without substance," said the deputy foreign minister. "It would certainly provide the ambassador with a response."

"And yourself," encouraged Danilov. "To achieve the publicity—photographs even—we could announce in advance your personally delivering them to the U.S. Embassy."

"We'll do it!" decided Georgi Chelyag, the man of ranking authority.

"I want it officially recorded that I oppose it," insisted Gromov.

"As I do," said Kedrov. "It's a pointless gesture."

"Which is precisely why it's so easy to make," reminded the president's advisor. To Danilov—but directing the remark to the stenographers—he said, "I want it recorded that Dimitri Ivanovich has made an extremely valuable contribution to today's discussion."

Only a few days ago it hadn't mattered to him whether he was vilified or not, thought Danilov. Now it did. It was like waking up from a sleep that had gone on too long. But still with too many terrifying nightmares.

Yuri Pavin waited until Danilov had finished his account of the meeting before saying "Do you want me personally to deliver the warheads to the Foreign Ministry?"

"No," said Danilov. "Someone else from the department."

Pavin frowned. "Is that a good idea?"

"I'm going to make it one," said Danilov. "Before you hand it over—before you even take it out of your car—I want you to scrape off some paint samples and break off some metal that won't be obvious. Keep one sample for me. Give the other one to forensics"—he took two envelopes of Gorki samples from his pocket, passing them across to the other man—"with these. I want them very specifically and separately marked and signed for as being from Plant 35 at Gorki, from Plant 43 here, and from the empty warheads going to the Americans."

Pavin didn't speak for several moments. "You think it's that bad?"

"Yes," Danilov said flatly.

"Then we'll never get anywhere with this investigation."

"We will," insisted Danilov. "People are trying to make me look stupid. I'm going to prove that I'm not."

"The pathologist says there are definitely two distinct sets of lung hemorrhage lesions," announced Pavin, moving on. "The worst torture both Nikov and Karpov suffered was to be partially drowned, revived into consciousness, and then brought to the point of drowning a second time."

Danilov stared down at the pathologist's report that Pavin put in front of him, carefully going through the injuries. Looking up to the other man he began, "That doesn't make sense," but stopped. "The same!" he started again. "Each was tortured in exactly the same manner and to exactly the same extent."

"Yes?" Pavin frowned, doubtfully.

"Nikov was a bull, a professional killer. Used to violence," reminded Danilov. "He'd have tortured like this himself, held out under questioning much longer than Karpov. But if Karpov had been interrogated about some information he had he would have broken, told whoever it was what they wanted to know long before so much was done to him. These were example killings, to warn others."

"It was good of you to come," said Cowley.

"I tried yesterday but it took this long to get a security clearance," said Pauline. "And there's a guard in the corridor. You really think they might try to get to you here in the hospital!"

"I don't. The bureau does. There's a lot the bureau and I don't seem to be agreeing about." Her hair was much shorter than she'd worn it the last time they'd met, and it was colored a deeper auburn. He thought she was slimmer, too. And looked terrific in the matching sweater and slacks.

"So how are you?"

"Better. The battle lasted all afternoon, but I compromised with the specialist in the end. I stay overnight and I can discharge myself tomorrow. He wants a waiver though. Which I'm giving him."

She sniggered, embarrassed. "You look funny with that great pad on your head. And you're going to look funnier when it comes off. They've shaved off half your hair."

Cowley laughed with her. "I did a deal on the waiver. Tomorrow I get a much smaller, less dramatic dressing. I've got a meeting with the director."

Pauline's face straightened. "You can't be well enough to go back to work, William!"

He'd always liked the way she'd called him William, never Bill. "I can see perfectly and my hearing's coming back. The head's practically healed and so's the rib." He hesitated, seeing the opportunity. "I could just maybe do with a little home help."

His former wife didn't pick up on the remark. Instead she said, "I think you're crazy."

"I sit in an office and make plans for other people to carry out."

"You walked into a building that might have been full of fatal germs and escaped being blown to pieces by a fucking miracle!"

"Rare," he said with attempted lightness.

"Don't, William. What have you got to prove?"

He felt warmed by the concern. "It's not proving anything. There needs to be a more experienced case officer: The panic's percolating down. And there seems to be a problem with Dimitri in Moscow." They'd met when Danilov had been in Washington the last time.

"I thought you got on well with him. Partners, you said?"

"I do. Others don't seem to. If there's a reason he'd tell me, *because* it's like partners. He trusts me. Not anybody else. It's instinctive in Moscow, in his position, not to trust people."

Pauline nodded to the bedside telephone. "You could call Moscow from here."

"Not a secure line," Cowley said glibly. "Let's stop talking about me. How about you? How've you been?"

"Fine. More than fine, I guess. Terrific."

"That sounds . . . I'm not sure what it sounds like."

"I was going to call, suggest we meet, before all this."

"Why?"

Her shoulders rose and fell. "It might seem funny, us so long over I mean, but I wanted to tell you myself. Not, I suppose, that you'd have heard from anyone else." She smiled. "I'm getting married again, William."

"That's wonderful!" he forced himself to say. "Really great."

"His name's John," she said. "John Brooks. He's an orthodontist. That's how I met him, at a dental practice. Can you believe that! He's just bought into a partnership on the West Coast, San Diego. So we'll be moving to the sunshine." She smiled. "Sunshine's good for people getting older, so they say."

"So they say," he agreed. "I wish you all the luck and love." Cowley had to force that, too.

"I knew you would."

Hollis had gotten to work intentionally early that morning, to be there when Carole arrived, which he watched her do from his window overlooking the parking lot, and called her extension the moment she reached her station. He'd rehearsed what to say—written it down, against his breath tightening—but she'd said she was busy for the rest of the week and didn't want to plan the next this early, so why didn't they take a raincheck and talk later. When he'd gone for coffee, she'd been sitting with Robert Standing and didn't even acknowledge him.

10

Cowley took the Tylenol the nurse offered and went to the bathroom to take another from the bottle with which they discharged him. As the bureau car drove downtown from the George Washington Hospital, Cowley gazed out at the White House and across the parks to the needle-like monument and the other memorials. He could see the nipple of the Capitol dome, too, over the far closer Treasury Building, and felt a lurch of despair at so many targets laid out like ducks at a shooting gallery. There seemed to be far more demonstrators than usual outside the White House. One of the banners read "Avenge the Innocent Dead" and the red paint had been allowed to drip, like blood. "Justice not Inaction" was written on another.

The car shuddered over the bureau's tire-tearing security ramp, jarring Cowley's chest. Just before he got out of the car he took another Tylenol. It was difficult to swallow without water, and the coughing hurt.

There was a lot of glad-handing in the entry lobby, where Leonard Ross's personal assistant was already waiting. On the way up in the elevator the man said he looked great, which Cowley knew he didn't from examining himself in a hospital mirror just before he left. Illogically, his size seemed to make the weight loss more obvious, and instead of minimizing the head injury the smaller dressing drew attention to how much hair had been cut away. Cowley thought that rather than look like a covering, the dressing itself looked like a deformity growing from the side of his head. Which throbbed, as his chest did, despite the Tylenol.

There was coffee and Danish already set out in the lounge area of the director's suite. Ross came across the room to greet him and afterward personally poured the coffee. Cowley tried to prevent any awkwardness—certainly any facial reaction to the jab of pain—as he came forward to accept the cup. He had wondered if Pamela Darnley would be included and was glad she wasn't: glad, in fact, that there was no one else except himself and the director.

The no-nonsense former judge said, "You look like shit."

The tone of the meeting had been quickly established, Cowley accepted. "Surface appearance. I'm fine. I told Pamela I wouldn't risk this investigation by not being fit enough to go on with it."

"And she told me," said Ross. "Your neurologist also told me he would have liked you to have stayed for another week."

"Every doctor's worried about his malpractice insurance." Pepper's parting words had been that he expected him to be readmitted in two or three days.

"I can't risk it, Bill. You any idea the sort of heat we're under? The bureau most of all."

"I've seen the coverage. Which is why I want to get back." He shook his head against an offered Danish and wished he hadn't.

Ross took one, crumbling it on his plate. "You want to explain that?"

"OK. I'm still slow, physically. But I can sit at a desk, think things through. You see that half-assed discussion on television after the funeral, some guy suggesting these bastards had frightened themselves so badly they wouldn't do it again?" He hoped he *had* properly understood the tone of this meeting.

"I heard about it."

"That really the guidance from here?"

"No!" Ross said positively. "I'm guessing at political pressure from the White House, although Norton denies it. Necessary for people to feel they can sleep safely in their beds at night."

"So by how much is the heat going to be turned up on us— you—here at the bureau when the next attack comes, which it surely will, and the fact that we didn't think another attack would happen is thrown right back at us!" demanded Cowley.

"I'm ahead of you." The director sighed.

"Doesn't the fact that I'm making the point prove I'm fit enough to come back here and think of things as a whole and not in panicked isolation?"

Ross smiled fleetingly. "Clever argument."

"*Valid* argument," insisted Cowley. He cautiously waved an arm toward the city outside. "You have any idea how many targets there are out there after the U.N. tower and the trade towers before that!"

"There's already extra security around all the obvious ones."

"Which again was leaked, from here, to the *Post* two days ago. So when the hit comes that'll be thrown back, too."

"Providing you're right."

"I am," said Cowley. The headache had gone and his chest was easier, scarcely any discomfort. "But there's an even stronger, practical reason for my being back here. Pamela doesn't think she's getting the cooperation from Moscow."

"That's why I agreed to see you today," disclosed Ross. "I thought there was a special relationship?"

"There is, between Danilov and myself," said Cowley, deciding that to succeed he had to go as far as he could and exaggerate as much as was necessary—knowing the conditions in Moscow, there was hardly cause to exaggerate. "Moscow isn't Washington and their Organized Crime Bureau isn't like us." He hesitated. The director set the tone, he reminded himself. "Here the only corruption is ambition, which I guess is how it should be. At Ulitza Petrovka virtually everyone from the janitor upward is on the take: Capone's Chicago was a kindergarten by comparison. More people—politicians as well as his own organization—are working against Dimitri than with him."

"You're saying you're indispensable," cut in the director.

"Yes," Cowley said unashamedly. "It's nothing personal against anyone here. But it's very personal with me. He's five thousand miles away, virtually unable to trust anyone within five yards of him in his own building. He needs to speak to someone he knows as a friend when he talks to us."

"A very, *very* clever argument," said the haphazardly dressed director, smiling longer this time.

"Very, *very* valid," echoed Cowley. He wished there was more facial reaction from Ross—something he might have been able to read.

"Pepper also told me he had you sign a specific waiver against premature discharge. Which he thinks this is."

Told *me*! Cowley picked up the phrase belatedly: The director of the Federal Bureau of Investigation *personally* talking to the physician of an injured agent! Could he have been working his ass off for a purpose that had already been decided? If he was reading the runes correctly, he was back! "The federal insurance people want me to sign the same exoneration?"

"Yes," admitted Ross.

"Why did we go through all this then?" chanced Cowley.

"I needed to be sure."

"Are you?"

"I think so."

"Am I still case officer?"

"Initially under the strictest—and personal—operational control. And I've agreed with the incident room being established here for that reason."

"You want me to sign the insurance waiver?"

"No."

"That makes it your personal decision."

"You feel competent to lecture *me* on law?"

"I wanted to make it clear that I understood the legal implications."

"If there was an alternative to bringing you back I'd have taken it. At this moment I wish there had been."

This really was trousers-down, ass-in-the-air time, thought Cowley. "I'm glad there wasn't."

"I want you to convince Danilov that Pamela Darnley can be trusted just as much as you can," demanded the director.

"In case I can't cut it?"

"You don't need me to explain what I'm saying."

"Thank you."

"This isn't for your career benefit. I don't want you imagining that this meeting gives you any special privilege, either."

"I don't. And won't. What about authority?"

"I appointed Pamela Darnley *acting* case officer. I'll tell her you're back."

"She'll be disappointed."

"I hope I'm not."

It was the first time he'd seen Pamela Darnley with total, unblurred clarity, and Cowley decided she was remarkably attractive: close, he supposed, to being beautiful. He tried to avoid the physical comparison with Pauline but couldn't. Like Pauline, she was richly auburn haired, although heavier busted—heavier altogether—which was compensated for by her height, which had to be at least five ten, maybe more. There was an elegance about the tunic dress without the edge-to-edge precision of Pauline the previous night, and worn with the insouciance of someone who either didn't care or knew she didn't have to try too hard. He suspected the latter. The heavy-framed glasses that had registered indistinctly during the hospital visit outlined deeply blue or maybe black eyes in an oval face spared, with the same insouciance, anything more than base makeup and pale lipstick. There was no wedding ring. Cowley was abruptly discomfited by an analysis—and most definitely by the comparison with Pauline—that was totally irrelevant. The incident room had been created from a small lecture hall, and Terry Osnan said it was good to see him back.

"It *is* good to see you back," Pamela said, settling into her chair in the cramped side office—surrendering the desk position to Cowley—and feeling the opposite.

"No, it's not, as far as you are concerned," Cowley replied at once. "You know I've just had a one-to-one with the director. I'm working the same rules now. And they'll apply in whatever the future is. You're not at all pleased to see me back. You saw this as your big chance—which it was and still is—but now you're thinking my being here screws everything. It doesn't. I'm not back here to watch my territory or my ass. We're not in competition. We don't have the time or the luxury to be. Any day now the bastards are going to hit again and we're going to be under more pressure than you ever thought possible. You *are* going to be glad I'm back then, to take some of the heat." Cowley paused. Then he said, "That's it, for openers."

Pamela didn't respond immediately because she couldn't. Neither did she show any facial surprise—any reaction whatsoever—to the pronouncement. Finally she said, "So I wasn't glad. Pissed, in fact. Now I'm not sure."

"Then you'll have to learn to be."

"OK," she accepted doubtfully. She hadn't known what to expect, but it certainly wasn't a conversation like this.

"What did you think of the suggestion that we don't expect any more attacks?"

"Total shit. Of course there are going to be. I wasn't asked an opinion until now."

Cowley smiled. "Now you're going to be asked; *we're* going to be asked. Before we are you'd better bring me up to date."

It only took minutes. The second forensic search in New Rochelle ("they even sexed the worms") had found nothing. In the intervening days since the disaster, they'd hit every known, possibly traceable and self-proclaimed radical group, from those that expected the world to end next week, through those that believed there was life on Mars, to those ("the freedom-of-expression Constitution's got a lot to answer for") that built shrines to Hitler and Satan, or both, and wanted to kill all the mentally ill, disabled, homosexuals, Jews, blacks, Catholics, and Protestants on the planet. There was no provable paramilitary group or organization in the area of the massacre, and the marina checks at New Rochelle and Norwalk had not produced a single sighting of any obvious reconnoiterer. The military hadn't come up with anything.

"Zilch!" the woman declared. "We also went through the Russian ghettoes at Brooklyn's Brighton Beach, where the links are to the mafias back home. No one expected to be knocked over by the rush of volunteers—a whisper would have been good. Nothing, not even for money and immunity. There was some copy-cat stuff, of course, from the crazies. One—a U.S. Army grenade—in Des Moines, two, both industrial dynamite, in St. Louis. No one got hurt, thank Christ."

Everything that should have been done according to routine, acknowledged Cowley. "Moscow?"

"The Moscow murders switched the attention from us yesterday and so far today. But all we know is what Danilov let us have. We haven't been able to add to it from here—establish a connection that makes sense, any more than he can." Pamela paused heavily. "Or any more than he's prepared to tell me he can."

"Or is *allowed* to tell us he can," Cowley picked up. "This *was* a

Russian missile. And the mines that killed seventeen Americans were Russian, too, according to the metallography findings. You weren't actually expecting the key to the store, were you?"

The woman made a vague, almost embarrassed gesture. "I hoped for more."

Cowley guessed Pamela Darnley was about thirty, thirty-five tops: a fast-track contender to be this high this young. He decided it was too soon to repeat the near lecture he'd delivered earlier to the director about the environment in which Danilov existed, quite irrespective of the political straitjacket into which the man was probably strapped, whatever public declarations there might be about full and frank openness. "I know it seems like forever but it's only been a few days." Exactly six, he realized, surprising himself.

"You want to convince the great American public they shouldn't be so impatient?"

"I'm not sure I could."

"I'm sure you couldn't. After September, 2001, and the anthrax outbreaks that followed there's a lot of frightened people out there." She consciously made her smile into a grimace. "A lot of frightened people in here, too. So what's our way forward?" Did he mean what he said about not cutting her out?

"I need to speak to Dimitri."

"Special friends?"

"Necessary friends," Cowley said, unconcerned by the cynicism. "Which brings it all back to us. I'm case officer as well as outranking you in seniority. But I'm not interested in playing that game. All I'm interested in is getting this wrapped up, whatever it takes. I want your total, unconditional input. You make the breakthrough, I won't steal it from you. Additional rules, OK?"

Pamela looked steadily at him for several moments. "OK," she agreed. If he wasn't sincere he had to be the world's best bullshitter. She'd go along with it because initially there wasn't any alternative. But only as long as it took her to decide if he was genuine or not. And if he wasn't, she'd have to do something about it. She wouldn't get another opportunity like this, and she sure as hell wasn't going to let it be taken away from her.

Why, wondered Cowley, had he made a commitment to Pamela

Darnley that it hadn't occurred to him to make to her predecessor? Reminded, he said, "What's the news of Burt Bradley? He taking visitors? Able to talk?"

There was another long look. "I thought the director might have told you. He died early this morning."

CNN made a news flash of the deputy foreign minister's arrival at the American embassy. Yuri Kisayev insisted on entering the building from the front, directly off Ulitza Chaykovskovo, personally carrying one of the awkwardly shaped packages, trailed by his more heavily laden driver. He paused at the babble of questions, refusing to identify what he was passing over but insisting it proved the Russian intention to cooperate.

Cowley said, "I'm guessing warheads."

"Very obviously a staged photo opportunity," said Pamela.

"Dimitri say anything about it?"

"I couldn't get him yesterday and he didn't call back," said the woman. "Nothing when we last spoke."

Only when he recognized Dimitri Danilov's voice did Cowley slot the receiver into the conference relay box. He began speaking in Russian. It was Danilov who switched immediately into English.

"How are you?" demanded the Russian. Cowley was back!

"Like shit on a plate, according to the director."

Danilov laughed. "But you're there?"

"Yes."

"And OK?" demanded Danilov.

"Good enough," dismissed Cowley. "This is a conference call. I've got Pamela Darnley with me."

"We've spoken. Hello."

"Hello," said the woman.

"CNN has just shown your deputy minister at our embassy."

"It's the duplicate warheads we spoke about before you got hurt," the Russian cut in.

Cowley hesitated. "That's good. Our forensic people are anxious for them."

"I can understand that." In his Moscow office Danilov smiled, relieved that Cowley was understanding, too.

"How closely do you think your murders are connected?" Cowley saw Pamela, on the other side of the desk, frown at the question.

"Perfect fit, I'd say. There are still some things to sort out here before I can come over. Will a delay be a problem for you?"

"Not at all," said Cowley without any hesitation this time. "How long do you think?"

"A day or two. Three maybe. Anything I should know from your end?"

"One or two useful-looking leads but nothing positive," said Cowley. "If there's a definite development I'll tell you at once. Otherwise I'll bring you up to speed when you get here."

"That sounds good. What about your not expecting another attack?"

Cowley hesitated. "You read that?"

"Had it suggested to me."

"Your side?"

"No."

"That's interesting."

"Thought you might find it so. True?"

"Of course not."

"Didn't sit comfortably with me, either."

"Pamela and I are working closely on this," said Cowley. "I'm going to be office bound for a few days, but if you come through and I'm not here, she'll have the handle on everything."

"Look forward to working with you, Pamela," said Danilov.

"And I with you," said the woman. Pointedly she added, "Finally."

Cowley supposed she was allowed the complaint. The frown had gone but there was a weary-faced resignation. He sat initially unspeaking after replacing the telephone, looking across at the woman. When she stayed equally silent he said, "Well?"

She shrugged. "I guess I got security clearance. I just wish we had been told something that needed it."

Cowley smiled at her. "We were. Welcome to the land—and the need—of double-speak."

Her face remained expressionless while Cowley sketched the difficulties under which Danilov operated. "The arrangement is that if

I initiate the call we speak in Russian. If he calls me, it's in English. A switch, like today, indicates he's got a problem—is being blocked or misled. Whatever, he can't speak freely. We never spoke, before the boat blew up, about his supplying duplicate although obviously empty warheads. Nor did we make—discuss even—any plans for his coming here. He was telling me a lot by seeming to tell me nothing. And if anyone was listening at his end, they wouldn't have understood a word."

Pamela's face relaxed at last. "Very Hollywood."

"Hollywood couldn't make it up."

Danilov *was* relieved at reestablishing his direct and very necessary link with Cowley. He felt a confidence he hadn't until now realized had been missing since the catastrophe in which the American could have died with all the rest. There was an excitement, too, at the thought of getting away from a dull, gray existence in a dull, gray Moscow to where there always seemed enough electricity to charge the people as well as all their neon and flashing lights. It might, also, temporarily resolve the immediate problem toward which he was driving, unsure what to expect when he got there.

Olga was at Kirovskaya, which Danilov half expected. What Danilov hadn't anticipated was the condition of the apartment itself. Or of his wife. The flat was tidier—cleaner—than he could ever remember it being. There were no discarded clothes anywhere, the couch and seat coverings were neatly arranged and looked freshly pressed, and the bed was made. Olga herself was in an unstained dress and wore a cardigan he didn't know she possessed, without elbow holes and with all the matching buttons still attached. Her hair was neatly arranged, although still in its several shades of blond.

"Can I get you something?" she offered.

"I'll do it myself," said Danilov. The stalagmite of dishes had gone and there was food in the refrigerator and ice for his vodka.

"I stayed with Irena," Olga announced before Danilov asked about her previous night's absence, which he hadn't intended to do. "We had a long talk."

Danilov nodded, with nothing to say.

"I don't know why I did it. Here, I mean."

"Does it make any difference? Has it ever?"

"I want to try again."

Danilov looked blankly at her, not understanding what she was saying.

"I mean you and me. Try to put our marriage back together."

"Olga! Don't be ridiculous. We don't *have* a marriage. There's nothing to put together."

"Please, Dimmy."

"Olga, there's no point. No possibility. You know that."

"I'm trying to say I'm sorry. That I'll never do anything like it again. Ever. I'll do anything!"

"Stop it, Olga! I've already decided I'll get another place."

Her face began to harden. "So you're throwing me out?"

"I said *I'll* find somewhere else."

"Like the place you found with Larissa!"

"I don't want to fight."

"That's what *she* said," blurted Olga, the bitterness overflowing, her voice shrill. "That I wouldn't be abandoned: that she'd always see I was looked after. *She* said that to *me*. Like she was doing me a favor! Making it all all right."

Larissa had insisted on that, Danilov remembered. Meant it, because of the sort of woman she had been, knowing there was going to be an upheaval and trying to do everything she could to cause as little hurt as possible. "She wasn't taking me away from you. You *drove* me away from you years ago. It was stupid, bothering to stay together. We both know that."

"You know what I did when she got killed?"

"I don't want to."

"I laughed."

"Don't, Olga! This isn't achieving anything." It was, he conceded. It was the only way she could hurt him, which she'd known. He wasn't going to argue—couldn't be bothered to argue. All he could do was hear her out—or rather try *not* to hear her out—closing his mind and his feelings to whatever or however she wanted to avenge herself.

"You'll pay!"

"I have already."

She snorted a laugh too heavily, so that her nose ran. She didn't try to wipe it. "So romantic! So touching!"

"I'm going to America," he announced, trying to stop her. "I'll start looking around when I get back. Until then, for the next two or three days, let's just try to be civilized. I'll only be here at night. Let's try to endure that as best we can."

She wiped her nose finally. "No!" she said. "You won't move out. I will. *I'll* find somewhere else while you're away. Somewhere nice, better than this rathole. And I'll see a lawyer, make sure I get all the money and support that a loyal, loving wife deserves when she's abandoned. You're going to regret the day you ever met me."

"I've been doing that for years," said Danilov. "You want to get into a competition about who betrayed whom first, you're welcome. I'm not interested."

"You've got more to lose than me," threatened Olga. "You'll become the joke, I won't."

Patrick Hollis had been physically sick. Even now, hours later in his locked den, he still felt nauseated. On the keyboard of his for once ignored computer lay the drawing that had been waiting for him, mixed in with that morning's mail. It showed a limp penis, the head drawn as a bespectacled, weeping face. Written beneath, in capital letters, was SORRY.

The explosion that blew away three of the tiered steps running from the top to the bottom of the Washington Monument came at 1:00 A.M. the following morning.

11

From the initial—but instantly withdrawn—Parks Department inspection they knew the explosion appeared to have separated the stairs that spiral from the bottom to the viewing gallery at the very top of the 555-feet monument, leaving a metal-tangled gap where the 304th, 305th, and 306th levels had been. It would have been impossible for Cowley to contemplate trying to climb that high, but at that moment the entire Mall, from beyond the Lincoln Memorial at 23rd Street up to 3rd Street and between Constitution and Independence avenues, was sealed to anyone on foot except the bomb disposal unit.

Cowley was as close as it was possible to get, in the team's control scanner halfway between the monument and the Sylvan Theatre, watching the instant television relay and listening to its accompanying commentary. It was tightly crowded. Besides the normal three liaison men, Pamela Darnley was there with him, together with a Parks Authority inspector with every available plan—as well as personal knowledge—to guide the team on anything that needed explaining once inside the hollow obelisk.

Which they weren't yet. Painfully, quite literally, aware of the New Rochelle booby-trap, Cowley had disregarded the impatient assurance from the bomb squad leader that they didn't require that sort of advice and urged that every inch of the surrounding ground be swept for mines, trip wires, or pressure sensors—for anything, in fact—before they even attempted to approach the monument itself.

They'd been doing that now for an hour, the scene made glaringly white bright by the searchlights of a concentrated circle of police and military helicopters. Other official helicopters revolved around that inner core to keep media machines out of what had been declared a civilian no-fly zone. All incoming and departing aircraft to Reagan Airport had been warned or diverted.

The body heat of three extra people inside the enclosed van was challenging its air conditioning. They were all in shirt sleeves—Cowley glad of Pamela's perfume—and all wore headsets and mikes directly linking them to the outside crew.

Just as he was beginning to be embarrassed by a feeling of boredom, the team leaders declared, "Nothing! We're going in. The park man there? Like to go through what we shouldn't be nervous about finding right inside the door?"

Before the man to Cowley's right could respond, another voice said, "Lambert here. It could help us if you filmed as much as possible as you go."

There was an overly heavy sigh from the team leader, Nelson Tibbert. "Trust us. We'll try to beat Spielberg to the Oscar before we get blown to hell. Which we hope we don't. And I wish to Christ people wouldn't keep telling us our job."

"Just doing my job, too, buddy," said Paul Lambert, who headed the FBI's forensic team. They'd waited throughout the outside search in a larger van immediately behind that in which Cowley hunched. Lambert added, "We're all holding our lucky rabbit's feet for you."

"Thanks," said the bomb disposal head. Nelson Tibbert was a black man as overpoweringly big as Jefferson Jones: Cowley hadn't needed the reminding comparison or the memory of six tiny, tightly closed faces.

Into Cowley's headset came the voice of Michael Poulson, the parks official fortunately jammed against his left, good side. The man didn't bother with his plans precisely to describe the entry vestibule, pay booths, and where the walkway would be found in relation to the central elevators. All the monument's electrical power had been cut from the mains, against the possibility of further explosives being connected to its operating supply—the up-and-down elevator current being the most obvious. Poulson set out where the mains and generator-activated emergency systems would be found. He also itemized the emergency firefighting and medical equipment at the various levels up to the three hundredth level.

"Followed you through on my plan," confirmed Tibbert. "And the door's open and welcoming."

It had been Cowley who'd ordered the service door left open by the quickly evacuated parks engineer who'd gone to investigate the alarm triggered by the explosion. Cowley's head ached, despite a second Tylenol, and he'd already smiled and nodded his gratitude to Pamela for straining away from any contact with his injured side.

The scene-recording cameraman was leading—with no one in view—and Cowley's immediate impression was of the minimally lit underwater television footage of the finding of the *Titanic*, even to the man's heavy breathing that interspersed his commentary. He matched his description to everything he closely filmed on the ground floor.

The engineer had told them he'd trodden on every step both going up and coming down ('You can't manage six hundred taking them two at a time'), which would have tripped any wire, but the ascent was still slow, hands coming into the frame, touching and gently probing every step and running up each support to the hand-rails on either side. Each step was methodically counted off as it was climbed. The breathing became louder. Every man was dressed in the heaviest of armored protective suits, Cowley remembered.

Cowley didn't have any irrational feeling of boredom any longer but just as irrational was the demanding, intrusive thought that he'd missed something—misinterpreted or misjudged—and the perspiration was more at the fear of that misinterpretation causing further death and injury than from the claustrophobic heat of the van. Pamela turned to him questioningly when he took off his headset, silently mouthing "What?" He shook his head, not bothering to hide the grimace at the sharp jab of pain. He turned down the earpiece volume, for a moment not wanting the distraction of the commentary.

Nothing had been overlooked—couldn't have been overlooked! He hadn't questioned the engineer alone, organized this alone. There'd been the bomb squad and their commander and a lot of other FBI personnel—Pamela among them—and the unseen, totally armor-suited men now groping with agonizing slowness around the pitch-black inside of the monument carried every sort and type of detection and neutralizing equipment. So there *was* nothing more. But Cowley couldn't shake the conviction that there was.

Pamela took her own headset off and leaned close to him, although still carefully not touching. "What?" she said again quietly.

"I've got a bad feeling. What haven't we done?"

She frowned, silent for several moments. "Nothing."

"I think there is. Something we haven't read properly."

Pamela laid her hand on his arm. "A lot of professionals are involved." He shouldn't be here! It wasn't the deal. She'd done exactly what she thought they'd agreed, by calling him after she'd been alerted, but hadn't expected him to come like this, not trusting her by herself.

"They haven't read it, either."

The gaping break in the stairway came abruptly into view. Cowley put his headset back on in time to hear the panting cameraman say, "Here!"

"Careful!" came Tibbert's voice. "Let me pass."

Cowley's underwater impression increased when the squad leader came partially into view. The metalled fabric of his armor and helmet glistened in the camera's strobe. From his back, which was how the man filled the lens, he actually looked fishlike: a prehistoric monster from some very deep lagoon. Adding to the imagery, Tibbert gently directed a heat sensor on the end of a hydraulically extended arm, moving it like a patient fisherman over every part of the hole and its surroundings.

"No register," Tibbert reported.

He repeated the process with what Cowley knew, from watching the equipment check, to be a device that could identify a variety of known explosive compounds from their odors.

"No register," he said again.

"Is it structurally safe?" demanded Cowley.

Tibbert probed with a stiff, rubber-encased rod before putting his weight on each of the intervening steps, until he reached the very edge of the break. "It would seem so. The perspective approaching the hole from below is confusing. The three steps have not been completely blown away. There is still some base left to every tread." As he spoke, the camera came up alongside, illustrating what he was describing. The picture was repeatedly whitened as another member of the squad took flashlit still photographs. "The damage is substantial, but my assessment is that it was a comparatively small charge. . . . I can see what looks to be explosive debris—"

"Please leave it in situ," came the urgent voice of Paul Lambert. "We don't want it moved. Touched."

Tibbert gave another of his heavy sighs. "Thank you for the timely reminder. We are now going to put an extension walkway over the damaged area to enable us to cross to continue the examination. And thank you in anticipation, guys, but we do know that they'd expect us to do exactly this, so it would be the place to set the trap."

But there wasn't one. The ascent, afterward, was even slower, testing for wires or trips, and it was a further hour before they reached the top.

Tibbert said, "I could never be bothered to wait in line with all the tourists, but this really is a hell of a view."

Relaxing too quickly, thought Cowley, unable to lose the foreboding. "This was obviously a timed detonation and there's still a lot of places—the elevator shaft and its workings the most obvious—where God knows what else could be waiting to go off. Don't you think you should get out of there?"

"That Special Agent Cowley?"

"Yes."

"We really do appreciate your concern, Mr. Cowley," said the man. "But while I'm admiring the view, the guys with me are running all sorts of checks on every electrical box and installation we can find up here, like we did at the bottom. And we've got some dinky little gizmos that can actually check the wiring in the shaft itself, even with the power off, for any nasty things that might be humming along it. And when we've done all that we're going to climb back down even more carefully, in case we missed something. 'Cause that's our job and we know how to do it."

Cowley moved to speak, but before he could Paul Lambert said, "A lot of guys who were friends of mine thought they did, too, up in New Rochelle. You watch your ass, Nelson, you hear?"

"I hear," said Tibbert, no longer patronizing. "And I'm sorry. Everything checks out up here. We're on our way down."

They did descend as carefully as the man promised. It took two more hours. By the time they emerged through the small service door it was daylight, and the only helicopters overheard were maintaining the air clearance. It was only when he stood that Cowley realized he seemed to ache in every part of his body, not just his ribs, from tensing against a fresh disaster. Pamela followed him from the van, stretching the cramp from her shoulders.

"I seem to remember some promise that you weren't going to get actively involved: just sit at a desk and think?" complained Pamela. If there was an understanding—or whatever the hell he chose to call it—then they had an understanding.

"I forgot," he said carelessly.

"Thank God your premonition was wrong." Son of a bitch! But it wouldn't be politically—personally—right to protest any more. She needed to remember, though.

Cowley shook his head. "There could still be enough explosives somewhere in there to blow away half of Washington. I want those forensic guys in and out of there in double-quick time."

A shout from one of the scanner operators stopped Cowley as he was about to join the FBI group, already in a debriefing huddle around the bomb disposal team.

"There's been a claim! And a message!" announced the duty officer at the bureau watch room when Cowley identified himself.

"Where from?"

"Bastards have hit the Pentagon again! But differently this time, thank God."

The message read:

AMERICA AND RUSSIA ARE ENEMIES, NOT FRIENDS. AMERICA IS BEING DECEIVED BY THE EAST. TO REGAIN DOMINANT WORLD LEADERSHIP CANCERS NEED TO BE EXCISED AND DECEPTIONS EXPOSED.

It was sighed THE WATCHMEN. Cowley and Pamela stood shoulder to shoulder, gazing down at the printout.

"The Pentagon?" demanded Pamela, baffled.

"And from the Pentagon they accessed www.fbi.gov—the bureau's home page—and put themselves at the top of the Ten Most Wanted list," said the duty officer. "They just don't want to terrorize us. They're humiliating us: showing the world how good they are and how bad we are. Which they've done, big time. They used the government's address—www.fedworld.gov.—to get not just to us but on every other United States federal department and agency home page. Even as we talk, this is being read by thousands everywhere in the country—maybe in every overseas embassy beyond. They're giving us the stiffest middle finger you ever saw."

"How can it be *simple*, breaking into what should be the most protected and secure system in the world?" challenged Pamela.

"Because there's no such thing as a perfect and totally secure system," the man said patiently. "There's always what's known in the trade as a back door. And always someone clever enough to open it. We've had hackers get into the Pentagon before. Once there was a kid of fifteen who endangered satellites, for Christ's sake! Anyone wrongly using an access is known in the business as a cracker!"

"If the distribution is anything like you say it'll leak to the media," Cowley predicted wearily.

"It already has," said the man. "It was a flash on the six A.M. radio and television news, right on top of what you've been doing all night out there in the Mall."

"What about tracing them, through however it is they got into the Pentagon system?"

"Forget it," advised the man. "The military will try, obviously. Got to. But guys this clever will have come in from another unsuspecting cuckoo's nest. We're in shit, Bill. And sinking."

"I knew there was something wrong," said Cowley, matching the cynicism. He said to Pamela: "The Watchmen?"

"Never heard of them," said the woman.

There was a downside to every move they made. Switching the crisis venue to Pennsylvania Avenue because of its more guaranteed security was at once picked up by the vulture-hovering media as yet another example of the bureau's reactive instead of proactive helplessness, but so overwhelming were the attacks that Cowley relegated them to the farthest edge of his consideration. At its forefront, while the conference was being organized, was the persistent nag that something had still been overlooked.

After suggesting the obvious additional people necessary that day, Cowley left the actual organization to the bureau director's assistant and Pamela Darnley at her own computer to return alone to the still-sealed Mall.

Washington was virtually gridlocked by the closure of its very heart, so the only way to move was on foot. And that was like edging, with wincing nervousness, through a Super Bowl crowd so big it was virtually shoulder to shoulder by the time Cowley got to 14th Street. There was, fortunately, a barricade-free lane for official vehicles, which Cowley walked along after identifying himself at the police line. He was almost into the park before he was recognized by anyone in the crowd. At once his name began to be called and there were a lot of camera clicks and flashes. He ignored it all.

Nelson Tibbert and his team were still there, although there were some new armor-shielded men just going into the obelisk when Cowley reached the scanner.

Tibbert recognized him and said, "Your guys have gone, with all they want. This is our fourth sweep. It's a bastard, trying to climb that high in this sort of gear. I'm sure there's nothing on the stairway itself. We're concentrating on the electrics, stuff like that."

"You know what's worrying me?" Cowley said, rhetorically. "Something going off when the elevator's run, full of people: a charge big enough to bring the whole fucking monument down."

"Ahead of you," assured the team leader. "The elevator *is* the most obvious. After this final sweep I'm going to crank the doors open manually, go through the shaft and the cabins. Actually using electricity is the last thing I'm going to do, and then by remote control. Take the elevator up and down, an itty bit at a time, in the hope of localizing any explosion."

Tibbert really did bear a remarkable resemblance to Jefferson Jones, thought Cowley. "How long?"

The man gestured uncertainly. "Couple of days from now. I ain't in no hurry."

"I don't want you to be." Looking at the solid mass of people lining every edge of the cordon he said, "If there is something in there the size of New Rochelle, those people going to be safe?"

"The monument's marble. Hard. If there's a blow it'll most likely be brought down, but the force will be contained. Maybe make their ears ring a little. Could do some damage to the White House glass."

A throwaway line to be taken seriously, recognized Cowley. "You got any kids?"

Tibbert frowned. "Four. Why?"

"Don't want any more orphans."

"Don't plan for there to be any more."

"You and me both," said Cowley. He stood on the knoll upon which the monument was built, looking around again, guessing the faraway crowd had to be a thousand strong, maybe more. Where was it? Where the fuck, what the fuck, was it that had to be as obvious as the arrow-straight marble dart pointing up into the clear morning sky but which he couldn't see, couldn't realize?

He accepted the offered ride from the crew of the police car on the perimeter, forcing himself into a gossiping conversation about bastard lunatics and agreeing it was good New York State had reintroduced the death penalty for crimes like New Rochelle and promising to take care when he got out at the J. Edgar Hoover building. He felt the sweep of dizziness as he walked into the enclosed forecourt dominated by the inscription of the bureau's credo. He grabbed the wall and covered the stumble by feigning problems with a shoe, lifting and easing his foot experimentally. The moment passed almost immediately, and he continued on to more gladhanding in the foyer.

Pamela was already in the conference room, waiting. He said at once, "Who are the Watchmen?"

She shook her head. "Not listed in any of our records. Got a help call out. What about you?"

"Our guys got all they wanted inside the monument apparently."

"The director's asked forensic to attend if they've got anything this soon."

"Who else, additionally?"

"Poulson, the parks guy who was in the truck with us. A general from the Pentagon with one of their computer guys. Some people, I don't know who or how many, from D.C. police. Al Hinton, our public affairs guy. That's all I know."

"Anything from Moscow?"

She shook her head.

"We're missing something, Pam. I know we are."

"What you're missing is the night's sleep you never got and the week extra you should have stayed in hospital." She paused, deciding not to let it go. "I called you because you're the case officer, not to come to the scene. That wasn't part of the deal."

"Couldn't sleep after I woke up."

The rib strapping made it difficult for Cowley to lean forward sufficiently to wash his beard-rasped face over the toilet washbasin. He did so frowning at his own reflection in the mirror. He *did* look like shit on a plate. Worse. He'd always had a heavy beard, and the unshaven growth made a black-and-white comparison against his deathly pallor. His eyes were sunk into his head and black rimmed, and the clothes he'd hurriedly grabbed—a sweatshirt and jeans—hung on him, sweat-wrinkled and baggy. Two cups of cafeteria coffee didn't give him the lift he'd hoped for, but they made swallowing the Tylenol easier.

The hastily arranged conference room—normally the biggest lecture hall in the building—was already filling. He was curious at what had been discovered forensically so quickly for Paul Lambert to be already there. The Pentagon general wore his uniform, complete with the name plate identifying himself as Sinclair J. Smith. There was a thin, nervous civilian with him. The bureau director's assistant bustled around the table, seating everyone, putting Cowley and Pamela together. From the arrangement Cowley saw that on FBI territory Leonard Ross was assuming the chairmanship.

Pamela leaned close and said, "We stink."

Cowley said, "That's what all the papers say. You want to bat first?" She smelled and looked early-morning fresh, not like someone who'd been up all night.

She turned more fully toward him. "You feel all right?" A genuine offer of a place center stage or a curve she couldn't see?

"You know as much about it as I do. I'll pick up as we go along." Cowley wanted to listen, hear what other people said, still searching for the trigger.

Leonard Ross was the last to enter, with the secretary of state and Frank Norton, the president's chief of staff. Al Hinton, the fat and balding public affairs chief, was in attendance, shepherding the three men ahead of him. Cowley realized gratefully that today's media coverage was limited to a press pool of one television and one still photographer and a solitary reporter. Cowley was conscious, too, of far less—in fact, scarcely none—posturing than before. The identification of Cowley was even quicker this time and the concentration on him just as immediate, but again he refused all questions beyond saying he'd recovered more than sufficiently to resume as case officer. As Hinton led the pool away, Norton said it was good to see him back and Cowley thanked him, conscious of the director's frown.

Leonard Ross showed no surprise, though, when Pamela responded to the update request, which Cowley at once decided she did brilliantly. She smoothly took everyone through a selection of still photographs of the scene inside the monument, even itemizing the electrical circuits and boxes that the disposal team had initially cleared, but stressed that the examination was continuing.

"And we've drawn a total blank on any protest or radical group calling itself the Watchmen. We've already asked friendly services—England and Israel—to check. Nothing back yet."

She looked invitingly at Cowley, who remained silent, although he was conscious of another frown from the director.

It was the president's chief of staff who spoke. Frank Norton said, "You got anything to tell us about this computer intrusion, General?"

"Too soon," said the soldier, who had a shaved marine haircut and a face that looked as if it had been carved from something very hard. He nodded to the civilian beside him. "Maybe you'd better hear from Carl."

"I'm head of Pentagon computer security, Carl Ashton," the man introduced himself uncomfortably. "We've got more than a thousand computers, terminals, and VDU stations, all at various levels of security, purpose, and program. If someone infects a system with a virus—the most common is one that replicates information until the file is totally filled, when it jams—then the problem's obvious. But if someone gets in a back door simply to use our machines and our servers as a conduit—giving themselves their own entry code and password—it'll take time to find them. It's possible we never will."

"Have I correctly heard what you've just said?" demanded Norton, spacing his words in incredulity. "A bunch of terrorists have gotten into the communications system of the military headquarters of the United States of America *actually to attack us*, and we're not going to be able to find them! Is that what the Pentagon is going to tell the president and the people of this country?"

"I think I should explain more fully—" tried Ashton.

"I really think you should," cut in Henry Hartz. "I don't like what I'm hearing at all, after last year. Neither will the American people." Irritation made the secretary of state's Germanic accent more pronounced.

Ashton's color rose and his hands fluttered nervously over the table. "No computer system can be declared totally beyond intrusion. There's always a back door, either left there by the installer for his personal gratification and amusement . . ." The man paused at the looks of fresh astonishment around the table. "Yes," he insisted, "even at the level of people who install at the Pentagon. More so, even: At the highest level of computer expertise a universal arrogance exists: they're Captain Kirks with their own *Enterprise* space ships, able to go where no man has gone before. There are websites—clubs—on the Internet where such people gather. Not physically or using their own names—pseudonyms by which one recognizes the other. Entry codes and passwords are swopped. All it would have needed in this case is for a disgruntled Pentagon employee to belong to such a club and the door's open."

"There's a check there!" interrupted the CIA's John Butterworth. "We need a list—"

"Which we keep, of every Pentagon employee who is dismissed or who leaves in circumstances considered likely to create resentment."

"This is absurd!" protested Butterworth. "Why don't we hit these cockamamie clubs, round the bastards up?"

Ashton, embarrassed, looked sideways to the low-profile general, who shrugged. The computer security man said, "Sir, these aren't places—buildings. They're websites. They only exist in what you've heard described as cyberspace: They have no actuality. We don't *know* where they are—how to access them. And if we did, we'd be committing a federal offense under the terms of the U.S. data protection legislation."

Stunned silence spread throughout the room. The pragmatic

Leonard Ross said, "So far you've told us what you *can't* do. What *can*—are—you doing?"

"I talked about various levels of security," reminded Ashton. "At its lowest administrative level we've got a lot of terminals without either a hard or floppy disk. They're VDUs operated from a central server. They're the most likely to have been breached. Those are the servers we're sweeping now: If our terrorists are there, we'll find them. Find the intrusion, at least. But we're assuming that these guys are good, professionals, if that's an acceptable description. They won't just have broken in and established their own little cave. They will have established their own burglar alarm when a trace is locked on them. They won't have come straight into the Pentagon. There'll be several cutouts in other systems—systems that might be on the far side of the world—and there will quite literally be a burglar alarm that might even ring a bell they can hear. And when they do—before we get close—they'll close down. That's what I meant by saying we'll probably never find them, not from putting on tracers."

"This is terrifying," said Hartz, almost to himself. "And I thought I had already used up all the terror I could feel."

"It's modern technology, Mr. Secretary," said General Smith, judging the moment safe to come back into the discussion. "It terrifies me, too."

"That's the lowest level of security," persisted Norton. "What else is there?"

"Machines with their own hard disks, their own programs. They're all swept, automatically, every month—in the most sensitive areas, every week—but we've already overridden that time frame. We're already sweeping every machine down to the war room itself. But even if we pick them up, they will have alarmed themselves, as I've just explained."

"Jesus H. Christ!" said Norton, exasperated. "Anyone here realize what the reaction would be from the American public if they knew this?"

"Probably close to the reaction they're showing at the moment to every other example of our helplessness," said Hartz.

"Bill," Leonard Ross said unexpectedly, "you got any point you'd like to make? Or would you like to sit this one out? You're really not looking at all well."

It was only then that Cowley realized he'd slumped down in his chair, even allowing his eyes to close as they'd been closed when the director spoke, although he'd heard everything. He said, "I was thinking—or trying to think—about something else."

"That's obvious," said Ross. "And for the case officer that's pretty worrying, as far as I am concerned. You've had a long day already. Why don't you rest a little?"

"I don't think the Pentagon break-in is our immediate consideration," declared Cowley.

He felt Pamela's hand on his sleeve and Ross said, "I think you'd better call it a day, Bill. My mistake, your mistake."

Cowley shook his head in refusal. To Paul Lambert he said, "You must have found something obvious to be able to be here this soon?"

"It was Semtex," said the bespectacled, crew-cut forensic scientiest. "Simplest thing imaginable: wrapped around a timer preset for one A.M. We're still checking for prints, obviously. Source is either the Czech or Slovakian republics: Czechoslovakia is the only country in the world still producing the stuff. We'll identify the timer before the day's out. But if the bomb squad doesn't find anything else, we're not going to be able to help you very much beyond this."

"They're taking it slowly," said Cowley. "Tibbert's talking of another two days—there might even be something intact."

"Two days!" protested David Frost, the diminutive police commissioner, sitting between two other uniformed officers. "It's going to become impossible! The city's already virtually gridlocked by that central area being closed just today. Even before I came in for this meeting I was getting reports of people coming in just to stand and look. If it goes on for two more days the city will have to close down, there'll be so many tourists."

"I don't think traffic control is very high on our list of priorities at the moment, Commissioner," said Ross.

"It is," said Cowley, softly at first. Then, more loudly: "Jesus, of course it is!"

Everyone looked in bewildered astonishment.

To the forensic chief Cowley said, "The charge! How big was the charge?"

The man shrugged his shoulders. "Maybe half a pound. Less, perhaps."

"Easily carried? And timed to explode when there wouldn't be anyone there to get hurt?"

"Sure."

"Wouldn't it have fit easily into a shopping bag or backpack?"

"Yes."

"And easily fixed?"

"Sure," Lambert agreed again. "Semtex is gray, same color as the steps. It was just slipped down the sides, against the outer wall."

"Bill—" Ross began sympathetically.

"Please!" demanded Cowley, remembering the stairwell gaps he'd looked at until his eyes ached earlier that day. "The gap between the stairs and the outer edge could have hidden much more than half a pound of Semtex, couldn't it?"

Lambert shrugged his shoulders in another helpless gesture. "If they'd wanted to plant more . . ."

"That's just it!" said Cowley, looking urgently to Leonard Ross. "They *didn't* want to plant any more. This isn't their speed, their way! They wanted to kill hundreds, certainly, with the warhead. Suckered us into the ambush at New Rochelle. Which is what this is! A decoy." He stopped, remembering the thick, solid line of people around the Mall. Trying to control his rising panic, Cowley leaned toward the police commissioner. "There's got to be a thousand people out there, all around the Mall. Two thousand. And there's another bomb, another device. Get it cleared! Get the Mall, all the roads, clear of people. Don't funnel them into the Smithsonian Metro. Close that. Just get everyone away as quickly as you can. Otherwise there's going to be another massacre."

No one moved. No one spoke.

Cowley looked imploringly at Leonard Ross. "Please!" he said. "I'm right. I know I'm right. This time they really do intend killing hundreds."

———

"Anne! We're talking seven bucks!" protested the Albany detective to whom Clarence Snelling had first complained.

"And forty-nine cents," she reminded.

"And forty-nine cents. I thought you guys were kinda occupied by something else?"

"So what have you done?"

The man spread his hands without replying.

"Not spoken to the bank?"

"No," said the detective. "I haven't spoken to the fucking bank! When I arrest the son of a bitch who killed the Seven-Eleven night man with a sawed-off twelve-gauge to steal maybe twenty bucks and then catch the bastard who raped the twelve-year-old on the Saratoga Road turnoff I'll really put my mind to Clarence Snelling's precious fucking seven bucks and forty-nine cents."

"So you wouldn't mind me doing it meanwhile?"

"Honey, if I hadn't seen your fucking shield you know what I'd do. I'd arrest you for impersonating an FBI agent."

"Don't worry," said Anne Stovey. "I won't arrest you for impersonating a New York State detective. Or for not knowing your criminal history."

12

It had become routine since the beginning of the investigation for Dimitri Danilov to keep his office television on and tuned permanently to CNN, so he learned of the Washington Monument bomb within seconds of arriving at Petrovka, for once earlier than Pavin. Danilov had slept badly on the couch and left the apartment before six, to avoid encountering Olga. She'd been snoring when he eased the door closed behind him. He put a call in to Cowley but was told both he and Pamela Darnley were in conference.

There was an overnight log note that Anatoli Sergeevich Lasin, one of the two men who had provided the alibi for the murdered

mobster, had been arrested during the night at his last known address, an apartment on Pereulok Ucebyi, in bed with a boy of fifteen.
Both were being held, separately, in basement cells.

Danilov at once saw the advantage, which was why he decided to
leave them there, wanting first to read the case file of the Osipov
mafia brigade to which Anatoli Lasin belonged. It had become instinctive to look for names that would personally mean something
to him from Larissa's murder, but very quickly, sighing in weary
professional recognition, he saw the obvious tampering and accepted
the pointlessness. The last criminal records photograph of the godfather—the brigadier himself, Mikhail Vasilevich Osipov—had been
taken twelve years earlier, when he'd been bearded and heavily mus-
tached. There wasn't any explanation for there being no updated
picture to accompany the two subsequent arrests. The beard and
mustache would have long gone, and Osipov would be unrecognizable from the only image they had on file. There had been insufficient evidence—due to loss, also unexplained—to prosecute on
either subsequent arrest, and there was even an assessment, un-
signed, that the brigade was fragmenting under pressure from other,
more powerful mafia families upon whom more attention should be
focused. From which Danilov at once knew it wasn't breaking up at
all but that after the territory wars to which Pavin had referred—
quoted in the assessment as evidence of the family's demise—it had
probably emerged one of the strongest in the city.

Who, wondered Danilov, was the well- but discreetly paid officer
within his Organized Crime Bureau ensuring that the Osipov family
remained protected from any irritating official intrusion? He was at
once annoyed—embarrassed—at asking himself the question.
Shouldn't he know? It was his department, and he'd taken up the
appointment as its director after exposing the corruption of the previous commanders with the burnished shield and sworn determination to cleanse it from the bottom as effectively as he'd cleansed
it from the top. And done what? Gotten rid of two of the most
obviously bribed inspectors, earned the obstructive animosity of
practically every other one, and after Larissa, in his swamp of self-
pity and disinterest, allowed everything to go on—get worse,
maybe—as it had before.

What about the other self-imposed determination, his supposedly always being honest with himself? The so-far avoided question. Which it was time to confront. His unease wasn't at his failure to correct the crookedness of others. It was at the thought—the vaguest, seductive wisp of an idea—of the only way he could maintain two homes and support Olga if she carried out her threat, which he had little doubt she would vindictively do.

But how could he? Danilov demanded of himself. Everything was totally different now from how it had been when he'd gone along with the accepted system. Which (excuse-seeking, he at once accused himself) in his case had not been dealing *with* the organized crime families. The reverse. He'd protected the small shopkeepers and businesses and independent entrepreneurs in the district he'd commanded as a uniformed militia colonel, facing down—arresting and prosecuting—the gangs who'd tried to extort protection money. For which those shopkeepers and businessmen and entrepreneurs had been grateful. He'd never exacted a levy or asked for any tribute. Whatever had been given had been offered freely: not once had he treated differently someone who had never given him a gift from someone who had.

But he wasn't any longer a uniformed militia officer with a comparatively small suburb of the city to administer, no longer the policeman who could take an offered apple from the stall. He was at the absolute center now—and at the pinnacle. What would his worth be to the brigade whose file was on the table in front of him or any of the other mafia groups who'd sliced the Moscow cake between them? Incalculable. Whatever car he demanded, whatever retainer he suggested, whatever rent-free apartment he chose.

Yuri Pavin's arrival broke the reverie, and Danilov was glad, actually embarrassed at the entry of one of the few truly honest men in the department while he had even been thinking as he had.

Pavin nodded toward the volume-reduced television. "Seems minor, thank God." Pavin was devoutly religious, a regular communicant at the new cathedral, sometimes stopping there on his way to Petrovka on weekdays as well as Sundays. The invocation of God was genuine, not blasphemous.

"I spotted Bill."

"So did I. You called him yet?"

"We'll speak later," said Danilov. "I've waited for you before seeing Lasin. What about the other one, Baratov?"

"Not at the last known address we have."

Danilov nodded to the Osipov dossier in front of him. "It's been doctored."

"I know."

"Who's their friend here in the building?"

"There's a lot to choose from."

"I've let things slip here," Danilov confessed abruptly.

"Maybe when this is over?" suggested the other man.

"Definitely," said Danilov. "Maybe today could be the beginning. And I want you to start making up a suspect list, OK?"

"OK." The deputy smiled.

As he stood Danilov said, "We don't have time to fuck around. We'll hit Lasin hard. I want results."

They heard the shouting long before they reached the cell in which the man was held. Danilov slid aside the peephole of the adjoining one holding the fifteen-year-old Vladimir Fedorin. It wouldn't, Danilov knew, be the boy's real name. His hair was long, almost to his shoulders, and richly dark. He was very slim, in a silk shirt and second-skin trousers. He'd been crying and the mascara was smudged. He looked up, unspeaking. Danilov said, "You're in serious trouble," and slammed the shutter closed. It would be very easy to use the terrified boy if it was necessary.

Lasin actually tried to leave the moment his cell door was opened and would have done so if Pavin hadn't put a spadelike hand against his chest, pushing him back inside.

"Who the fuck do you think you are that you can do this!" demanded the man. "I want a lawyer now! Some fucking desk sergeant took all my belongings: watch, rings, bracelet. I'll never get them back. I want everything accounted for. I don't get them back, I'm going to sue."

"Don't be ridiculous," Pavin said, calmly. "Sit down." He and Danilov did, leaving Lasin standing. He was a small, wire-thin man who nevertheless conveyed an unsettling impression of coiled-up strength. He, too, wore trousers as tight as his lover's next door, and the sweater was silk. The hair was very obviously dyed, a yellow blond. Danilov decided it was too good to have been done by Olga's hairdresser lover.

"What can you tell us?" demanded Pavin.

"About what?"

"Nikov's murder. And about Valeri Karpov."

"Nothing. There'll have been things stolen from my apartment, too. I'll sue for that, as well!"

"I told you to stop being ridiculous," said Pavin.

"The arrest sheet lists four handguns—two American Smith and Wessons—found in your apartment," said Danilov.

"Not an offense," said Lasin.

"Nikov and Karpov were shot. You think we might find the bullets came from one of your guns if we did a ballistics test?"

"Wasting your time." The man sneered.

"Maybe we should extend the tests: compare the bullets recovered in other murders and shootings? There was a lot when the Osipov brigade fought for control of the Vnukovo Airport area." Pavin spoke to Danilov, not the gangster.

"That's a good idea," accepted Danilov. "We'll do that."

"All right!" said Lasin with impatient bravado. "What do you want? However much it is, call Vladimir Leonidovich and he'll pay you."

"Shouldn't we negotiate through someone here in the building?" Danilov asked casually.

For the first time Lasin regarded them warily. "Who are you?"

The recognition was obvious when Pavin identified them. Lasin sat down. He said, "I want a lawyer."

"You've been seeing too many American films," said Pavin. "The only rights you have are those we allow you, and we're not allowing you any."

"What am I being held for?"

"Suspicion of murder, until we complete all the ballistics tests on those guns," said Pavin. "Could take a long time."

"Weeks," agreed Danilov. "Not safe, leaving your apartment empty for weeks. Not in a place like Moscow."

"I don't know anything about Viktor Nikolaevich's killing," said the slightly built man.

"But you knew he was in Moscow?"

"He was often in Moscow. He dealt in cars. So do I."

"Cars stolen in the West?" said Pavin. "We'll check out the ones you've got, see if there's anything we can make a case on. That'll take even longer."

"I don't know anything!" protested the man. "Viktor Nikolaevich arrived two weeks ago. We did a bit of business—car business. I thought he'd gone back. I haven't seen him for more than a week."

"What did he tell you he was doing?"

"Looking at cars."

"What else?"

"He said he had some people to see. He didn't say about what."

"Selling weapons?" pressed Pavin.

"I don't know anything about selling weapons."

"You knew he did. You alibied him before."

"I didn't do anything with him."

"How did you know him?"

"We grew up together in Gorki."

"You got a resident's permit to be here in Moscow?" said Pavin. "You could be sent back if you haven't. You could have a lot of problems, one way and another."

"The only dealings I had with Viktor Nikolaevich were about cars."

"What about Igor Baratov?" demanded Danilov.

"I don't know. Ask him."

"Where is he?"

"I don't know."

"He do business with you?"

"Sometimes."

"Dealing in cars?"

"Yes."

"What else?"

"Nothing."

"Not weapons?"

"No."

"Osipov deal in weapons?"

"I don't know."

"Why don't you know?" Pavin cut in. "You work for him."

"I don't know all of what Mikhail Vasilevich does."

"But you do work for him?"

"I look after—service and maintain—the cars he uses in his businesses." All the bombast had gone. Lasin was sweating, even though it wasn't hot in the cell.

"So you must know what his other businesses are?" Danilov came back into the questioning.

"*No!* People come to me, say they work for Mikhail Vasilevich and he's told them to bring their car to me. I check and if Mikhail Vasilevich says he knows them, I do the car."

"You must see a lot of people," encouraged Pavin.

"A few."

"Hear a lot of interesting things?"

Lasin didn't reply.

"You ever hear about other brigades dealing in weapons?"

"There's a lot of weapons around, now the army's been reduced."

"Special weapons? Like germ warheads?"

Lasin shook his head. "Don't know about special weapons. Warheads."

"What about ordinary weapons?"

"No."

"How long have you and Vladimir been together?" demanded Danilov, nodding toward the adjoining cell.

Lasin blinked at the abrupt change of direction. "None of your business."

"You choose him that young so he wouldn't have AIDS?"

"That's nothing to do with you, either."

"I don't like you," Danilov said conversationally. "I don't like your attitude, and I think there's a lot more you could tell us that you think you don't have to. So here's how I see it. We'll hold you while we check out those guns against the Nikov and Karpov murders. And the other killings during the turf wars. I'm sure we'll be able to make a case against Osipov for having some stolen cars in that fleet you look after for him. No need to hold your boyfriend, though. We'll let Vladimir go. Tell him why we're keeping you, so he'll know you're being cooperative. Won't have to worry you're being roughed up in here at least."

"I haven't helped you with information about stolen cars!"

"You ever been to Lefortovo?" Pavin broke in. "Hell of a prison. That's where you'll be held while we're checking all this out. They don't use condoms. That's how AIDS got so bad there in the first place. You watch yourself, Anatoli Sergeevich. It won't be easy but try to choose your partners. Whatever happens, don't get gang raped."

"No," pleaded the man in a soft voice. "Please, no. You can't. You do this I'm dead, either way."

"You recognized our name," said Danilov. "So you know about us. Know we do our jobs properly, mean what we say. Have to check out information we get. I don't see any other way. . . ."

"Osipov *has* got someone here, someone inside. I don't know who but I'll find out—tell you."

"I'm not investigating internal corruption." Danilov dismissed his offer. "This is more important."

"Outside!" blurted the man. "Outside bulls. That's the story going around. Brought in specially to make the hit on Nikov and the other man."

"Brought in from where?" asked Pavin.

"I don't *know*. I honestly, genuinely don't know. What I've told you is *all* I know. About the killing, I mean."

"What did Nikov tell you?" demanded Danilov.

"He was meeting people. Setting up a deal."

"With a germ warhead?"

"I think so."

"Did he have one when he was here?" Danilov asked urgently.

The man shook his head. "I'm not sure. I don't think so. He said there was a lot of money involved and that he'd cut me in for that alibi. That all I'd have to do was drive up and down to Gorki a few times. I assumed he meant to transport something."

"Did he see Baratov while he was here?"

"He said he was going to. I don't know if he did."

"Where's Baratov live?" said Pavin.

"Ulitza Krasina 28. Third floor."

"Where did Nikov live, when he was here in Moscow?"

"This time at the Metropole. Said he wanted to impress the people he was going to meet."

"You sure you don't know who they were?" said Pavin.

"*No!*"

"Who do you *think* they might have been?" pressed Danilov.

"I don't know! I've helped you all I can."

"For the moment you can stay safely here and not in Lefortovo," Danilov decided.

As they walked back toward their offices, Pavin said, "How much do you believe?"

"The suggestion of the hit being organized from outside is intriguing," judged Danilov. "Not something he would have made up without trying to bullshit us with suggestions of where they might have come from we couldn't check out. And I'd say the Metropole was the first-choice hotel for westerners—Americans—with a lot of money."

"You think there's any point in testing his handguns ballistically?"

"Not for these two killings. He didn't seem very comfortable when you talked about the turf wars."

"I doubt any of the forensic or ballistics stuff will have survived."

"Just check," suggested Danilov.

"What about the kid?"

"Leave him where he is. He could probably do with the rest. I want you to check out Ulitza Krasina." He paused at the top of the stairs. "I ever personally investigated Igor Ivanovich Baratov?"

"Not as far as I can remember," said Pavin, knowing how Danilov—to the neglect of everything else—had tracked every member of the two gangs involved in Larissa's killing.

"Why do I think I know the name from somewhere?"

Danilov had naturally anticipated the initial concentration being on the overnight Washington explosion, but neither Cowley nor the woman was available when he'd called again just before leaving for the Interior Ministry.

At once Viktor Kedrov, the security chairman, said, "You think they're stalling, avoiding your calls?"

"No," said Danilov, ever conscious he was between the rock of the old and the hard place of the new. "I think they're fully occupied with the latest attack, which perhaps we should be if there's a trace back to us. I'll talk to them sometime later today. I intend, incidentally, to go to Washington in the next day or two."

"Why?" demanded Georgi Petrov.

"Because I need to meet, face-to-face. Until I do it won't be the joint investigation we've undertaken. And it's more practicable for me to go to them." He looked to Kisayev. "More visibly what the people are expecting to see, don't you think?"

"Definitely," agreed the deputy foreign minister.

"So you don't believe they're fully sharing?" persisted Kedrov.

"Something else I won't be able to assess fully until I get to Washington," said Danilov, pleased with the direction of the conversation. "Cowley, whom I deal with and trust, only came out of the hospital yesterday. We've scarcely had an opportunity to speak to each other . . . exchange *any*thing." He looked again to the deputy foreign minister. To get the official attitude on record, he said, "What's the government guidance on biological weapons being stockpiled?"

Yuri Kisayev said, "I've instructed our ambassador in Washington—and told the American ambassador here—officially to assure the secretary of state that we are in the process of complying with the terms of the 1993 agreement but as they will understand from being in the process of dismantling their own, similar weapons, it's a long procedure that cannot be hurried."

Georgi Chelyag smiled in open admiration. "An extremely astute diplomatic response." He turned to the deputy defense minister. "Which brings us to you, General. And the point of this reconvened meeting."

Sergei Gromov coughed and shuffled some obviously old papers that he'd laid out in front of him while they'd talked. "So far—and

I mean so far, because the search is continuing—we have been unable to find any distribution records matching the 19-38-22-0 or the 20-49-88-0 batch numbers on the warhead fired at the United Nations building." He tapped one of the yellowing pieces of paper. "They were certainly the identifying codes for the joint sarin-anthrax weapon. There's some limited cross-references, confirming the production of this particular weapon in a total of eight different factories—two in Belorussia as well as one in the Ukraine and another in Latvia—but it's incomplete." He produced another archival sheet, like a card from an ancient pack. "This is a ministry instruction, dated 1975, that records could be disposed of as well as the weaponry itself following the abandonment of the program."

The man was the focus of total incredulity from everyone else in the room. Danilov decided that virtually the entire explanation had an element of truth because even in a society destroyed after seventy continuous years of chaos, inefficiency, criminal manipulation, and mismanagement, it would have been impossible to invent such a lame explanation of bureaucratic ineptitude.

It was Chelyag who seized the advantage. "The Ministry of Defense doesn't know how many such missiles were manufactured or where they are now!"

"No," admitted Gromov. Desperately he said, "It is a situation we inherited, can't do anything to correct."

"It is a total, unmitigated disaster," said Chelyag. Looking directly at Danilov he said, "Something that can never be admitted to anyone in the West."

"If there is another attack—more than one attack—using missiles of the same design, there won't need to be an open admission," Danilov pointed out. "What about the telephone number?"

"Allocated for this particular production. Dispensed with when the program was abandoned and never allocated to anything else," said Gromov.

"What about the Ministry of Science?" demanded Kisayev. "What about their records?"

Gromov shrugged his shoulders. "There hasn't been time to extend the search."

"*I'll* do it," Chelyag decided quickly. "And stipulate the security upon the inquiry." He looked, almost too theatrically, to each man in the room. "None of you here must ever discuss this, hint it, to another living soul outside these walls. Is everyone clear—*absolutely* clear—on that?"

There were shuffles and head nodding and mutterings of assent. Danilov wondered how one side—which side?—would try to use the fact against the other. He was sure one of them would try.

"There is no complete documentary evidence about this particular weapon—how many were produced in which countries?" demanded Viktor Kedrov.

"No," acknowledged the uniformed general.

Chelyag said, "What has been disclosed today amounts to a state secret."

Which, wondered Danilov, did that knowledge make him: very powerful or very vulnerable? Like so many others, it was a question that could be answered both ways. He didn't like either.

Pavin followed Danilov into his office the moment he got back to Petrovka. "I've got Igor Baratov downstairs in cell three. Guess what he says?"

"What?"

"He's not involved with Osipov anymore. He's got married, has a baby, and is a legitimate businessman."

"Running a garage?" suggested Danilov.

"You guessed it."

Cowley was aware of his name being called from a long way away and then of the discomfort—although not pain—at being gently shaken before finally emerging into wakefulness, but not immediately recalling where he was. Then he saw Pamela bending over him, frowning and asking if he was all right, and remembered the meeting being suspended and the cot being moved into his office—as well as one into Pamela's—and of everyone else going to the director's private dining room for lunch.

He tried—and failed—to lever himself up on one elbow and thanked Pamela for helping him.

She said, "I was worried. It took a hell of a lot to wake you. I thought you'd collapsed."

"What's happened? What time is it? What . . . ?"

"It's a quarter after two." She turned briefly to his desk, coming back with a disposable razor, a toothbrush, toothpaste and a can of shaving foam. "I went shopping for you."

"What's happened?" he demanded, swiveling his legs off the cot, pleased there wasn't any pain from his rib.

"You just won gold." She smiled. "They found enough explosives packed in and around the Lincoln Memorial to blow it all the way to California. It's going to take at least another hour to defuse it all, so you've got time to clean up before we go take a look-see." She turned back to the desk. "I have salt beef on rye—a pickle's optional—coffee, Tylenol, and water to take it with."

"I'll pass on the Tylenol," he said.

"That's a good sign."

So was this personal attention, thought Cowley.

The bank manager regarded Anne Stovey with roughly the same surprise although none of the cynicism of the metro detective to whom Snelling had earlier complained, shaking his head in expectation of something more. "It's computer error," he said. "What else can it be?"

"Aren't you worried about it?"

"It's pennies," dismissed the man. "It's not uncommon. We've always credited Mr. Snelling."

"No other customer complaints?"

"Not a one." He smiled invitingly. "The fact is that Mr. Snelling is the sort of man whom banks don't particularly welcome as customers."

"Because he keeps such a close eye on his account and expects it to be in order?"

The smile went. "He's a pedantic man."

"How long have you been in banking?" asked Anne.

"Twenty years." The man frowned.

"I really thought you would have heard of one of the most successful computer scams ever directed against a bank," said the woman.

The man was completely serious now. "What scam?"

"Happened very soon after banks were computerized," said Anne. "It's lectured about at Quantico, the bureau's training academy. Can't, for the moment, remember the bank, although it was certainly in New York State. A teller calculated that most people had a good idea of the dollar balance in their checking accounts but never knew to within ten to fifteen pennies how many cents they had. So he opened his own account, under a fictitious name, in a branch in a nearby town and creamed off a few cents from the most active accounts. In a year he had a country house in Westchester, with a pool and a tennis court, to which he stupidly invited people from the bank for weekends. Just as he stupidly drove a new Cadillac into work every morning. When anyone asked he said there'd been an inheritance from a rich aunt, only when there were a few isolated complaints—like the ones you're getting from Mr. Snelling—bank security couldn't find any rich aunt."

"What do you want me to do?" asked the man, completely serious now.

"Check to see if there are any more accounts from which penny-ante amounts seem to have disappeared, like they have from Mr. Snelling."

13

The president had been helicoptered to Camp David from the White House, which had been evacuated. So had all the buildings in the federal triangle down to the Agricultural Department and every government office farther along Constitution Avenue, at Foggy Bottom, which included Henry Hartz's State Department and went up as far as the Kennedy Center. The barricading of Pennsylvania Avenue, to provide a clear route for emergency vehicles, began at the FBI building. Cowley and Pamela walked on the outside of the fencing behind which people were jammed ten deep. Cowley was recognized long before he reached the television and press pen in front of the

Willard Hotel and walked a gauntlet of name-shouting and camera-clicking. It became a flash- and strobe-light dazzling clamor at the media enclosure. Cowley walked carefully, shaking his head against the interview demands, grateful there was no sudden burst of pain.

Abruptly they were alone in another moonscape more desolate than the emptiness into which he'd flown in Manhattan. This clearance had been organized and orderly, and there were no haphazardly abandoned vehicles. The only movement was far away at the memorial itself, a seething of black, antlike activity in which the figures did not become recognizably human until they had passed the now-ignored Washington Monument.

Pamela said, "I don't know why we couldn't have used a car, if they're sure there's no risk of a vibration setting something off. You sure you're OK?"

"I keep telling you I'm fine," insisted Cowley. He was. There was no headache and he didn't have any difficulty going along the avenue, although Pamela was, considerately, walking quite slowly. The tightness to his chest was caused by the strapping, nothing more.

At that moment a car carrying the police commissioner swept by without stopping.

"Truculent bastard!" accused Pamela. "Just because you realized the danger and he didn't."

"He's a political policeman among politicians."

"He's certainly not a policemen's policeman. There's a couple of calls logged from Dimitri."

"We need to talk; see if 'Watchmen' means anything to him."

"We've drawn a blank from everyone else we've run the name by."

Cowley saw that the monument scanner had been moved to the closed off half-circle in front of the Lincoln shrine and was drawn up alongside three additional vehicles, one the commissioner's car. David Frost was standing by the main control vehicle, flanked by the two other uniformed officers from that morning's suspended meeting. As Cowley and Pamla arrived, a yawning Nelson Tibbert emerged, stretching, from a van. He still wore his body armor, although it was unbuckled. Paul Lambert came at the same time from the Doric-columned re-creation of the Greek temple in which the Lincoln statue sat. Cowley realized both men had been summoned by the commissioner.

"Right now!" Frost said briskly. "What have we got?"

Lambert ignored the police chief, talking instead to Cowley. "Word is it was you who thought this might be set up."

The commissioner's face became tight. Cowley wondered who had told the head of the bureau's forensic team. The normally fresh-faced Lambert was hollow-eyed and sag-shouldered from fatigue, and Cowley thought how much better he felt after being able to sleep and to shave. He said, "Lucky guess."

"Deductive guess," contradicted the scientist. "Thank God you made it." He nodded behind him. "We've deactivated everything but we're leaving it all in place to get it on film. None of my people—or Nelson's—has ever seen anything like it before. It'll be a visual training manual."

"You sure that's safe?" demanded Frost.

"Yes, sir," Tibbert said wearily. "If it wasn't, you wouldn't be here."

"What is it?" asked Pamela.

"Semtex, mostly," said Lambert. "Haven't weighed it yet, but provisionally I'd say over a thousand pounds. So we're talking about half a ton—"

"And rigged like a firecracker," Tibbert broke in, rubbing the sleep from his face. "The way it was set it would have destroyed the entire thing." He led the way up the steps toward the huge sculpture.

Standing in front of the statue, Tibbert pointed to the folds fashioned in the marble of the frock coat. "Look. Two separate charges there alone, with fragmentation antipersonnel mines on top. The funnel effect of the carving would have acted like a gun barrel. The mines are shrapnel-packed but in addition the marble would have splintered like razors."

"And our estimate is that we cleared over three hundred people from in and around this area alone, not counting those lining Constitution Avenue," supplied Frost, in shocked awareness.

Lambert said, "Those who didn't die—and most of them would have—would have been mutilated."

"How many mines?" asked Cowley.

"Six," said Lambert. "All Russian made. I'll confirm it in a day or two, but I'd say identical to the ones used in New Rochelle. They weren't just set here around the statue. The wires link on to the North and South Halls. All the plaques and inscriptions of Lincoln's Gettysberg Address and his second inaugural speech would have been blown away. And the Guérin murals, of course."

"I'd say the crater would have been eight, maybe ten feet deep. That's all that would have been left, one damned great big hole," said Tibbert, yawning hugely. "If the Arlington Bridge hadn't been destroyed outright, the foundation structure would certainly have cracked. Whole thing would have needed to be rebuilt."

Cowley gestured toward the White House. "What about that?"

"There wouldn't have been a pane of glass left," said Tibbert. He pointed to some more charges to the left of the statue. "They're funneled again. The shock and the shrapnel is directed straight toward the White House. There would probably have been some structural damage, as well as just glass breakage. If the president had been in the Oval Office or in his side office he'd have been hurt from the glass alone. State Department would have been wrecked, too."

"We'd like the ten-dollar tour," said Cowley.

Every conceivable place in the statue or the chair upon which it was carved was packed with Semtex or a mine or both. Where the space was too shallow for the explosive to have been completely hidden, it had been painted the same off-white color to merge with the Colorado marble. So, too, had all the connected detonating wires and the clamps holding it virtually invisibly in place. All the detonators had been removed. Where they'd been was marked with bright red clips.

Pamela said, "How was it all going to go up?"

"Simple timers," said Lambert. "Again I'll need a day or two, but I think they'll match what set off the Washington Monument charge. Here there were twelve in all. Russian. Standard design, according to our ballistics guy. Most of it prewired and connected in a safe house somewhere before being brought here. Each set to explode precisely at six tonight."

"The time when a lot of home-going workers would have joined the rubberneckers already here," mused Cowley. "And when the Arlington Bridge is at its rush-hour busiest."

"I told you it was training manual material," said Lambert.

These guys got jungle training for sure, Cowley thought. "Who the hell are we up against here?"

"People good enough to *train* professionals," stressed Lambert. "This genuinely is state-of-the-art insurgency expertise. Although a lot was prepared elsewhere, they'd have to set all this up at night, unseen by any park guards or police despite the lights that are kept burning. Look at the way the wire's hidden! Always tight into the crease or bend, never awkwardly left to become obvious. Since it's all been made safe we've gone over every inch. There's not a fingerprint or an indentation in the Semtex or a stray hair or a single piece of fiber. We've even tested the floor for detergent traces or cleanser: I'm sure we'll find they actually cleaned the floor before they left."

Pamela said, "Jesus!"

"It scares me shitless, too," said Lambert. "I like being better than the bad guys. This time I think they're better—cleverer—than us."

"I don't want that opinion spread about too much," warned Cowley.

"Bill!" exclaimed the scientist, his face pained. "In just fifteen hours we've had a decoy bomb go off in the Washington Monument, just avoided half a ton of explosives destroying another, killing or maiming hundreds—one possibly the president—had to evacuate the White House and hundreds more people, reducing the capital of this great and good country to a helpless standstill! You really think I'm the only guy likely to realize we've got a serious problem with some very serious people?"

"Serious, yes. Cleverer, no," said Cowley. "We stopped them blowing this place to hell, didn't we?"

"You called it luck," reminded Lambert.

Leonard Ross didn't. He called it brilliant. So did the secretary of state, followed by Frank Norton. By the third repetition Cowley started to think the praise was as much to reassure themselves as it was to accord him credit. It worsened, too, the obvious discomfort of the police commissioner in front of whose car Pamela had stood, demanding a lift back to the J. Edgar Hoover building. It meant Frost's two assistants having to walk.

A palpable, horrified disbelief permeated the reconvened meeting by the time Cowley finished recounting how narrowly disaster had been avoided. No one hurried to speak when he stopped, everyone needing their own time to digest it.

"Carnage," said the president's chief of staff, finally and in virtual conversation with himself. "Absolute, total carnage . . . a massacre like the Trade Towers."

"Quite clearly the president has to remain at Camp David, where security can be guaranteed," John Butterworth declared positively.

"Absolutely," agreed the police commissioner, anxious to make a contribution. "We should move some National Guards to Maryland, too. Create a visible presence around the retreat."

"I don't think so," rejected Norton, at once. "The president and commander-in-chief forced to quit the capital! That doesn't sound the right message to me. In fact, it sounds like the totally wrong one."

"Definitely," said Hartz, just as quickly. "We don't need to give the media anything more to beat us with—they've got more than enough already. And it would give the Watchmen almost as great a coup as they've been denied."

"The mistake was underestimating by how much security needed to be increased," said Cowley, careless of the sharp look from the police chief. "That won't happen again, not after today, will it, Commissioner?"

"It won't," Norton broke in. "I'll personally brief the Secret Service myself." He, too, looked at David Frost. "You'll liaise with all the necessary civic authorities, of course?"

The police commissioner colored further at what amounted to an order. "I spoke with the mayor from the car. It's already in hand."

"I'm glad something is," said Norton, as close as he'd openly come to criticizing the D.C. police department.

"Lambert says there isn't *anything?*" pressed Ross.

"Not from the preliminary examination at either scene," said Cowley.

"Provisionally the whole area will remain closed until tomorrow afternoon, when we'll review it again," said Frost.

"How are we going to take this investigation forward!" said Butterworth. He'd intended it to be a critical demand, but to Cowley it sounded more like an admission of defeat. From the shift around the room it was clear others thought so, too.

Looking to the parks authority inspector, Cowley said, "We didn't finish talking about the Washington Monument. What's the system for climbing up and down the stairs where the decoy went off?"

"You don't go *up*, not normally," said Michael Poulson. "A climb like that, five hundred and fifty-five feet, wouldn't be medically safe for a lot of people. Tourists always go up by elevator. Part of the history of the obelisk is the different pieces of marble contributed by various states when it was being built. There are tours twice a day—one at ten in the morning, the other at three in the afternoon—when people can walk *down* with a guide who points out the gift stones."

"Only two a day!" seized Cowley. "You'd have the names of yesterday's guides, particularly the one in the afternoon?"

"They'll be on the roster," guaranteed Poulson.

"There any restrictions about taking photographs on the way down?"

"We advise people to buy the official postcard prints," said Poulson. "But sure, tourists can take their own shots."

It still wouldn't be simple, Cowley acknowledged: Tourists at the monument the previous day could be on the other side of the continent by now. But tracing and questioning everyone who'd used the stairway the previous day—and days before that—about anyone who might have behaved suspiciously was something practical, a recognizable routine, to pursue. Realizing a way to make it even more practical, he looked to General Smith and the computer security official beside him. "These people you've listed as being possibly aggrieved at being let go by the Pentagon? Do you have security photographs as well as names?"

"Yes, sir," Carl Ashton said at once.

"So what do I tell the president?" prompted Norton.

Cowley set out the material—and its catastrophic potential—recovered from the memorial and said, "The people who did this are specialized soldiers. That—hopefully—could narrow down who we're looking for." He looked at the two Pentagon officials. "Which won't, I don't think, come *directly* from the Pentagon. The men who attacked the UN and set the monument charges are active field people—operational soldiers."

"You suggesting a conspiracy?" demanded the general.

"I would have thought that was already established." Cowley frowned. "What I'm suggesting is a link between an active service unit—and it would have needed several men to rig the Lincoln statue—and someone, maybe only one man, with access and knowledge of the Pentagon communications and computer systems. And I'm not restricting the profile to men. It's probably too soon to judge from just one message, but I'd guess that message to be from the most extreme of hard-right extremist terrorist organizations. So far we've failed to locate any group calling itself the Watchmen. Psychologically—bear with me on the use of that word—they've already proved themselves people determined to commit mass murder. If they're ever confronted as a group—cornered with no chance of escape—their last act will be to destroy themselves, causing as much damage and harm to anyone else as they do it. Waco and suicide plane hijackers all over again."

"Russia." The president's chief of staff stopped, not needing to provide any further prompt.

Cowley was conscious of the particular attention with which Pamela Darnley was concentrating on him, enjoying it. "I still need to liaise properly with Moscow's Organized Crime Bureau. The Watchmen obviously have a Russian source. Since the end of the Cold War the country and some of its former satellites have been awash with every conceivable sort and type of weaponry. The trade is Russian mafia controlled. If it isn't in this case, it's a linkup between a fanatical far right group here and an equally extreme body of people in Russia who want to go back to the old, confrontational days of the Cold War."

The CIA director voiced disbelief. "That's totally and utterly absurd! We've got nothing to suggest—"

"Believe me, sir, no one hopes more strongly than I that you're right and I'm wrong," said Cowley. "Because if I'm right we've got an escalation I don't think we want to contemplate."

"I certainly don't," said Henry Hartz.

"I *won't!*" insisted Frank Norton. "But the computer message fits that analysis."

"The Watchmen have a worryingly substantial supply up to and including biological weaponry from a Russian or Eastern bloc source," Cowley reminded. "So, whatever their motivation—politically, psychologically, or philosophically—they've got access to a great deal of money. Millions, even. Terrorist groups normally finance themselves through crime, frequently making political claims in doing so. I'm not aware of any singular criminal activity in the last few months I'd put down to terrorist financing—"

"There hasn't been," insisted Pamela. "I ran a check. And I've circulated the query to all the field offices."

"I don't recall anything, either," said Ross.

"I don't like this Doomsday scenario," complained Norton.

"There is a slight upside," Cowley pointed out. "The Lincoln Memorial bombing *was*, quite obviously, planned as a spectacular: something they wouldn't have needed to repeat. We've recovered an enormous amount of materiel and know what they used before. They might just have exhausted their arsenal. Which could give us two things! a respite and the chance, through Moscow, of discovering their source or supply line."

"What if they've got another biological warhead?" demanded David Frost.

"They'd have fired it," Cowley judged flatly. "Capitalized on Manhattan. Today would have been bad enough. To have released a germ warfare device would have been worse."

"What we now need to discuss—and decide—is as much public

reassurance as we can create," declared Norton. "Which the Lincoln Memorial gives us. We beat them. That's got to be our message, and I'm going to suggest to the president that he give another television address to deliver it."

"I'd certainly endorse that," said Henry Hartz.

"It'll also be a challenge to them," cautioned Cowley. "If I'm wrong, if they have got another warhead, they'll definitely use it."

"You arguing against the idea?" asked Norton, genuinely asking an opinion.

"No," said Cowley. "They don't have to be told we beat them. If they've got something else they'll use it, whatever we do or say."

Igor Ivanovich Baratov was a thickset, undistinguished man with none of the swagger or bullying confidence of Anatoli Lasin, still in his cell farther along the Petrovka corridor. Baratov's suit was western but conservative, and there was no flashing diamond and gold jewelry among his belongings. The watch was actually Russian, a Sekonda. There was a picture of a very attractive, dark-haired girl with a tousle-haired baby in his wallet. Aware of how quickly valuables disappeared in Russian militia buildings, it was the only personal item Baratov asked about within minutes of Pavin and Danilov arriving in his cell. Danilov guaranteed its safety because it was valueless. He let Pavin begin the interview, intently studying and listening to the man, unable to lose the feeling that there was a previous encounter, even briefly wondering if there might have been an association—or more likely a confrontation—when he'd been the uniformed colonel in charge of a district. He'd already checked his personal records and knew the man's name had never emerged during the investigation into Larissa's death.

"I don't know anything about anything," declared Baratov. "I don't run with the Osipov Brigade anymore. I don't run with anyone. I've got a wife and a child and all I want is to be left alone."

"We've been told Viktor Nikolaevich Nikov came all the way from Gorki to see you," exaggerated Pavin.

"He called from Gorki," Baratov admitted at once. "Two, maybe three weeks ago. Said he had a big deal and wanted to cut me in for helping him before. I said I wasn't interested."

"Did you see him when he got here?" asked Danilov.

"I told you, I wasn't interested."

"What was the deal?"

"I didn't ask him. Didn't want to know."

"Who was it with?"

"Americans," identified the man without any hesitation.

"What Americans?" Danilov demanded, eagerly.

Baratov shook his head. "He didn't talk names. He said he'd made this great contact with some Americans, that there was a lot of money in it and that he was setting himself up and did I want to come in with him. I told him no, that all that was over for me and that there was no point in our meeting. So we didn't."

"What did you think setting himself up meant?" asked Pavin.

"Going independent from the Myagkov Brigade he was with in Gorki, setting himself up here in Moscow."

"Doing what?" pressed Danilov.

"Cars. That's why I didn't want to know. I thought he was setting up some deal to bring in American cars and wanted to use my garage as the outlet. There's a big market for American vehicles." He spread his hands. "You know the system: I'm not telling you anything. I pay to operate. It's the way. It works. I didn't want any jealousies, any big increase in my cash-only premiums."

"What do you think now?" asked Pavin.

"Now I think I'm even more glad I said no, otherwise I might have been floating in the river with a bullet in my mouth."

"Who are the Moscow brigades dealing in weapons?"

"I don't know. I got out more than a year ago. Didn't know even then."

"You expect us to believe you're reformed?" demanded Danilov.

The man spread his hands palms upward. "I can't make you believe anything. I drove for Osipov, OK. That's no secret. But that's all I did. Drove. The money was good and there was respect." He rolled up his left trouser legs. Where his calf should have been there was a huge, scooped-out indentation. "It was a shotgun. I almost bled to death. Thought I was going to lose my leg at least—probably would have if Svetlana hadn't been my nurse at the Kliniceskaja hospital. Hell of a way to fall in love. Great way to decide how to go on living, though."

"You don't have any connections anymore?"

"No," said Baratov.

"You still see Anatoli Lasin?"

"I trade cars with Anatoli Sergeevich, that's all."

"He ever tell you what's going on?" Pavin tried hopefully.

"I don't want to *hear* about what's going on. All I want to do is go home to my wife and baby. I was lucky to escape. That's how I want to stay, lucky. And out of it."

"It all checks out," assured Pavin. "Even to Svetlana Dubas being his nurse at Kliniceskaya." When Danilov didn't respond his deeply religious deputy said, "Sinners *do* repent."

"What about the ballistics check on Lasin's guns?"

"There's nothing left from the turf wars," said Pavin.

"The paint samples we gave to forensic?"

"Nothing back yet."

"Who volunteered to deliver the warheads and mine casings to the foreign minister?"

"Senior Colonel Investigator Ashot Yefimovich Mizin. You want him under any special observation?"

"No," decided Danilov. "You release Baratov and the boy. I'll deal with Lasin."

"You want any sort of surveillance on them?"

"I don't think so. For the moment I want everyone to imagine I'm totally confused. Which isn't too much of an exaggeration."

Lasin stood almost respectfully when Danilov reentered the cell, drained of all bravado.

Danilov said, "It's important that you listen and understand what I am going to tell you, Anatoli Sergeevich. We're going to keep all your handguns and we're going to run ballistics on all the turf killings. And when we get a match"—Danilov smiled—"even, perhaps, if we don't, I'm going to arrest you again and we'll go on with that conversation about Lefortovo."

"What more do you want from me?" wailed the man. "I've answered all your questions."

"Not quite," said Danilov. "I'm going to let you go for a reason. You're going to find out the name of the officer here who's on Osipov's payroll and you're going to have it ready when I ask. And if you don't have it—the right one, no bullshit—we're going to prove that a bullet that killed someone in the Osipov turf war came from one of your guns. You understand all that?"

"Yes," said Lasin. He kept his mouth so tight the word hissed from him.

"That's good," said Danilov. "You really wouldn't like Lefortovo."

Anatoli Sergeevich Lasin said nothing.

When they were finally connected that day, Danilov told Cowley the Watchmen had no significance for him but promised to check it out as fully as he could.

"There's a lot to talk about," said Cowley.

"When I get there." Danilov stopped.

What would he do when he found Osipov's militia source inside Petrovka, Danilov wondered as he drove home. Purge the man or ask him to arrange an introduction?

Patrick Hollis knew Carole had never intended him to make love to her. It had all been an obscene joke, set up by Robert Standing. That day, knowing he was watching, Standing had made an exaggerated gesture with a limp forefinger, and everyone at their table, including Carole, had laughed.

He'd punish them, Hollis decided. He didn't know how he'd do it, just that he would. Hurt them, humiliate them, as much as they'd humilated him.

Tonight would be the start, cracking into the online main branch of the bank from another hideaway system before entering their branch and accessing Standing's personal account details. From Standing's regular payments Hollis knew he could get other information, like his medical records through his insurance. And the man's log-in password code with which Standing himself accessed the branch's computer.

He was going to find out everything there was to know about Robert Standing. And then use it.

14

It was the uneven surface of the parking lot that caused Cowley to stumble. He wouldn't have fallen but Pamela was immediately at his side, cupping his elbow.

He said, "It was the loose gravel."

"Sure. I'll see you up." It had been her idea to give him a lift home to Arlington. Helping him up to his apartment was a spur-of-the-moment decision. She had things to learn, experiences to absorb. Ambition—even an ambition as absolute as hers—wasn't enough. It had to be supported by the sort of forward-thinking and analysis that Cowley had demonstrated that day. In fact, in an almost complete reversal of her earlier thinking, Pamela decided that she actually needed the man.

"I'm not an invalid, for Christ's sake!"

"Sure," she said again.

There were some other residents barbecuing in the pit in that part of the landscaped garden area just before the communal pool. One group, none of whom he knew, recognized him and waved. Cowley gave a halfhearted response. He said, "This is a pain in the ass."

Pamela said, "It could be if your address becomes known. What do you think about a security detail, like there was at the hospital?"

"No," he said positively.

"You're hardly in shape to look after yourself. You're not even carrying a weapon."

"No," he repeated. She held the apartment block door open for him and Cowley said, "Stop it!"

"Enjoy the service."

"I'm not." He waited for her to enter the elevator first.

"Grouch."

He smiled back at her. "It really was the gravel. I'm OK."

"We're on our way up now. And the president's address is in five minutes. Mind if I watch from your place?"

"Not at all." Cowley couldn't remember how he'd left the apartment. He couldn't actually remember leaving it, whatever day it had been. He was surprised how tidy it was. Pamela didn't appear to notice, going at once to the window that overlooked the river.

"Nice," she said. "And sorry."

"What for?"

"The presumption." She encompassed the apartment with a wave. "There could have been someone . . . ?"

"There isn't," he said. "I've only got scotch."

"Scotch is good," she accepted. She stayed by the window, watching as he took the bottle from the cabinet and poured her drink.

He turned on the television as he passed it to get water and ice from the kitchen. The address was timed to coincide with the evening news, which was still running. The air exclusion had been lifted, and from the helicopter camera there was a startling contrast between the emptiness of the Mall and the surrounding government buildings against the gridlocked chaos in the rest of the city. There was a lengthy interview with Commissioner Frost during which he claimed the Lincoln Memorial discovery to be entirely due to the vigilance of the police.

"Asshole," said Pamela.

Cowley said, "Look at that concentration of traffic and people. It's a target that couldn't be missed if they've got another warhead. Or anything else, for that matter."

"What's the answer?"

"I don't have one."

Opening the presidential speech with a long shot, clearly to show the man in control and in the Oval Office, was the obvious political and reassuring necessity that Frank Norton had talked about at that afternoon's meeting but at the same time through the window and beyond the Rose Garden the TV shot showed the desertion of the Mall. The president at once declared that the terrorists, who called themselves the Watchmen, had been beaten. An intended atrocity had been foiled and a great deal of vital information and intelligence gathered from what had been recovered from the Lincoln Memorial.

The terrorists were now hunted men, frightened men. In their desperation they probably would attempt another outrage. The public had to remain vigilant. When the killers were caught, which would be soon, they would face the maximum penalties prescribed by American justice.

"What vital information and intelligence?" demanded Pamela as the speech finished with the customary presidential blessing upon those watching.

"All part of the reassurance," said Cowley. "At least it was a damned sight better than last time. But it was too much of a challenge, claiming they were beaten. Everyone knows they're not beaten!" He leaned over to where she was sitting and topped off her glass as well as his own.

"How's it going to fit the next attack?"

"He covered himself with a warning for vigilance."

"What's going to cover the bureau?"

"Shit, after it hits the fan," said Cowley. He used the remote to turn off another studio analysis featuring the two men who'd earlier talked of the New Rochelle massacre frightening the group against another attack. "I didn't mean to sound ungrateful down there. I'm not. Thanks for the concern."

"It's been a busy day. You're allowed. And I've got an agenda."

"Shouldn't the patient know a little about his nurse?"

Pamela looked directly at him. It all fit the change of mind, she decided. "Thirty-two. Divorced. Unattached at the moment and not concerned about it. MA in psychology. Headquarters transfer from Miami two years ago. Determined to run with the big career chance until I drop." He wouldn't be able to accuse her of lying, deceiving him in any way.

"That what they call a potted biography?"

"As potted as it gets. Your turn."

"Forty. Divorced. Unattached. Director of the bureau's Russian desk for three years. Consider this the worst nightmare imaginable and, to coin Paul Lambert's telling phrase, I'm frightened shitless."

She nodded toward his drink. "Not sure scotch mixes well with Tylenol."

"We'll soon see."

"That was presumptuous, wasn't it?"

"Yes."

"Pissed at me?"

"No."

"You didn't eat lunch. What have you got?" Would this be another mistake? She hoped not.

"I'm not sure."

She carried her drink to the kitchen. "Eggs and ham," she called. "I do great omelettes."

"How about omelettes?" Cowley said. He had no idea where this was going but he was enjoying the ride. Ensuring Pamela was out of sight, he refilled his glass.

Pamela said, "By the time you set the table, they'll be ready."

They were. She'd found garlic he'd forgotten he had and lightly fried the ham with it before adding it to the omelette, which really was great, he told her.

"We screw up on this, maybe I'll open a restaurant. Think you could be a waiter?"

"That's all I seem to be doing at the moment, waiting."

She looked away, not speaking for a moment. "Seems to be my night for saying sorry but I'm sorry, too, for resenting your coming back so soon. I wouldn't have got the Lincoln Memorial, and I'm supposed to be the psychologist."

Cowley grinned at her. "Psychology was my major, too."

"Am I trying too hard?"

"No." He actually thought she was, but it didn't upset him.

"I meant what I said, about running as hard and as long as I can with this: It *is* my chance."

"OK," Cowley said doubtfully.

"So don't misunderstand."

"What?"

"I want to stay over."

Now Cowley was silent for several moments. "I'm not sure—"

"That a sofa bed?" she stopped him, pointing to where she had been sitting.

"Yes."

"You look dreadful. *That's* why I want to stay over, not to screw the boss. Who couldn't anyway, because of a busted rib. Quite apart from the bad psychology of it all. I want to because I need you: The moment I'm up to your speed, I'm on my own, but I'm not there yet. What you've done today would exhaust a fit man and you're not fit, whatever you say. So I think it's a good idea for someone to be around: my own agenda, remember?" Could she be sexually attracted to him? In other circumstances—other jobs, other places—perhaps. But there were too many obvious barriers even to contemplate the question. Pamela was actually curious about her own sexuality, unsure of a criteria. She liked sex but hadn't slept with anyone for the past six months, a mistaken weekend visit from an airline navigation officer trying to keep alive an already dying affair. Now, she supposed, she was repressing sex with her job determination. Sometimes she thought she would have enjoyed the singles' bar era, able to make her own unencumbered, uninvolved choice. She added, "I'm not at all sure that came out in the right order, but I think you understood."

"I think I did," said Cowley.

"So?"

"I don't know how comfortable it is." All he did feel was exhaustion, but he liked the idea of her being in the apartment.

"One condition. I get the shower first."

"OK." Her night for apologies, his for agreeing to everything.

"Can I go on being presumptuous and give you some advice?"

"What?" he said.

"Shoot that sweater and those jeans: It's the humane thing to do."

Cowley awoke to the smell of coffee and a note from Pamela that she'd be back to pick him up by eight, which she was.

"I made it through the night," he said.

"Loudly," she said. "You snore." She accepted the offered coffee. "And I'm glad I wasn't needed."

"Thanks just the same." He wasn't sure now why he'd agreed so readily to her staying and felt vaguely discomfited.

"The start of the routine slog," she declared.

"It's what solves crime, according to all the manuals."

"Let's hope they're right."

There was an attempt to ease the rush-hour congestion caused by the Mall and Arlington Bridge remaining closed by introducing a contraflow across the Roosevelt and George Mason bridges, but not enough commuters had heard the police announcement and the jams were worse than they might otherwise have been. They got to Pennsylvania Avenue only minutes before the Washington Monument guides and initially split, Pamela checking the incident room for overnight developments—which there hadn't been—and Cowley escorting the guides to an interview room.

Regulations required that a tally be kept, so John Barclay, a timid man whose speech hesitation was only just short of a stutter, knew he'd taken fifteen people from the top of the obelisk on the 10:00 A.M. tour. There had been three teenagers—he guessed one at eleven, the other two slightly older—and thought the adults divided between seven men and five women. He couldn't remember anyone behaving suspiciously during the descent or more specifically at the level where the bomb had gone off. The routine was to lead the party down, so he would have been looking back up at them, pointing out the gift stones, and could be expected to see anything unusual, which he hadn't. He couldn't recall how many people carried or used cameras, but most tourists usually did.

Janice Smallbone, who'd conducted the afternoon tour, was in fact a large black woman. There'd been seventeen in her group, all adults, seven women and ten men. She remembered one man wearing the sort of jungle-suit camouflage jacket veterans sometimes wore for their vigil at the Vietnam Memorial. She thought he'd been with another man. Both had short military-type haircuts, but that's all she could remember and she didn't think she could identify them again or describe them sufficiently for an artist's or computer-generated impression. Neither they nor anyone else had acted in any way to attract her particular attention. There would have been cameras but she didn't know how many and couldn't remember any being used during the descent. There probably had been.

By noon four people—two men and two women—who had made the monument descent on foot responded to the FBI appeal to come forward. Unprompted, one of the women, a kindergarten teacher

from Houston named Hillary Petty, talked of the man in the camouflage jacket. "It seemed such an odd thing to wear, to someone
like myself, from Texas. He wore a black beret, too, as if it was part
of a uniform." There had definitely been a second man, who'd carried a satchel from a strap over his shoulder. She was sure they'd
been the last of the group to come down because she'd been the
next in line, at the rear, but she hadn't seen either of them do
anything to suggest they might have been planting a bomb. She
guessed both their ages between thirty and thirty-five. Although
both had military haircuts, she didn't remember more than that to
provide enough for a detailed description. She said of course she'd
look at the photographs that Cowley was expecting sometime that
day from the Pentagon—she wasn't leaving Washington until the
end of the week—but she really wasn't sure she could identify anyone. She listened several times to the Highway Patrol copy tape of
the New Rochelle cruiser fire report but wasn't able to recognize the
voice as being that of anyone she had heard during the tour. She'd
taken several photographs herself on the way down and surrendered
her film, which was immediately developed. Neither man was shown
in any of the prints, but two more people in the afternoon group—a
man and a woman—were sufficiently recognizable for the photograph to be published in a renewed plea to contact the bureau.

"How much credibility can we put on it?" asked Pamela.

"It's more than enough to describe as a positive lead," judged
Cowley. "But cautiously. Not too much detail—not even whether it
was on the morning or afternoon tour—for them to realize how little
we have. Hillary's photograph will help: We can talk about other
prints, as if we do have pictures of the two men. We might just
spook them into a mistake."

At that moment Cowley's direct line rang. Carl Ashton, the Pentagon's head of computer security, said, "You won't believe what
the bastards have done. I don't believe it myself. Call up the government's home page."

There were only two words—THE WATCHMEN—-replicated
thousands upon thousands of times until the Pentagon's VDU server
was totally full, immobilizing the system. In doing so the virus in-

fected subsidiary, linked programs, causing computer crashes in the Commerce, Agriculture, Welfare, and Social Security departments.

Cowley stood with the telephone cupped to one ear, not fully comprehending the screen in front of him. Ashton said, "What you're seeing isn't the worst of it."

"What else?" asked Cowley.

"Computers generate static—glue, dust and hair, stuff like that, to the screen. So there's antistatic bands that attach to the supply lines. Computer shops sell a gizmo identical to antistatic bands. It fits on to the main feed and can record, for later downloading, the ten most recent access numbers and entry codes dialed from a machine."

"Jesus!" Cowley exclaimed, numbed. "How many?"

"We're still sweeping," said Ashton. "So far every lower-level VDU and fifteen stations with their own hard disks. There'll be more."

"Any way of knowing the complete access they've achieved?"

"Every operator keeps a work log, but it'll take weeks. But all that will tell us—hopefully—is the last ten from each individual machine. Which they've had God knows how much time to get into and move on. They can just ride piggyback on any call that's made, anywhere else from their new host number."

"Make it simple for me," said Cowley.

"The Watchmen could already be, unknown and undetected, inside as many as five thousand programs anywhere in the world. There's not a chance in hell of tracing them. And they can cause the sort of blocking chaos they've done with the official government page whenever they feel like it."

"How are they doing that specifically?"

"It's called a Trojan horse, which is self-explanatory. There's no way of telling when one's been lodged in a system or when it'll open up. That happens when a code word or phrase is entered. Once that happens it becomes, quite literally, a computer infection, compounding and compounding itself over and over again. People die from virulent medical infections; programs die from virulent computer infections. Same principle. And we probably caused it ourselves."

"Help me with that, too," demanded Cowley.

"It would have been their burglar alarm," said Ashton. "I've got thirty operators sweeping everything it's possible to sweep. When one of them got close to the dormant Trojan horse, the alarm would have gone off, opening it up. It's an absolute disaster."

"What about the disgruntled list?" asked Cowley. "That on hard copy or disk?"

"That's part of the disaster," said the computer expert. "We were a third of the way through printing it off."

"Which could be what triggered the alarm," Cowley suggested at once. "The closeness to a particular name."

There was no reaction from the other end for several moments. Then Ashton said, "I didn't think of that! But it could easily be the way it happened."

"The list alphabetical?"

"Yes."

"And there was no master, backup file?"

"There should have been. But there wasn't. An inquiry's already started."

"What other way could there be?" said Cowley, the question as much to himself as to the man at the Pentagon.

"There isn't one," said Ashton. "We're looking at the failure of modern technology."

"No," refused Cowley. "What's the system for letting people go? They get severance, vacation money, stuff like . . . ?"

"That could be it!" accepted Ashton, understanding at once. "No idea how long it might take but it could be a cross-reference."

"And there's the photographs," reminded Cowley, recalling the arrangement with Hillary Petty. "That's another check, surely?"

There was another silence. "Part of the problem," admitted Ashton. "They're digitized."

"You mean they're on computer, too? No prints?"

"We'd run off some before the crash."

"You know what I always thought?" said Cowley. "I always thought the Pentagon was the super-efficient institution that fought wars and kept the free world safe."

"We had a mole in here," said Ashton. "Someone we didn't know about."

"If that's supposed to be an excuse, it isn't," said Cowley. "I wouldn't offer it to anyone else if I were you."

Pamela Darnley had stood at his side throughout the exchange, mostly staring at the screen. She said, "I heard enough to understand. Ashton's right. It's a disaster."

"Not quite," contradicted Cowley. "There hasn't been another missile. Or any more bombs."

"Yet," qualified Pamela.

Dimitri Ivanovich Danilov eased the seat back and closed his eyes even before the plane leveled off, uninterested in seeing the Moscow hinterland disappear beneath him. He scarcely had sufficient data to justify the trip this soon, he knew. But equally—more so in fact—he needed personally to be in Washington to evaluate the forensic tests, even though he was sure what the results would be. The big uncertainty was what to do when he got the confirmation: assessing—if he could even then—the obstacles and obstruction he was facing. At least he'd be free of the distraction of Olga. Who was confusing him even further. There'd been no threatening belligerence before he'd left. She'd been positively docile and actually wished him a good trip as he was packing. He couldn't remember her doing that when their relationship had been amicable. It probably would all be changed by the time he got back.

"There are certainly disparities," said the head of bank security, a thin-faced, blinking man named Hank Hewitt.

"Thefts?" insisted Anne Stovey.

"The surprising thing is that apart from Mr. Snelling—and one or two people who believe there are discrepancies, since we've begun to check specifically—no one's actually complained. There has to be a complaint to constitute a crime, doesn't there?

"It's a legal point," said Anne. "How much, so far?"

"It's still far too early to tell. As you yourself warned, the discrepancies never amount to more than a few cents, a dollar at the most."

Anne refused to be irritated. She'd gotten the same reaction at three different banks she'd asked to check. One had even refused outright, if there hadn't been a complaint from a customer. "If, over a long period, four or five cents have been taken from the checking accounts of all your bank's customers, in all your branches, how much could have been stolen?"

The blinking man tried a disdainful laugh, which didn't quite work. "That's an impossible hypothesis. And an exaggerated one."

"Indulge me," coaxed Anne. "If it's been going on for say two to three years, I think we could be talking of hundreds of thousands of dollars, don't you?"

"I really won't go into a hypothesis like that," refused the security chief.

"It has to be a bank employee, doesn't it?"

"Accounts never balance at the end-of-day trading."

"What checks can you put in place?"

"I don't know, apart from making a visual examination at the beginning and end of each day's trading against deposits made during that day. It would be totally out of the question."

"I'd like you to spread the inquiries through all your branches," insisted the woman. It was time to respond to the memorandum about possible robberies that could be financing the terrorism.

In the locked study of the Rensselaer house Patrick Hollis surfed through the sites where he customarily played his war games. Posted on two was a message that read: THE GENERAL IS CALLING THE QUARTERMASTER AT THE USUAL PLACE AND TIME.

Hollis had been disappointed by his probe into Robert Standing's background. The man had no medical history that could have been embarrassing and his financial records were haphazard but disclosed no excess or irregularity.

Hollis sat looking at the screen and its message for a long time before the idea began to germinate. Robert Standing was the sort of person whose account he plundered, Hollis recognized: someone who'd never be sure to the last cent—even the last dollar—what his balance was.

Hollis called up the screen-filling list of bank account numbers he had accumulated over the years, choosing at random. It was going to work, he knew; work very well indeed.

15

The photograph had given Pamela Darnley an identification but not an impression of Dimitri Danilov, and for a moment she remained unmoving by an arrivals hall pillar, studying the man. A good six inches shorter than Cowley and much slighter, thinning blond hair carefully combed to cover where it was already receding, Slavic cheekbones giving his face a leanness: inconspicuous but confident, at least outwardly, not looking around anxiously to be greeted, intentionally just apart from the bustle all around him, making his own space. A man accustomed to being alone; maybe preferring it.

Danilov's look encompassed the hall at the same time as she picked up the taxi direction sign, toward which he moved after just the briefest hesitation. It brought him toward her, so all Pamela had to do was step out into his path.

"Dimitri?" she said. "Pamela."

He took the offered hand, the direct, unsurprised look confirming her inference of confidence. He said, "Thank you for bothering."

"It's no bother. Bill's become a little too publicly recognizable, and a hospital appointment clashed anyway."

"Is there a problem?" The concern was immediate.

"Having his stitches taken out. He should be back at the bureau by now. You want to go straight there or stop off at the Marriott? It's the nearest."

Pamela had driven to Dulles in her own car and used the return journey to bring Danilov completely up to date. With the Arlington Bridge still closed, the traffic began backing up along the George Washington Parkway before they got as far as Langley.

Danilov said, "They're being very successful at making everyone look ridiculous."

"The fear is what they'll do next," said Pamela.

"Let's hope Bill's right about them exhausting their supply."

"How do we block their resupply?"

"I wish I had a better idea," admitted Danilov.

"Have you got one at all?" Pamela immediately demanded.

"I'll be better able to answer that after talking to your forensic people," said Danilov.

"They've already got what you shipped earlier," said Pamela.

"But not the way I want it examined," said Danilov. "How strongly are you treating this sighting of the man in the camouflage jacket?"

"It's the most hopeful lead so far."

"How many have you traced from both tours?"

"Six from the morning descent. Seven in the afternoon. And no useful photographs."

Danilov slumped into such contemplative silence that Pamela wondered if he'd actually fallen asleep after the flight. But then she saw his eyes were open and realized he was someone not discomfited by silence. She said, "I hear it's not easy for you to work properly in Moscow."

Danilov looked at her across the car, caught by the directness. Cowley must be working very closely with her to have told her. Was their relationship entirely professional? Pamela Darnley in person was even more attractive than he had thought her to be from TV. The briefing had been impressive, as well: A succinct, factual account spared any unsupportable opinion or conclusion and gave Cowley the credit for preventing the Lincoln Memorial explosion. Danilov said, "Sometimes it can be useful."

The Key Bridge was blocked, stopping them. She turned to look directly at him, expecting him to elaborate, but he didn't. The traffic became freer after Washington Circle but clogged again at the detour that had been imposed around the White House.

Cowley was back at the bureau building. He held up a warning hand as Danilov entered the incident room and said, "No Russian bear hugs." He touched his head. "And you might as well laugh at this and get it over with."

No dressing had been necessary after the removal of the stitches, and the two-inch-wide furrow along the entire side of Cowley's head, where the hair had been cut away, made it look as if his scalp had slipped sideways. Pamela did grin and said, "If it's a fashion statement, I can't say I like it."

There was definitely an easiness between the two of them, Danilov decided. "It's not as if I have that much hair to spare."

The relaxation was brief. Cowley said, "I'd rather you gave me now what you couldn't from Moscow."

"I need to give it to the forensic team who've got what was delivered to your embassy."

In Paul Lambert's section they were greeted by a mixture of curiosity at Dimitri Danilov—a Russian in the heart of America's counterintelligence organization—and undisguised amusement at Cowley's appearance.

Danilov said, "You've tested what was sent from Moscow? Compared the paint and the metals?"

"Not a single match," dismissed the scientist.

"Good." Danilov smiled, although he'd already known there would be some disparity when there shouldn't have been.

"That prove something?" demanded Cowley.

"I hope this will," said Danilov, taking from his pocket the envelopes he'd carried with him at all times since Gorki and added to after collecting the samples from the Moscow plant. Opening two separate, carefully labeled envelopes he said, "Is that enough metal?"

"Should be," said Lambert.

"What about the paint?" asked Danilov, opening the other identified envelopes.

"More than enough."

"How long?"

"Twenty-four hours, to be absolutely sure."

"That's what I've got to be, absolutely sure," insisted Danilov.

"What are you trying to prove?" demanded Pamela.

"Where the UN missile definitely came from," replied Danilov. To the forensic scientist he said, "Have you made a positive comparison between the stenciling on the UN warhead and what was sent to you, marked as coming from Gorki—specifically the name itself?"

Lambert coughed uncomfortably. "I need to double check that."

"Do," urged Danilov. "Should you be able to tell if the template from the two separate Gorkis is the same or different?"

"A simple matter of enlarging photographs of both names sufficiently to compare their outlines," said Lambert. "It will show up the imperfections in the manufacturing stamp for each letter. If the imperfections are different, then so are the templates."

"Gorki is the important word but I'd like every letter checked. And those from the Moscow plant: the words on the mines as well as the warhead from Kushino."

Back in his office Cowley said, "What do you expect to find?"

"Quite a lot of effort to lead me—us—in the wrong direction," said Danilov.

"How?" asked Pamela.

It took Danilov almost an hour to explain. Even then he omitted the cell threat to Anatoli Lasin and the importance he attached to Ashot Mizin, the man who had eagerly volunteered to deliver the warheads and mines from militia headquarters to the Russian Foreign Ministry. Long before he finished he was aware of Pamela's skepticism. When he did stop, she said, "It can't be as bad as that."

"I'd like not to think so. But I do. That's what I meant in the car by saying how misdirection of which we are aware could sometimes be useful."

"You any idea *how* to use it yet?" asked the less doubtful and more pragmatic Cowley.

"Let's wait for the results of the scientific tests."

"Is there anything else?" said Pamela, making no more effort to hide her disappointment than she had her skepticism.

"Viktor Nikolaevich Nikov made two visits to America, one in January, the second in August of last year," disclosed Danilov. "He'd have had to complete a visa application form with a contact address in this country, wouldn't he?"

Cowley smiled broadly. "Absolutely!" he said.

"Both visits were on a passport in the name of Nikov," added Danilov. "But there's a possible alias, Eduard Babkendovich Kulik. He had a Russian driver's license in that name. Which—"

"—he could have used to rent a car, which a man with an interest in cars would almost automatically do," completed Pamela excitedly. "And rental agreements require residency addresses!"

Although Danilov telephoned from the J. Edgar Hoover building to warn of his impending arrival, there was still confusion when he got to the new Russian embassy off Wisconsin. The obvious initial reaction was that he was a deluded imposter. The jet lag that began to engulf him didn't help his heavy-eyed, disheveled appearance, either, and he began regretting not waiting until the following day, which Cowley had suggested, when there might have been more on the suspect in the camouflage jacket. He spent more than half an hour alone in a bare room into which he was shown by an unnamed and clearly disbelieving reception clerk who demanded his passport and militia credentials before the door abruptly burst open and a gray-haired man, red faced with anger, demanded, "What the hell's going on!" It was the start of a further hour of outraged demands, anger, threats, and quite a lot of communication by telephone and fax with both the White House and the Foreign Ministry in Moscow.

"I forbid you to behave in such a manner, imagining you can work totally independently of this embassy and my authority," declared the ambassador, Andrei Guliyev, virtually at the moment of their meeting. "You will communicate through me—and only through me—at all times and do nothing without my prior approval. It's also ridiculous for you to expect to live outside the diplomatic compound."

"Hasn't there been notification of my coming from the president's office?" queried Danilov. This far from Moscow he had no way of protecting himself between the conflicting pressure from the Duma and the White House.

Guliyev looked to his head of chancellery. Timor Besedin said: "Our notification came from the Foreign Ministry."

Why hadn't it come from Georgi Chelyag? thought Danilov. "At most I don't imagine needing more than the intelligence bureau's secure communication facilities."

"I have not been officially informed of this," protested the embassy's security chief, Ivan Fedorovich Obidin loudly. "The militia has no right of access to my *rezidentura*. It's out of the question. I expect, however, to accompany you on inquiries you make while you are here in America. I shall contact Moscow suggesting this. That way the secure *rezidentura* facilities can be used. By me, to relay what's necessary."

Danilov sighed, holding back the irritation he felt for the president's chief of staff not personally sending the message. He hadn't expected to make friends but to make enemies here would serve no purpose. And there would, he was sure by now, have been a lot of separate conversations and instructions from Moscow to each of these men from their respective superiors. "I'm fully aware of the pressure you have personally been under since all this began. Which is precisely the reason *why* there has to be a separation. The FBI has no positive leads. Neither have I, from Moscow. There will be more outrages—atrocities even. If I am attached to this embassy and living in the Russian diplomatic compound—and my presence here in Washington becomes known—then it will be to this embassy and you, Mr. Ambassador, that fresh demands and criticism will be directed. Working independently of the embassy *is* diplomatically essential, in the opinion of the president." He paused, confident the inference of ultimate, inner sanctum access was necessary. "I don't need secure facilities to talk to Chief of Staff Chelyag. Any telephone will do."

"I'm not being obstructive," the local intelligence chief said uncertainly.

"No one is suggesting that you are," Danilov said easily.

"If the purpose of the conversation with the president's office is to ensure we each understand your position and function here, there's surely no reason why we can't hear it?" the military attaché, Colonel Oleg Syzdykov, said with a smile.

Danilov forced himself to smile back, recognizing the military intelligence chief to be the most formidable opponent and warmed by a further realization. Chelyag hadn't personally sent the advisory cable, and they believed he was exaggerating his authority! "None whatsoever."

Guliyev gestured toward the telephone bank beside his expansive desk.

Danilov booked the call in his name through the embassy switchboard, turning to face his audience. Who was calling whose bluff? Hardly a bluff, in his case. He'd made it quite clear to Chelyag how he needed to work in America, and at the very first crisis meeting the presidential aide had precluded the direct involvement of any other agency. But there was something close to overconfidence in the attitudes of the people facing him.

The telephone rang and the ambassador again held out his hand in invitation. It was a secretary, a voice he didn't recognize. Danilov repeated his name, feeling the perspiration prickling his back, and said he would not give a message but that he wanted Chelyag to be told personally who was calling from Washington. It was difficult to keep his voice even. The line went dead, as if the call had been disconnected.

Syzdukov said, "I think there really has been a misunderstanding!"

And then Chelyag came sharply on to the line. "What!"

Instead of immediately replying, Danilov leaned across the ambassador's desk and pushed the button for speaker phone, so that Chelyag's impatiently repeated demand echoed into the room.

"I am speaking to you from the office of His Excellency Ambassador Guliyev," Danilov established formally. "Also with me are Head of Chancellery Timor Besedin and security officers Oleg Syzdykov and Ivan Obidin." The first flicker of apprehension registered with the security chief. "There's an operational difficulty that needs resolving.

The collapse of the four men was practically visible, their strings going slack. The ambassador tried anxiously to talk over Danilov, but Danilov refused the interruption, bulldozing on with the insistence that the separation was to spare the embassy embarrassment until Chelyag himself broke in.

"Is this line open, for everyone to hear? There's an echo."

"Yes," said Danilov.

"Good," said Chelyag. The lecture was terse, each man addressed individually by name. Any difficulty experienced by Dimitri Iva-novich Danilov would be considered positive obstruction, to be ex-plained to the White House. Danilov was to be given every assistance and embassy facility without question or interference. Each of their department heads—the foreign minister himself in the cases of Am-bassador Guliyev and Timor Besedin—would be notified of these instructions within the hour and asked why it had been necessary to reissue them, in view of the specific directives each had unequiv-ocally been given.

"Dimitir Ivanovich?"

"Sir?"

"Anything further that needs to be made clear?"

"I don't think so," said Danilov. This whole episode had, he guessed, been set up. Some sort of loyalty test in the continuing internecine Moscow infighting in the middle of which he remained caught.

It was almost seven-thirty before Cowley and Pamela, working smoothly together from the communal incident room, organized all the searches possible from Danilov's leads. The car rental companies hoped to complete their computer records check by the following day, but the Immigration Department thought it might take longer to trace the written visa slips, which weren't transferred to com-puters and needed, therefore, to be gone through by hand.

Terry Osnan, pleased at last to be able to do something more than assemble records, said, "This has got a positive feel to it."

"We hope," said Cowley.

"Dimitri's not the sort of guy I thought he would be," said Pa-mela.

"Different how?"

She made an uncertain movement. "I don't know. Quieter, I guess. If the forensic results turn out like he expects, it's going to point toward some official complicity."

"It's something I want to talk through with him when we get the findings." Cowley hesitated. "How about my buying you a thank-you dinner for last night?"

She looked at him silently for several moments from her desk. "I really was going through my angel-of-mercy routine, you know."

"I know," said Cowley, angry at himself. Shit! he thought: shit, shit, shit.

"I don't want anything to get complicated." Not unless it's on *my* terms, she thought.

"Neither do I."

"Maybe some other time."

"Sure. Some other time."

It was Cowley's extension that rang. Carl Ashton said, "They're jerking our strings again. All the blocked screens have cleared. And there's another message, signed the Watchmen. It says within twenty-four hours they're going to prove the hypocrisy that exists between America and Russia."

"Where's it being sent from?"

"They're still using the Pentagon, for Christ's sake! Proving we can't catch them even though we know they're there somewhere."

"You think we should wake Dimitri up?" asked Pamela, when Cowley relayed the message.

"There's nothing he can do to stop it happening, whatever it's going to be," said Cowley. "We can give him a few more hours."

"What can we do to stop it?" Pamela said rhetorically.

"Nothing except wait."

"What if they've got another missile? Or more bombs?" she said, still in self-conversation.

"Then we've got a new catastrophe," said Cowley.

Anne Stovey took great care with her memorandum to Washington, believing that quite alone she'd found a lead—maybe even *the* lead—to the terrorist financing but not wanting to overstress the claim, in case she hadn't.

But it had to be more than a coincidence that the security departments of four quite separate, unconnected banks had finally acknowledged complaints of irritating customers like Clarence Snelling that there had been nickel-and-dime differences in their accounts.

She rewrote her message three times, her conviction wavering at every attempt because there was so little to support her theory. For an hour she even considered saying nothing until the inquiries she'd asked the security departments to make produced something. An impossible task, she remembered, according to each security chief she'd spoken to. Her fourth rewrite included that phrase. It was late afternoon when she finally faxed it, quoting the reference from the terrorist inquiry incident room.

"Can't it wait until we get home?" demanded Elizabeth Hollis.

"He might not be there if we wait." Hollis hadn't wanted another scene so he had taken his mother, announcing the sudden need to use the phone as they got close to the mall.

"What is it?" demanded the woman.

"A guy at work had a problem he couldn't work out. I promised I'd think about it, try to find the answer. I think I have." In more ways than Robert Standing would ever think possible, he thought.

"Maybe I'll come with you. Look at Penney's."

"It's too crowded. You'll get tired. Stay in the car and listen to the music."

"Perhaps you're right."

Hollis had allowed ten minutes and felt a lurch of anxiety when he saw a woman using the telephone. He placed himself obviously outside the booth and just as obviously she turned her back to him. There was only a minute to go when she collected the unused coins from the ledge. He hurried forward, holding open the door. As she emerged she said, "Don't worry, honey. She'll wait, hunky guy like you," and laughed. He could smell that she hadn't showered. The phone rang.

"You've disobeyed orders!"

"I'm here."

"Make sure you are in the future. You're part of the struggle."

Using pseudonyms and phrases was all right cracking through the Web and playing war games. Verbally it sounded ridiculous. Hollis said, "I've got some more account numbers."

"How many?"

"Ten."

"That's not enough!"

"It'll have to do. I'll get more."

"Don't be insubordinate. We want you to work. We need a lot of money."

"No more than cents. Otherwise you'll be picked up."

"I give the orders. Be here on time, for the next contact. And I want you personally to raise $20,000."

"That's impossible!"

"You invented the system. Make it work."

"All sorted out?" his mother asked as he got back into the Jaguar.

"I think so," Hollis said contentedly. There was no way thefts of the size the General was talking about could be restricted to cents and therefore no way they could go undiscovered.

16

The Chinese-initiated debate intended internationally to humiliate both America and Russia—the one unable to protect the world's UN statesmen, the other the treaty-ignoring manufacturer of weapons of mass destruction in the hands of terrorists—was destroyed as if by another bomb by the new, unspecified threat. Within an hour of its being made and relayed worldwide, the favored analyses of the intelligence and terrorist pundits in permanent—sometimes unshaved for effect—residence in television studios and newspaper offices was that the United Nations complex was to be targeted again.

Within almost the same time frame Beijing realized there wasn't the remotest possibility of its carefully cultivated supporting army of podium attackers from Africa and Asia getting within fifty miles of Manhattan for the beginning of the assembly but refused an unthinkable loss of face by asking for a postponement. The impasse was resolved again by UN Secretary-General Ibrahim Saads, who ordered that the complex be evacuated once more. That announcement convinced the already uncertain New York mayor to declare the city closed the following day to all incoming commuters with the advice to residents to leave immediately.

The exodus was only slightly less chaotic than before, and there was almost a familiarity about the aerial television coverage of people in unthinking flight. All the city's airports, including Newark, closed, although some landings were allowed for refueling. After Canada warned that its East Coast and central airports might not be able to cope with the rerouting, departures from Europe and eastbound from within the United States began to be canceled. Grand Central and Penn Central railway terminals were shut. There was looting and arson. By 3:00 A.M. seven looters had been shot.

The mayor of Washington stopped just short of officially ordering the evacuation of the district, gauging from the migration accounts of an increasingly overwhelmed police commissioner that so many people were already on the move that the advice was unnecessary. Besides, he wanted nothing later to prove an albatross around his already aching neck. The closure of the Mall and all government offices was extended to include the Capitol and all its administrative buildings, and thirty senators and House representatives issued individual declarations that their duty required them to be at home with their constituents in times of national crisis. Other congressmen who weren't quick enough to think of the reelectorally correct escape were glad they hadn't, so cowardly facile did the virtually identical statements sound, and left without attempting to justify their hurried abandonment of the as-yet unsinking ship. Dulles and Reagan airports closed down, as well as D.C.'s Union Station. Three blacks died when police opened fire on early-morning looters who started torching shops in Anacostia, just beyond Capitol Hill.

Throughout the long night there were equally frantic efforts made to guard other likely targets through the country. All army, airforce, and naval bases—including the already penetrated, previously and derided Pentagon—were placed on full alert. So were the Kennedy space launch site in Florida, Houston Control, and the Mojave space shuttle landing facility. Disney World and Disneyland announced their closure. After McDonald's declared it would not be opening until the threat was understood and prevented, all the other fast food franchises shut, too.

With nothing more—no way of predicting more—than a five-line message registered on the federal government's Internet-accessible home page, the crisis team that assembled within two hours at the White House was limited to Frank Norton, Henry Hartz, the directors of the FBI and CIA, and Peter Prentice, the president's media spokesperson. Prentice stood by the Oval Office television that was permanently left on, relaying developing frenzy throughout the country.

"I've got to say something, but what the fuck *is* there for me to say!" demanded the president. "If I go on television again with the same speech rewritten the fourth time I'm the dumbest-ass chief executive in history. Which is what I already am in the ratings history."

"The bureau assessment is that it's an overreaction," suggested Leonard Ross. "Cowley sees the Watchmen's message as some kind of embarrassing disclosure." Ross had spent the entire journey from his home to the White House on the car phone to the incident room.

"About what?" demanded the president.

"We don't know," Ross conceded lamely.

"Thank you for that, Mr. Director! That really tells me how to convince the American people we've got everything under control and that there's nothing to panic about!" He jerked a finger toward the television. "Look at it out there, for Christ's sake!"

"We *don't* have anything to say," declared Frank Norton, ever mindful that he needed the endorsement of a respected departing president to further his own ambitions and that therefore the man had to be safeguarded from mistimed public appearances. "So it would be wrong to make another personal television address. Even worse to face the press, where you'd have to take questions. The announcement's got to be in your name but by Prentice. It's got to make it very clear that you're still here in the White House, the president who definitely didn't run—"

"What's the announcement say?" demanded the man, not needing the paint-by-numbers explanation. "There's got to be some substance."

"Russia," said Hartz, as the idea came to him. "Call the Russian president personally. Maybe invite the Russian foreign minister here to talk to me. It's positive. High level. And shows you're standing up against the demands the Watchmen made in their first message, protesting the detente between the two countries.

"That's good," Norton agreed.

"Yes," said the president more slowly, digesting before regurgitating. "Yes, that's good. You following this, Peter? Put out something right away on the wires: that there's soon to be an important announcement. Promise each of the majors personally—tell them I told you to—it'll be in time for their late news. But insist I'm too occupied—occupied's the word, not "too busy," as if I don't know what I'm doing—to do anything on camera myself." The man began to make rolling motions with his hand. "We're refusing to give in to terrorism . . ." He looked at the FBI director. "You say that Russian guy's arrived?"

"Earlier today," said Ross.

"Good," said the other man, picking up the briefing. "Senior Russian investigators already here . . . combined, highest-level cooperation . . . nowhere to hide . . . that sort of stuff, got it?"

"I think so, Mr. President," said the public affairs spokesman, a mop-haired man who talked a lot with his hands. "I think we should have a picture I can issue. You on the telephone to Moscow . . . world leader to world leader?"

"It's building well," congratulated the politician. "The pose will be important. Shirt sleeves and loosened tie, president hard at work in a crisis? Or jacket and tie, calm, refusing to be panicked? Which do you think?"

"Difficult one," said the media specialist, frowning at the seriousness of the decision. "Shirt sleeves, I think. But maybe not loosen the tie, like you're anxious."

"Any thoughts?" the president invited generally. "This has got to be exactly right."

"Shirt sleeves," said Norton, the other White House professional.

Hartz and Butterworth nodded in uncomfortable agreement. Leonard Ross refused to become involved.

Prentice said, "I think we should stress, too, that it's we who initiated the direct approach to the Russian president. Puts the pressure on Russia to respond after whatever the attack is. Spread the pressure."

"Perfect!" agreed the president. "Get to it. You've only got an hour. And Peter?"

"Mr. President?"

"Change that tie. It's too bright. We don't want a happy mood image. People could die."

Cowley woke Danilov in time to watch Peter Prentice face the White House press corps on his hotel room television. Cowley and Pamela saw it from the incident room. It was followed immediately by a roundup of the intended evacuations and closure precautions, the footage on every channel that of miles-long head- and-taillighted streams of fleeing, going-anywhere vehicles. When they talked again Cowley told Danilov he was going to use the office cot, but there wasn't any practical reason for the Russian to come from his hotel simply to sit around and wait: He could get to the bureau from 14th Street five minutes after the Watchmen carried out their threat, whatever it might be.

"This is clever," said Danilov. "Psychological. Military. Professional insurrection training. You thought of extending the disgruntled search beyond the Pentagon to the CIA?"

"Not until now," admitted Cowley. It was a valid but numbing suggestion.

"There was a lot to learn—and be taught—from Vietnam. Africa before that. And Latin America: Chile particularly. That's the time—and the attitude—reflected in that first Watchmen message."

Pamela decided to go home, which Cowley discovered for the first time was north, a condo in Westminster. He was surprised that he actually slept and for so long, from just after midnight to five. He thought it was the sound of a telephone that woke him, but the night operator came on asking what he wanted when Cowley snatched it off his desk.

There were no fresh towels or soap in the mess washroom where Cowley went to shower, and to shave he had to try to lather the sliver he did find. He managed without cutting himself and was glad there wasn't any discomfort from his rib or head. He spent several minutes studying his lopsided appearance in the mirror and decided it might look less ridiculous if he had the rest of his hair cropped much shorter than it was. Would Pamela judge a crew cut as a better fashion statement? The coincidence of the new threat had wiped away any embarrassment at her dinner rejection, but he'd clearly and badly misjudged a situation. Which she was right about, he further accepted. They couldn't allow the intrusion of even the most basic of social relationships, which it hadn't seemed as if she would have welcomed in other circumstances. What about himself? Hardly a rebound reaction from Pauline's marriage announcement, after almost three years of divorce. He'd been flattered, he acknowledged, at someone—not just someone, but an attractive, intelligent woman—seeming to show some interest in him. And got it wrong. Been naive. Laughably so. Lucky to have gotten away with it. No risk of it happening again.

The television commentaries this early were all replays from the previous night and very early morning, so he turned the sound down. The footage was virtually all repeats, too, although there were some new but familiar shots of an empty New York and Washington. The voice-over reporter added that the volume of early-morning commuter traffic was averaging less than fifty percent of normal in every major American city. Over the previous night's still photograph of the serious-faced, shirt-sleeved president on the telephone to Moscow came the promise of a response during the day from the Russian White House.

Pamela included Danilov in the coffee and Danish that she brought when she got back at six-thirty, which was fortunate because the Russian arrived only five minutes behind her. She would have been earlier, Pamela apologized, but her normal coffee shop and the one after that were closed. There was virtually no conversation while they ate, watching the repetitive newscast. The only fresh item was the worldwide stock market slump, with overnight panic selling in Tokyo triggering a plunge in London, Paris, Frankfurt, and Hong Kong. There was speculation that trading on Wall Street might be suspended even before its opening in an effort to break the cycle.

Pamela said, "This is driving me nuts!"

Danilov said, "That's what it's meant to do! Drive everyone nuts. It's called psychological warfare—as infectious and as deadly as anthrax or sarin."

Cowley said, "Makes a change from everything moving so fast we can't keep up."

Leonard Ross came on to Cowley's direct incident room line at seven demanding a complete update in time for an eleven o'clock presidential briefing. When he learned the Russian was in the building, he asked that Danilov come along, as well. Seizing that as an excuse—in reality as impatient as Pamela by the inactivity and needing to move—Danilov borrowed her car to drive along deserted streets to the Russian embassy. The head of chancellery accepted at once there was no point in a meeting with the ambassador if there was nothing positive to advise the man about. Ivan Obidin came to the foyer himself to escort Danilov to the Security Bureau's communications center, and Danilov decided that ironic and rare though it might seem, there was sometimes benefit from operating in the cesspit of Moscow deceit. This was actually amateur by Petrovka standards.

On their way to the communications facilities, the nervous intelligence chief hoped the previous day's difficulties had been totally resolved. He certainly hadn't intended any personal offense or obstruction and wanted to make his own office available. Danilov came close to feeling sorry for the man.

Obidin's office was remarkably large and comfortable—almost as expansive as the ambassador's suite—and very much the man's own territory. Obidin's various promotion testimonials and commendations were framed on the walls and on a low bookcase. There was an official, full face portrait of the man at a citation ceremony. Next to it was an official group photograph of what Danilov assumed to be the rest of the *rezidentura*. On the desk was a photograph of a plump woman flanked on either side by two boys in their early teens. St. Basil's Cathedral in Red Square was in the background.

Seeing Danilov's look, Obidin said, "They've already gone back. My tour ends in three months."

The system on Obidin's desk appeared to be an ordinary five-telephone console, the security route through which the lines were channeled—and to the sort of soundproof booth in which Danilov knew he should actually have been shown—in another part of the complex. Danilov wasn't surprised his conversation was being monitored, in the hope they could achieve the sort of control they'd imagined possible the previous day. He would have eavesdropped in the same circumstances, with the same facilities.

He talked on the assumption that he was being listened to, keeping any deference from his voice when he was connected to Georgi Chelyag to maintain the impression of upper-echelon access and equality. Danilov told the presidential chief of staff there was no indication what the threat could mean or when it might be carried out, although it was expected sometime that day. He hoped later to get some insight into Washington's genuine political attitudes, and if he did he'd call immediately. It would be helpful—show the required cooperation—to be able to hint what that was in Moscow. The FBI had two suspects for the small explosion in the Washington Monument but the lead was very slender. He believed the bureau was being totally cooperative and wished he was able to contribute more. And he thanked Chelyag for the requested guidance that the American leader's offer might be accepted, although Moscow wanted a neutral venue to avoid the impression of the Russian foreign minister having to come to Washington to meet the secretary of state.

Danilov went into more detail about the tourist in the camouflage jacket when he was connected to Yuri Pavin, although again for the benefit of any listener he said the likelihood of tracing the man and his satchel-carrying companion wasn't promising.

"Anything you want me to follow up here?"

If there was he'd call from another phone, Danilov decided: maybe even from the FBI building itself. "What's there been from Reztsov in Gorki?"

"Promising to come back in twenty-four hours."

Obidin came from a room farther within the *rezidentura*—proof that Danilov didn't need that the security chief had heard him terminate his conversation—as Danilov emerged from the man's office. As they walked back through the embassy, Obidin disclosed that on Moscow's instructions, security had been tightened around the building and the compound. Danilov held back from asking how they intended stopping a missile. A clearly alerted Timor Besedin intercepted them in the final corridor before the entrance to ask if everything had gone satisfactorily, volunteering the just-made announcement that Wall Street wasn't opening. Danilov made his way back to the bureau building unsure if their obviousness was openly to mock him and his belief that he was beyond their control or if they were simply inept.

Cowley had agreed that they should remain vague about the purpose of the forensic tests until what Danilov knew partially to be a fact was fully confirmed. Leonard Ross himself decided not to promise too much from the visa applications or car rental checks on Viktor Nikov's two American visits. "Everyone's too eager to clutch at straws: We'll get the criticism if it comes to nothing." Cowley told his director that they'd identified and eliminated all ten tourists on the Washington Monument stairs in the morning of the explosion and only had the two male suspects and another man and women on the afternoon visit to eliminate. Anticipating that the Watchmen would make another claim or boast after carrying out their threat, Carl Ashton had assembled a squad of twenty computer specialists at the Pentagon to attempt a source trace, and every available bureau technician at Pennsylvania Avenue had been briefed to do the same, the moment a new message was posted. Others were at the communications centers of all the major telephone companies, whose engineers were mobilized for the hunt. Ross expected that Moscow's reservations regarding the foreign minister's visit to the American president had already been sent to Henry Hartz or maybe the American White House direct but thanked Danilov for the guidance.

"We're doing everything we can—and should—do, but it's not enough," summed up the director. "They can carry out whatever threat they damned well like."

Pamela Darnley was hovering impatiently at the incident room door when Cowley and Danilov returned. "Lambert's got the forensic results!" she announced. "But he says he doesn't understand them."

"Let's hope I do," said Danilov.

The forensic scientist had assembled everything in a small conference room off his working laboratory, what had been sent from Moscow and what Danilov had later brought laid out as if for an exhibition but very distinctly separated. Each item was just as distinctly labeled. The now-empty United Nations warhead was on its own table. On another table next to it were the defused mines, Semtex and timers recovered from the Lincoln Memorial, divided from the debris lifted from the Washington Monument. Lambert's team of specialists were grouped around their supervisor, as if for a lecture.

Lambert said at once, "We've got some inconsistencies."

"I expected there to be," said Danilov. "Take me through it all."

Lambert patted the UN missile. "Here's our attack weapon. We've subjected it to every forensic test and examination available in metallography. We've also analyzed the paint and"—he paused, looking to Danilov—"made photographic enlargements of the stenciled identification lettering. From each we are able to make a positive comparison with similar weapons, their metal, paint, and lettering."

The man moved to an adjoining assigned table. "These mines and this explosive came from the Lincoln Memorial. The mines have been subjected to the same metal, paint, and lettering tests. He picked up an intact timer in one hand and the shattered remains of the Washington monument detonator in the other, lifting and dropping his hands as if weighing them. "These are identical, the metals and wiring match, and there's enough lettering actually left on the side of the monument device for us to be certain they formed part of the same production batch, off the same assembly line." He shrugged. "Semtex is Semtex. It was the monument explosive."

He replaced the timers, moving back to the larger table. "Here, to the right, are the empty warheads, mine casings, and paint samples which were shipped from our embassy in Moscow to compare with the material we already had. None of it—either that marked as coming from Gorki or what came from Plant 43 in Moscow—makes any metal or paint match.

"What about lettering?" broke in Danilov.

"The first inconsistency, although not against our original warhead," said Lambert. "On the sample that came from the embassy marked as having come from Gorki, the name itself—Gorki—has quite definitely not been applied by the same stencil as the rest of the lettering. It's a different template. And it doesn't match the lettering on the UN missile, either.

Beside him, Danilov was aware of Cowley and Pamela shifting uncertainly. He looked in time to see the woman shake her head in bewilderment. Danilov said, "Now tell us about what I brought personally."

Again Lambert used both hands, holding both up for everyone to see. "This is a firing pin—the sort that fortunately broke off and stopped anthrax and sarin being released in Manhattan—and this is a casing clasp which you can see here"—he pointed—"on the mines from the Lincoln Memorial."

Lambert paused theatrically, a magician with a trick he knew would work. "The pin was marked as having come from Gorki and is a perfect metal match to the UN missile. The clasp marked Plant 43, Kushino, is a perfect metal match to the mines from the Lincoln Memorial."

"A match in both cases!" Danilov frowned.

"Absolutely," insisted Lambert. "And so, again, is the paint you gave me, from both Plant 35 and Plant 43. He paused. "I can explain the science but I'm damned if I can make sense of anything else."

"I can," said Danilov.

Before he could continue, the door jarred open behind them and Terry Osnan said, "It's started! Hurry!"

17

They did hurry—Cowley too fast and quickly forced to slow by the pain in his chest—but it wasn't necessary. They got to the full but subdued incident room to see every computer screen split between digitized photographs of two men, beneath each of whom appeared a comprehensive biography.

"What . . . ?" demanded Cowley.

"That's the last of Beijing," said Osnan. "The full staffing of our CIA station there compared one to one with that of the Russian's Federal Security Bureau. The transmission opened with a repetition of the mistrust declaration, then a promise to disclose America and Russia's hypocritical spy presence in every major world capital."

At that moment on to the screens came a photograph of Ivan Fedorovich Obidin very similar to the one Danilov had seen in the man's embassy office, now coupled with that of the CIA's head of Moscow station. The pictures went, match for match, through the intelligence personnel in both stations and then switched to military intelligence, with a photograph of the Washington embassy's Colonel Oleg Ivanovich Syzdykov against the FBI's agent at Ulitza Chaykovskovo.

"Jesus H. Christ!" said someone.

"We *have* to get a trace!" insisted Pamela. "They can't go on doing this without our being able to find where they're doing it from!"

"I want everyone able to move the moment we do," Cowley said generally. "This has got to be their big mistake." Cowley said to Osnan, "Get on to the Pentagon now. See how they're doing."

"We've got two men with Ashton and his people," protested the incident room supervisor.

"Do it!" said Cowley, at once regretting the impatient loudness.

Pamela answered the ringing telephone in their office, handing it to Cowley. "Not yet," he said, to Leonard Ross's demand. "We're checking the Pentagon at this moment. As soon as we hear—'

On the screens all around them the kaleidoscope continued. London led the European capitals, after the complete listings in Washington, Moscow, and the United Nations in New York, to go in sequence to Paris, Rome, Madrid and Lisbon. Tokyo picked up the Asian identifications from Beijing.

Cowley said, "We copying all this!"

"Three terminals, printing as fast as we can," called an operator at one of them.

Osnan replaced his telephone and said, "I don't understand the technicalities, but Ashton says it's not coming from one server. They're using several. As soon as one of Ashton's sweepers think they're getting close, they run into what Ashton calls a firewall, which in computer-speak is exactly what it sounds like: something they can't get past. Then the program starts up from another server and they've got to start all over again."

"Bastards!" Cowley exclaimed.

Pamela broke away from a screen upon which the photographs and names of the CIA and FSB personnel in Canberra were being disclosed. Dimitri Danilov was perched on a table edge, chin reflectively cupped in his hand, smiling faintly. She said, "I miss something funny?"

"Something that could help us," said Danilov. "Maybe not their *big* mistake, but it could definitely help."

After Johannesburg came the Russian and American intelligence presence in the six major Middle East oil-producing states, headed by Saudi Arabia and followed by Kuwait, and after that the full American and Russian espionage staffing in Israel.

Pamela again moved to take one of the two ringing telephones, putting her hand at once over the mouthpiece. Excitedly she said, "There's a positive Manhattan trace: The office there is already moving on to it."

A man on the second line called out: "Seattle. Looks like the procurement division of Boeing. We're moving there, too."

"At last!" said Cowley.

"Let's not get too hopeful," cautioned Danilov. "I don't understand computer technology, either, but if they put up barriers against some pursuit, why aren't they doing it to others?"

"I don't know and at this moment I don't care," said Cowley, still impatient. "I just want to have *something* positive."

Into the telephone she was still holding Pamela said, "Son of a bitch!" Covering the mouthpiece again she said, "It's the computer program in the United Nations' library: the one that stores the index of all the issued pamphlets and reports and Assembly debate transcripts. Or did, until a minute ago. It's been wiped, along with their bug. All that's left is a message that says the Watchmen came calling. Just that. Those four words."

"It's stopped," someone said.

The computers suddenly were filled by another split-screen picture of the American president in his shirt-sleeved pose of the previous night, seemingly face-to-face with a photograph of the Russian leader, also talking into a telephone. The caption beneath read:

TRUSTED FRIENDS SHALL SPEAK UNTO TRUSTED FRIENDS. BUT NOT BELIEVE WHAT THEY HEAR BECAUSE THEY KNOW THEY ARE LIARS.

The final screen image appeared to hold for a long time, although in fact it was only seconds. It faded to be replaced by another Watchmen message:

ALL THOSE REASSIGNMENT AND RELOCATION EXPENSES!

"They're certainly right about that," said one of the terminal operators. "They did thirteen countries, if we include the UN. Averaging five people in each station, we've just witnessed sixty-five officers, American and Russian, totally blown."

The man was right, thought Danilov. Ivan Fedorovich Obidin wouldn't have to wait three months now before rejoining his plump wife and two teenage sons. Danilov wondered if the significance of what the Watchmen had just done would have registered with him so quickly if he hadn't sat that morning in the bald man's memorabilia-packed office of stiff-faced official photographs. It certainly didn't appear to have occurred yet to either William Cowley or Pamela Darnley. Maybe it would when they studied the computer printout more carefully, had the complete selection of images directly in front of them.

It didn't.

Between the three terminals they managed to get printouts of every disclosure, which was then photocopied and made up into full sets. Danilov went through his individually, confirming the idea that had come to him as he'd watched the procession of identities come and go on the screens. He spent longer doing it than either Cowley or Pamela, for whom the greater urgency was following the separate leads thrown up by the transmission.

Pamela retreated to a separate office for a single but protracted telephone conversation that went back and forth between Carl Ashton, at the Pentagon, and the bureau specialists who were with him and who'd sat in during the attempted entrapment. Cowley established contact at the Boeing factory with agents from the FBI's Seattle office. After listening to their preliminary findings with the New York team at the UN, he realized almost at once, with a sinking feeling of renewed frustration, that neither was going to produce anything worthwhile. Cowley quickly warned the bureau director it didn't look like the breakthrough they had all hoped for.

It was almost an hour before they reassembled in Cowley's incident room office. He said at once, "Looks as if they just got into the UN and Boeing systems—the Trojan horse thing that Ashton told us about earlier—and simply relayed their photographs through two or three intermediary terminals. New York and Seattle reckon they'll be able to locate the intermediary computers—"

"Ashton's people already have," Pamela interrupted, although no longer with any excitement, knowing it was a cul-de-sac. "That's how they made the trace, going back from the Pentagon through each invaded system. It gave them numbers and passwords in sequence. Ashton's also already established, from user logs, that the intermediary links and the Boeing and UN numbers would have been on two of those phony antistatic bands they found attached to the feed cable of their computers. It's not going to take us anywhere—" Her head came up quickly, toward Danilov. "Hey! What mistake?"

Cowley looked at the two of them, bewildered. "What are you talking about?"

Danilov unpicked the staple holding together the hard copies of the digitized pictures of the Russian and American intelligence officers, carefully laying them out so the entire collage was presented at once. "What do you see?" he demanded.

"Well, I'll be . . . " Cowley smiled in instant awareness. "You think so?"

"Do I get to know the code we're talking here?" protested Pamela, still confused and fervently—angrily—wishing that she wasn't appearing so lacking in the presence of the two men.

"Look!" insisted Cowley. "What's different between the photographs? In every case?"

"Too obvious to see!" Pamela recognized at last.

"Every picture, of every American, is snatched: not always sharp. *Surveillance* photographs. Every Russian is an official personnel file print."

"You actually suggested a disaffected or disgruntled CIA officer might be involved," remembered Cowley.

"Or former KGB," said Danilov. "Which is where I think all these came from. From Lubyanka records, taken by someone who doesn't have a job anymore because of the scaling down of the service."

"As a result of the detente which the Watchmen are protesting against," offered Pamela, anxious to contribute.

"Or someone still there with access," suggested Cowley.

"And there's a way of finding out which," Danilov pointed out. "The CIA will know at once if all the officers exposed today are still on station. And if not, the date they were reassigned. And that date of reassignment will tell us how current these disclosures are. And a time frame against which to check KGB dismissal of officers with access to counterespionage archives."

"Haven't a lot of ex-KGB people crossed the street to join your mafias?" pressed Pamela.

"Most of them," Danilov admitted easily. "Which, with luck, will continue taking us in the right direction."

"What about the cooperation we'll need from the FSB who took over your external intelligence service?" asked Cowley.

"I don't know," Danilov further conceded. The reasons for his returning to Moscow were building, and he'd scarcely gotten over his arrival jet lag.

"All this interrupted us downstairs," reminded Pamela.

Danilov didn't respond at once. Then he said, "I hoped—we all hoped—there was just one source for what was coming out of Russia. What your forensics found most obviously gives us two, but like a lot of what emerged in Gorki and Kushino, it might not be as obvious as it seems."

"I can't quite reconcile that to what you've already told us," complained Pamela.

"The colonel in charge of organized crime investigation in Gorki drives a BMW he would need a lifetime's salary to buy," said Danilov. "When they realized I wasn't part of the system, I had the constant attendance of him and the major supposedly in charge of the actual case. When I got back to my hotel room after picking up a comparison missile at Plant 35 I snapped off a detonating pin—just as it was snapped off the missile that hit the UN building—and scraped off a lot of paint." He smiled bleakly. "It was switched: The one I took back to Moscow had both pins intact, but I'd kept the one I'd broken off and the paint with me. I detached a clasp off one of the mine casing samples I collected from Plant 43 at Kushino and scratched off more paint before they were delivered to the Foreign Ministry and from the ministry to your embassy. I kept that clasp and paint permanently with me, until I got here and personally gave them to Paul Lambert. From what Lambert said downstairs—what he *didn't* find in what came ahead of me supposedly from Plant 43—they were switched too."

"We talking crooked cops or official interference?" broke in Pamela.

"Crooked cops, certainly," said Danilov. "But there's a lot of people—some still in government and in ministries—who think communism worked better than the reforms that have bankrupted Russia: reduced it as a world power. And would be happy to return to the old ways and the old days. Who would, in fact, like the sort of confrontation the Watchmen seem to regret doesn't exist between Moscow and Washington anymore."

"Are you suggesting there might be a group in Russia linked to the Watchmen here?" demanded Cowley.

"I'm suggesting it wouldn't be difficult to find people there thinking the same way, even if they aren't definitely part of the same organization—certainly prepared to cooperate."

"Wouldn't that fit your theory of former KGB—succeeding FSB even—being involved in what we've just seen on all these screens?" wondered Pamela.

"Yes," agreed Danilov.

"So now we're into global conspiracies!" said Cowley.

"Put together what we know so far," urged Danilov. "It's not difficult to make that sort of pattern."

"I wish it were," said Cowley. "I'm not happy offering this to the director or the crisis committee, whether some parts fit or not. I want more before I throw this fox into the henhouse. Accepting the situation in Moscow—which I do—you think there's a chance in hell of your getting anywhere?"

"A lot further than I have already," promised Danilov. "And here's another theory, based on the autopsies on Viktor Nikov and Valeri Karpov. They were horrendously tortured, half drowned, revived, and tortured again before finally being drowned and shot. I think that was done as an example to others. And Karpov worked at Plant 43 at Kushino."

"So what's the theory?" Cowley frowned.

"Gangs—brigades—falling out or fighting," said Danilov. "I might have a way of infiltrating or exacerbating it."

"That could produce something," agreed Cowley.

"I'm not sure, though, that it would lead us to the connection we need between Russian suppliers and our unknown Watchmen," cautioned Danilov. He was glad he'd taken the chances he had, in Gorki and in Moscow. He was sure he had unsettling bombs of his own to detonate to see which way people ran for cover. His bigger uncertainty was his own crisis group—even some of its members, maybe.

The door into the office opened and one of the incident room agents said, "There's two guys downstairs think you want to talk to them. One's wearing an army camouflage jacket."

"Looks like we just hit another firewall," said Pamela.

In the FBI office in Albany Anne Stovey was thinking roughly the same thing about her overnight communication with Washington, although she accepted that the day's terrorist sensation would be occupying everybody at headquarters, to the exclusion of everything else.

Which it was. Her memorandum about missing pennies from banks had already been greeted with snorted derison and filed under nonaction miscellaneous by Al Beckinsdale, seconded on to the investigation from his normal role as agent in charge in Philadelphia.

Anne supposed she'd have to allow another day or two for a reaction, but she hoped it wouldn't be any longer than that. Ridiculous though it might seem, she instinctively felt it was a significant lead.

There was a temptation to leave Robert Standing's personal bank log-in on all the accounts he'd supplied to the General, but its being there had to look like Standing's carelessness, so Patrick Hollis restricted himself to three. It meant accessing them, of course, and because he'd downloaded the accounts when he'd chosen them, he was easily able to see that amounts as high as fifteen dollars had already been withdrawn. It wouldn't be long before the internal investigation began.

18

Pamela's firewall prediction *was* right, and the rest of their day, until the very end, continued in another downward spiral.

Brad Piltone wore his camouflage jacket and the same shaved haircut as his friend, Duke Lucas, who carried his shoulder satchel. Beneath their respectful demeanor—awe at actually being *in* the headquarters of the Federal Bureau of Investigation—there was the faintest indignation at the thought of their setting a bomb at the monument to America's first president. Piltone said the sons of bitches who'd do a thing like that needed punching out and he'd like to do it, and Cowley believed him. They were both twenty-eight and lived in the same street in San Antonio, Texas. Piltone was a linesman for the telephone company, Lucas was a body repairman in a garage. The jacket had belonged to Piltone's father who'd been killed in Pleiku, Vietnam (which Piltone called Nam) and whose name inscribed on the Constitution Gardens Memorial Wall was the main reason for their first, week-long trip to Washington. They'd gone to the memorial before going to the Washington Monument. Lucas had taken several photographs of Piltone pointing to his father's name on the camera he had in the satchel and which he willingly handed over for the film to be developed.

Pamela took it to the bureau laboratory and continued on to the incident room from where she called the FBI office in San Antonio. Agents there took only fifteen minutes to confirm both men's addresses, employment details, and that neither had any local police record. Lucas's film had four frames of Piltone in front of the Vietnam shrine—his father's name clearly visible in two—three from the top of the Washington Monument, and three of their descent on foot. One showed the half face of the man who hadn't yet been traced, the other partially the back—but nothing of the face—of the still-unknown woman, who was wearing jeans and a plaid shirt and had her dark hair in a pony tail. Neither man had seen anyone behave suspiciously as they walked down the monument stairs or remembered anything particular about the untraced man or woman or anyone else in their group.

"I wish I had," said Piltone, to his friend's nodded agreement. "It would have helped, wouldn't it?"

"Probably more than you can ever know," said Cowley.

Within an hour the last remaining unknown man called the FBI's Charleston, North Carolina, office to say he wasn't sure if he was one of the people for whom they were appealing. He was wearing the same windbreaker as in Duke Lucas's wired photograph when he arrived, as requested, at the local bureau building. Part of the identification procedure for the morning and afternoon descents had been to photograph everyone who had willingly come forward. Hans Bohl, the taxi driver son of a German immigrant, positively remembered eight from among his afternoon group. Prompted by Lucas's picture, he thought the pony-tailed girl had been around thirty years old and "not American," Hispanic or maybe Asian. He also recalled her bending to do something to her shoe as they came down, because he was at the back of the line and now he remembered her running to catch up. She'd been carrying in front of her the backpack that wasn't visible in Lucas's snapshot: He thought it had been green, with yellow buckles. Bohl spent a long time with a facial reconstruction technician trying electronically to re-create an image of the girl, which Cowley thought looked like the Disney animation of Pocahontas when it was wired down to Washington. Both Pamela and Danilov agreed it was unpublishable in a fresh appeal. Instead Cowley wired it, along with Lucas's partial picture, to every regional office to which identified tour participants had come forward. He sent incident room agents to the hotel and motel addresses of those still in Washington to get their impressions and improvements.

When he spoke, quite alone in Cowley's permanent office, to Georgi Chelyag in the Russian White House, Danilov claimed it was an American conclusion that the intelligence officer identification was from an official Russian source and that they hoped to establish a time frame from CIA records.

"Is there going to be an open accusation?" demanded the presidential aide at once.

"I don't know," admitted Danilov.

"Do you think it valid?"

Danilov smiled to himself. "Very much so."

"It would put even more pressure on us here."

"Deservedly, if it's true. What's the reaction to the disclosures?"

"There's already been a formal protest note from Beijing. Everyone named is being expelled. We'll do the same to their agents here, of course. And bring everyone back from everywhere else. What's Washington doing?"

"I don't know that, either," admitted Danilov.

"You learning enough from being there?" Chelyag demanded pointedly.

"I think so," said Danilov, who hadn't told the man of the American forensic findings. "The CIA reassignment check could produce an important lead."

"Leads here in Moscow, if Moscow is the source," said Chelyag. "If it does I want you back here, handling it personally."

"What about Chairman Kedrov?" Danilov asked uneasily. Once more in the firing line, he thought.

"I'll want you back here," insisted the chief of staff, refusing the question. "If we're the source of everything that's happening there, this is where you should be. Finding it."

How positive—and determined—would Georgi Chelyag be when he discovered it? wondered Danilov. The qualification was immediate: *If* he discovered it. It came to Danilov again when he got back to the incident room at virtually the same time that Cowley returned from briefing the FBI director. Pamela Darnley looked at the two men and said, "Immigration says it'll take at least another three days to find the visa applications for Viktor Nikolaevich Nikov. And neither Hertz nor Avis has come up with any rental in the Nikov or Eduard Kulik names. The only glimmer is that Ashton says he'll have some of the possible disgruntled Pentagon dismissals by tomorrow."

CIA Director John Butterworth was furious that the suggestion of the Internet's disclosure source—and possibly how to date it—had come from Leonard Ross and not from anyone within the counter-intelligence unit of his own agency. "It's certainly a simple check to make," he had to concede.

"Then let's make it," urged Frank Norton. "We could turn this back on the bastards! Could be our first break."

"Beijing has formally complained about American spying," said Henry Hartz.

"Posturing, for public consumption," dismissed Ross. "My people had already identified every Russian agent from Wisconsin Avenue on today's list. So will every counterespionage agency in every other country."

"I'd like to think my agency is more successful overseas," said Butterworth.

"You might like to think so," said Ross. "Surely what we all sat and watched this morning shows you're not."

"It's public consumption we're here to discuss," said the White House chief of staff. "What's our response?"

"We're in a bind with a Russian detective actually here, cooperating with the bureau," said Hartz. "What I've proposed to Moscow, through Ambassador Guliyev, is that instead of formal, tit-for-tat protests and expulsions they simply withdraw their people and we withdraw ours."

"That sounds the most practical," agreed Norton, although looking at Ross. "What we really need is something positive in the actual investigation."

"We've narrowed the Washington Monument list down to one suspect," said the FBI director. "By tomorrow we might even have an eyewitness compilation good enough for an electronic reproduction and a physical description."

"We could go with that now," Peter Prentice said quickly. Sonorously, as if reading a headline, he said, "Washington Monument Bomber Known!"

"Except that she isn't," deflated Ross.

"*She!*" echoed the media spokesman, who thought in headlines.

"We definitely don't want the fact that it's a woman made public, not until we've traced her," demanded Ross. "And it *is* still a process of elimination. The timer could have been set days before."

"How about 'closing in on the suspect'?" negotiated Prentice. " 'Dramatic breakthrough expected in twenty-four hours'?"

"It sounds good," encouraged Norton. "I like it."

"Definitely nothing about it being a woman," insisted Ross.

"Agreed," acceded Prentice, moving on. "I've checked the clips on this guy Danilov. He got quite a lot of space when he was here last time, when the joint investigation system was established, and there's been demands to know who the Russian investigator is after last night's statement. What about giving his name?"

"Not until I clear it with him and he gets Moscow's OK," Ross replied. "Cowley's not happy about the exposure he's already got, says it gets in the way. And let's not forget the personal danger."

"Let's keep it in mind, though?" persisted Prentice. "We don't feed the media every day, it's us they bite."

That night Pamela did go out to dinner with Cowley, as joint host to Dimitri Danilov. They went to a French restaurant on Georgetown's M Street, which the Russian remembered from before and declared the vodka better than he could get in Moscow. Cowley tried to pace his scotch in time with the other two—Pamela went straight to wine—but his glass was always empty first.

She jerked her head toward the waitress's station and said, "They've made you already."

"I know," said Cowley. He wondered when he'd be able to get to a barber to even up the freaky hairstyle. The waitress who recited that day's specials and took their order called Cowley by name.

"It's good to be anonymous," said Danilov.

"You going to tell the director no?" asked Cowley, who'd relayed Prentice's request to release Danilov's identity.

"There's no practical benefit, which would be the only reason to do so," said Danilov.

"Safer to stay anonymous," insisted Pamela. Difficult though the case was, she didn't imagine there were many investigators who would have dismissed the offer of personal publicity for the reason Danilov had just given.

Cowley was curious at the concern and was then immediately surprised at himself. Why shouldn't she be concerned, show some personal interest? It had been obvious for Pamela to accompany them, but Cowley wished it could have been just he and Danilov. That was an irritatingly unnecessary thought, too. There'd be time enough to renew the friendship—talk about other things—in the coming days and evenings.

But for the moment, in the noise-obscuring restaurant, the conversation was inevitably a continuation or reexamination of what had been discussed in the incident room. Almost at once Cowley wondered if he and Danilov really would have the time he'd imagined when the Russian recounted the exchange with Georgi Chelyag. If they didn't get an American address for Viktor Nikov in the next two or three days he guessed he'd have to go back to Moscow to examine more closely what was possible from Paul Lambert's forensic findings.

"It was a long way to come to confirm your own guys were cheating on you," Pamela said with her usual directness.

And probably settled a personal question, Danilov realized. He'd have to expose the corruption within his department, not fantasize about becoming part of it again. Which was all it had ever been, a fantasy. He was embarrassed he'd even allowed himself to think of it. "It was the only way scientifically to do it."

"You could still be obstructed," said Cowley.

"It might be more difficult for that to happen if you were with me," suggested Danilov.

Pamela was about to speak when her pager sounded. She rose from the table, checking the caller, and returned from the restaurant phone booth in seconds. She said, "Eduard Babkendovich Kulik rented a Lexus from Budget for five days. The address on the agreement is Bay View Avenue in Brooklyn." She smiled and added, "That well-known and much-loved ghetto for Russian emigres."

Patrick Hollis decided that the Internet disclosure of Russian and American intelligence agents was brilliant, as brilliant as using the

Web for all the other mockery. Better than committing—or trying to commit—any more atrocities. Would the General be doing it personally, or were there other nerds equally as good at surfing? There had to be a lot—a unit—to carry out the bank thefts. Would the General maintain the telephone-at-fixed-times division between everyone else that the man had insisted upon with him as being necessary to prevent their being discovered? Hollis smiled at the question, knowing of one man who was soon to be discovered.

19

It made operational sense to split up, Cowley and Danilov flying up to New York by bureau plane leaving Pamela Darnley in Washington to supervise the individual checks on the former Pentagon employees on the following day's promised list.

A bureau lawyer flew with them to make the application for a search warrant and wire tap on 69 Bay View Avenue to a judge roused by the Manhattan office and waiting in chambers by the time they got to the city. By then two agents from the Manhattan office had driven out to Brooklyn and made one pass by the house, a neglected clapboard owned by a property company in Trenton, New Jersey. No lights had been burning and it looked deserted. On Cowley's orders from the incoming plane from which he was coordinating everything, they hadn't attempted any neighbor inquiries but parked as inconspicuously as possible to wait and watch. The police commander of the local precinct was called at home, told of the bureau presence—and why—and asked that no foot or vehicle patrol interfere if they realized a surveillance was under way. The police chief said there weren't any foot patrols in the area but he'd alert traffic. If there was anything he could do, all Cowley had to do was ask.

The telephone company night-duty supervisor with whom Cowley discussed the telephone tap assured him that the billing records of calls into and from the Bay View Avenue house would be available within five minutes of the clerical staff arriving at 8:00 A.M. the following morning. The tap itself was installed by 10:30 that night, to be monitored around the clock by a rotating task force of eight operatives. Cowley took them with him on the plane, freeing up the Manhattan office for the twenty-four-hour surveillance for which Cowley asked for intentionally battered, Midwest registered and apparently much used communications and observation vehicles. They were to be driven up from Washington overnight, with the exception of the one available in New York, which Cowley rejected as too new and likely to attract attention in the neglected suburb. He also ordered six vehicles hired by the following morning—none four-door Fords, the too-recognizable federal pool choice—so that no regularly parked cars or vans would arouse any suspicion.

The largest room at the bureau's New York office on Third Avenue was turned into an incident room. On the first of the exhibit boards were pinned a blown-up street plan of Bay View Avenue and its surrounding waterfront roads. There also appeared photographs of Viktor Nikolaevich Nikov, one official militia arrest photograph of the man when he'd been alive, two more of him after his body had been recovered from the Moskva River.

At midnight Cowley demanded, "Anything not in place that should be at this stage?"

"I don't think so," said Danilov. He was, in fact, awed by the speed and completeness with which the entire operation had been organized in little more than the three hours since Pamela's paged alert in the Georgetown restaurant. At its fastest—and most unobstructed—Danilov couldn't have achieved it in Moscow in under two days. He'd also adjusted to the now-familiar curiosity at his presence on an FBI investigation, although he didn't think the Manhattan office had, not fully.

"Let's have a drink and make sure," said the American.

Their reservations were at the United Nations Plaza. Cowley had taken Danilov to the bar there on his earlier visits to show off its glass-and-chrome Americanism.

Danilov said, "There's a lot of this in Moscow now. And dollars—and crime—rule more than ever." This time he joined Cowley in scotch. It would be the first time he could speak properly to the American, and Danilov wanted to. It seemed absurd, but he supposed Cowley to be his only real friend.

"You really think Nikov's our man?" said Cowley. He really did intend a review of all they'd done as well as having a drink: The lift he was getting was more from the adrenaline than from the booze. Why was he even thinking about it anymore? His drinking was under control.

"Obviously part of it. It's part of *what* that I can't make up my mind about."

"We'll give it twenty-four hours before we exercise the search warrant," decided Cowley. "I'm hoping they're still there. Will lead us somewhere."

"Don't you intend picking them up if they are?"

"I want all of them, not just one or two. People this determined wouldn't give us the rest under questioning. They'd consider themselves prisoners of war: not even name, rank, and serial number."

"Dangerous strategy, if we lose them."

"Legally there's no proof—no suggestion even—of a crime committed here in America," Cowley pointed out. "Let's hope we get enough for you to pick up in Moscow. And that people don't get in the way."

"Nothing's gotten any better there. Worse maybe." Danilov hesitated, looking down into his drink. "The great anticorruption crusader stopped crusading. It was too much trouble."

Danilov wanted to talk, guessed Cowley. "What happened?"

"I destroyed them," Danilov declared, quietly, not looking at the other man. "The Chechen Brigade that ordered Kosov's car bombed, with Larissa in it, for not earning the money they were bribing him with. Created a war between them and an Ostankino Brigade and watched them picked off, one after the other, until all the hierarchy we knew about were killed." The Russian looked up at last. "Doesn't that tell you how it is in Moscow: letting them kill each other because I knew they'd bribe or murder their way out of any charge I legally brought against them!"

Cowley shrugged. "Not the first time a policeman's done that anywhere in the world. You couldn't have proved the guys in charge gave the order for Kosov to be killed."

"I wanted them dead," said Danilov. "Would have killed them myself if any I knew about hadn't been taken out."

"You sure about that?" Cowley queried, in disbelief.

"Quite sure," Danilov insisted at once, coming up from his drink again. "I'm still not satisfied. I broke the gang—destroyed the men responsible for Larissa being killed—but I never found the bull who actually planted the explosion."

"Stop it, Dimitri!" urged Cowley, although sympathetically. "You're going to eat yourself away with hate like that."

"Maybe I already have." The Russian shrugged. "After the gang war I gave up trying with anything else within the department or the militia. There's too many and too much for one man—a squad of men."

"It was a vengeance crusade. Not the same thing."

"I still stopped."

"So start again."

"Maybe." It wasn't important enough—wouldn't mean anything— to talk about the divorce from Olga. Danilov looked pointedly at Cowley's gesture for refills and said, "How are you managing?"

"OK," Cowley said at once. Not for the first time—unaware of Danilov's earlier, matching reflection—Cowley thought how odd it was that the only person aware of a problem that could end his career was a Russian who so few years ago would have been an enemy and considered the information a weapon. Instead of which Danilov had saved his career, smothering the sexual blackmail the Chechen gang had attempted during their last combined investigation in Moscow, posing him helplessly drunk to be photographed naked with a gymnastic hooker.

"You sure?"

"I haven't slipped for over a year," insisted Cowley. "I won't, not now. I'm clean. Well and truly."

"That's good."

"I think so. It's good to be able to talk like this, too." He paused, feeling he should offer something in exchange. "Pauline's getting married again."

"You ever hope to get back together?" Danilov asked presciently. A dark-haired, slightly built woman, he remembered. Not unlike Pamela Darnley.

"I'd thought about it after I got straight."

"What about her?"

"We saw each other a few times as friends. Which we still are. But I let her down a lot when I was drinking. One girl in particular, but there were others I threw in her face. I don't think she would ever have been able to believe I could change that much."

Danilov snorted a laugh. "Couple of maudlin old failures, aren't we?"

Cowley finished his drink, putting the empty glass down firmly on the table to make an unspoken statement. "No failure this time. There can't be."

"No, there can't be," agreed Danilov. To which of them was it more important to prove themselves *to* themselves? About the same, he guessed.

The Bay View Avenue clapboard remained empty throughout the night, which they knew before arriving at the bureau office because Cowley's instructions had been for him to be called the moment there was any movement. The telephone billing records arrived exactly at 8:05 A.M. They were in the name of an Arnie Orlenko.

"Orlenko's a Russian name," Cowley identified at once.

"And Arnie is an easy Americanization of Arseni," suggested Danilov.

"Wouldn't it be great to get a break just once?" mused Cowley.

"That only happens in detective novels," reminded Danilov.

Pamela Darnley assembled her intended task force controllers before 8:00 A.M., too, which was a mistake because the expected list hadn't arrived from the Pentagon. She started to fill the time briefing the eight male and two senior-grade female agents on what she knew from Manhattan, which was obviously very little. Even more obvious—she guessed to the rest of the incident room as well as to herself—was that she couldn't possibly have answered at least three

consecutive questions from Al Beckinsdale. Irritated, she acknowledged a fact she scarcely needed to remind herself about: that she
was in sole supervisory control of a specific task force, without the
physical authority of William Cowley, the case officer. She also acknowledged that Beckinsdale had to be at least fifteen years her
senior. What she judged to be the first opportunity to justify herself
to Leonard H. Ross, director of the Federal Bureau of Investigation,
this chauvinistic son of a bitch saw as showoff sex challenge time.
So be it.

"Case this important, I'm surprised we haven't been able to get
things faster from the Pentagon or Immigration, that being the only
lead we've got after all this time," persisted Beckinsdale, a fat man
who perspired and rarely fastened his collar or tightened his tie. He
lolled back in his chair, legs stretched out in front of him.

"The Pentagon computer was sabotaged, as you know," Pamela
said, evenly. "And Immigration's a physical check through God
knows how many individual pieces of paper."

"Can't imagine that would have been much reassurance to people
who'd lost family if the Lincoln bomb had gone off. Could have
killed a lot of people."

There was an uneasy shift from among the group facing her. One
agent said something Pamela couldn't hear to the man next to him,
who smiled.

Pamela said, "But it didn't go off. We prevented it."

"Bill Cowley prevented it."

The two female agents were in head-bent conversation now, looking annoyed.

"Prevented it brilliantly," agreed Pamela. "But you're right, Al.
It has taken a hell of a time—too long—and none of us is doing
anything at this very moment, sitting around here with our fingers
up our asses. So here's what I'd like you personally to do. I'd like
you to get over to Immigration and you tell the superintendent in
charge—his name's Zeke Proudfoot—you tell Zeke Proudfoot how
pissed off we all are that it's taking him and his people so long and
that's why you've been seconded to them, to put a burr under their
blanket. Let's get that address off the visa application by the end of
the day, OK?"

The two female agents were smiling now. None of the men were.

"Now let's just wait a moment here—" began the man.

"What, Al?" stopped Pamela.

"I thought we had a specific role here. A task force?"

"Of which I'm supervisor, like I'm deputy case officer of the entire investigation." Pamela smiled. "Which has got to be flexible. I'm open to persuasion and you've persuaded me. You give me a call around midday, tell me how you're getting on: If we're all out, leave a message with Terry Osnan. If I'm here I'll probably know the answers to those other questions you were asking earlier about Manhattan."

The man stood and remained staring at her for several moments before storming from the room. As the door slammed behind him Pamela said, "I mean it, about flexibility. Anyone else got any suggestions that might be useful?"

No one spoke.

"Here's how we'll do it then," resumed Pamela. "I'm assigning each of you your own four-person group. The Pentagon is providing the personnel records of everyone it's referring to us. The reason for their being let go is primary, obviously. Get everything checkable— Social Security number, medical details, everything and anything that is publicly traceable—you can use to find things they won't have volunteered. Lied about. Like criminal convictions. Any previous military record is a concentration, among civilians. A hidden court-martial, you win the kewpie doll. Membership in *all* organizations if we can find them. The guy—or girl—we're looking for is a computer freak, and all the steers we're getting from the experts is that computer freaks are arrogant, sure they can never be caught. Check out every one if you can for an Internet address, through the telephone company against the addresses the Pentagon will have. We've got ten manned terminals here in the incident room, all ready to be used. I don't want anyone confronted personally without our being able to catch the lie: We go in unprepared, they're not going to be there waiting for us when we go back a second time." She paused. "Anyone got any improvements on that?" Another pause. "And this time I *am* looking for input."

Again no one spoke.

"Let's find who we're looking for," Pamela concluded. She was on her own, in charge, and determined that everyone knew it, Leonard Ross most of all.

The couple—a dark-haired, big-busted girl of about twenty-five, the fair-haired, bull-chested man older, maybe thirty-five or even more—arrived at 69 Bay View Avenue by yellow cab at 10:45 A.M. They had luggage, a suit bag and a matching airline carry-on grip, in red tartan.

The photographer in the observation van got three exposures, one very good of the two of them full face. Another agent got the number of the cab and telephoned it to the first of the four backup cars parked the most convenient to the direction in which the taxi moved off. They identified it easily on Neptune Avenue but waited until it turned on to Copsey before pulling it in. The driver, a third-generation New York Italian, said he'd picked them up outside Terminal 2 at LaGuardia just before ten. They hadn't talked a lot—not at all to him, apart from giving him the address—but when they had it had been in English. The girl had an American accent but the guy hadn't, although he hadn't been able to pin it down. German, maybe: guttural like Germans speak, from the back of their throats. He couldn't positively remember anything they'd said. He thought there'd been a John or a Joe mentioned. Someone had been difficult: The girl had definitely called someone a son of a bitch. They hadn't seemed particularly close, not sitting together or holding hands or anything like that, like he would have done, a girl with tits like that. He hadn't seen—hadn't looked for—a wedding ring. The driver demanded to know who was going to pay for his time when they asked him to follow them in to the Manhattan office to make a formal statement. They told him they would.

The observation photographer's film was already there by then, ferried in for development and multiple printing by a second standby car. Within thirty minutes it led three other cars and ten agents back to Terminal 2 at LaGuardia. The third Brooklyn car had gone directly there the moment the cab driver named the airport, to hold as many of the terminal's morning and already landed airline staff as possible.

During the two-hour period before ten there had been eight long-haul arrivals and five shuttles each from Boston and Washington. The FBI squad divided, half trying to prevent as many crew as possible from leaving the terminal—discovering at once that four shuttle crews were already returning on commuter flights—the other five attempting to shortcut the search by obtaining passenger manifests. Which paid off. A Mr. and Mrs. A. Orlenko had boarded an American Airlines flight in Chicago that had originated in St. Louis, and the crew was still in the building, waiting to return to the Missouri hub as passengers.

A sharp-featured senior stewardess named Mary Ellen Burford identified the couple from the photograph as having occupied seats H7 and 8 in her section. Two agents immediately began naming and trying to locate from airline records people who sat in every surrounding seat. Two others tried but failed to get aboard the aircraft before the cleaners reached row H. They still lifted five different sets of fingerprints from the plastic meal trays and from the magazines in the front pockets.

Mr. and Mrs. Orlenko were just ordinary, unremarkable people, said Mary Ellen Burford. As far as she could remember, the woman had refused breakfast and slept most of the way, using eye shields. The man had drunk two spicy Bloody Marys. When the woman had been awake, they hadn't talked much. From her minimal contact—serving the drinks and breakfast to the man—she didn't remember any discernible accent.

In the bureau's Third Avenue office, from which Cowley was coordinating the investigation, the telephone records of 69 Bay View Avenue proved immediately productive and later curious. From the country and city codes, Danilov at once recognized the listed international calls—three outgoing, two incoming—as Russian. The two incoming and one outgoing were from the same number in Gorki. The other two outgoing were to Moscow. The last was dated two weeks before the attack on the United Nations.

When Danilov spoke to him, Yuri Pavin said he hoped to get names and addresses by the end of the day. He'd try, said the colonel, to bypass the Gorki militia and deal directly with the telephone authorities there. The wired photographs of the couple were already being run, with the names, against Moscow criminal records, and he wouldn't have any alternative but to go to Reztsov and Averin for a Gorki comparison. He was ready for the aircraft fingerprints, when they were wired.

"Seems to be a lot happening there," suggested Pavin.

"Routine but impressive," agreed Danilov.

"The White House has been on—Chelyag himself. Wants to hear from you. Belik, too."

"What's the reaction to the intelligence exposure?"

"I've not been included officially. Newspapers and television have picked up the hypocrisy line."

"The message of the Watchmen," Danilov pointed out. An NBC survey that morning had discovered quite a lot of similar comments, mostly in the Midwest but some from the South, too.

"At least people aren't dying."

"Yet."

Danilov hung up to find Cowley in deep discussion with the team leader supervising the trace of every American number on the Bay View Avenue listing. Cowley said, "Got ourselves a funny pattern."

"What?"

The American offered a photocopy of the bill. Marked on it were several blocks of numbers, alphabetically identified. "All outgoing from the Orlenko house. All to public booths. Chicago, Washington, New York, and Pittsburg. How'd you read that?"

Danilov stared down at the paper for several moments. "I can't."

"We've got to work it out somehow. There's a reason for it."

Danilov remained looking down at the list again. "Repetitions, in every city. Any chance of getting taps at their end?"

Cowley shook his head doubtfully. "Public lines. Judges would take a lot of persuading. Our tap on the exchange should give us two-way conversation. But we need to get into the house now—get some microphones installed to hear all that's said inside."

Danilov tapped the paper. "If this *is* caution, we'll need a lot ourselves to avoid them becoming nervous: certainly nothing as obvious as their telephone going out of order."

Cowley regarded the Russian with a pained but unoffended look. "I'm not going to be as obvious as that. Honest!"

The planning came close to overwhelming its objective; certainly Al Beckinsdale wasn't missed. Only nine names, accompanied by photographs and supplied biographies, arrived from the Pentagon. To Pamela Darnley's furious, lost-chance silence, the exasperated Carl Ashton said, "They wrecked our goddamned systems! I told you that!"

"How many do you guess we lost?" she demanded, the telephone seemingly heavy in her hand.

"Maybe another nine."

"*Maybe,*" Pamela repeated. "More than nine or less than nine?"

"Fifteen, certainly."

"So we're wasting our time, aren't we? They'd have taken their own guy out first, wouldn't they?"

"Maybe."

"Carl! You want to do me a favor, for fuck's sake stop saying "maybe" to everything I ask you! I want—I need!—a straight answer. What are the chances of the person we're looking for being among the nine we've got? Against the chances of whoever it was wiping themselves first?"

"Not good," conceded the Pentagon's computer security chief. "But it's possible. We put up firewalls in every system the first day—the first hour—we discovered the intrusion. The wiping would have been automatic, Trojan horse stuff, but it's got to be triggered by a command. The nine you've got were behind three separate firewalls. They'd have gone if we hadn't put the barriers up to stop the password getting through."

"What chances of getting any of the rest—finding them somewhere?"

"Nil. The severance pay idea doesn't work without a name. There is good news though. We've actually narrowed the penetration. It *is* low level: administration data, stationery ordering, car pool and parking records, stuff like that. Virtually no security risk at all. National Security Agency's clean, all our sensitive areas."

Pamela allowed another aching silence. "Carl! For the past week—using administration, stationery ordering, car pool and parking record computer access so unimportant it's hardly got a clearance—

some organization called the Watchmen has made the president, the Pentagon, the FBI, the CIA, and the State Department look absurd. They're responsible, at the last count I can remember, for the deaths, one way or another, of sixty-five people. They came close to killing hundreds more, the president among them. They've closed cities— and the government offices of this country—and cost millions of dollars. And we've most likely lost our chance of finding who the guy was, eating alongside you over there in the cafeteria, riding the elevator with you in the morning and at night. Now here's my question. Take your time. Let's get it right. I'd like you to tell me what you'd call *really* bad news and then what's stand-up-and-cheer good news? You think you can do that for me?"

"You pull wings off butterflies when you were a kid?" demanded the defeated man.

"And then pinned them in the display case while they were still alive," said Pamela, putting down the telephone.

She didn't wait for any comment—curious if there would have been any after the earlier confrontation with Beckinsdale—but began the assignment distribution with the warning that what they had was the best they were going to get but they still had to run it into the ground, hopeless though it might be.

Only when she went one by one through the biographies and reasons for each of the nine Pentagon dismissals did Pamela fully recognize just how hopeless the selection seemed.

Two security duty marines on the list had been dismissed for two separate offenses, both for brawling in Crystal City bars while in uniform. One civilian suffered a broken jaw. A civilian male chauffeur had tested positive for marijuana during a random drug test, as had a twenty-year-old girl in the secretarial pool in another random sweep. A storeman had been caught on a security camera, stealing stationery for which he was responsible. He also was unable to account for two computer terminals for which he'd signed receipts. A security camera had provided the main evidence against a female army sergeant found responsible for thefts over a year from a women's locker room. An army sergeant had been dismissed from the service and the Pentagon after being found guilty by a military tribunal of sexual harassment; four female employees under his command had complained. A female computer operator, judged incompetent, had been fired after her reference had been more thoroughly checked and found to be forged. Another chauffeur, a woman, had been replaced after twice being involved in accidents, one with a chief of staff general as a passenger.

Despite Pamela's earlier warning, one of the male team leaders who'd been amused at Beckinsdale's performance said, "Most of these wouldn't know a computer if it came up and bit them in the ass."

"How about one of those horny marines screwing some secretary and persuading her to get a few passwords he can hand on to someone who would know if a computer bit him in the ass!" demanded Pamela. "Or our light-fingered lady sergeant, forty-six and single according to her record, wanting to prove how good she is apart from in the sack to a younger stud? I told you: This is all we've got. I want everyone traced, the way I told you I want them traced, and by the end of every interview I want to know what their grandmothers had for breakfast the day they died."

Cowley had just been alerted that Mr. and Mrs. Arnie Orlenko had been photographed outside 69 Bay View Avenue, when Pamela spoke to him for the first time.

She said, "Seems like it's moving for you?"

"Too early to get excited," cautioned Cowley. "You told the director about the Pentagon?"

"What's to tell? It's a mess. End of story." She'd let him learn from others of her confrontation with Al Beckinsdale.

"Keep him informed," advised Cowley. "The Pentagon will try to get out from under. Don't get dumped on."

Pamela smiled to herself in the office off the incident room. "You spoken to him yet?"

"Briefly. I want to let these two run, follow them. Ross isn't so sure. I'm holding on to the argument that they haven't committed an offense in this country."

"What's Dimitri think of the Russian connection?"

"That it might fill in a blank, but that there's still too many."

Pamela said, "From the look of things you're likely to get more than me."

He said, "You never know."

Which was meant to be reassuring and turned out to be prophetic, although in the beginning it didn't appear so. Keeping strictly to their brief, the assigned teams tried first for everything possible from public sources and records on their individual targets. The most consistent—and quickest—discovery was that during the two-year period covered by the Pentagon list, only four had remained in the D.C. area. Pamela personally briefed the necessary local FBI offices as each new location was found, e-mailing everything they had at Pennsylvania Avenue so far with specific instructions to do nothing more than confirm the new residence until all possible background was complete.

The female army sergeant had a month to serve of her court-martial sentence in a stockade in Virginia. Her sexually harassing counterpart was an instructor in a health club in Baltimore, where he lived. The accident-prone chauffeur had a home in Frederick, where she now worked in a haberdashery shop. And according to the welfare agency details—she'd only left the Pentagon a month before and hadn't gotten another job—Roanne Harding, the references forger, had an apartment actually in D.C., off Lexington Place close to Stanton Square.

Almost at once it emerged that her Pentagon references weren't the only variable documents in Roanne Harding's thirty-two—or sometimes twenty-eight—year life. She was only Roanne Harding on her Pentagon personnel records, which gave her age at twenty-eight and her birthplace as Roanoke, Virginia. The date on her birth certificate issued there made her thirty-two and included the middle name of Roland, which had been her mother's maiden name. The computer-copied photograph accompanying the logged details of her Washington, D.C. driver's license matched the Afroed, light-skinned black woman whose matching digitized picture had been supplied by the Pentagon. The license photograph of Joan Roland, from the same address in Roanoke as that of her parents, was of a woman with the same facial features but with long, straight, almost shoulder-length hair. Duke Lucas's photograph of the girl who'd descended with them from the Washington Monument showed only the back of her head. Pamela decided at once the hair could be the same held back in a pony tail. She dispatched two agents to find Lucas and Piltone, she hoped at their motel, and three to Roanne Harding's Lexington Place address—with instructions to make discreet neighbor inquiries but not make any direct approach. She also got Leonard Ross's authority to brief a bureau lawyer for a search warrant and wire-tap application to a judge.

Piltone and Lucas were brought into the J. Edgar Hoover building and immediately—although separately, to avoid one influencing the other—identified the Roanoke picture of Joan Roland as the girl who'd been in their party.

The report from Lexington Place was that Roanne Harding hadn't been seen for at least a week. Her mailbox hadn't been cleared, and the janitor had had complaints of a gas leak smell from other residents.

William Cowley was patched from the Manhattan office to take part in the conference call discussion with Leonard Ross and Pamela Darnley. Cowley pleaded against immediately exercising the warrant, arguing that the woman was a more direct link to the Watchmen whom they should follow, not arrest. But he was overruled by the director, who insisted the publicity would have warned Roanne Harding and her group and that there was sufficient evidence to bring her in for questioning.

Pamela went to Lexington Place with the bomb disposal team and ordered no one clearing the apartment block and three immediately adjacent buildings to disclose it was an FBI operation before she authorized the entry. The door and its frame were X rayed for explosive devices or connections before the bureau locksmith even began to work, which he did with painstaking slowness and encased not only in protective armor but from behind a thicker, armored shield.

There was no booby trap but the smell of leaking gas was so overpowering that the coughs of two of the bomb disposal team turned into choking. Pamela, armored like the rest of the agents she was leading, wished they had nose clips. From the doorway where she was waiting, she could see that the main room had been trashed.

From another unseen room the bomb squad leader called: "It's not leaking gas. In here."

Roanne Harding was naked and on her back, legs splayed on a bed wrecked like the rest of the room. She had been shot twice in the head, and there were already maggots in the decomposing body.

In Brooklyn an electrical power cut followed at once by a surge totally distrupted the appliances in fifteen streets—including Bay View Avenue—in the Norton Point district. Deep freezers died, televisions blew, fire and burglar alarms went off, and a lot of home computers crashed.

The maintenance director of Con Ed said to Cowley, "You satisfied with that?"

"Completely," said Cowley.

"I wish to Christ I was," said the man. "And knew what it was all about."

"If you did you'd be proud of the help you've given," promised Cowley.

20

It was Dimitri Danilov's idea ("if they're worried and they're both Russian that's what they'll speak in front of strangers") to go into the Bay View Avenue house as part of a supposed repair team. There was confirmation from the surveillance vehicles that some genuine electric company vans were already in the Norton Point area and a lot of people were in the streets, Orlenko one of them, talking to neighbors on both sides. He'd hurried inside when a local news television crew had appeared. On the way to Brooklyn in the repair truck that was their necessary cover an enthusiastic professional linesman, Peter Townley, rehearsed Danilov and a bureau electronics technician, Jack Harrison. The technician, a lean-faced would-be stand-up comic, insisted he'd done this sort of thing a dozen times and didn't need to be told how to appear as if he knew what he was doing, because he did know: All he needed was for them to distract the people so he could get his bugs in "to make the place one great big sound box."

Townley said to Danilov, "You're supposed to be my supervisor, OK? I'm doing the work, you're making sure I do it right. I'll throw in a lot of technical crap means nothing. If I ask your opinion about something, I'll keep my left thumb on the piece of equipment or the wire it's the correct one to choose. How's that sound?"

"Fine," said Danilov.

They passed a proper repair truck on West 37th Street, and Danilov spotted the FBI surveillance vehicle parked not in Bay View itself but on the corner of Seagate. In Danilov's opinion the area wasn't so much rundown as wind- and sea-swept, fronting on to Gravesend Bay: great in the summer, not so good in winter. He wondered what rent the Trenton company was charging. Arnie Orlenko certainly didn't appear short of money: according to the LaGuardia taxi driver, he'd dropped a $20 tip on top of the fare.

They parked visibly but some way away from 69, and they didn't go to it immediately. A man in the first house they called at said he'd already talked to his lawyer and was getting all his appliances checked by an independent firm and intended to sue for any that couldn't be put right. A woman in the next said what could they expect, so close to all those Coney Island illuminations. It shouldn't be allowed.

Arnie Orlenko opened the door. He was wearing the same shirt and jeans of his morning arrival but his hair was wet and he was barefoot. There was a heavy smell of cologne. His accent was quite pronounced when he asked what the hell was going on. Danilov, who'd studied linguistics at the university with the original intention of using a natural talent before deciding on a police career, guessed English was a comparatively new language for the man. Danilov easily adopted his supervisory role. It was, he apologized, a major breakdown they didn't yet know the reason for. Although the power was restored, they needed to check for line faults to prevent it happening again. The whole area had been affected and so far a cause hadn't been found.

The woman met them in the hallway. She'd changed from the arrival picture. The bulging breasts were straining a halter top that left her midriff bare, and she wore tight, knee-length shorts. Like the man, she was barefoot. The blond hair was a bubbled explosion around a surprisingly freckled, ready-to-smile face. She wasn't smiling now. She said, "Everything's gone. The television went bang."

Danilov decided there was no foreign intonation in the voice. She smelled freshly showered, too. Conscious of the FBI man's need, he said to Townley, "Maybe we could specifically look at the TV, try to help."

"You're the boss, so if it's all right with you," said the man. "Right now or shall I look at the boxes first?"

"I can do the boxes," offered Harrison, on cue. To Orlenko he said, "You want to show me where they are?"

The living room had an odor of a place stale and unused and was untidy, which was useful because Danilov immediately recognized the Cyrillic print of two discarded newspapers as well as the English of that morning's *Chicago Sun Times*. As he passed, he saw the Russian newspaper was *Moskovsky Vedomosti*. He was aware that Orlenko had remained with Harrison. So far there was none of the hoped-for Russian between the man and the woman and after hearing her speak Danilov didn't expect it.

Townley had the back off one of the largest television sets Danilov had ever seen—much larger than his indulgence at Petrovka—with separate speakers on either side. The woman was leaning across from the other side, showing an appreciative Townley a deep cleavage valley.

Townley unclipped a circuit board and went through the charade of testing it with a power meter. He said, "This could be it." He allowed himself a cleavage glance and called, "Sir. Sir, can I see you? And Jack . . . ?"

The FBI man, carrying his toolbox, came in just moments after Orlenko. Townley gestured to Harrison with the microchip board and said, "You think this could be it? It doesn't give a reading." To Orlenko he said, "You get the set locally or in the city? You might have to go back to them."

"Rented locally," said the man.

Harrison almost had his head inside the set. Emerging, he said to Danilov, "Don't you always say go for the most obvious?"

"Always," agreed Danilov, following the lead.

"Then why don't we check the plug fuse?" Harrison shuffled on his knees to the wall socket, dragging his box, and within seconds turned triumphantly holding up a blackened fuse. "And I've got another one with me! Why don't you put the circuit board back, Pete?"

Danilov said, "That's a helluva set: never seen one that big. Shouldn't you check for overload?"

"Not a bad idea," agreed the FBI man. "I'll do that. Wouldn't mind you running over the boxes. I think they're all right but we need to be sure, don't we?"

"Can you show us?" Danilov asked the hovering Orlenko.

The electrical boxes were in a closet by the stairs, and it was a tight squeeze for two of them, with an attentive Orlenko wedged half in as well, to see what they were doing. Danilov responded to a lot of left-thumb guidance from Townley, who attached a variety of meters to a variety of wires for the needles to rise and fall impressively.

"Looks like Jack did all he had to here," said Townley. "This where all the boxes are as far as you know?"

"As far as I know," said Orlenko, looking back in the direction of the living room in which he'd left Harrison. "This going to take long?"

"Gotta be sure," said Townley. "No point in rushing it and getting it wrong."

It was fifteen minutes before they returned to the main room overlooking the bay. Neither Harrison nor the women were there, but there were voices from the kitchen. Townley said, "Better see if Jack needs a hand."

As Orlenko moved to follow, Danilov pointed to the pulled apart *Moskovsky/Vedomosti* and said, "Foreign, right? What's the language?"

Orlenko stopped uncertainly, aware Danilov wasn't going with them. "Russian." He looked back and forth between Danilov and the kitchen. There was a laugh from the woman.

"You from there!" demanded Danilov, emphasizing the interest. "How long in this country?"

"Coupla years," said the man.

"Is it as bad as they say it is? Nothing in the shops, lotta crime?"

"It's better here. What's your accent?"

"German," said the linguistically able Danilov, prepared and able to speak it if the other man spoke it, too, and tried to test him. "Came here as a kid but my parents spoke it at home. Useful. Gave me a second language. Your English is good."

"How much longer you going to be?"

"Almost through now. Always wanted to go to Russia. What part you from?"

"Moscow." There was an impatience in his voice and he looked again toward the kitchen.

"You think I should go to Moscow? See for myself?"

Orlenko made a half move toward the other voices. "Your choice. What are your guys doing in there?"

"Their job," said Danilov. "Company don't like things like this happening. Bad for customer relations."

"It's certainly pissed me off."

The woman led the other two men back into the room, smiling. "Jack fixed the toaster and the stove."

"Just fuses," said the bureau technician. "You were lucky."

"What about bedrooms?" demanded Danilov, wanting to see as much as he could. "Anything electric there? Blankets? TV?"

"TV and it's OK," said Harrison. "Mary showed me."

"I'd better cast an eye over it," said Danilov, maintaining his supposed role. Everyone trailed behind him, like a tour party, into the kitchen, where he feigned an examination of Harrison's appliance guidance. There were dirty breakfast plates and two cups in the sink, but Danilov decided the couple still had a lot to learn from Olga. He wondered how far Olga had gotten with her intended divorce settlement. He wasn't looking forward to returning to Moscow.

"You finished?" Orlenko demanded truculently.

"Not quite," said Danilov. The suit bag and carry-on were on the unused bed. "You going on a trip?"

"You want to hurry up and get this over with?" insisted Orlenko. "I'm busy."

"Sorry," said Danilov. If the woman had been able to speak Russian, there'd have been an exchange by now.

Silently he completed the examination performance and said on the doorstep they were sorry to have troubled them. Orlenko said he was sorry, too, and remained at the door, watching them. They hadn't intended to leave immediately anyway. They went through a similar charade in three more properties in the avenue, so their van could remain in sight for almost another hour, before Townley summoned a regular relief team and made a show of handing over the check. Orlenko had gone back inside but Danilov was sure the man was watching from behind the net-curtained window.

On their way back into Manhattan Harrison said, "If you guys had spent another five minutes in that closet I'd have had Mary giving me head. Did you ever see tits like that?"

"No," Townley said. "Should have been cast in stone."

"What *did* you get?" asked Danilov, impatient at the relief-in-the-front-line camaraderie.

"A fly farts in that place, we hear it," promised Harrison. "And a lot more besides. . . . Hey, we made a great team, the three of us. We should all be in movies—the new Marx Brothers." He erupted into laughter at his own joke, prodding Danilov. "Get it, you being a Russian. Marx Brothers, like . . . ?"

"I got it," Danilov said soberly. "It's very good: very funny."

Pamela argued essential continuity to have Paul Lambert lead the forensic team, which was enlarged by the inclusion of a D.C. police pathologist, a bald doctor who only just tiptoed beyond being a dwarf and seemed prepared to confront anyone. He had, fortunately, brought nose clips, which everyone was now wearing: having come close to losing her lunch—as well as her credibility in front of men waiting for her to throw up—Pamela would have marked her cross on a ballot paper to elect the man president. The pathologist scarcely had to bend to remove the bullet-split pillow that had been put over Roanne Harding's face. There were two bullet wounds, one in the center of the forehead, a second that had destroyed her left eye. Both sockets were maggot filled.

Lambert surveyed the room and said, "I'm not happy with this."

"I shouldn't think Roanne Harding is, either," said Pamela. "What's your point?"

"What do you see?" demanded the scientific examiner.

"Dead woman, maybe sexually violated. Apartment turned over, searching for something. . . ." She paused. "There *is* something," she said.

Lambert called to one of his team, "What's the count?"

"One," the fingerprint expert called back. "Hers, I'd guess. No way of getting anything from her, decomposed like that. But her prints are on the personnel file we got from the Pentagon."

The boyish forensic head raised a warning finger at the approach of the police surgeon and said to the man, "How's it look to you?"

"Intrusion," said the pathologist at once. "Guy breaks in to an apartment he thinks is unoccupied, starts to toss it. Girl wakes up, naked. He takes the diversion, rapes her, shoots her through that pillow to deaden the sound. Zips his fly, takes what else he wants. Goes home to watch the *Letterman* show. I'd have said it was all in a night's work."

"Except for what?" pressed Lambert.

"For you guys being here. This should be PD, not bureau. She the girl from the Washington Monument you guys been looking for?"

Pamela didn't answer. Instead, waving her arm around the destroyed room, she said to Lambert, "This is neat, isn't it! Tidy trashing?"

Lambert smiled broadly. "Right! It's my job to go through tossed rooms. This stuff has been *put* down."

Pamela said, "Might help if the Watchmen thought we'd bought it."

"Give us a little time, at least," agreed Lambert.

She said, "I'll get the director to talk personally with Commissioner Frost. Have it released as a homicide not connected with us. The surrounding apartments were cleared because the danger was a gas explosion. No one was identifiably Bureau."

Pamela was aware of Lambert shifting beside her and the doctor looking at her questioningly. She said, "Let's give it a try, at least!"

The doctor shrugged. "All I'm responsible for are the medical findings."

"Which are?" pressed Pamela.

"Decomposition has stages," said the man. "From the maggot samples I've taken, forensic entomologists will be able to date the death to within a day or two. I've taken vaginal samples but there won't be any semen left, for DNA. No fingernail debris, either: There aren't any finger ends."

"We got a long way to go," said Lambert, exasperated.

"We always did," said Pamela. She hoped Lambert would spread the word on how she'd recognized the intended deception.

Jack Harrison most definitely had turned 69 Bay View Avenue, Brooklyn, into a sound box. And just as definitely got a lot more besides. Arnie Orlenko had married Mary in a drive-through ceremony in Las Vegas eighteen months earlier—cajoling from her the actual, traceable month, May, by telling her that he'd arranged his divorce on the anniversary of his wedding to his first wife—and that she and Arnie had been in Chicago for the previous two weeks, seeing import-export business friends of Arnie's. She hadn't liked Chicago, her first visit: The wind was too cold, coming off the lake, even in summer. She didn't like where they lived in Brooklyn for the same reason. They'd move, maybe. Arnie was always talking deals, about moving on. If they did move, she hoped it wouldn't be to Chicago.

"And she slipped me her number!" declared the ebullient FBI technician. "As if I didn't have it already."

"Let's test," suggested Cowley, pressing the replay button for what had been recorded during their return journey from Brooklyn.

"Brooklyn's out, for fuck's sake! What are you worrying about?" Mary's voice.

"The day we get back?" Orlenko.

"What's that got to do with it?"

"That's what I mean."

"I know cops. Can smell cops. They were dumb-assed electricians probably jerking off right now from the memory of the titty show I gave them."

"What did you tell that guy you were with most of the time?"

"Small talk. Nothing! But if they had been cops, you'd have rung bells with your tight-assed number."

"Show me exactly where he went! What he did."

"He fixed the things that broke, for fuck's sake. Put funny things on wires and stuff, made needles jump." There was the sound of movement, people walking. "Now what the fuck are you doing!"

"Looking."

"For what?"

"Won't find it!" intruded Jack Harrison.

"I don't know." Orlenko.

"That's why he won't find it," said Harrison, talking to the ceiling.

The noise of scratching and squeaking, as screws were unscrewed, came loudly into the Manhattan office.

"So!" demanded the woman.

"Looks all right."

"The fucking trucks are still driving up and down the street, for Christ's sake! You seen too many movies."

"What's the time?"

"Ten after four."

"I'm going to nap before we go out."

"You wanna fuck? Fool around a little?"

"I wanna nap."

"Just offering value for money," she said.

"Jesus! The waste!" Harrison moaned.

"Las Vegas found the registration," said Cowley. "Mary's full name is Mary Jo James. Born in Montana. Orlenko is Arseni Yanovich Orlenko, born—wait for it—in Gorki, June 10, 1958. Job description on the marriage certificate is engineer. Got a match for Mary Jo from a forefinger print on one of the in-flight magazines from the flight. She's got three convictions for prostitution, two for the larceny of her Johns' wallets. Served three months in a correctional institute in Billings five years ago. Nothing recorded since then."

"Time I called Moscow," said Danilov.

Pavin reminded him that the fingerprint comparison had to be made mechanically and visually, against a named offender, because none of their records was computerized. Having Orlenko's full name might help, but nothing had shown against any of the Orlenko's so far checked.

The positive connection came from elsewhere. The Gorki number from which two calls had been made to 69 Bay View Avenue and to which one had been returned was a garage rented by Viktor Nikolaevich Nikov. The Moscow number to which the two other outgoing international calls had been made from Bay View Avenue was to a newly opened restaurant named the Golden Hussar on Pereulok Vorotnikovskij, off the inner ring road. There was no intelligence of its having been adopted by any known organized crime brigade.

"We've got our link!" Cowley exclaimed in quiet triumph.

"*A* link," cautioned Danilov. "Leading where?"

"To as far as it goes," said the American.

The sound of renewed movement started in the Bay View clapboard at 5:20 P.M. Orlenko woke up irritable, complained Mary Jo should have called him earlier, and insisted he wasn't taking the car, even though it was a long way to walk.

"Easier to see if we're followed, going on foot."

"For Christ's sake, how long we going to go on with this shit!"

"Until I say so."

"Can we go to the Odessa after you get your call? I like the blinis there. And I'm hungry."

"Maybe."

Forewarned, Cowley alerted the surveillance van and the agents in the four backup vehicles against any pursuit on foot. Working from the exhibit board map, he moved one car close to the junction with West 37 and Neptune and put another nearer to the Coney Island strip, at the join with Atlantic Avenue. Both vehicles, in constant radio contact with each other as well as with Manhattan, were able to see Orlenko's constant turning, to check for followers.

The observer in the Atlantic Avenue car said, "From the look of things, Mary Jo's giving him hell for making her walk."

There were so many people along Surf Avenue and Riegelmann

Boardwalk that there was no risk of Orlenko identifying any pursuit. There was still thirty minutes left of happy hour in the bar that Orlenko headed for so obviously that two agents from the Atlantic Avenue car, now on foot, were able to get in ahead of the Russian. The third man alerted the field teams to the location of the targets, so the surveillance could be rotated, which was an unfortunate professional precaution because it was a topless bar called Bare Necessities.

Orlenko drank beer, Mary Jo vodka martinis, straight up with a twist. They didn't talk a lot. At precisely 6:25 he left her alone at a table by the stage on which a disinterested girl with a G-string and unmoving, rock-solid breasts was gyrating to "Simply the Best" and walked to the pay phone booth. He went in but didn't attempt a call. At precisely 6:30 the telephone rang. The observers later reported that he appeared to listen more than he talked. The conversation lasted two minutes and thirty-five seconds. Orlenko didn't bother to sit when he returned to their table but stood, waiting for his wife to finish her martini. He left his beer unfinished.

In the Manhattan office Cowley said, "It's a pattern. But of what?"

As he spoke the fax machine began relaying what turned out to be the corporate record material on the Trenton, New Jersey, company that owned 69 Bay View Avenue.

"Here's more to go with it," said an agent, taking the sheets as they came off the machine. "Two of the listed directors have got Russian-sounding names."

Anne Stovey decided to give it one more day before approaching Washington again. They'd probably laughed at her like everyone else. Foul-mouthed her, perhaps, for wasting their time. So what? She'd responded to an all-stations request and she deserved a reply, even if it was to go to hell and stop bothering them. Another written message or a phone call? No hurry. She had twenty-four hours to make up her mind.

21

In the bedroom closet Pamela Darnley discovered the green back-pack with yellow buckles in which Lambert was later to isolate Sem-tex traces. It was when she was using the apartment telephone to obtain its billing records that she found the cassette had been removed from the answering machine. In a locked bureau drawer that one of Lambert's technicians easily opened with a pick lock there was a series of photographs showing a child that could have been Roanne Harding in the arms of a man—quickly identified by the Roanoke team as her father, Albert Johnson Harding. It was posed in front of what appeared to be a shrine to Malcolm X. In two the child, whom Pamela guessed to have been no more than four, was aping her smiling father's clenched-first, Black Power salute.

Pamela used the apartment telephone for a second time to run the check on bureau records, from which Albert Johnson Harding emerged a civil rights activist in the early 1960s. So did a woman in the photographs, whose name on FBI files was Angela Jane Roland. There was no criminal history against either.

There was no activist or criminal listing for the girl herself, under the name of Roanne Roland Harding or Joan Roland. She had lived in Lexington Place for only four months. Two of her immediate neighbors claimed not to have seen her at all since she'd moved in and the two others hardly ever. Roanne Harding had made no effort to be friendly—positively ignoring them when they had encountered her—and neither could remember her ever having visitors. The Realtor traced that first day admitted not having checked the woman's tenancy references, from a credit rating agency and a law firm, both in Chicago and both, upon immediate check, proving to be forged. Roanne Harding had always paid her rent, in cash, on its due date and had given the required two months' notice to terminate the tenancy three weeks earlier. There were no personal letters, credit card receipts, or bank statements anywhere in the apartment—or in her handbag found in the same closet as the backpack, with a discarded and empty wallet alongside as apparent evidence of robbery. The uncleared mailbox only contained advertising fliers and junk mail. There were no old newspapers, magazines, or any books. The clothes closet contained just two business suits and a dress, which had been left undisturbed in the phony ransacking. There were only three pairs of briefs and no bra, despite the girl being comparatively large busted. There was no computer or TV—nor obvious evidence of there having been either—in the apartment.

William Cowley had just learned of Arseni Orlenko's 6:30 P.M. public telephone conversation in the Bare Necessities when Pamela came on the line from the J. Edgar Hoover incident room.

"Sounds like you've had a busy day, too," he said after they'd exchanged accounts.

"More productive for you than for me," said Pamela. "*Everything* about Lexington Place is phony. She didn't live there, not properly. It was like a hotel room. Nothing personal. The photographs were the only things."

"You think they were planted intentionally to be found?"

"Could be," accepted Pamela, wishing she'd offered the suggestion.

"You've done well in a few hours," praised Cowley. "Realizing the place hadn't really been trashed but getting it logged as an unconnected homicide was brilliant."

"Like to know what was possibly on that answering machine tape."

"And I'd like to have heard Orlenko's incoming call at the titty bar," said Pamela. "We've put a tap on Roanne's line and another tape in the machine, just in case there's a call. I've got a field team in Roanoke, which is our only positive lead, although mother and father died two years ago within six months of each other. I'm on my way to the Pentagon to talk to her work supervisor." She hesitated. "The bastards are still so far ahead they're out of sight."

"There's dust on the horizon," said Cowley, gauging her depression.

"I can't see it," said Pamela.

The evening rush was easing by the time Pamela crossed the re-opened Arlington Bridge to pick up the Pentagon feed road. Carl Ashton was waiting for her at the gate, as promised, and accepted without comment her insistence that she shouldn't be introduced as bureau but as D.C. homicide.

"Looks like we got our intruder after all," said Ashton. The self-satisfaction was obvious after all the criticism.

"I wish it told me more," said Pamela. That's what she needed, to deduce or find something that the director would recognize as taking the case substantially forward. "You sure we've got everything you had on her?"

"You already asked me that," reminded the security chief. "I checked, as I promised I would. You've got it all."

"You spoke to her supervisor?"

Ashton shook his head. "Only told her Roanne's been murdered. Her name's Bella Atkins and she's pissed being kept late."

"Doesn't sound like she's sad about it."

"Decide for yourself," suggested the man.

Bella Atkins was a commanding, severely dressed woman with heavy features and graying hair. She was very obviously unmoved at learning that someone she'd known, albeit slightly, had been killed. She didn't ask how it had happened.

"Shouldn't have got past the entry qualification," insisted the woman, as if it had some relevance. They were in Ashton's office, overlooking one of the inner courtyards.

"How did she?" asked Pamela. It was hardly a homicide detective's question, but it didn't seem to occur to the other woman.

"You tell me," said the supervisor indignantly, looking demandingly at the computer security chief. "She wasn't right from the start. We're working current Microsoft and she said she was only used to old systems, 3.1 stuff. So allowances were made when she first arrived. I had doubts by the end of the second week."

"You're in the ordering division. Supplies, stationery, office equipment," Pamela said. "Did she have access to other departments?"

"Nowhere beyond her own room," said the woman. "But she

moved around that enough. I guessed she was asking for advice from other operators."

Instead of which she was busily attaching phony antistatic bands, Pamela thought. "You say she didn't really know what she was doing, working a terminal?"

"No, ma'am. She was hopeless. She hardly knew anything more than absolute basics: scarcely more than how to turn on and off, touch type—she was as slow as hell, needing to look at the keyboard all the time—and what a mouse was."

"Are we talking about the *Pentagon?*" demanded Pamela, looking in disbelief at Carl Ashton.

"I filed a complaint at the end of those two weeks," said the woman. "The process, against suit for wrongful dismissal, took another two and a half months. Would you believe she'd actually learned to type faster in that time!"

"What about people she met here? Made friends with?"

"She didn't. Some of the other girls got to calling her "lonesome." It was the same with guys, too. She was kinda pretty but as far as I know never agreed to date, not once. Never tried to share a table in the cafeteria or want to share hers with anybody else. Left promptly on time, catching the first staff bus into D.C." Bella Atkins looked pointedly at her watch. "Even the last one's gone now. Lucky I brought the car."

"Always the first bus?" qualified Pamela. "Never volunteered to work late?"

"Asked her twice. Refused twice."

"You had a girl who didn't know her job, didn't *want* to know her job, and didn't want to make friends—acquaintances even—with anyone. Didn't she strike you as one hell of an unusual girl?"

"Put it in my first complaint," insisted Bella Atkins. "I know the sensitivity of this place, even though we're low security. Suggested there should be a psychological assessment."

Ashton nodded and said, "Bella did just that."

And I'm only hearing it now, thought Pamela. She was supposed to be D.C. homicide, not FBI, she remembered. "That in the stuff you let me have earlier?"

"Personnel decided to let her go instead. Putting that on file might have affected her getting another job," said the man.

Even though it was supposed to be a straight murder inquiry, it would be logical to ask about the computer intrusion, Pamela decided. "What do you think about the hacking?"

Again Bella looked accusingly at the security man. "Hardly surprising, when you think someone like Roanne Harding got in, is it?"

"It occur to you she might have been somehow involved?"

"Roanne! Don't be ridiculous! I'm department supervisor because there's nothing I don't know about computers or can't make them do, including jump through blazing hoops. And *I* didn't even know there were such things as phony antistatic bands. A bunch of terrorists want to infiltrate the Pentagon—the *Pentagon*, for God's sake!—they're going to choose an expert, not someone as dumb as she was."

She wouldn't have thought so, either, conceded Pamela. But there was no benefit in discussing it further with this woman. "Doesn't look as if you can help me, then?"

"Wish I could," said the department head, letting a little stiffness ease away. "What actually happened?"

"Looks like a break-in that went wrong," recited Pamela, sticking to the cover story. "Roanne was in bed, naked, asleep probably. Intruder rapes then shoots her."

The older woman shuddered. "Poor kid."

Who was part of a conspiracy to slaughter hundreds by blowing up the Lincoln Memorial, thought Pamela. "Yeah," she said. "Poor kid."

As Ashton walked her to her car, Pamela said, "So what about your worm or whatever you call your intruder?"

"We're satisfied it was low level. Every VDU server has been swept. Twenty using hard disks have been replaced."

"So you're clean?"

Ashton paused as they reached Pamela's car. "We hope so, inside here. But they got a hell of a lot from those goddamned bands."

"What about your employment procedures?"

"There won't be another Roanne Harding," insisted Ashton.

"One was enough," said Pamela.

Paul Lambert came on to her car phone as she was returning over the Arlington Bridge. "Didn't know if you were coming back in," said the man. "Thought you'd like to know we got a positive match with the fingerprints on Roanne Harding's Pentagon file and several of the supposed antistatic bands. She was our girl, all right."

"*Was*," Pamela said heavily. So much for Bella Atkins's doubt. But then what she appeared to have done didn't amount to much more than wrapping a Band-Aid around a cut finger.

Waiting for Pamela at the J. Edgar Hoover building were the results of the CIA check suggested by Dimitri Danilov, which dated the intelligence agent photos published by the Watchmen to be almost exactly a year old: In the same month—May—there'd been a rotation of officers wrongly identified in the computer revelations as still being in Tel Aviv, Canberra, and Tokyo. Also on her incident room desk, marked for her personal attention, were the billing records of Roanne Harding's Lexington Place telephone. From Manhattan Cowley had had transmitted the complete account of that day's investigation there, so Terry Osnan could maintain up-to-date dossiers.

It was when she was preparing her own up-to-date file on Roanne Harding that Pamela stopped, although not immediately knowing why, just that there was a connection. For several moments she remained staring down, unfocused, at everything spread out on the desk in front of her and the adjoining evidence table. Comparisons. What was there—what could there be?—to compare with what had happened that day in Manhattan and here, in Washington? She couldn't miss it again: *Wouldn't* miss it again. What then? Where? A common denominator. It had to be a common denominator. And then she saw it and found what had registered, initially subconsciously, and felt the satisfied warmth.

Pamela put both sheets of paper on the desk in front of her, marking each, deciding as she did so against showing her excitement by first telephoning Cowley. Instead she had both faxed, timing her call to Manhattan to coincide with their arrival in the New York incident room.

"Roanne Harding made four telephone calls from Lexington Place to the same public booth in Chicago as Arseni Orlenko from Bay View Avenue," Pamela announced triumphantly.

"And all on the same days," agreed Cowley, looking at the telephone accounts.

Four hours later—at precisely 2:30 A.M. Moscow time—the projectile was fired from a car that paused briefly on Ulitza Chaykovskovo, near the U.S. Embassy. Part of the building is hedged by barbed-and mesh wire netting. The missile ricocheted off the metal thicket, deflected completely from the legation toward the boxlike diplomatic compound at the rear. The deputy cultural attaché, his wife, and their twin eight-year-old daughters were killed instantly. So flimsily constructed was the Russian-built complex that the rocket's explosion destroyed two adjoining apartments, killing a further five Americans.

Dimitri Danilov was already awake when Yuri Pavin telephoned him at the UN Plaza Hotel in Manhattan. When he recognized his deputy's voice Danilov cut him off and said, "I've already heard: I need to know everything you've got!"

"Mikhail Vasilevich Osipov got blown up last night. Three others died. But that could have waited until later."

"What?" demanded Danilov.

Pavin said, "Olga's dead."

22

It was the Washington political carousel, finally and inevitably spinning up to the White House, rather than the more practical other-side-of-the-world logistics that created the twenty-four-hour hiatus. So frenetic was the activity that followed the attack upon the US Embassy in Moscow that none of those in the far from calm eye of the storm were aware of either a respite or even a delay. And that was minimized as much as possible by Cowley's task force being allocated *Air Force Two* for the eventual flight to Moscow.

Some of the most outspoken critics declared from the very beginning that it was a diplomatic mistake for the U.S. ambassador in Moscow, with the personal authority of the president, to invoke international protocol in declaring the embassy and its compound technically U.S. territory and therefore beyond any Russian jurisdiction or entry. By so doing he adopted the same stance as the Chinese after the destruction of its United Nations quarters.

Deciding—and announcing—that stance after a series of White House and State Department meetings was the major cause for the delay in taking not just Cowley and Danilov as well as a full forensic team headed by Paul Lambert but also Secretary of State Henry Hartz. The aircraft was fitting transportation in which to return with sufficient state solemnity the coffins of the dead to their grieving relatives and a carefully modulated, unsteady-voiced president waiting at an Andrews Air Force base ceremony.

Lost in the Russian fury at the implied distrust of Moscow's ability successfully to investigate the embassy attack was that by coming to them, Hartz overcame the still-unresolved Russian reluctance to appear the supplicant in meetings at secretary of state to foreign minister level. Also lost was the attempt to assuage the America-in-charge impression by having Dimitri Danilov publicly identified for the first time in the carefully choreographed arrival photo opportunity.

What wasn't anticipated but perhaps should have been and what stoked the angry Russian resentment were the additional, although nonviolent, Watchmen attacks.

There were two, both equally humiliating to Washington and Moscow.

One of the first U.S. presidential decisions was that no details should be publicly released of the missile that wrecked the U.S. compound until the arrival of American investigators. Even before the team boarded the aircraft, the terrorists posted, not just on supposedly swept U.S. government sites but on Russian government screens as well the full specifications of the American-manufactured 66mm single-shot M72 A2s rocket, including its weight and the fact that it was shoulder-fired from a throwaway telescopic launcher. Within four hours of Washington's diplomatic insistence of U.S. jurisdiction over the embassy—when the investigatory team was only just airborne—the second Watchmen statement was posted on official American and Russian websites.

It read:

> SO RUSSIA SURRENDERS ITSELF TO BECOME A LICKSPIT-
> TLE COLONY OF AMERICAN IMPERIALISM. TWO WHITE
> HOUSES BUT ONLY ONE PRESIDENT.

On Russian screens it was in Cyrillic. And there was a computer graphic of the American Stars and Stripes fluttering from the Kremlin flagstaff.

By the time *Air Force Two* landed at Sheremet'yevo Airport, the American president had made another television address to the nation. In his anxiety to reassure the country after more American deaths he fueled the diplomatic outrage by allowing the assumption from his renewed arrest pledge that any trial would be under American, not Russian law. His attempt to ridicule the already posted Watchmen declarations was equally bad, almost an ambiguous confirmation rather than his intended denial.

Henry Hartz's arrival statement was more carefully prepared—he had winced at the president's efforts, patched into the aircraft television during the flight. In it he insisted that the investigation remained totally mutual and jointly cooperative. Danilov stood self-consciously next to him. But by the time the American cavalcade reached the heavily guarded embassy, the banner-carrying imperialism protesters were estimated at more than two hundred and growing. In the Duma, Russia's lower-house parliament, a motion was tabled criticizing the Russian president for allowing an American investigation in the heart of the Russian capital. Its proposer talked openly of possible impeachment.

Dimitri Danilov did not travel in to the city with the American party but was met, by arrangement, at Sheremet'yevo by Yuri Pavin.

"Who have you assigned to the Osipov killing?" Danilov demanded as their car moved off.

"It happened during Mizin's shift. He began before I was told. I left him heading the investigation until you got back."

"There seem to be a lot of coincidences involving Ashot Yefimovich Mizin."

"You want me to take him off it?"

"No. Leave it as it is. All the forensic samples sent to America were switched."

Pavin nodded. "Mizin used a pool car to deliver the warhead to the Foreign Ministry. I checked the garage log. He was out for three hours. I could walk it in fifteen."

"What about Gorki?"

"Reztsov says he's got a definite suspect, from Plant 35. I told him I'd go if there was an arrest."

"If there is one we both will," decided Danilov.

The burly deputy said, "Chelyag's demanding to see you immediately at the White House. But there's time to stop at the Kliniceskaja Bolnica. Olga's body is still there."

Danilov guessed that despite the apparent acceptance—and sympathy—it had always been difficult for his deeply religious deputy to condone the situation with Larissa. Now the man would despise him further for imagining he'd maintained a married relationship with Olga—that he might even have known about the pregnancy before going to America.

The obstetrician, a young, fresh-faced man whose hair was so blond he appeared scarcely to have any, also despised him. There was no handshake, and the man said at once, "I opposed the termination. Your wife said you were insistent."

"We hadn't spoken at sufficient length about it," said Danilov.

"That was obvious."

"What was the cause?"

"Septecemia. It's easier to get ill than get well in Russian hospitals. Once the infection began to spread we couldn't stop it."

"How pregnant was she?"

The doctor regarded him curiously. "Did you speak at *all*?"

"How pregnant?" Danilov repeated.

"Nine weeks. It should have been quite straightforward." He

paused heavily. "As a proper birth would have been."

Whose baby would it have been? wondered Danilov. Igor, the hairdresser, who kept his own bouffant a better color than Olga's? Or someone else he didn't know about? *I want to try again,* Danilov remembered. And then *I mean you and me. Try to put our marriage back together.* She would have known then: hoped for them to make love, which they hadn't done for years, to be able to claim he was the father. Which he was going to allow the few who needed to know to believe. For whose benefit? Olga's, who might not even have known herself? Or his, to hide in death just how much and for how long he'd been cuckolded in life? For Olga, he decided. He had an abrupt recollection of Naina Karpov and her words echoed in his mind, too. *I don't have anywhere else. Anyone else.* He said, "Did Olga come alone?"

"Yes. I told her there was still a lot of time—that she could wait until you got back—but she said she didn't know how long that would be. And that you wouldn't change your mind."

Danilov ignored the open contempt. Poor, lonely Olga. It didn't matter—hadn't mattered for too long—how much she'd lied and cheated and whored, she hadn't deserved, no one deserved, to die all alone. "No one came to see her? Inquired about her?"

"No one," said the doctor. "It would have been a boy."

Danilov nodded, not knowing what to say.

"There are formalities. Identification."

"Yes," accepted Danilov.

He walked, unspeaking, with the other man to the mortuary. Olga's frozen pallor made her multihued hair look even worse than when she'd been alive. He nodded and said, "Yes," and then, "I'll make the arrangements. Get the body collected."

"As soon as possible," urged the man.

"By tomorrow," promised Danilov. "And thank you for what you did."

"It shouldn't have happened. Any of it."

"Far too many things happen that shouldn't," said Danilov.

"It's my job to try to prevent them," said the younger man.

"Mine, too," said Danilov.

———

The American party divided immediately inside the embassy, Henry Hartz being hurriedly escorted to the waiting ambassador. The Moscow-based FBI agent, Barry Martlew, was also waiting and led Cowley, along with Lambert's team, to the shattered compound.

At Lambert's insistence everything had been left, except the bodies. The scientist patiently pointed out the shrapnel from the explosion and said, "The bastards were right, of course. It's an A2 version of the M72, bazooka adaptation."

"I didn't doubt it would be," Cowley said wearily.

From the dead children's bedroom one of the team called, "Got a piece with markings here. Code designation is Mojave."

"There's an arms dump there," Lambert said to Cowley.

"Hardly significant," Cowley said dismissively. "Had a check run after the Watchmen identification. Seems we gave these things out like candy at an orphanage party, officially and unofficially. Equipped Israel with them, and the CIA supplied them to the mujadeen during the Russian war in Afghanistan. And to the Kosovo Liberation Army in Yugoslavia. It could have come from anywhere."

"That'll be lost in the fine detail," predicted Lambert. "The only fact that matters is that it's American."

Cowley nodded toward a burn-blackened piece of metal. "You likely to get anything from that?"

Lambert shook his head. "I doubt it." He turned to Martlew, a heavily bespectacled, unsmiling man. "The launcher for this thing *is* throwaway. We got it?"

Martlew shifted uncomfortably. "Seems the Russian militia guard outside the embassy picked it up."

Lambert groaned audibly. "They still got it?"

Martlew said, "They refused to hand it over after our announcement of jurisdiction."

"Great!" said Lambert.

"There could be a lot of other forensic stuff apart from this we'll need your help on," said Cowley.

Dimitri Danilov had just finished setting out the differences between the Russian and American forensic findings in the White House office of Georgi Chelyag. For several moments the presidential aide remained silent. Then he said, "It would be deliberate, of course. The tampering as well as everything else."

"It has to be," said Danilov. He was not sure how much of a risk he'd taken detailing all the obstruction and misdirection he'd encountered. But if he had any chance of breaking through it, he needed authority at the highest level. He would have liked the conversation to have been protectively recorded but none of it had been.

"The Americans know about it?"

"The intended forensic deception, certainly."

"Which they could make public totally to justify their carrying out their own embassy investigation?" accepted the politically astute chief of staff.

"Yes," Danilov agreed.

"Might they?"

Danilov thought the question too sweeping. "Not at my level," he restricted himself.

"I can't risk their doing it at mine," mused Chelyag, thinking aloud. He shook his head at a further awareness. "Or risk purging—arresting as they should be arrested—the militia people who've done what they have to you. If it become public that we had—as it could too easily do—it would be even more justification for America."

"Yes," agreed Danilov, intrigued by a different sort of mental deduction.

"So to the Duma—and the communists—we'll appear to confirm their accusations of willingly being subservient to Washington."

"I don't know the answer to that," said Danilov. Could he get an answer to another uncertainty?

"I'll find one," said the politician.

Danilov acknowledged that he'd fully committed himself, telling Georgi Chelyag everything he knew and what he suspected from it. He might as well take things as far as he could. He asked, "There was a lot of initial confusion at the Washington embassy?"

The humorless man allowed himself the briefest of smiles. "I needed to test others. It was obvious you'd come on to me as you did. It was the only thing you could do."

"Test for what?" persisted Danilov.

"Loyalty. Attitudes," the political aide said generally.

"And?" questioned Danilov. He'd known from the beginning he was the puppet, so it would be ridiculous to be irritated by the manipulation. Instead he had to use it in any self-protective way he could, as he was now sure that there was some official involvement in the switching of the warhead evidence.

"There's a lot of support for the old ways over the new."

Surprising honesty, decided Danilov. "How does it affect the investigation?"

"You have *my* total support," declared Chelyag. "And there'll be no more shared sessions with anyone else."

"I am officially answerable to Interior Minister Belik," reminded Danilov. "I've been summoned immediately after this."

"It's countermanded by presidential authority. Which Belik will be told," said the other man. "The same authority will get—through me—the personnel dismissals and changes you believe important in the old and new intelligence service."

He was, Danilov recognized, very definitely between a rock and a hard place.

Pamela Darnley was excited. Unable quite yet to believe how the opportunity had finally come about. Sufficient that it had. No point—no reason—for any analysis. She'd had time to learn from William Cowley's leadership. Now, as she'd told him at the very beginning, she was going to run with her chance. Prove herself as head of the American part of the investigation. Alone. In total, unshared control. She wasn't frightened or unsure. She knew she could do it. Even knew how she was going to do it, surprised that it hadn't occurred to anyone else, Cowley or Danilov in particular.

She hadn't actually been sidelined in all the frenzied activity of the preceding twenty-four hours, but one of the first decisions had been that she should remain in Washington and she'd seized it, reanalyzing, reassessing, rereading all there was, seeking the opening. When she'd realized it she'd almost laughed aloud, it was so obvious.

She also had put some hope on the search for Viktor Nikolaevich Nikov's visa application and the American address he'd listed on it, but when it had finally been located by Immigration it had been 69 Bay View Avenue, Brooklyn. She got no satisfaction from telling the even more resentfully hostile Al Beckingsdale they not only already had it but that it was wired. She didn't want anyone claiming any credit for what she'd worked out.

Pamela was actually refining her intended use of the Orlenko monitor when Terry Osnan appeared at her office door and said, "My number three at Albany—a good agent—is on line three: says she thinks she knows how it's all being financed."

"What's the lead?" demanded Danilov.

"The possible supplier of the warhead," said Reztsov, from Gorki.

"You've got a positive identity?"

"We expect to in the next couple of days. And there's a possibility of a connection with the Zotin Brigade."

"I'll come for an arrest," Danilov told the man. "Tell me when you're ready to move."

23

There was every career-advancing reason for Pamela Darnley to go up to Albany rather than to bring Anne Stovey to headquarters, totally emptying the bureau office there being among the considerations, but impatient though she was, Pamela determined that everything had to have its priority, and Chicago—and her agonizingly simple suggestion—dominated that. But the Albany message now gave her possibly two breaks. In addition, she had guaranteed access—visible, in-his-face recognition—to the director, to ensure all the credit was properly accorded.

The diligent Terry Osnan had followed the bureau's evidence collation procedure to the letter, and that required the initialed identity of every examining agent recorded against each incoming item and message. Because of this it took only minutes to identify Al Beckingsdale as the incident room agent who had discarded Anne

Stovey's original alert and caused the delay in responding to it.

Despite being acting case officer, Pamela's grade was insufficient to dismiss Beckingsdale. She continued strictly to follow procedure, verbally warning the blustering man before handing him his required copy of her written request for Leonard Ross instantly to remove the Pittsburgh agent in charge from the investigation.

Her summons came within the hour.

Leonard Ross didn't rise at her entry. He remained behind the desk upon which her memorandum was laid out and disappointed her by appearing to ignore the link between the Chicago telephone number and both Roanne Harding and Arseni Orlenko. Instead, he asked her to refresh his memory about the original bank theft. He genuinely wanted only that—unlike Pamela, who'd needed a full account from Anne Stovey in Albany—because the first "penny-pinching" case had come to trial soon after Ross had been elevated to the New York circuit bench.

"We've got four separate banks with God knows how many branches admitting it's happened—or *is* happening—to them," concluded Pamela. "That isn't coincidence."

"I don't think so, either," agreed the director. "It could answer one of the many outstanding unknowns."

"So could putting a tap on the public phone in Chicago," urged Pamela, eager to get the conversation back to her agenda. "We've got an even more definite connection there."

"All sorts of legal difficulties, state *and* federal," cautioned the man.

So he hadn't realized the other way! "And practical, from the sheer volume of what will have to be listened to," accepted Pamela, taking her time now. "But surely we've got to do it: *try* to do it."

"I'll discuss it with the attorney general," Ross said. "Talk to the White House about getting the Illinois governor involved, if necessary. You heard anything from Moscow?"

She sure as hell wasn't going to lose her big moment talking about Moscow, from which she hadn't yet heard anyway! "Chicago's a street phone. We could avoid involving anyone at all apart from ourselves by putting it under permanent bureau surveillance. We know every call that's made from Brooklyn, as soon as a number is dialed. The moment we identify Chicago, we alert the observation team and pick up whoever's at the Chicago end."

Ross regarded her without speaking for several moments. Then he said, "Nothing's more obscure than the obvious."

What the hell was that, recognition or praise or what! Cautiously—knowing Cowley's intention to let the Brooklyn couple remain free, to guide them further toward the Watchmen—she said: "We'd have to pick up the Orlenkos, too. But they would have served their purpose, giving us whoever it is in Chicago. Who's clearly farther up the ladder, dealing with them *and* Roanne Harding."

"Who was the Pentagon infiltrator and now a murder victim, providing just cause to arrest them," completed the former judge. "I like the way you're bringing this together."

Acknowledgment, at last! "Thank you. I'll talk to New York and Chicago before going up to Albany." And get my name on the detailed instruction briefings, she thought. "Agent Stovey isn't convinced the banks' security people are taking it seriously enough."

"Make them," Ross demanded shortly. "What about Beckinsdale not taking it seriously enough?"

"You have my memorandum," said Pamela, equally brief. All the necessary details were there. It would be wrong—impolitic—for her to offer any comment or opinion.

Once more the man remained momentarily silent. "You're making an impressive contribution. It's being noted."

"Thank you," Pamela said again.

Terry Osnan was waiting to follow her into the side office when Pamela got back. Al Beckinsdale wasn't in the incident room.

Osnan said, "You really play hardball."

"Come on, Terry!"

"Mistakes happen."

"Not on my watch, not if I can help it. He's been a pain in the ass from the start. I want team play, not resentment."

"Anne could be wrong."

"If it's a blowout it still doesn't alter the fact that he didn't react properly."

"OK," capitulated Osnan.

"What about Anne Stovey?" demanded Pamela. "She get things wrong very often?"

"No," said the woman's station chief. "Hardly ever."

"Good," said Pamela. "It'll be a welcome change."

There was immediate female recognition between the two women.

Pamela Darnley identified the graying, sensibly dressed, sensibly shod Anne Stovey as a state capital stalwart, probably born within twenty miles of the office in which she'd remained, by choice, throughout her entire career. One framed photograph on the woman's desk in the office they'd just left showed her as part of a family group of husband and son. The other had father and son proudly posing with pole and line and a fish half the size of the boy's arm.

Anne Stovey saw the sveltely dressed, tightly coiffed, seriously bespectacled Pamela Darnley as an interested-in-nothing-but-a-career woman prepared to run up the downward escalator in her total determination to get to the top. In the fifteen years that she had served in Albany, Anne had seen the attitude in a lot of male agents—for whose families she felt sorry—but never in a female one. She was curious about the experience to come.

"You've done well," Pamela praised at once. "I'll see it's properly noted. The delay was ours, in Washington. That's been noted, too."

"I appreciate it," said Anne, who didn't, particularly. Anne was driving, Pamela twisted toward her in the passenger seat. "It could still be nothing: normal bank discrepancies, as they all say."

"And it could be everything, hidden behind reluctance to admit they're either fallible or can be robbed or both."

A little more of Anne's remaining uncertainty went. "How's Terry getting on?"

"He's doing a great job, too. Got the incident room running like an engine."

"You close to anything?"

"Not close enough." But they would be, soon enough. The Chicago street phone on Lake Shore Drive and 14th Boulevard had been under total surveillance for the last two hours, the control car permanently linked to the Manhattan office to be notified the moment a call was initiated from Brooklyn. Pamela had already decided to go up to Chicago when the arrest was made to conduct the interrogation personally. She'd packed enough clothes to go on from Albany if it happened soon enough. The instructions were for her to be told on her cell phone the moment a call was made.

"Maybe this will get us somewhere."

"If it's there, I'll find it," said Pamela. If she established the finance route as well as the Chicago arrest, virtually everything would be down to her. She wished she'd said "we" instead of "I." The other woman appeared not to have noticed.

When she'd called to arrange the second meeting, Anne Stovey had been referred to Christopher Jackson, the senior vice president of Clarence Snelling's bank, not the security chief, Hank Hewitt. Hewitt emerged from the building with a second man when Anne pulled into the slot reserved for them. Pamela had already decided that the involvement of a vice president was intriguing. So, too, was the effusive greeting before they were led into the building through a side door, avoiding the crowded main hall. Jackson was an urbane, white-haired man whom Pamela guessed spent more time on golf courses, encouraging customers, than in his bank office, luxurious though this one was. In the other man's presence, Hewitt's blinking was even more pronounced.

Jackson said, "I want to thank you for bringing this to the bank's notice.

"I thought it was a customer, Clarence Snelling, who did that," said Pamela. There was no purpose in—or time for—verbal niceties. She didn't like the man or his unctuous attitude.

"Quite so," agreed Jackson, smiling. "The extent, I mean."

He hadn't meant to say that, Pamela knew. "That's what we've come here to learn about, the extent."

Jackson looked at his security chief, shaking his head, before saying, "Our internal auditors would have picked it up, of course."

"Why haven't they already?" asked Pamela.

"No books balance out with total accuracy at the end of any day's trading," the bank executive lectured patiently. "Some days there's a shortfall, sometimes a slight excess. That's why we *have* internal audits. As I think Hank explained, shortfalls are made good. It's the way it works."

Anne Stovey said, "Are you telling us you still think these differences are the few cents you're accustomed to being short in normal bank business?"

"We've no reason to think otherwise, have we?" Jackson's question was addressed to his security official.

"I don't believe so," Hewitt said dutifully.

"How many cases have you discovered in addition to Mr. Snelling?" demanded the local agent.

"A few. Again only pennies. The sort of differences Mr. Jackson is talking about."

Pamela allowed the silence, hoping Anne wouldn't break it. Only when the security man shifted uncomfortably did she say, "Mr. Hewitt—Hank—I'm not getting the feeling you're offering us the cooperation we should expect. *How* many? And *how* much?"

"Just twenty-eight dollars in total. From thirty accounts," said Hewitt, a faint note of triumph in his voice.

"Nothing to worry about?" coaxed Pamela, at once.

"On the contrary, we consider it too high," insisted Jackson. "That's why I've already thanked you for bringing it to our attention. We're taking the proper steps, I can assure you."

"Doing what?" persisted Pamela.

"The internal audit I talked about."

"You familiar with the famous case of the teller here in New York State who stole a million in pennies, nickels, and dimes?" said Anne.

Jackson's smile was vaguely patronizing. "Of course."

"You don't think history could be repeating itself?" broke in Pamela. She curbed her anger, convinced now of the way the bank, in the person of the smoothly persuading Christopher Jackson, imagined the matter was going to be resolved. As the other banks doubtless imagined.

"Of course not."

"Hank, when Anne first spoke to you a few days ago, she asked you to check other branches?"

"Yes?"

"Did you?"

"The larger ones in town." He stopped himself from looking toward Jackson.

"How many?"

"Three."

"What's the shortfall in each?"

"The highest is forty dollars."

"The other two?"

"Twenty-three and thirty-one."

She'd had enough condescension, Pamela decided: enough of men thinking they were superior because she couldn't piss up the wall like they could. "Mr. Jackson. You're the victim of a clever thief. You know it and we know. We also know that you intend making up the pennies he embezzles, hoping to find him in an internal audit and fire him. That way there's no publicity and your bank customers don't lose confidence and move their accounts elsewhere. But there's a problem you're not aware of, not yet. You haven't got a clue how long he's been doing it and how much money he's stolen from you alone. But it *isn't* from you alone. We're checking out losses in three other banks—two your primary competitors—with branches all over the state and links with other financial institutions beyond the state. . . ." She paused, expecting an attempted contradiction that didn't come. "The FBI has a highly trained and expert fraud division. I want to move investigators and auditors into all the regional offices that handle accounts from your smaller branches, which I intend asking all other involved banks to agree to my doing. I would like that to be at your—and their—invitation, but if it's not I can—and will—do it by court order. Which unfortunately could result in your bank being publicly named, something I do not seek nor want to do."

"All you've told me about is, I repeat, normal end-of-day shortages!" protested the senior vice president. "I certainly don't intend giving that permission. In fact, I think it is something my board will have to take it up with Washington."

"I'd like you to do that as soon as possible," said Pamela. "It's urgent. I still have the other banks to meet."

"Urgent! The FBI considers the loss of exactly one hundred four-teen dollars, in nickels and dimes, urgent!"

"If the losses are far greater than that and are being used to finance even bigger crime."

"What evidence have you got for that!"

"That's what we want to find, evidence. And why we want your cooperation," said Pamela. "Why don't we have my director talk to your chairman right away? Save a lot of time."

Jackson tilted his head to one side, frowning. "You're quite serious, aren't you? Imagine you can make that happen?"

"Quite serious," agreed Pamela. "Can I use that phone?"

Patrick Hollis was, as usual, drinking his coffee alone in the cafeteria when Gilliam Carling, a junior programmer in his loans and securities division, came in, smiling expectantly for someone she knew. When she only found Hollis the smile faded but she still came over, needing someone in her excitement.

"Guess what?"

"What?"

"The director of the Federal Bureau of Investigation has been talking personally to the chairman at Main Street! How about that!"

"I don't believe you," said Hollis. It was like an operation, without anesthetic, his stomach being gouged out.

"And there were two agents there in person," insisted the girl, pleased with his shocked reaction.

"It can't be right."

"Janet, my roommate, works on the switchboard there, for Christ's sake! She put the call through from Jackson's office."

"What about?"

"She didn't *listen*! Just handled the call. But it must be important, big, mustn't it?"

"Yes," agreed Hollis. "I suppose it must."

When they were eventually reunited late that night—after Henry Hartz, with the Russian foreign minister beside him at a televised press conference, identified the embassy missile to be American—William Cowley and Dimitri Danilov tried to compile their list of priorities. Like Pamela Darnley earlier in Washington, they decided the first had to be the Moscow connection to the house—or rather the telephone—at 69 Bay View Avenue, Brooklyn.

Which was the Golden Hussar on Pereulok Vorotnikovskij. No American calls had been made to or from it after those listed on the Brooklyn billing records. Cowley and Danilov reluctantly judged they were too publicly recognizable to visit it personally. Yuri Pavin was told to take his surprised wife out to dinner and the FBI's Moscow-based Barry Martlew had to miss the departure party of the Internet-identified CIA station chief to remain outside with one of the newly arrived Washington forensic team, photographing customers.

Photographs took up a lot of their discussion. There was no criminal records trace of Arseni Yanovich Orlenko. Danilov had brought with him the FBI's New Jersey surveillance pictures of Vyacheslav Fedorovich Kabanov and Ivan Gavrilovich Guzov, the two Russian directors of the company that owned the Brooklyn house.

"Will the personnel photographs of the KGB people who were let go within the CIA's timeframe have been kept?" wondered Cowley. They were in the bar of the Savoy, where Cowley was staying.

"I don't know."

"Be a bitch if they haven't." Cowley was relieved to be in Moscow, spared overcrowded committee discussions that got nowhere. "What about tying up all the ends you left hanging when you came to Washington?"

"Anatoli Lasin, certainly. Even if he gives me a name, I don't think we're able to move against anyone else here in Moscow yet. I think we should go to Gorki."

"So do I," agreed the America. "As soon as possible." He hesitated, knowing he had to say it. "I'm sorry about Olga."

"Yes," said Danilov.

Cowley waited but Danilov didn't say anything more.

The Kirovskaya apartment would be as she left it going to the Kliniceskaja Bolnica for the abortion, Danilov realized. And as he would have expected it to be, if she had still been alive. There were discarded clothes, even underwear, on the living room couch and the bed was unmade, a jumbled heap of blankets and sheets. The familiar stalagmite of unwashed dishes jutted from the kitchen sink.

He found an old cardboard suitcase with only one clasp that worked and heaped all the living room trash into it before adding the rest of Olga's clothes from the closet and drawers in the bedroom, surprised there was so much because she'd always seemed to wear the same things, day after day. He found a separate supermarket bag for her four pairs of shoes, all of which needed repairing.

He realized for the first time that nowhere in the apartment were there photographs of them when they first married—when he at least had been trying to make it work—and found three, including a wedding picture, him in his militia uniform, in a box at the bottom of the bedroom closet. Their marriage certificate was there, too. He left it all as it was and carried everything that had belonged to his wife out into the entrance hall, convenient for the following day.

He should, he supposed, tell her friends about the funeral, but the only one he could remember—knew even—was Irena. And Igor, the hairdresser. He decided to clean up the mess in the kitchen first.

24

The expected but unwelcome call from Interior Minister Nikolai Belik came within minutes of Danilov's arrival at Petrovka the following day.

"I have been told, ordered, that I am now directly responsible to—and operating under—presidential authority." Danilov thought his remark sounded like the schoolboy-to-schoolmaster recitation it was.

"I am your superior," said Belik.

"A point I made to Georgi Chelyag. I was told you would be advised of this changed arrangement." This wasn't so much the sort of loose end he and Cowley had talked about the previous night— more of a rope with which he could so very easily hang himself.

"I am not challenging any new arrangement. You are, additionally, to report to me."

"I have not been told that by the White House."

"You don't have to be told by the White House. *I'm* telling you."

Danilov felt the telephone becoming slippery in his hand. "That's not my understanding—my orders—from the White House."

"They're your orders from me. Which you will follow."

Damned if he did—and Georgi Chelyag found out—and damned if he didn't, by the man who *was* his ultimate superior and whose instructions were unquestionable. Why was the situation—the cliché itself—so constantly the same? "I think the matter needs to be clarified."

"There is nothing whatsoever you need to clarify with anyone—any other authority—except me. Nor will you." Belik paused. "Although perhaps, Dimitri Ivanovich, your proper political understanding is lacking. Which is something else upon which you will take guidance from me and no one else."

Danilov's curiosity began to grow. "Perhaps I would benefit from some political clarification."

The pause this time was longer, the man at the other end making a decision or maybe arranging his words. "There is going to be widespread political fallout at the very highest level over this. The Duma resolution is not an empty gesture."

"I realize that," encouraged Danilov. It had been spelled out at the first of their joint meetings, which, like Cowley, he was glad was over.

"Then perhaps you should also realize that it's important you give support to those upon whom you—and your future—most depend."

The telephone was still greasy in his hand but Danilov felt a physical chill. Unformed thoughts—awarenesses—jostled in his mind, very much indeed needing to be clarified, put in their proper order. It had been Belik's voice when he'd lifted the telephone. So the call hadn't come through either the ministry or militia switchboard. Officially it wasn't taking place. Belik was positively ordering him not to approach Georgi Chelyag. Uncertain, then, despite the heavy-handed innuendo about choosing the right side. So which *was* the right side? The traditionalists in whose camp he'd already put Belik, along with the security chief and the deputy defense minister? Or the supposedly reforming presidential faction increasingly threatened by the communist-dominated—and therefore traditional— Duma? It was very much a matter for political judgment. Danilov's problem was reaching it.

"Dimitri Ivanovich?" prompted Belik.

"I appreciate your guidance," Danilov said emptily, needing more time. Uncertain, he thought again. It hardly mattered whether this telephone conversation was deniable or not. Nikolai Mikhailovich Belik was taking an astonishing—desperate—risk approaching him like this, scarcely bothering anymore with clumsy innuendo.

"It's important that you take it," said the politician. "I accept you already have arranged commitments with the Americans. What's a good time in your schedule for us to meet?"

The word "desperate" echoed in Danilov's mind again. No longer demanding. Accommodating. "I'll need to get back to you."

There was yet another pause, the longest yet. "Make sure you do, Dimitri Ivanovich. Make sure you don't make a mistake you could very easily and very soon regret."

Danilov had a joint schedule with William Cowley, but he moved on to it distracted, unsettled by the choice demanded of him.

If the obvious comparison between the technology-controlled and gleaming FBI building on Pennsylvania Avenue and the cracked Bakelite and the unswept corridors of Petrovka registered with Cowley, the American didn't show it. But then, remembered Danilov, he'd been there before, knew what to expect. Or rather was *not* to expect. Danilov was still glad of the improvements to his own office: His television was actually bigger than Cowley's. He'd left it on CNN while he'd gone down to greet the American, and when they reentered that day's renewed demonstrations outside the Ulitza Chaykovskovo embassy were on the screen. The voice-over commentary claimed the crowd was larger than the previous day, despite Henry Hartz's televised assurance of full cooperation with the Russian foreign minister, and Cowley said that was very definitely the impression from inside the building. To avoid running the gauntlet he'd come directly to Petrovka from the hotel. Immediately after the television report of an intended meeting between Hartz and the Russian president, there was a live interview with an English-speaking communist deputy from the Duma insisting that the resolution criticizing the president would definitely become an impeachment debate.

His mind still very much upon the conversation with the interior minister, Danilov said, "What do your State Department people traveling with the secretary say about that?"

"Haven't discussed it with anyone in detail." Cowley shrugged. "Takes a hell of a long time to impeach a president, either here or at home."

"Unless they're forced out by the threat, like Nixon was," reminded Danilov.

"Then it comes down to how hard-assed your guy is," said Cowley. "A political problem, not ours."

"Yes," agreed Danilov, wishing it were true. Should he talk to the American about the Belik conversation: ask Cowley to circulate the question of the Russian president's survival among Hartz's support staff? There would be an exaggerated show of confidence from the Russian White House in front of Hartz and his people, so any playback would be misleading. And apart from the sort of television pictures on at that moment, the Americans had little way to gauge the parliamentary opposition's strength or weakness.

Cowley held up his hands against the reunion with Yuri Pavin becoming too effusively bear-hugging, and the Russian avoided any reaction to the American's hair ditch along one side of his head. The greetings were quickly over.

"So how was dinner at the Golden Hussar?" demanded Danilov.

"The food was better than the chances of recognizing anyone— which I didn't—but it definitely has the smell of a new brigade location," Pavin said at once. "A lot of available women, men in their favorite shiny suits and just slightly more Mercedes than BMWs. Accepts every Western credit and charge card and the menu's priced in U.S. dollars." Danilov nodded to the gesture toward his desk, and Pavin unrolled a white tube of paper he was carrying, pinning the edges open with the telephone and pen holder.

"Architect's drawings of the restructuring work carried out less than a year ago. No record of their being approved but they've been carried out, so someone paid someone." As Danilov and Cowley came to either side, Pavin moved his finger in explanation and said, "And here's our problem. Long bar, immediately after the main entrance. Restaurant, supposedly for sixty people, directly beyond that. Kitchens, closed off obviously, halfway down the left-hand side and from them, leading out into an alley quite separate from an adjoining road, are two doors." The finger traced on. "And here's what's listed as office and administration space. See, here, here, and here are three more doors, designated fire exits, but in fact closed off from the restaurant itself by this full-length wall." He looked to each man. "Two of them lead again into separate roads. Five different ways by which people can come and go, unseen, unless we're going to surround the place by what would need to be a squad of at least twenty observers."

"If I was a cynical FBI investigator, I'd say the Golden Hussar was a custom-designed mob place," said Cowley. "Lambert's photographer went through four rolls of film last night, although he's worried about the light and the quality. Thinks they can get prints to put against your criminal records by the end of today."

"All of people going in through the front door," reminded Pavin. He took a colored booklet from his inside pocket, laying it on top of the plans. "The official pictorial brochure, handed out with the bill. Gives you some idea what it looks like."

There were a lot of long-leafed plants, small trees almost, around the walls, and in the very center there was more jungle-type greenery around an ornamental, fountain-fed pond.

Pavin said, "The pond has real fish."

"What about telephones?" demanded Danilov.

"Two public, to the side of the bar. Neither is the number listed on the Bay View Avenue billing account. That has to be somewhere in the back, in one of the offices."

"What about a tap from the exchange? Any problem getting a court order for that?"

"A bigger problem would be finding someone here who'd put it on without telling the Golden Hussar with his hand out," said Danilov. Who, he wondered, would the homosexual Anatoli Lasin name as the mafia source within Petrovka?

"Lambert's got a bunch of guys sightseeing and buying *matroyshka* dolls in the Arbat," said Cowley.

Danilov had lowered the sound but kept the television on: The banner-carrying crowd seemed to have increased since he'd last looked. He said, "If your people installed it, the monitor would have to be from inside your embassy."

Cowley followed Danilov's look, toward the screen. "We're wired at the Brooklyn end. Maybe it's not a good idea to try to connect up here after all."

"What about continuing the surveillance?" asked Pavin.

"I think we need to know how many people—and get identification if that's possible—use the rear doors," said Danilov.

"Let's hope the identification isn't of Americans doing it," said Cowley, accepting the unasked request.

Pavin opened a farthest, functional flap of the restaurant brochure still lying on Danilov's desk. "The bill. We both had goose. It was excellent, like I said. But very expensive."

At the height of the KGB's all-pervasive, all-intrusive power, the supposed militia guards on Moscow's foreign embassies had all been KGB—America's more heavily covered than any other. With the diminishment of the organization, the concentration had been scaled down although not completely abandoned. Danilov recognized at once that the bearded man, so big he dwarfed Pavin, was not just basic street-level but basic street-mentality militia. The uniform was soiled, shining from grease and wear, and the felt of his regulation-issue winter boots, which he was still wearing in early summer, was scuffed through to the canvas lining. He smelled.

His immediate, apprehensive concentration was on the obviously American William Cowley, and his suspicious eyes flickered between Cowley—whom he also dwarfed—and the plastic-wrapped missile launcher that Pavin had collected from the Petrovka forensic department on his way to escort the embassy guard from the vestibule.

Danilov said, "We want you to tell us about the attack."

"I acted correctly picking up that thing. It was evidence," the man said at once, defensively.

"You're not here to be accused of anything."

"Nothing much to tell," said the guard. "It was raining. Hard. I was in the hut, trying to keep dry. Heard a car but didn't see it, not at first. No cars around, not even on the ring road, that late. Looked out and saw it had stopped, although the engine was still running. Then someone got out, bundled up. I saw him bring something up to his shoulder but it was too thick to be a rifle. Suddenly there was an explosion and a flash, as if something was blowing up, and then I heard a crash from farther down the alley beside the embassy and a very big explosion. I didn't see him drop that thing, but when the car drove off I realized something was lying where the car had been. I pressed the alarm button and picked up the frame from the road. I knew it was important so I put it inside the shelter and didn't give it to the Americans who came out. I waited for a militia colonel to arrive and gave it to him. He said I'd done the right thing. That's all. A lot more officers came then. Took over."

"Were you wearing gloves when you picked it up?" asked Cowley.

"Yes. It was cold. Wet."

"What about the officer you gave it to? Was he wearing gloves?"

"I don't know."

Maybe—just maybe—the chance of a fingerprint if the officer could be eliminated, thought Danilov, following the direction of the questioning. "Tell me about the car. What make was it?"

"Foreign. American," said the embassy guard at once.

"You sure about it being American?" demanded Cowley.

"I worked for two years with GIA: traffic."

The man's size alone would have terrorized motorists into handing over the expected bribes rather than be issued fabricated tickets, Danilov thought. He wondered whom the man had failed to bribe to keep the job. "Do you know the make?"

"It was big: bigger than a Zil. It went up at the back. The design, I mean."

"Fins?" suggested Pavin.

"Yes."

"Mercedes are foreign. So are BMWs. There are a lot of those in Moscow?"

"Mercedes and BMWs don't go up at the back, like this car did."

"What about a number?" pressed Pavin.

"I didn't get a number. It was over too quick. And it was raining. And I thought he had a special gun."

"What about a color?"

"Dark colored, not light."

"There's sodium lighting on that road!" insisted Pavin.

"It was two o'clock in the morning. Raining. I couldn't make out a proper color."

"What about the man who fired it?" urged Danilov.

"I didn't see him. Just a shape."

"Was he wearing a coat? A hat?" said Cowley.

"Both. A coat and a hat. And I thought at first he was very tall, but he wasn't, not really. It was the gun thing he was pointing upward like you hold a rifle upward."

"You mean like a soldier holds a rifle properly?"

"I suppose so," the man said doubtfully.

"How did he fire it? Simply stand upright and put it against his shoulder? Or did you get the impression he was doing it in a special way, again like a soldier would have properly done it?"

The man didn't immediately respond. "I don't know how these things are supposed to be fired. Maybe he was crouched a little."

"How many people were in the car?" said Pavin.

"I couldn't see. Two, certainly. The man who fired got out of the rear seat and got back into the rear afterward."

"Was anything said between the man who fired and whoever was in the car?" said Danilov.

"Not that I heard. It was a long way away."

"You think you could recognize the car again?" asked Cowley.

"Maybe," said the man, again doubtfully.

As the man left, again escorted by Pavin, Danilov said. "American car, American bazooka, American embassy."

"And the weapon held correctly, as a trained soldier would have held it," completed Cowley.

The American was standing beside the bagged-up rocket launcher when Pavin reentered. He said, "According to our forensics, it's clean."

"That's what Lambert was frightened of," remarked Cowley.

There were four of them.

The intention was to go directly from the funeral to confront Lasin at his Pereulok Ucebyi apartment, so it was convenient for Cowley to have come with him, but Danilov hadn't expected the American to suggest it. He was glad he had. It was Cowley who'd reminded him about flowers, which they'd stopped on the way to buy. He'd never needed reminding about flowers for Larissa's grave, which was in another part of the Novodevichy Cemetery. He couldn't see it from where they were but knew exactly where it was. If Cowley hadn't been with him he would have gone there afterward, but he wouldn't now.

Danilov hadn't told Igor, who stood on the other side of the open grave, head bowed for the end of the interment oration, but he guessed that Irena had. Irena's hair appeared as haphazardly streaked as Olga's had been. Danilov supposed Igor was Irena's hairdresser, too. The bearded priest was promising that Olga was going to a happier life. Danilov hoped it was true, because she probably hadn't been very happy for much of the one she'd just left. He wondered if there were better hairdressers in Olga's heaven. He hesitated when the priest offered him the trowel but then bent and tossed some earth on to the coffin. Instead of handing the trowel back to the priest, he offered it directly to Igor. As he threw earth into the grave, Igor began to cry. Irena did, too. They backed away to let the gravediggers complete the filling in but remained separate. Danilov couldn't think of anything to say to the other two so he nodded.

It was Igor who spoke, brokenly. "I'm sorry."

Danilov wondered what, exactly, the man was apologizing for. "No one was with her. That's sad."

"I didn't know. She didn't tell me." His voice caught, from his crying.

So Igor was the father. How many children did he have by his legal wife? "There are some photographs," Danilov offered.

"That would be," started the man. Then he said, "Thank you. I . . . ?"

"I'll send them to Irena."

"Thank you," Igor repeated. His voice caught again.

As they walked toward their car Danilov said: "Larissa's buried over there."

"I know," said Cowley. "I came to her funeral, too."

Danilov waited for the question, but it didn't come.

Yuri Pavin, who'd been sent ahead to establish that Anatoli Sergeevich Lasin was at Pereulok Ucebyi and keep the man there if he was, opened the apartment door to them.

Danilov said, "How is he?"

Pavin said: "Going through the routine. He says a bracelet was stolen when he was at Petrovka. I've told him he was lucky that was all and to have survived the turf war, but he needs to shout a little longer."

"He can shout as long as he likes providing he tells us something. He alone?"

Pavin nodded. "I was surprised about that."

"Is he frightened?" asked Danilov.

"Concealing it well, if he is," said Pavin.

The wire-thin, blond man was wearing the same sort of second-skin trousers and silk sweater—both in complimentary shades of blue—as he had during their first encounter but this time all the jewelry—with the possible exception of the missing bracelet—was glitteringly in place. Lasin's immediate concentration was on William Cowley.

"I told you I'd be robbed!" protested the man, at once.

"We're not here to talk about your bracelets, are we, Anatoli Sergeevich?" said Danilov. "We're here to talk about things much more important than that."

"A lot of people have died. Here, now. More, in America," said Cowley. "And your own brigade got hit—Mikhail Vasilevich Osipov himself."

"What have you got to tell us about that?" picked up Danilov.

"Nothing."

"You're being stupid, Anatoli Sergeevich. And irritating," said Danilov. "You know why we're here?"

"Of course I know why you're here!"

"No," contradicted Danilov. "*Here*, in your apartment. We're here so that no one in Petrovka—and no one *outside* Petrovka—is ever going to know we've had this meeting."

"Keeping you safe," added the rehearsed Cowley. "That was the undertaking, wasn't it? Keeping you safe?"

Lasin's eyes flickered snakelike—blankly, as snakes' eyes are blankly unresponsive—before he said, "Osipov's dead. The brigade's smashed. That's all I know."

"Who killed him?" demanded Pavin.

"How do I know?"

"We're sure you do," insisted Danilov.

"I do the cars, that's all. There was a war a few years back. I wasn't with him then. Ask the brigade he fought then."

"Can we tell them you sent us?" asked Pavin.

The bravado began to crumble. "I don't know!"

"Our deal," reminded Danilov. "You were going to get me a name I needed?"

"I couldn't," the man refused, bluntly.

Silence grew up in the opulent, flower-overwhelmed apartment, like building blocks for a wall. Danilov said, "You seen all those people outside the American embassy?"

"Hasn't everybody!"

"Don't worry, we'll get through," said Cowley, to Danilov. "Don't worry about it."

"Not unseen," said Danilov, back to the American.

"We'll try," said Cowley.

Danilov spread his hands toward the Russian gangster. "You can't say I didn't try to keep my side of the bargain."

"What the fuck you talking about now?"

"The same thing, keeping you safe. Not letting anyone know you're helping us," said Danilov.

"You're not making sense," jeered the man, although uncertainly.

"Can't be many foreign cars—European, American—you can't

recognize, being in the business like you are?" suggested Cowley.

Lasin's eyes flickered once more, but he didn't speak.

"Got a lot of pictures of American cars at the embassy," said Cowley. "What we want you to do is look through them, see if you can match any to a description we'll give you of the car used in the attack on the embassy."

"Pity you couldn't give me a name from Petrovka," said Danilov. "And tell us about the Osipov killing. Wish I had enough people to guarantee your safety after you've been to the embassy, but we're as stretched as hell. Sorry."

"Bastard!" said Lasin.

"It's the business we're in—makes us like that," said Pavin. "We all ready?"

Cowley and Danilov moved toward the door together.

"Mizin!" blurted the man. "Ashot Yefimovich Mizin! "

Who'd volunteered to deliver Plant 43's double-headed missile—the missile that had been switched in transit—to the Foreign Ministry and the self-appointed investigator of brigade godfather Mikhail Vasilevich Osipov, thought Danilov. "You see, you *can* help, when you really try."

"Now let's talk about American cars in Moscow," picked up Cowley.

"And after that we're going to go back to who killed Mikhail Vasilevich and destroyed the Osipov Brigade."

"You'll get me killed! You know you'll get me killed!"

"You help us, we'll help you," promised Danilov.

"Motherfuckers!"

"We don't enjoy it, either," said Cowley. "Just part of the job."

Pamela Darnley was pissed off: irrationally, which she knew and which didn't help, angry but with no one and no target at which to vent it. It had begun so well, so seemingly *complete*. All it needed was one simple, fucking 25 cent telephone call—why was everything in nickels and dimes!—and she'd have been there, wherever *there* was. There with a SWAT team and helicopters—a fucking army, maybe—and they'd have all been in the bag, tied at the neck, the national emergency over and done with.

But there hadn't been a call between 69 Bay View Avenue, Brooklyn, and a public street booth on the corner of Lake Shore Drive and 14th Boulevard, Chicago.

In the thirty-six hours since she'd established the monitor, the Chicago surveillance team had racked up $480 in overtime and taken 250 unnecessary photographs, including three sets of street hookers who used the telephone for business. And the Manhattan listeners knew what take-out pizza toppings Arseni and Mary Jo Orlenko preferred, that when she was out jogging on the bay road he called telephone sex lines, and because the house was live to every sound that he enjoyed oral sex when she came back, before she showered.

There was an equally frustrating paradox about the bank investigation, too. Within the thirty-six hours that the bureau auditors had moved in to the regional offices, there'd been the breakthrough that the siphoning from three banks in New York City and four in Philadelphia had gone beyond pennies: at two, in Philadelphia, three separate amounts of ten dollars had disappeared. The frustration came with the caution from the fraud team supervisor that while she—and Anne Stovey—had probably locked in on a substantial crime, it was still going to be difficult to isolate the embezzlers.

Pamela was actually in the Manhattan office, listening to the conversation between the couple on Bay View Avenue, when the fight began that alerted them.

Pamela said: "This could be something!"

It was but not at all—or anything—what any of them wanted, Pamela Darnley least of all.

Patrick Hollis had been panicked, open-boweled, for the rest of the day after Gillian Carling's cafeteria announcement and sleepless that night in his locked den. But he was better now. Totally calm. It would not be just difficult, it would be impossible to catch him. And he'd always intended Robert Standing to be hurt, as badly as possible, for what he'd done, although more by an internal bank audit than by an FBI investigation.

Because it *was* an FBI investigation he still had to be careful, Hollis acknowledged. Better to get rid of the Jaguar than need to explain it, despite the inheritance cover he'd created. It was, really, a small sacrifice to make.

Senior Colonel Investigator Ashot Yefimovich Mizin was a thin, round-shouldered man who didn't make the mistake of flaunting his additional income with impeccable tailoring, like Reztsov and Averin in Gorki, but there was the faintest attitude of superciliousness as he came into Danilov's office.

Danilov said, "I thought I should have an update on the brigade murder."

Mizin shrugged. "Another turf war, like the ones a few years back."

"Who's the opposition brigade?"

"I'm not sure, not yet. I doubt we'll be able to bring a case even if I do find out."

"I don't want it written off," said Danilov. "I want it properly investigated."

"Trust me," said Mizin.

"Of course I will," said Danilov.

25

The argument was again about walking instead of driving to the Coney Island strip.

"I'm wearing heels!"

"Change your shoes."

"You're fucking paranoid!"

"I'm fucking careful."

"It'll be the Bare Necessities," predicted Pamela, to no one in particular. "Fuck it! And fuck the D.A. most of all: He's going to sleep well when half Manhattan gets wiped out in the next germ attack!" The dispute between Leonard Ross, the New York District Attorney, and the attorney general remained unresolved three days after Pamela had renewed Cowley's already once refused request to tap the public telephone in the topless bar.

"We'll get in place ahead of them," said New York agent in charge Harry Boreman, who didn't like what he considered Pamela Darnley's unnecessary intrusion on his turf on her way back from Albany to explain the importance of the Brooklyn–Chicago monitor, which they understood every bit as much as she did.

A surveillance team did establish itself in the bar ahead of Orlenko, but other observer cars got in place as before along the seaside approach roads, keeping the couple constantly in view as a precaution against their going somewhere else. Mary Jo had refused to change her shoes and was hobbling before they got on to Riegelmann Boardwalk. It took them forty minutes, Orlenko constantly searching around, staging pauses to look for pursuit.

"Funny thing, but he seems more nervous than he was the day we blacked out the area, when he had more reason to be suspicious."

"Agreed."

The voices of two separately motorized observers, both of whom had watched the earlier public telephone routine, echoed into the Manhattan incident room. Pamela made a conscious effort to dismiss her irritation, acknowledging the unprofessional stupidity at it. She'd too rigidly made her mind up that the break was going to come from Chicago—which it still might—and wasn't paying sufficient attention to alternatives. Such as why, without any apparent summons of which they were aware—certainly nothing involving the telephone or discussed between Orlenko and his hooker wife in the totally wired house—the couple was seemingly on their way to another contact. Or why Orlenko was behaving more apprehensively.

"It's the same titty bar," came an observer's voice.

"We've got enough people inside. Let's not overcrowd the place," ordered the agent in charge.

"Spoilsport," came the same voice.

The search for a table closer than the previous occasion to the public telephone was obvious, inside the Bare Necessities. They ordered the same drinks, straight vodka martini for Mary Jo, beer for the Russian. Mary Jo seemed more interested in the stage show, two black girls needing a lot of body touching helping each other to undress, than Orlenko whose attention alternated between his watch and the use of the boxed-in telephone. Without saying anything to his wife, he got up from his chair at 6:25 to claim the booth. Once inside he took a notepad from his pocket, followed by two pens, exposing both ballpoints and testing each.

Again the incoming call was precisely at 6:30. After what could only have been the briefest of identification Orlenko began to write, painstakingly slowly—as if he were printing the words, according to one observer later—and just as pedantically reading each line back once he'd completed it, visibly stabbing the pen from word to word. It took a full ten minutes for the dictation to be completed.

Once more Orlenko didn't sit down when he rejoined Mary Jo, urging her to finish her drink. They appeared to be arguing as they left the bar, although Orlenko at once hailed a cab back to Bay View Avenue.

"You promised blinis at the Odessa again!" were the first shouted words that echoed into the FBI's Manhattan office.

"Shut up! I've got to make a call first. Alone. Go and clean up the shit in the kitchen."

"I can't understand what the fuck you're talking about anyway."

There was the sound of a receiver being lifted, numbers being punched. The FBI operator at the front of the electronic equipment said, "One zero seven is the Russian country code. Nine five's Moscow."

The Manhattan agent in charge snatched up his own phone and said, "I'll tell Cowley," ignoring Pamela.

A woman answered, on the second ring. She said: "Yes?"

"Arseni," identified Orlenko.

"You've had a call?"

"Yes."

"I knew he would. He had to. How was he?"

"Like he always is. Where did you get the American rocket?"

"They're everywhere." She had a throaty voice, deep.

"He was impressed about us keeping our side of the bargain."

"Pity for him and his great big cause that he didn't keep his. He say anything?

"Most of the time talked a lot of shit about battles and wars."

"Let him talk about what he likes."

"You have any problems?"

It was a dismissive laugh. "Not good, working with outsiders. Not ones who think they know it all, arrogant cunts. Didn't even have transport. And when it came to it they couldn't hit the embassy building itself."

"Going on to Russian government websites in Russian was a good idea, though."

"Our idea, from here."

"He wants us to be very careful."

"Like he should be, in future. All he's got to worry about is the money and realize no one can do better than us."

Orlenko hesitated. "He says he doesn't want what happened last time happening again. That he hopes everyone got the message."

"He tried the side deal!"

"He meant the missile not detonating."

"There was an obvious answer to that: It didn't come from us. But you didn't remind him of that, did you?" The contempt in her voice was obvious.

"He reestablished contact, came to *us*. He was admitting his mistake doing that." Orlenko hesitated again. "I'm sorry, incidentally."

"It was business—only ever business."

"Still unfortunate."

"What does he want?" Now the tone was impatient.

"Quite a lot. Certainly another microbiological missile: one that will detonate this time. A conventional rocket, if you can get one. More than one, if possible. That's why I asked about the embassy rocket, although it's American manufactured. Antipersonnel mines. Semtex. And detonators and timers."

"Quite a lot," she echoed.

"I know."

"They shouldn't have used everything on the memorial."

"It would have been spectacular."

"Except that it wasn't and they lost everything. He admit that was a mistake?"

"Talked about it being an unfortunate battlefield loss."

She snorted in disgust. "They're mad, you know? Him and his group."

"He thinks it's working in America. Says there's a lot of anti-Russian feeling, particularly after the intelligence revelations," said Orlenko. "Told me to ask what the real political feeling was there: whether the Duma move against the president would come to anything."

"I'm not interested in politics, revolutionary shit. I'm only interested in business."

"So, can you meet the order?"

"Of course."

"How long?"

"What about the money?" she countered.

"He said it would be ready."

"*Would,*" she qualified. "Not *is?*"

"No."

"The bastard's got to be fined for what he was prepared to do."

"What do you mean?"

"A germ warhead will be a million. Rockets a quarter each. We've already got most of everything else. A half a million for that."

"Two million, two million plus?"

"Depends on how many missiles and rockets I can get. I thought you said he wanted everything we could get hold of?"

"I need to check with him. And tell him the price. What if he says no—to the price, I mean?"

"If he had another supplier he wouldn't have come back like he has. He's created the momentum; he's got to keep it up. Hasn't got time to come all the way here again, start from scratch."

"Gavri gave him a coup with the intelligence identities. Maybe, with his contacts, Gavri could introduce him to someone else?"

"The intelligence deal was separate. Just Gavri. If Gavri had a different source they would have used it, wouldn't they? But they didn't. *They* came to *us,*" insisted the woman.

"I guess you're right."

"Of course I'm right."

"You think Gavri would do another separate deal?"

"Of course he would, if he had something to sell."

"I didn't like what he did, cutting us out: saying we had nothing to do with it and didn't deserve a cut."

"Maybe we don't need him anymore," suggested the woman. "Maybe nobody needs him anymore."

"If he's killed it would bring attention to the legit business. And through that to me."

"I'll think about it. I didn't like what he did, either. What's the arrangement for the next contact?"

"Him to me, as always. But not the topless bar anymore; says we've used it enough. I have to go through the routine of getting a new number, to be ready when he calls."

"Mad, like I said. Playing at being soldiers."

"With germ warheads and real bombs."

"I'll be waiting to hear."

The phones were put down without any farewells.

The call timed out at eleven minutes forty-five seconds, and it took Cowley and Danilov exactly twenty-three minutes to get from the Savoy to Pereulok Vorotnikovskij. Immediately after alerting them the bureau duty officer, at Cowley's instructions, had told the telephone-linked surveillance teams—particularly those at the rear—that every woman had, without fail, to be photographed leaving the Golden Hussar.

Danilov, who was driving, parked some way from the restaurant, but that was an unnecessary precaution, too. Vehicles—predominantly Mercedes and BMWs, as Yuri Pavin had reported—overflowed from the parking lot into adjoining streets. As they moved unobtrusively through the crush both men looked for American models. There were some—at least three Cadillacs—but none with upthrust rear fins and none were dark in color. They had, in fact, taken with them to Lasin's apartment photographs of the three cars—two Oldsmobiles and a Lincoln—the embassy guard thought might have been the vehicle he'd seen, but Lasin claimed not to know of such vehicles in Moscow. Would there be any recognition from the supposedly gang-retired Igor Ivanovich Baratov, who ran a garage? Danilov wondered.

Besides a lot of cars there were a lot of people—not just from the vehicles but on foot. Danilov said, "We're not going to get photographs of every woman here."

"I know," agreed Cowley, and repeated the same acceptance to each of the three surveillance teams as they were located. He also accepted that, by comparison to the brightly lit front of the Golden Hussar—complete with a neon depiction of a plumed and cloaked soldier—the rear of the building was almost too dark even for the fastest of infrared films on the longest of exposures.

Cowley used the mobile telephone of a rear car driver to summon replacement teams. The current ones would return to the embassy to begin developing their prints, then come back afterward with Danilov to the easier concealment of the jammed parking lot.

"There'd be no purpose, even if there wasn't the risk of our being identified, in our going in there," said Cowley. "But there's a woman probably still inside who could tell us all—a hell of a lot, at least—of what we want to know. And there's no way of knowing or finding out who she is. That's crazy. Downright fucking crazy."

"No way *yet*," qualified the equally frustrated Danilov.

"Manhattan relayed the conversation to a copy tape back at the embassy."

"No real reason for our hanging around," said Danilov.

"No real reason for us coming here in the first place," Cowley said bitterly. "Downright fucking crazy."

There was a printed transcript and English translation by the time they got back to Ulitza Chaykovskovo, but they still listened, twice, to the recording.

Cowley said, "They're going for their germ warfare massacre."

"We knew they would, if they had another warhead. Which they haven't, not yet," said Danilov, more objectively. "We've got time and we've got Bay View Avenue."

"Which we mustn't lose." Cowley checked his watch. "I'll speak to the director—Manhattan, too—when everyone wakes up in America." They'd both already given up any idea of sleep for what remained of that night.

Danilov tapped the transcript. "There's a lot here, if we can see it."

"Gavri?"

"Doesn't sound Russian. Greek maybe."

"Where's that leave the theory of the intelligence agent identification being KGB?" queried Cowley. "KGB didn't employ foreign nationals in Moscow Center, did they?"

"Not as far as I know, although Feliks Dzerzhinsky, who founded the service, was a Pole," admitted Danilov. "I'll check. If it turns out to be a working code name, we've got our KGB search down to one."

There were only the two of them in the FBI section. Martlew, at Cowley's suggestion, had provided a bottle before leaving to check the picture development. Cowley and Danilov were on their second drink.

"Gavri has to be in America if killing him risked bringing attention to Orlenko," said Cowley. "But what legitimate business was Orlenko talking about? You remember any reference to a business in anything we've heard from Bay View Avenue?"

"Not from the bugging," said Danilov. "But when we were wiring the house she told Harrison they'd been in Chicago seeing import-export business friends of Arnie's. And that Arnie was always talking deals."

"There'd need to be an import-export front to bring in weapons," said Cowley. "And Chicago's a port."

"If Orlenko's name was on the register of an import-export business based there we'd have the route," said Danilov. "And Chicago's on the telephone list."

"About time," insisted Danilov.

"The Watchmen are definitely a fanatical military group," said Cowley, looking down at his own transcript copy.

"Operating like an insurgency group in enclosed cells: like the booby trap at New Rochelle was insurgency," said Danilov.

"What's *new*, leading us somewhere?" complained Cowley.

"Torture," said Danilov, to himself.

"What?"

"It fits," insisted the Russian, still reflective. "Remember I told you how Nikov and Karpov had been tortured before being tied together and finally thrown in the Moskva? As an example to anyone else? Now look at the conversation between Orlenko and the woman. There was a falling out: someone trying to cheat. I'd say that someone was Vitali Nikolaevich Nikov, who got mutilated and murdered for doing it."

"With Valeri Karpov, who worked at Plant 43 and had access to double war-headed missiles," said the American, going along with the reasoning.

"According to Lasin, the story is that the killings were carried out by Americans," recalled Danilov. "You think some of the Watchmen came in personally to set the example of what happens when something goes wrong?"

" 'Hasn't got time to come all the way here again' " quoted Cowley. "Could be interpreted that way."

"And Nikov stayed at the Metropole Hotel, the favorite of American visitors," filled in Danilov.

"So," said Cowley, underlining passages in the transcript as he talked. "The Watchmen set up a deal to buy a germ war-headed missile. Get a better offer—they think—from Nikov, who supplies them with one that doesn't go off. They also think it's his fault, that he sold them a dud, so he gets tortured and killed. So does Valeri Karpov, his supplier, by a Watchmen group. Who then have to go back to their original source."

"Problems," cautioned Danilov, lifting the paper toward the American. "This is Arseni Orlenko, a boyhood friend of Vitali Nikov—to whose garages in Gorki we know calls were made, and received, from Bay View Avenue—talking to the Watchmen's original supplier. So who's Orlenko running with?"

"Both?" suggested Cowley.

"Wouldn't he have been tortured and killed, as another example, if he was?" asked Danilov.

The room became silent, both men hunched over their transcripts.

"Why was Orlenko sorry?" demanded Cowley, not looking up. He quoted: " 'I'm sorry, incidentally. . . . It was business—only ever business. . . . Still unfortunate.' What was? What's that all about?"

"I don't know," admitted Danilov. "What we do know—can be

positive about—is that for the moment there aren't going to be any more outrages in America because their arsenal has gone."

"It's not empty here," Cowley reminded. "Who are the outsiders she refers to? And the deal? She's only interested in business, not in any revolutionary shit, so why's she involved, as she obviously was, in the attack on the embassy?"

"Another question that has to go on hold," said Danilov.

"Which plant are the warheads coming from, Moscow or Gorki?" demanded Cowley.

"Karpov had to be Nikov's supplier: That's why he died tied to him," said Danilov. "Which points to Gorki. But the stenciling on the UN missile was wrong compared to the sample your forensic people checked. It could be either plant. Or one we don't even know about." He went to his transcript yet again. "She's got virtually all the conventional stuff the Watchmen want. And the type of bazooka that hit your compound is everywhere—sixth line from the top."

A gray dawn was spreading across the city outside, slowly, as if it really wasn't interested in starting a new day. Cowley wasn't sure if he was, either. He took a third scotch, ignoring Danilov's look. Cowley said, "I think I'll call the director."

"What are you going to tell him?"

"That we know there's most likely going to be another disaster and we don't know how to prevent it."

It wasn't the defeatism of the remark that unsettled Danilov. It was the feeling that he'd missed the most important thing in the telephone conversation between Brooklyn and Moscow. As Cowley went into Barry Martlew's office to make the Washington connection, Danilov pressed the replay button for the third time and listened to the tape in its entirety. The unsettled feeling didn't go; it actually increased. "Told me to ask what the real political feeling was there: whether the Duma move against the president would come to anything" echoed in his mind and stared up at him from the printed page in his hand. Was that it? The reminder of what he'd done by ignoring not just the early-morning demand but the repeated afternoon telephone calls that Pavin had relayed from Interior Minister Nikolai Mikhailovich Belik?

Pamela Darnley was unsettled, too.

She'd carried a transcript and a copy of the telephone conversation with her on the first morning shuttle to Washington—calculating that professionally and politically the J. Edgar Hoover building was the place for her to be—refusing the irritation at Cowley talking directly with the director from Moscow, just as she'd discarded what she now embarrassingly accepted to have been an irrational disappointment that Orlenko hadn't called Chicago.

There had been nothing to detract from what she'd achieved in sole command. From the long conversation she'd just concluded with a tired-sounding William Cowley, it appeared they were still going to need a miracle—several, maybe—to benefit from the tape or identify the unknown woman who'd featured on it. If anything concrete was going to emerge it would be linking Arseni Orlenko to a Chicago import-export firm. If she did that, it would again be to her credit, despite the lead coming from Moscow. Letting her mind run on, Pamela recognized that although, objectively, it would have achieved nothing—and risked destroying the only positive Russian lead they had—Cowley's explanation why he and Danilov had not gone into the Golden Hussar, that they didn't have the slightest clue to whom the woman was, had sounded lamely facile. She wondered if Leonard Ross had thought the same.

She had posed a number of questions to herself the previous evening in the Manhattan incident room. And she'd come up with some more since. Besides initiating the Chicago company search, it was time to regain a total overview: to look down from the top of the mountain of what they had, searching for what might have been overlooked.

"I'll try not to get in the way."

"There's more than enough room," said Patrick Hollis. He encompassed his office with a gesture. "If you like I could move out of here into the open room and you could have it all to yourself." He felt totally relaxed, unfazed: enjoying it even. It was being interrogated by the enemy after being captured. Except that he hadn't been captured. And wouldn't be.

"That desk and the terminal out there are all I need," Mark Wittier said. The FBI auditor was a dry, thin, bespectacled man whose overburdened briefcase sagged, strained against its side straps.

"You change your mind, all you've got to do is say. You think you'll be here long?" Hollis had read books on interrogation technique: how to resist and throw questioners off the scent. This was classic so far. Affably willing to cooperate in every way, become the questioner rather than the questioned.

"Depends what we find. Sometimes it's months."

"What, exactly, *are* you looking for?" Still the questioner.

"What do you imagine?"

Careful: turned it back on him. "The gossip is that you're in a lot of branches. If that's true—a lot of branches, I mean—it's a pretty substantial fraud." He paused. "That's what I've guessed."

"You ever come across anything that seems out of order?"

Clever again. Avoid the question and ask another. Still not fazed, still in command. "Out of order?"

"Disparities. Things not quite adding up as they should?"

The moment for indignation. "Not in my department, Mr. Whittier! I've had AI in-house audits ever since I got appointed, and I'm proud of it. We talking a loan or securities fraud here? If we are, then I think I need to be told about it!"

Whittier's supposedly reassuring smile clicked on and off, like a light switch. "Actually it's customer accounts. Day-to-day transactions, things like that."

Hollis was sure he allowed just the right amount of relaxation. "Afraid I can't help you there. Not my division."

"I know," said Whittier. "That's why it was thought best I work out of here: out of the way of everyone in the bank who deal day to day. Less upsetting."

He had a reaction ready for that one. Hollis actually counted, in his head, stretching the apparent surprise. "You mean you believe the fraud is being committed from someone *within* the bank! An employee!"

"That's how these things usually turn out."

But not this time how the auditor imagined, thought Hollis. And even more certainly not how Robert Standing imagined, either.

26

When the Chicago agent in charge complained that the manpower drain to carry out a local shipping companies' registration check, in addition to the rotating surveillance on the Lake Shore Drive public telephone, Pamela Darnley told him all other ongoing cases should be suspended and promised an immediate authorizing fax, which she sent with the promise to draft in more personnel if it became necessary. From the equally quick, unargued acceptance of everything she said, Pamela wondered if her confrontation with Al Beckinsdale had already been churned out through the gossip grinder. There was constant communication among Chicago, Washington, and New York, and from the hostility she could have bruised herself against in New York it was obvious it was common, apprehensive knowledge there.

She wasn't unhappy to be tagged a ball-breaker. Rather it was the reputation—the fear—she wanted. All it needed for her to be sucked down into quicksand oblivion was one mistake—someone failing instantly to react or recognize, as Beckinsdale had failed. She hadn't realized, in the beginning, how useful that episode would be.

Based on her newly acquired cover-your-ass headquarters' expertise, she enclosed a copy of her Chicago authorization to Leonard Ross that a register check was a way to locate the U.S. entry route of the next germ warfare weapon. It wasn't, however, her major communication. Aware of Cowley's direct contact with the man, Pamela turned her memorandum accompanying the actual tape and its transcript into an analysis, stressing what she considered an overwhelming priority.

A tap on the now clearly abandoned Bare Necessities telephone would have provided the number from which the weapon ordering call had been made, giving them a voiceprint. Knowing now, as they did, that another combined germ and biological attack was planned, there surely couldn't be any constitutional or legal argument against tapping the public telephones on the Bay View Avenue billing records not just for Chicago but for Washington and Pittsburgh.

Terry Osnan arrived while she was in the middle of composing the memo. Without stopping Pamela handed him the Golden Hussar transcript and companies' search instructions to Chicago.

He waited until she'd finished before saying "If we'd spoken last night, I could have set this up then."

"It was even later in Chicago and only eight A.M. there today—two hours before the company records office opens—when I organized it all. We didn't lose any time." She hoped the incident room coordinator, who'd argued against her Beckinsdale complaint, wasn't going to become a carping pain in the ass.

"It could be good," judged the man.

"I want the master file. I'm going to do a complete review personally."

There was a visible stiffening in the slim, fair-haired man. "I review everything in context as it comes in."

Pamela sighed. "This isn't any sort of attack, criticism. *I* haven't reviewed everything in context—know, properly, where the pieces fit and where they don't. I'm the joint controlling case officer but I've only been involved in parts. I need to know—*should* know—everything as completely as I know just some. OK?"

"OK," Osnan said doubtfully.

Feather-smoothing time, Pamela decided; ball-breaker was all right, scalpel-wielding emasculator wasn't. "So help me, Terry. What have I missed out, failed to do?" Quickly she corrected, "What might Bill and I failed to have done?"

"Nothing," the man said tightly. "If you had—either of you—I would have pointed it out, obviously." He waved the transcript he still held like a flag. "And as I said, the Chicago lead here really could be a step—a lot of steps—forward."

"Do me a favor," said Pamela. "Run a check, where we've withdrawn people, where there's people we could still bring in. Just in case we've got to build up even more."

"Chicago's isn't the only complaint," said Osnan. "I've had it from Los Angeles, Houston, and Minnesota. And that was before we virtually took over the entire fraud division for the bank investigation. And sent half of forensic to Moscow. We get a major, competing crime and the overstretch is going to snap."

"What would you say is a major crime likely to compete with a biological germ attack on an American city?"

"Just doing what you asked me, flagging up the hot spots," said Osnan.

"And I appreciate it," said Pamela. "Anne sends her love. I'm recommending a commendation for her picking up like she did."

Pamela read the master file steadily, unhurriedly, breaking off more than once to go out into the larger room with the folder in hand to look at the scene-of-crime photographs of the United Nations building, the New Rochelle massacre, and the Washington Monument bait for the failed Lincoln Memorial trap. Each had its own individual pinboard, but Pamela remained in front of photographs of Roanne Harding in her Lexington Place apartment longer than the rest, finally stepping back to see all the illustrations at the same time.

After returning to her office, she abandoned the master file for the complete evidence dossier of the murder, which was cross-referenced to her own inquiries at the Pentagon. There was still an FBI team on the case but as a murder investigation, it was totally stalled. As Paul Lambert had warned, the apartment had virtually been polished clean of any forensic evidence and the decomposition had destroyed any evidential medical finding, certainly semen traces for a DNA match if Roanne Harding had been raped, which he also couldn't prove.

Although Roanoke did appear to have been her hometown, the bureau team there had failed to locate friends or anyone who remembered her in any useful detail, despite local newspaper appeals that included publishing the Pentagon personnel photograph. Her teacher ("a quiet child who had difficulty in learning") believed she'd left the town after grade school ("I thought the whole family had moved on"), and whatever had attracted the FBI to the parents' black protest activities hadn't been registered by the local police, who had no record whatsoever of the family. The graves of the mother and father were in the Baptist cemetery. There was no reference on the headstone to the grief of any child at their passing.

It didn't fit, Pamela decided abruptly.

The UN missile had failed to explode because of a fluke, and the Lincoln Memorial explosion had been prevented by William Cowley's clever lateral thinking, but both had been painstakingly—brilliantly, by terrorist criteria—conceived. As had the New Rochelle booby trap and the monument lure. But somehow—she couldn't at that moment decide how—killing Roanne Harding seemed different: unconnected, although it wasn't. And despite the efforts of the killers to make it appear so.

So what didn't fit? Roanne Harding herself, perhaps? A girl with two names but no friends, no family, no lovers, no past, no future. A good choice, objectively, to infiltrate the Pentagon and its computer systems and humiliate America throughout the world. Except that she *hadn't* been a good choice. She'd attached the phony antistatic bands upon which her fingerprints had been found, giving the Watchmen incalculable access. But she'd drawn attention to herself— gotten fired—because she was so incompetent at the job she was supposed to do. Was that it? Was attaching the bands all she'd had to do? After which she became, quite literally, disposable? No, Pamela answered herself at once. Roanne had also had to wipe the personnel records of possibly disgruntled dismissed employees. But hadn't erased her own. Predictable, typical incompetence? Or . . . Pamela experienced the briefest feeling of numbness. It took her only minutes to find the notes—her own—that she wanted. And after that Paul Lambert's forensic reports on the antistatic bands upon which Roanne Harding's fingerprints had been found.

Hurriedly she reached for the telephone.

There were 120 photographs of women—the majority accompanied by men—from the Golden Hussar. Having been there, Cowley openly admitted the impossibility of photographing everyone and demanded an honest assessment of how many more might have been missed. The combined estimate, from the front and rear surveillance, came to twenty. Bad light and obstructing vehicles and people blurred the definition of ten of the 120 beyond any reasonable identification and the quality on a lot of the others was bad. The bristlechinned Cowley said, "Another fucking waste of time! What's going to tell us who she is, even if she's on one that's half good!"

"Maybe something we haven't yet got," said Danilov. An hour later he said, "And this could be it," after Pavin called from Petrovka to say that the records of 230 former KGB and Federal Security Bureau personnel had been delivered, with a note from the archive supervisor that there could be that many more again still to come. Nikolai Mikhailovich Belik was also demanding contact.

Cowley said, "We're being buried under paper."

"Which might be the idea," suggested Danilov. He thought the cynicism might actually be true when he returned to Petrovka. Some of the dossiers were more than two inches thick, and Pavin had taken over a small lecture room adjoining his office to accommodate them all.

Pavin said at once, "I've got the key and as far as I know there's only one spare." He extended his hand. "And that's it. What about Mizin?"

"You know one of the favorite mottoes of the old KGB? The spy you know is better than the spy you don't know. Mizin stays until there's a use for him."

Pavin said, "The minister's called again."

"It's best I spend as much time as I'm doing at the U.S. Embassy: It distances you—you and the few others we might be able to trust here."

"I didn't realize you were that exposed."

A totally unconnected thought suddenly presented itself. "Does your church do charity work?"

"Of course."

"I've got all Olga's things—dresses, stuff like that—in the car. Could you find a use for it?"

"That's very thoughtful of you."

He still had to give Olga's photographs to Irena to pass on to Igor. Igor who? he suddenly wondered, realizing he didn't know the full name of the man who'd made Olga pregnant. The name wasn't important or necessary. He'd keep one, he decided—their wedding photograph. He didn't know why. It just seemed the right thing to do. An easier decision than the one he'd made about choosing professional sides.

Danilov's office television was showing the early-morning buildup of protesters outside the U.S. Embassy and promising coverage of the public appearance of Henry Hartz and the Russian president, expected later in the day. The alley beside the legation had been sealed off by Moscow militia, but it was still possible to see the blackened and burst-apart side of the compound over the shoulder of the CNN reporter who was suggesting that the absence of any FBI statement indicated a total lack of progress.

The American axiom Danilov had always liked about being caught between a rock and a hard place didn't seem so slick now that he was the one in the middle. Committed, he reminded himself. Too late now to change his mind. All he could hope to do—*had* to do—was cushion as much as possible one of the hard surfaces between which he was being squeezed.

Danilov was connected at once to Georgi Chelyag, who listened without comment to his and Cowley's interpretation of the intercepted telephone conversation. When they did start to discuss it, Danilov patiently put up all the middle-of-the-night arguments against sealing off both the Moscow and Gorki plants they knew to hold germ warfare weapons or doing anything to disclose the importance of the Golden Hussar.

"We know we've got time," stressed Danilov, trying to direct the conversation. "There's Chicago and now the intelligence files."

"I can order Kedrov to produce Gavri—identify him—if it's a code designation."

"I don't think it is. I don't see the point of Orlenko and the woman continuing to use it and he's in America, not here. All we'd risk is alerting them, if there is still a link with the Security Bureau."

"I think we're standing back too much," protested the presidential aide.

"Is that the White House view? Or that of the rest of the control group?" demanded Danilov. The moment of truth or of suicidal self-destruction? He could easily have already pressed the self-destruct button.

A response was a long time coming. "The inference from that question—those *two* questions—is that one is very different from the other."

"They might be."

"From what? Or whom?" demanded Chelyag.

There was no purpose in continuing the ambiguity. "I have been ordered to duplicate my reports to the interior minister."

"Which I have forbidden."

"And which puts me in the impossible position I feared would arise. And has."

Nikolai Mikhailovich Belik's call came within thirty minutes. "I warned you against choosing the wrong side."

"I don't regard it as choosing sides. I'm following orders."

"Don't you think you might have overlooked something?"

"What?"

"How long, constitutionally, a man is allowed to serve as Russian president. And how, when he leaves office, all his acolytes and supporters are swept away with him."

Pavin appeared at the door, gesturing that the other call on Danilov's blinking telephone console was important.

"I told you to wait!"

"We didn't have any direct evidence. We needed a confession, which we got," said Reztsov. "Your jurisdiction doesn't extend to Gorki."

"That of the White House does. Having got the confession, why didn't you tell me before going to seize Zotin!"

"We needed to arrest him, too. Wrap everything up."

"So the maintanence man at Plant 35 who confessed to supplying Nikov with the UN's warhead committed suicide in his cell and Aleksai Zotin died resisting arrest?"

"That's what happened. There is the confession implicating Zotin. And the evidence of an entire *spetznaz* squad of his brigade fighting to prevent Zotin being taken into custody. Six others died. The theft from Plant 35 is solved."

Not even Reztsov's arrogance would have been as great as this without the confidence of official support. "Everything wrapped up."

"That's what I said," reminded Reztsov.

"But I meant it differently from the way you did," said Danilov.

It had been Georgi Chelyag's suggestion during the morning conversation that the impression of a combined investigation could be achieved—after announcing the intention in advance—by publicly bringing an FBI group from the embassy to Petrovka. There was an additional, practical benefit of giving them more space in which to compare the Golden Hussar photographs against those in the personnel files of ex-intelligence officers.

To protect their identities, the American group left Ulitza Chaykovskovo in an enclosed minibus, which actually got hammered by some of the protesters both leaving the embassy and arriving at militia headquarters. The closed vehicle minimized much of what Chelyag had hoped by the exercise but at least provided new television footage.

Danilov relied entirely on Yuri Pavin's selection of three junior-grade militia detectives for whose honesty the man vouched to comprise the Russian contingent. All three were young, none more than thirty.

They'd been given the records of redundant employees from every department of the old and new intelligence organization. Danilov concentrated the search upon the First Chief Directorate, exclusively responsible for overseas espionage. Following the logic that only someone attached to that directorate or one of its subdepartments—most likely the archival—would have had access to so many CIA identities. That reduced the 230 possibilities to 52. Six were women.

"We can always extend—we will, whatever the outcome—if nothing comes from the first search," he told his deputy.

While the groups were divided up, with Pavin the liaison officer, Danilov drew Cowley aside from the American group to recount his conversation with Gorki.

Spacing his words, Cowley said, "That is quite simply beyond belief."

"They don't think so."

"They must be very confident."

"Or to have chosen the wrong man in Reztsov."

"You told Chelyag?"

"Not yet."

"Let him know that *we* know."

Danilov was surprised at Cowley's political awareness and at once wondered why he should be. "America knowing is probably my greatest protection."

Very quickly there was more. When they went back to the American contingent, Paul Lambert, who declared he'd come along for the ride, said, "Guess what was on the A2 launcher?"

In sighed resignation Danilov said; "What?"

"Alcohol," announced the scientist. "Might even be vodka. Alcohol's a great cleaner, and that's what it was used for." Abruptly he smiled. "But whoever did it did it badly. Left a very good forefinger print on the trigger guard. We were even able to tell that the shooter was left-handed."

Cowley nodded to the stacked folders and said, "I wonder if there's been an attempt to sanitize those."

There hadn't been.

One of the young Russians made the match within the first hour, approaching Pavin with a print in either hand, visibly relieved at the large man's shout of "Got something!"

The Golden Hussar photograph was one of those in which the woman was too blurred to be identified. But quite clearly, although pictured at such an angle that it was impossible to be sure if he'd actually been with her, was a smiling man named in his First Chief Directorate file as Yevgenni Mechislavovich Leanov. His job was given as translator and one of the four listed languages was English.

Cowley turned over the Golden Hussar print and said, "It's one taken at the rear. They weren't using the public entrance. It's beginning to move!"

It didn't stop, although what amounted to a virtual breakthrough wasn't pictorial and was found by the detail-attentive Yuri Pavin checking through a folder that had already been scrutinized. He gestured for Cowley and Danilov to move out of the hearing of the searching groups before offering it to them.

"Ivan Gavrilovich Guzov," he said simply.

"Codirector, with Vyacheslav Fedorovich Kabanov, of the New Jersey company from which Orlenko rents 69 Bay View Avenue, Brooklyn," Cowley recognized at once.

"Gavrilovich is an Armenian patronym," continued Pavin. "It's quite customary to shorten it to Gavri."

"How many?" demanded the General.

"Five," said Hollis. He painstakingly dictated the codes, enjoying ordering the other man to repeat them back to him.

The General said, "They big? We need customers with substantial accounts."

"Yes," said Hollis. He was quite sure of the customer assets of one. It was his until now untouched own branch, where at that very moment an FBI auditor name Mark Whittier was monitoring computer movement, hunting a thief.

Carl Ashton, who was waiting for her at the Pentagon gatehouse, said, "What the hell's the panic?"

"We got it all wrong," Pamela Darnley said simply.

27

"I didn't think it fit because it wasn't as cleverly planned as everything else. But now I'm sure it is! I even think it's brilliant." They were in Ashton's inner courtyard office, Pamela leaning forward eagerly to convince the Pentagon computer security chief. She didn't feel numb anymore. She felt excited.

Ashton sat behind his desk, blank faced, her first, gabbled explanation beyond him. "Run it by me again."

Pamela sighed. "Roanne Harding was the one person who risked being identified from planting the Semtex in the Washington Memorial."

"Right," accepted Ashton. "That's why they killed her. If you'd arrested her, she could have led you to them."

Pamela smiled. "Obvious conclusion—my conclusion, your conclusion, everyone's conclusion. What about their accepting that we'd find her and setting everything up to lead us *away*!"

"This is where you lose me," protested Ashton. His hands were constantly moving about his desk, as if he were physically groping for something.

"And where I need your guidance to tell me I'm understanding it at last," encouraged Pamela. "When did you start looking for the worms inside your computer systems?"

"The day the first Watchmen message was posted, when we realized there'd been an unauthorized entry. I told you that."

"The fifteenth?"

"Yes."

"That was the actual intrusion. When did you discover the list of possible security risk employees had been wiped?"

"Not until the eighteenth."

"Why did the nine—including Roanne Harding—survive?"

"I told you that, too. By then we'd put up firewalls."

"We had a spat, remember? You kept saying 'maybe' and I asked you to be specific and you said fifteen names had been erased. *How* did you know it was precisely fifteen?"

"I'm beginning to understand." His nervous fingers stopped. Now he gripped the edge of the desk as if he needed to hold on.

"How, Carl?" she persisted. It had to be spelled out, the pieces numbered.

"The suspect dismissals were on a separate program. Sometimes, when information has been deleted, it can be recovered simply by hitting undelete; it's a built-in fail-safe. We didn't get the files back—they'd been properly wiped—but we recovered the date of the deletions."

"Which was?"

Ashton was flushed now, acknowledging the oversight. He groped into a drawer, taking out his own investigation records and thumbing through them for several minutes. He looked up, swallowing. "All on the same day. The thirteenth."

"How long would it have taken to wipe the entire program?"

"Seconds."

"How *many* seconds?" pressed Pamela.

"Not seconds," the man corrected. "It's instantaneous."

"So, on the thirteenth—two days before you put up firewalls—fifteen names were erased instantaneously. Five days later you were still able to find nine more names, Roanne Harding's among them?"

"Yes."

"You remember agreeing with me, during that argument we had, that logically the identity of the person who'd planted the Watchmen worms would have been the first thing to go?"

"Yes," the man, said tightly.

"How can you explain those nine still being in the system if it would have taken less than seconds on the thirteenth to take them out, as well? And destroy the link between Roanne Harding and the Pentagon from which we made the connection to the Washington Monument?"

"I can't."

"Her name wouldn't have meant anything to you if she had been identified in newspapers as a murder victim?"

"No."

"So we had to be led to her: and from her, led here, to the Pentagon."

"Why?"

"To make us think—as we *did* think—that Roanne Harding was the only Watchmen intruder."

"She has to be!" It was a groan.

"The message after the Moscow embassy attack was posted on your site." She felt very sure of herself, convinced she was right.

"The phony antistatic bands!" Ashton threw back. "I told you we'll never be able to calculate how many passwords and codes Roanne made available by fixing those damned things. The fact that the Moscow message *was* posted from here proves we haven't kept the bastards out by changing the lower security systems!"

"That's one of the cleverest things," said Pamela. "I went through our forensic findings, location by location, before coming here. And then read again what you and Bella Atkins told me—Bella in particular. She told me Roanne Harding's access was officially restricted to the stationery and office ordering division, which was her workplace, but that Roanne had obviously moved far beyond that. Roanne's fingerprints were everywhere, on all the bands."

"Yes," the man agreed doubtfully.

"Roanne shouldn't have been allowed access, for instance, to the gatehouse ID computer system, should she?"

"No."

"Remember you found a phony band on one of the garage terminals that shares the gatehouse database?"

The man nodded agreement.

"Although it's part of the ordering division, the accounts and invoice office is separate, isn't it? Actually on a different floor, according to the plan you gave me?"

Ashton nodded again. All the color had gone from his face. He was swallowing a lot, as if he were trying to force back the need to retch. His hands had gone back to the edge of the desk, holding on.

"There was a band there, you'll remember. And that other one in the mail room: on the computer system that records incoming and outgoing mail—including the e-mail—in the building. Roanne shouldn't have gotten anywhere near any of those: different floors, different security-classified divisions that her pass wouldn't have accessed. And do you know what, there's no forensic evidence that she actually did! Her fingerprints are over all the others, where her pass *would* have allowed her. But not on those three. There are prints, but they're smudged too badly to be positive. But because there were so many elsewhere, we *assumed* she'd fixed those, too."

"What are you saying?" demanded Ashton.

"I'm saying that Roanne, with a supposed Black Power background, was the deception, the decoy: like the virtually harmless explosion at the Washington Monument—with which she was also connected—was a deception. And littering the Pentagon with so many false antistatic bands was a deception."

"To achieve what?"

"The concealment of the real cracker the Watchmen have here that we were never supposed to find: someone who really knows how to use a computer and is probably responsible for all the website postings that we've believed—because we were *supposed* to believe—came from outside, through all the back doors Roanne opened for them."

The man looked solemnly at her for several moments. "How *are* we going to find who it is? Prove you're right?

"I don't know. But we might prove whether I'm right or not by checking the new antistatic bands at really sensitive levels—the ones you checked once and found to be safe." She stopped, trying to think of something she might have missed. "The ones that, having been guaranteed safe, wouldn't be checked again until the next regular security sweep."

"You know what they could do—disrupt or destroy even—if they've penetrated the higher levels: gone sideways to one of our connected agencies!"

"Communication satellites: intelligence-gathering satellites?" guessed Pamela.

"Dear God, I hope you're wrong," said Ashton in a voice that sounded as if he didn't think she was.

Danilov insisted they take what they considered quantum-leap discoveries back to the security-guaranteed U.S. Embassy, leaving Pavin to supervise the extended search through the remaining intelligence records. They did so discreetly and with Paul Lambert, the two breakthrough dossiers hidden in briefcases—one Lambert's—before quitting the lecture room to go through the corridors of Petrovka. They avoided the chanting protesters just as discreetly by entering the legation from the bordering alley on which Aleksandr Pushkin's house is preserved as a monument to the poet.

The date of his dismissal made Ivan Gavrilovich Guzov a victim of the KGB disbandment. The file picture was of a heavily built man with the swarthy skin and swept-back, deeply black hair of his Armenian ancestry. Compared against the snatched surveillance photograph Guzov had gained at least ten pounds, maybe more. From the listed date of birth in his dossier, he was now thirty-eight years old. He was described as a bachelor. When he read that Guzov had been a middle-ranking finance officer in the First Chief Directorate, with special responsibility for North America and Canada,

Cowley, the counterespionage expert, said, "Paymaster for overseas deep cover or diplomatic agents."

"Who as paymaster would have had details—and access to their archives—of all those agents," completed Danilov.

"At last a shape, a pattern!" said Cowley.

"Was the realtor business from which Orlenko is renting Brooklyn the legitimate business he was referring to if anything happened to Guzov?" wondered Danilov. "If it is, there's no purpose in continuing the company search in Chicago."

Cowley considered the question. "It's already been started. I'll let it run. And add Guzov's name. Chicago seems to come up a lot, and it *is* a shipping entry point into America."

Yevgenni Mechislavovich Leanov had also worked at Lubyanka for the old KGB. He was forty-two years old and ironically had attended the same Moscow University language college as Dimitri Danilov, although two years later. Leanov had joined the intelligence organization directly after he had graduated, with distinction, and for two years acted as deputy supervisor for the English language department. The last listed Moscow address was Ulitza Krymskij Val.

Cowley said, "I'm surprised they let him go."

"There's never any logic in Russian bureaucracy," said Danilov.

"The file says he's married," Cowley pointed out. "Be interesting to hear what his wife's voice sounds like?"

"We're getting a voice analysis from the intercepted conversation, incidentally," came in Lambert. "Arriving in tomorrow's diplomatic bag." The forensic scientist stopped at the sudden expression on Danilov's face. "What?"

Danilov frowned, shaking his head: "I just had the oddest recollection. Stupid. There was something about the tape when I first heard it: couldn't think what it was, but now it's come to me. I thought I'd heard the woman's voice before."

Now Cowley regarded the Russian quizzically. "How? When?"

Danilov was embarrassed, particularly in front of Paul Lambert, whom he scarcely knew. "It's ridiculous. Forget it."

Lambert said, "The analysis is that it's a Muscovite accent. Age range between thirty-four and forty-five, which is pretty wide."

Danilov shook his head again. "It's ridiculous," he repeated.

"You want to listen to the tape again?" offered Lambert.

"We've got more positive leads to follow," dismissed the Russian.

That was Pamela Darnley's thought when she got back to the J. Edgar Hoover building to further developments and a coincidence about voice recognition that had occurred to her and Danilov within an hour of each other.

Besides reacting to Cowley's instructions to add Guzov's name to the Chicago company search, Terry Osnan had liaised with Manhattan, from which the New Jersey surveillance was being coordinated, to suggest it be intensified. He handed Pamela the list she'd asked for earlier and said, "We could draw a total of fourteen people from Seattle, Austin, and Atlanta for that and to build up Chicago."

"Let's do it," she decided. Pamela didn't fill the incident room coordinator in on her Pentagon visit, wanting the further confirmation of Carl Ashton's promised computer sweep to announce her deduction as an unarguable fact instead of a theory based for the moment on an inexplicable date difference.

Instead she went back to her earlier review. Because she'd urged the tapping of the public telephones, she concentrated on the billing from Bay View Avenue from which the calling pattern had first emerged. She began searching for patterns additional to those already established in the four cities, even though there'd already been a computer comparison that hadn't thrown up any extra ones. She created her own handwritten pattern blocks, listing on a yellow legal pad Chicago, Manhattan, Pittsburgh, and Washington against the dates of the calls for more repetitions that hadn't already been eliminated, curious now that she knew the added significance of the New Jersey property company that no calls were recorded to its number from Orlenko's house. On impulse she even looked for a call from Brooklyn to the public booth at the New Rochelle mall from which the booby-trap massacre had been initiated. There wasn't one.

At the end of half an hour the only thing Pamela noted was the absence of contact between Trenton and Brooklyn. She noted it on her pad, although she was unsure of its importance or relevance. She was looking too hard, wanting too much, Pamela warned herself.

If she was right about the Pentagon, which she was convinced she was, it would be her unqualified, unshared success—probably reaching the president himself, for the earthquake it would cause—and that had to be enough. *Was* enough.

It was probably because earlier she'd looked for the New Rochelle number on Orlenko's records that Pamela played the Highway Patrol copy tape of the burning cruiser report. She did so absently; for the first few seconds of what lasted less than a minute Pamela only half listened. But then, abruptly, she rewound the tape to the beginning.

There's what looks like a large fire in the woods by the New Rochelle creek . . .

Can you give me a name, madam . . .

It could be a boat with people on board. You'd better get there, check it out.

Madam. . . . ?

The sound of the telephone being replaced.

She'd heard the voice before. Just as quickly as the certainty came to her, so did the stupidity of it. She found the voiceprint analysis from Osnan's meticulous indexing, the doubt growing with its first line that an obvious attempt had been made at disguising distortion, although the intonation had been from a Southern, not a northern, state. She listened to it several more times and then to the first eavesdropping on Bay View Avenue, concentrating on Mary Jo's voice. Mary Jo, she remembered, who had been born in Atlanta, Georgia, but whose Southern accent was not immediately recognizable. There was a similarity, but . . . Looking too hard, wanting too much, she thought. But there was no record of a scientific comparison being made, when there should have been. Another oversight to be corrected.

It was midafternoon, long after she'd given the voice comparison instructions, when Leonard Ross personally told her the attorney general—and all four district attorneys, even the reluctant New York legal chief—had agreed to the requested taps on all the public telephones.

Carl Ashton's contact was an hour later. "We found a phony band on a terminal line of one of the Joint Chief's secretaries."

"Oh, Jesus!" said Ross, when Pamela called him back.

Patrick Hollis had been particularly careful that the workstation allocated to the FBI auditor was directly outside his own glass-walled
office. Mark Whittier was in his sight line at all times without Hollis
appearing constantly to watch the man.

Hollis was sure he detected the physical reaction—a slight,
pushed-back-in-his-chair start, then a quick coming forward over
the keyboard—when Whittier detected the first intrusion. Because
he was so attentive, Hollis saw the beginning of the instinctive glance
of triumph toward him from the man and was able to turn away,
appearing to look into a drawer, before it was completed. When he
stared back into the open plan room, Whittier was already talking
animatedly into the telephone.

To have registered as positively as it had with the auditor the
transfer would have had to have been exactly what he'd warned
against, dollars instead of cents, Hollis knew. What good was a general who ignored intelligence? That was the recipe for losing battles,
not winning them.

28

The Pentagon discovery caused the earthquake Pamela Darnley anticipated, the aftershocks rippling from Washington to Moscow—
and Henry Hartz—and back again. Crisis meetings were convened
at varying levels in both capitals, for people unsure what to do to
sound—to themselves, at least—as if they did.

Pamela rode expectantly to the American White House with
Leonard Ross but was disappointed by the meeting. Although it
established her personal recognition at the highest level, the encounter was chaired by Chief of Staff Frank Norton, not the president himself. She was ready, if a further chance came; prepared to
make it, if it didn't, although aware that she had to be careful of
her self-promotion appearing too obvious.

Hartz was patched through—visually, by television satellite, as well as audibly—to announce he was informing the Russian president as a precaution against knee-jerk retaliation to whatever and however the terrorists utilized their access.

"They may not intend to, not immediately," intruded the FBI director, briefed more completely than anyone apart from Pamela, whose presence was advisory. For the first time Ross outlined the intercepted conversation between Brooklyn and Moscow to the entire group. He said, "They've had the Pentagon access we didn't suspect for a week. Instead of using it, they want more weapons, germ and biological as well as conventional. Which we believe we know how they're financing. If they'd wanted to use the Pentagon access they could have done so already."

"You got any more maybes, mights, and on-the-other-hands?" demanded CIA Director John Butterworth. "We can't make any sensible decision based on those hypotheses!"

"We can," insisted Ross, the calmest person in the room. "There's one very necessary and very sensible decision that's absolutely essential. It's that the Russians mustn't make our Pentagon disaster public. They must limit it, even within their own White House. If the terrorists get the slightest hint of how much we know, they won't wait. They'll use their Pentagon intrusion to do God knows what."

It was Norton who posed the question to the Pentagon officials. "What *could* they do?"

"Virtually whatever they damned well like," said General Sinclair Smith, making it an accusation against Carl Ashton, sitting beside him. "Realign—misdirect—satellites. Access operational secrets up to the security level of presidential decision. Send ships and aircraft around in circles with false orders." He spread his hands helplessly. "Think of your worst-nightmare scenario. Treble it and try to imagine something worse. You'll be getting there."

"You're telling us it's out of control?" said Norton.

"Is that what I'm saying, Carl?" the general asked the man next to him.

Ashton said, "We're working—already started—from the top

down. All satellite operational and activating codes are being changed. *Every* password, entry code, and system is being switched and reprogrammed. And not just firewalled but iron-boxed—"

"What the hell's firewalled and iron-boxed!" Hartz broke in impatiently from Moscow.

"A firewall is a barrier between a cluster of machines and outside use," said Ashton. "An iron box is an added precaution that's sometimes better described in hacker—or cracker—jargon as a flytrap. Any unauthorized entry is caught, and if the connection is long enough, it can be traced. Any unauthorized ID—which in this case would be the old entry codes and passwords, all of which we know—will be picked up immediately."

"A question," announced Butterworth. "You've been tricked, right? Some son of a bitch is still *inside* the Pentagon—some son of a bitch who really knows how to use a computer and can do what he likes with it. It doesn't matter a damn how much we keep it all under wraps, hidden from the public. *He'll* know, won't he? But we don't know who it is so we can't stop him finding out."

"All the satellite changes aren't being made from *inside* the Pentagon for that very good reason," said Ashton. "It's being done by the National Security Agency, and it'll be completed by midnight tonight. By dawn tomorrow—again by the National Security Agency—everything at presidential level will be reprogramed—"

"What about ballistic missiles?" broke in Norton. "Russia is supposed to have retargeted their intercontinental stuff away from us. We done the same?"

Smith shifted, looking toward the television picture of the secretary of state. "Everything will be by this time tomorrow. That's a precaution ahead of changing firing codes. And there are two, quite separate, for every one: One, by itself, won't activate anything until there's human—which means presidential—confirmation by the second. Without that, they can't be fired. Those codes are switched every two days, which means there've been at least two changes from the time we believe the terrorists have had access. Despite the fact that the firing needs presidential authority, we're actually deactivating them, making them inoperable.

"What about China?" demanded Hartz, from afar.

The general's shift was even more discomfitted. "Being changed, too."

"Deactivated?" pressed Norton.

"That order hasn't yet been given."

"Give it," instructed the chief of staff. "Stand everything down."

"That would leave the United States of America totally vulnerable," protested General Smith.

"We can talk—*are* talking—to Moscow," said Norton. "We can't talk to Beijing: We couldn't trust them not to go public, after the United Nations attack. If they did—and the Watchmen managed to launch something against China—Beijing would retaliate. That's a greater risk than the United States being, in theory, *vulnerable* to attack: We're not; only from terrorists who already think we're bare-assed anyway."

"I speak on behalf of the Joint Chiefs of Staff," said General Smith formally. "I mean no personal or official offense to you, sir, but the Joint Chiefs will not accept a standdown of this magnitude without the explicit, written authority of the president as commander-in-chief. It's the required chain of command."

Norton nodded, unoffended, accepting both the argument and the protective security system. "You'll get the written order. Going back to an earlier question, we're not out of control, are we? Badly exposed but recovering."

"I think there's more we could do," urged Hartz, over his link. "They might not wait; certainly won't if there's any delay or failure to get their weapons resupply from here. Which we're doing everything to prevent. They're into spectaculars. As well as doing everything that's been outlined—and I'm going to speak directly to the president about deactivating our Chinese missiles—we've got to identify the Watchmen's most likely targets. I'll order my analysts to do that and suggest you do the same at the agency, John."

"It's an ongoing program, from the time we prevented the Lincoln Memorial explosion and expected them to do something else," assured Butterworth.

She wouldn't have to make her chance, Pamela recognized, deciding she could even take Ross's sideways glance as an invitation, whether it was or not. "The space shuttle," she declared. "It's an obvious target: It could actually be the explanation for their not having used the Pentagon access yet. There's a launch scheduled in two weeks, I think."

Ross's second look was sharper.

"Could they have gotten into NASA? And the shuttle's onboard computers?" demanded Norton.

"Yes," confirmed Ashton.

"That's the sort of analysis we want," congratulated the secretary of state.

On their way back to the FBI, Ross said, "Why didn't you mention the space shuttle to me before the meeting?"

"It didn't occur to me until Hartz asked for the most likely targets," Pamela said easily. It was a lie, like her seeming uncertainty about the actual date of the next launch, which she'd checked before leaving for the White House. It was scheduled for exactly two weeks from now, and two Russian astronauts were included in the crew. Pamela had never imagined it would all go so well.

By yet another twist of logic, the way the Pentagon situation unfolded actually sidelined Dimitri Danilov, creating something of a respite. Despite how closely he was working—and was known by the Americans to be working—with William Cowley, there was no question of his being part of the crisis meetings at the U.S. Embassy that followed the Washington alert. And Henry Hartz's decision—made before the satellite link to the matching Washington meeting—fully to brief the Russian president meant all Danilov had to do was advise Georgi Chelyag in advance, as William Cowley had in turn told him.

In the time before Cowley was summoned by the secretary of state, he and Danilov agreed on their surveillance on Yevgenni Mechislavovich Leanov. Because, in daylight, men wearing easily identifiable American clothes were too much of a risk, they detached the four Russian detectives from the ongoing intelligence archive search to the Krymskij Val apartment, where the instant bonus was establishing that Leanov still lived there, apparently alone. They also agreed the surveillance—more so from its rear than from its front—

had to be maintained on the Golden Hussar in the hope of connecting, and picturing, the now-identified former KGB linguist with a woman. And because it would be covered by darkness, that observation should remain an American assignment.

Danilov still felt so underemployed that on his way from the embassy to Petrovka he delivered Olga's photograph to Irena, whose comparable work shifts he knew, to pass on to Igor. Irena asked him what he intended to do, which Danilov thought an odd question although he understood its point. He replied that his job was very demanding and occupied most of his time. She told him if she could help in any way, all he had to do was ask. Danilov found that even more odd, considering the woman's obvious connivance in Olga's affair with the hairdresser.

Danilov drove on to the Organized Crime Bureau building, his mind more in the past that in the immediate present or future. For a reason he didn't bother to define he regarded the handing over of Olga's picture to be the final separation—the end. The final, definite act had been to keep his own single recollection—their wedding photograph and marriage certificate—although again for a reason he couldn't define. He just had it. Even the need, which he'd never imagined being able to lose—had never wanted to lose—to mourn at Larissa's grave was over.

Irena's question presented itself in his mind, demanding more than platitudes. What *did* he intend to do? Work was the only thing he had left—had been, since Larissa. But for how much longer would he even have that, after the choice he'd made? Not made, he corrected at once: had imposed upon him. Hardly an important qualification. Whether he liked it or not—which he didn't, because he didn't want to follow any factional banner—he was in the presidential camp. If that fell, so did he. He was abruptly, deeply, worried by an uncertainty beyond his ability to resolve.

The uncertainty remained while he disclosed the American Pentagon debacle to Yuri Pavin, before going on to talk about the division of the surveillance assignments.

"We're being stretched very thin of men we can trust," warned Pavin.

"And still with too many loose ends," accepted Danilov. "Any lead on the American car used in the embassy attack?"

His deputy shook his head. "We know it's an old design, from the guard's description. The brigades—the entrepreneurs—are only interested in status symbols as new as tomorrow. I don't think the guard saw the vehicle properly: might have recognized it as American and imagined the tail fins."

"What about Igor Ivanovich Baratov?" remembered Danilov, briefly caught by the man having the same given name as Olga's lover. "He runs garages but said he didn't want to get involved in American cars with Viktor Nikov. Why don't we run the description by him?" He stopped and Pavin waited, curious.

"No!" said Danilov. "No, we won't." He laughed. "I know! I know who the woman is from the Golden Hussar."

Patrick Hollis had established the pattern of joining the FBI auditor in the cafeteria, savoring the cachet of association in front of Carole Parker and Robert Standing and all the others who despised him. Whittier smiled invitingly at his approach, and Hollis eased into the opposite seat. He knew everyone was looking, even though he had his back to the room. "How's it going?"

"Pretty good," said the man.

"You've certainly been hard at it."

"That's the job."

Hollis jerked his hand vaguely toward the room behind him. "Everyone knows who you are and what you're doing by now."

"Inevitable," accepted the auditor. "Too late for anyone to hide their tracks, though."

"You got someone?"

"I can't tell you that."

"Of course not. I'm sorry. It was just . . ." Hollis stumbled intentionally, sure he was acting out the apparent difficulty exactly right.

Whittier held up a hand with the forefinger narrowed within a fraction of his thumb. "I can tell you that we're that close."

There was more progress than setback for Pamela Darnley when she arrived in the incident room. Silently Terry Osnan handed her the

Chicago printout upon which Ivan Gavrilovich Guzov was listed, together with Arseni Yanovich Orlenko, as a codirector of Over-Ocean Inc. The Chicago office had already applied to a judge in chambers for a telephone tap.

There was also a report from the audio science department. There was no match between the voice of Mary Jo Orlenko and the woman who had called the Highway Patrol from the New Rochelle shopping precinct.

29

There was too much activity at too high a level at the U.S. Embassy and Petrovka was too porous, so at Cowley's suggestion they gathered at his suite at the Savoy. Cowley, who'd needed to excuse himself from the continuing embassy preparations for Henry Hartz's meeting with the Russian president, said, "You sure!"

"As sure as I can be without scientific proof." It was the first time Danilov had been in Cowley's room. There was a bottle of Glenfiddich scotch, with glasses, on a tray on a side table.

Yuri Pavin, who had to be included because Cowley couldn't be involved in the intended confrontation and whose presence was a further reason for their not having met at the American legation, said, "I think so, too."

"Jesus!" said Cowley. He wondered why, when it began to happen, the resolution of cases invariably seemed mundane compared to the crimes themselves. A premature reflection, he realized. A resolution to an investigation of this enormity was always going to seem an anticlimax, and at the moment they were as far away from concluding it as they'd ever been.

"It could provide a lot of answers," encouraged Danilov. "Explain the murders. Why Osipov and Zotin got killed. Even double warheads from two separate plants."

"Valeri Karpov was tortured and killed!" reminded Cowley.

" 'It was business: only ever business,' " quoted Danilov.

"Jesus!" Cowley repeated.

Danilov turned to Paul Lambert and the technician the forensic chief had brought with him. "Will you be able to make positive identification from a telephone call?"

"That's the level of distortion we're working on from the Golden Hussar, with the addition of a distance factor," Lambert pointed out. "It should be enough. A less relayed—less diluted—exchange would be better."

"We'll try for both," decided Danilov. "Advance warning doesn't matter."

The technician wired Cowley's room phone and tested the pickup by calling Barry Martlew at the embassy. The equipment worked precisely as it should have. The technician rewound and wiped the tape. "All set, when you're ready."

"You," announced Danilov, to his deputy. "It would more likely be you, wouldn't it?"

The telephone table and nearby chair appeared too small for the huge man. From his reaction, the reply at the other end was very quick. Pavin played his role to perfection. He was very sorry. He didn't intend to intrude. The return was a necessary formality, which he hoped wouldn't cause any distress. He was sorry he didn't have any news, but they could talk about that when he got there. He was grateful for the understanding and cooperation. He could certainly be there in an hour. It wouldn't take very long.

They listened heads bent, attentively, to the instant replay. Danilov realized he was breathing shallowly, as quietly as possible. He thought the others were, too.

Cowley said, "I think you're right."

Lambert said, "I do, too."

"Let's make sure," said Danilov. He and Pavin stripped to the waist and stood self-consciously while the sound technician taped them with body wires.

The man said, "I'm afraid it will hurt when we tear the tape off, but I've got to put this much on to keep it all as close and as inconspicuously as possible against your skin."

Danilov was surprised that he had far more body hair than his deputy. Larissa had called him her bear, he remembered. The technician fed the wires and microphones through their clothes as they dressed, standing back to check the concealment, patting each to ensure he'd fixed the wires to avoid their being detectable if either man was touched. The final preparation was to test the recordings and sound levels, which again were perfect.

"How's it feel?" asked Lambert.

"Like I'm trussed up, ready to be cooked," said Danilov.

"You're doing the cooking," said Cowley.

On their way out to Pereulok Samokatnaja, Pavin said, "All we need is talk, isn't it?"

"And to avoid arousing the slightest suspicion," warned Danilov.

When Naina Karpov opened the door of the converted apartment, he said, "Thank you very much for seeing us like this."

Naina Karpov was as neatly dressed as before, in a sweater and skirt, and again there was no makeup or jewelry. The attitude of uncaring resignation had gone, though. Today there was no child watching television, either.

Danilov said, "I thought I'd come, too. Just in case you'd remembered something since last time." She was curious. Understandable: no cause for concern. There was more danger in over- than underreacting.

"You gave me your card to call you, if I did."

Danilov shrugged his shoulders. "You never know."

"No," said the widow. "I haven't remembered anything since last time. Can I offer you tea?"

Quite calm, unworried, Danilov recognized. How it should be. He refused tea. So did Pavin.

"I'm glad your daughter's better," said Danilov.

"It was nothing. What have you found out?"

The voice, which they'd thought on the first occasion to be the huskiness of grief, sounded just the same, deep in her throat. Danilov said, "Nothing at all that helps."

"You actually think Valeri Alexandrovich was involved in all this other business?"

"He worked for a factory that manufactured weapons," Pavin pointed out. "But we've no proof. It's embarrassing for us. And the Americans."

"I'm sure he wasn't." Looking to Danilov she said, "I read—or maybe I saw it on television—that you'd been in America?"

"It's a joint investigation. I'm the liaison."

"More seems to have happened there than here?"

"They were lucky, preventing a terrible explosion. But nothing's led them anywhere."

"Was that all it was, luck?"

"Entirely. A park attendant saw something he didn't understand on the statue."

She shuddered. "I still can't believe that Valeri Alexandrovich knew gangsters—people who would do things like that. That's what the papers said: that the man he was found in the river with was a gangster and that he worked for a crime group whose boss was killed, too. Is that true?"

"We've nothing to connect your husband to the crime group, only the man who was killed at the same time," said Danilov. "And we haven't been able to find out how they knew each other."

"But it wasn't another woman, was it?"

Danilov had forgotten her persistence at their first meeting. "No. We've found nothing about another woman."

She looked at Pavin. "You said you had things to return to me?"

"Your husband's belongings," said the colonel. "Wallet and what was in it. His watch, although it's stopped. And your wedding ring." He offered the plastic container.

Naina Karpov looked briefly away, apparently composing herself, before reaching out to accept it. "Thank you."

"We didn't think you'd want anything else . . . clothes . . . ?" said Pavin.

"No," the woman said sharply. "Certainly not that. This is all I want."

"We're sorry to have troubled you," apologized Danilov. "If—"

"I know." she stopped him. "I've got the card."

"It's her," said Pavin, back in the car.

"I know," said Danilov. "And that's only the half of it."

"Do you think she believed two supposed detectives couldn't have made more progress than we said we had?"

"Easily," said Danilov. "This is Russia."

The technician hadn't exaggerated. It hurt like hell when he pulled off the tape holding the wire in place.

"How!" demanded Cowley. He'd insisted on opening the whiskey in his suite and given Lambert and the technician a drink before they returned to the embassy. Now only he, Danilov, and Pavin remained. They were on their second, and now the bottle was less than half full.

"It was clearing up Olga's things," said Danilov. "I've kept our marriage certificate. And a photograph. In a box. Which was how Naina Karpov kept her things: She showed them to us when we saw her the first time. Then we were trying to find her husband's connection to Viktor Nikov: find anyone who might have met Nikov when he arrived from Gorki. We had been told one might have been Igor Baratov, a name I thought I'd come across searching for Larissa's killers—"

"Wait!" stopped the American, holding up his hand. "I'm totally lost!"

"It didn't consciously register with me that I was keeping things in a box, the same as Naina Karpov. Not until this morning. It was only the coincidence, at first. Then I remembered her voice. But more important what I'd read on her marriage certificate."

"What?" Cowley frowned.

"Baratov," Danilov said simply. "It was Naina's name before she married." He paused. "She's related to a man—a brother, I'd guess—who knew Nikov and who admits talking to him after he arrived from Gorki. But says he didn't want to get mixed up in a deal he thought involved American cars. His full name is Igor Ivanovich Baratov, and he was a bull for the now supposedly broken up Osipov Brigade, before he almost got killed and quit to run a legitimate car business."

Cowley was smiling now. He topped off all their glasses and said, "Now the pieces are really fitting!"

"If it's proved scientifically to be Naina Karpov's voice, which I think it will," said the careful Pavin.

Danilov said, "It took me a long time to realize it. Which was a mistake I shouldn't have made."

"For Christ's sake!" protested Cowley. "We've only had a voice to compare for forty-eight hours! Less."

"I meant the Baratov name. I shouldn't have missed that." His fixation with Larissa's death clouding everything, he thought.

"We've caught up now."

"Have we?" challenged Danilov. "None of us doubt it, so let's work on the assumption it *is* Naina Karpov. We know, from the Golden Hussar tape, she can get another warhead. Who from, now that her husband, who worked at the plant, is dead?"

Cowley stopped smiling. "We also know, from the tape, that there was a double cross. What if Valeri Karpov *wasn't* his wife's supplier?"

"And she had him killed?" questioned Pavin, disbelievingly.

"It was supposed to be someone from America," reminded Danilov.

" 'It was business: only ever business' " quoted Cowley, in reply. "Not heartbroken if she didn't actually take out the contract."

Danilov looked at his deputy. "Do we know, definitely, that the Osipov Brigade broke up after his killing?"

"No," Pavin admitted immediately. "Like so much else, it came from Ashot Mizin."

"So it's a lie," dismissed Danilov, at once. To Cowley's frown, Danilov said, "We know Mizin's on the payroll, and I'm very glad I did nothing about it. You think it's too much to speculate that Naina Karpov has become head of what was the Osipov family?"

"It wouldn't take a lot to convince me," accepted the American.

"It isn't the most important question," said Pavin. "We still don't know who her supplier is."

"Or how to find out," completed Danilov.

Pamela Darnley immediately realized the leads made possible linking the two Russians with OverOcean Inc., the most obvious and important being the name of a consignee to whom anything might have been shipped from Russia.

Yet another telephone tap was granted, after a bureau lawyer applied—and explained—to a judge in chambers. By the time that happened Frank Norton, at the White House, had invoked presidential authority to sweep aside the traditional obstructive hostility between the FBI and the IRS to get the company's tax returns made available to one of the bureau's few remaining auditors not involved in the embezzlement investigation, which had spread to sixty-four branches of four different banks operating in four eastern states.

OverOcean's accounts were immaculate and all its taxes fully paid up. Its complete financial returns provided a detailed record of the company's operations over the preceding two years of its incorporation, from which a list was compiled of every shipping company it had ever used, particularly any with obvious connections with Eastern Europe. Very quickly it was seen that although there was no direct Russian trading during those two years, OverOcean had six times shipped cargo from the Polish port of Gdansk aboard freighters operated by the Cidicj line. The last had been one month before the attack upon the United Nations.

With dates to work from, Pamela assigned four agents freed from the Lake Shore Drive public telephone tap to trace the cargo manifests declared to U.S. Customs on arrival. In every instance the cargo had been containerized and described as farm equipment returned for refurbishment. According to Customs' records, no container had ever been opened for examination. Each had been marked for Chicago dockside collection, for onward delivery by OverOcean itself.

A disappointed Pamela Darnley exclaimed, "As easy as that!"

"Not next time," promised Terry Osnan. "Now we know how to put the stopper in the bottle."

"We hope," said the unconvinced woman.

In his Moscow hotel suite, Cowley replaced the telephone and smiled at Danilov. "It's definitely Naina Karpov's voiceprint. Congratulations."

"There are two garages that we know about," Pavin set out. "The larger is on Nikitskij Boulevard—that's Baratov's outlet for Mercedes. The other one is on Ulitza Kazakova. Mostly Zils from there."

"Selling or repairing?" asked Cowley.

"Both," said Pavin.

"Stock?"

"Seemed a lot available. I only went once to each place."

"And everything's legit?"

"Looked like it," said Pavin. "But it wasn't in any detail—not like the need is now."

"If he has a lot of stock, he'll have other places to keep it," guessed Cowley.

"They'd suspect something if we openly approach him so soon after seeing the woman," said Danilov. "We'll have to split the Leanov surveillance."

"If they've taken over the Osipov Brigade, Anatoli Lasin would know about it," Pavin pointed out.

Cowley shook his head. "I don't think we can risk going anywhere near anyone. It's a bastard that even now, we still haven't got anything *legal* we can move on spread like this between America and Russia!"

"Sometimes," said Pavin, "the law gets in the way of enforcing it."

The other two men took it as truism, not cynicism. Neither smiled.

Pamela Darnley wasn't smiling, either, because the development that should have been to her credit ended, in her opinion if no one else's, in more frustration than the unqualified success it should have been.

Because there was no precedent, it had been impossible to predict the volume of calls from or to the limited number of public telephones on the contact list from Bay View Avenue.

It was so great that it overwhelmed every physical monitor; within two hours that had to be abandoned for duplicated sound recordings. The delay in reading the transcripts built up to three hours before one of the Washington technicians listening to the targeted D.C.

phone heard what they were waiting for. By then the conversation—between the Washington telephone and that on Chicago's Lake Shore Drive upon which Pamela had reduced physical surveillance—was three hours and seven minutes old.

Pamela wasn't satisfied that the Washington voiceprint proved to be that of the woman who'd made the booby-trap call from New Rochelle. Or that they had a new voice trace from the man who'd spoken from Lake Shore Drive, who was obviously a leader—maybe *the* leader—of the Watchmen. And they'd lost him.

30

Once again there was no identification. The man said, "Any problem?" It was a deep bass voice. American. No discernible accent.

"They haven't got a clue." Her voice was deeper than how she'd distorted it from New Rochelle.

"They won't find anything?"

"No way they can until it's too late. More surprises than they can ever guess."

"We're going to mount another operation first."

"What?"

"A warhead. One that works this time."

"How can you be sure?"

"Because we showed them last time what happens if it doesn't."

"United Nations?"

"Not decided yet. There'll be some other stuff, too. I've got a lot coming in."

"Separate, you mean?"

"One after the other, bang, bang, bang." He laughed. "That's good: bang, bang, bang!

She laughed obediently. "I've been working my ass off getting the money." There was another laugh. "Kinda fun, helping ourselves."

"How much *are* you taking, for yourself?"

There was a pause. "Cab fare is all."

"That's OK. And we've all been working at it."

"We got enough?"

"Whatever we're short I'm going to fine the asshole for going AWOL."

"What'd he say?"

"He had a virus."

"You think it's true?"

"He got chicken: changed his mind."

"You want me to go on having fun and helping myself?"

"Gotta get a price from the Russians yet; maybe put it on hold for a coupla days."

"Any hard feelings there?"

"I guess but so what? We're the buyers, they're the sellers. What choice they got, they want to make money?"

"We would have been there by now, that fucking thing gone off like it should have."

"It will next time. And maybe we'll do something else in Moscow. That worked better than we expected."

"What?"

"Need to speak to them there: See what ideas they got."

"America taking over the Moscow investigation was good."

"You see the speculation there could be government changes there—the president even?"

"I saw it. Be good to claim credit. Prove our strength."

"We *will* claim credit. We'll deserve it."

"When do you want me to call?"

"Friday. Same time. But not this number."

"Security change?"

"It's time. You got the next number?"

"Of course. What about an announcement on the Net like before?"

"Need to finalize the target first. Might even do Moscow before here. We'll talk about that on Friday, too."

"Take care, brother."

"And you, sister."

Pamela was glad the director insisted on time to read everything. It gave her the matching space to talk it through with Terry Osnan— lessen her fury at the setbacks that couldn't have been avoided and the stupidity that could—and read what had come in from Moscow. She also made several phone calls.

When she did finally enter the fifth-floor office Leonard Ross greeted her with "We got a new ball game here?"

"New game plan, certainly," she agreed. There was no way to avoid some of the responsibility. It might be an idea, maybe, to admit at least to part.

"Talk it through."

A sudden awareness further dampened her anger. She *had* made it! She'd attended the topmost planning session at the White House—and been acknowledged—and here she was, by herself, being asked for opinions by the director of the Federal Bureau of Investigation, who called her by her first name. Which made today such a bastard, she thought, the annoyance flaring again. She had to think of everything she said before saying it. "After all the effort, the public telephone taps are useless, now they've changed their numbers."

"What about picking the new ones up from Orlenko's billing, like we did the others?"

"Maybe, in time. But we don't know how much time we've got. Or if Orlenko will call them, like he did last time. We can't rely on it."

"Didn't we have Lake Shore Drive under physical surveillance? Cameras?"

Careful, Pamela warned herself: Apportion as much blame as possible away from herself. "With the tap in place—and Chicago stretched, checking out OverOcean—I agreed the surveillance could be reduced. I *didn't* mean—or approve—that reduction in any way including cameras."

Ross regarded her steadily for several moments. "Nothing?"

"I don't know," Pamela admitted. "We have the conversation specifically timed. The photographic coverage is estimated. There might be a half hour overlap."

"Damn!"

"I know."

"That's a bad mistake, Pamela. A hell of a bad mistake."

Pamela said nothing.

Ross waved the transcript at her. "This could be the man in charge!"

"I recognize that." She didn't think Damn. She thought Fuck! fuck! fuck!

"What about the taps on OverOcean? And the Trenton company?" demanded Ross. He was only just controlling the anger.

"Everything strictly business. Nothing relevant at all."

"And the two Russians, Guzov and Kabanov? What the hell we doing about them?"

Still only just in control, judged Pamela. "Both houses bugged from the exchange. We didn't think we could risk another entry like in Brooklyn." William Cowley didn't think, not "we." Should she have qualified the decision? Too late now. The encounter was far more critical than she'd anticipated. Wanted. Hurriedly she added, "Twenty-four-hour physical surveillance, of course. Including communication vehicles. Nothing so far."

"I'd like a legal reason to bring the bastards in—cut the thing off at the head."

Could she risk the argument? She had to, because there was one to make and because there was more than enough in the conversation to stage at least a partial recovery. "We would not be cutting them off at the head. We don't know who or what that head is."

"What the hell *do* we know, then? Know that takes us one inch forward!"

Pamela snatched the chance. "We know the New Rochelle trap was baited from Washington, so if we identify the voice, we can consider multiple homicide as the legality you're looking for. We've got positive confirmation that they *are* inside the Pentagon—or have access, at least—and that something's already been set up that they don't expect us to find: 'more surprises than they can ever guess,' " she quoted. "That could mean more than one thing. We know that they intend using a warhead they don't yet have in two, not one, separate attacks and that the UN could be one of the targets. We know they're thinking of doing something else in Moscow and from that one remark—'need to speak to them there: See what ideas they got'—I'd say there's a contact route we don't know about, not involving Brooklyn and the Golden Hussar. And I'd say it's more than likely we've confirmed how they're financing everything—" She straggled to a breathless but intentional stop, worried she had begun to sound too strident.

"But what can we do about any of it?"

"The finance guys we've got in the banks are setting electronic traps they say could give them a trace."

Ross lifted and dropped the transcript. "He just told her to stop."

"He doesn't yet know the price Naina Karpov is asking, which we do. We still don't have a definite figure, but the estimate is that from all the banks we know are being robbed, the total is just over a million. They're short. They'll have to start up again."

Ross smiled at last. "Yes they will, won't they?"

"And we've got OverOcean," continued Pamela. "Chicago's *got* to be their entry: their base, even, judging from this intercept."

The FBI director went back to it. "Who's the asshole who's got to be fined?"

"Their bank source, obviously."

"*How?*" demanded Ross. "Four banks! That many branches!"

"Banks deal with other banks," said Pamela. "But to have that access he'll have to be fairly high."

" 'Brother,' " quoted the director. " 'Sister.' Black-speak? Roanne Harding?"

"Could be. Copied a lot by Caucasians, though. The voice intonation doesn't give any indication."

"Could the limited Chicago photographs be of any practical use?"

"I'm running every one through records here. Been doing that from the beginning. The army still insists any comparison is impossible with discharged personnel." She paused, creating the division. "I've already told Carl Ashton about the conversation. He said it was confirmation he didn't need. And I've sent the entire transcript to Moscow, of course."

"I talked with Bill," said Ross.

"He told me. That you'd talked, I mean. Not in any detail."

"In detail it came down to what we've decided: that we still can't move," said the exasperated director.

In Moscow neither Cowley nor Danilov had decided they couldn't move, either separately or together, although they'd both reached the same furious conclusion as the FBI director and of Pamela Darnley before him.

"You had the Watchmen's leader," said Danilov.

"And lost him," agreed Cowley.

Georgi Chelyag's call anticipated Danilov's by thirty minutes, and Danilov went directly from the American embassy to the Russian White House. He avoided the continuing protests by using the side-alley route but was reminded by some of the banner slogans of the impending Duma vote of no confidence in the president. That automatically led his mind to the interior minister's direct threat, after his initial complaint to the presidential aide. In the last twenty-four—or was it thirty-six?—hours he'd consciously avoided thinking about it, but now it forced itself into his mind, demanding attention. Which achieved nothing. What was the point—more important, the protection—in raising it further? The conversation itself was something else about which he had insufficient proof. No proof at all, in fact. So to complain—seek Chelyag's intervention for a second time—would simply worsen an already irrevocable situation between that familiar rock and that inevitable hard place, with no way out. It really was a shitty expression. He had to stop using it, even in his mind.

He was ushered immediately into Chelyag's overly ornate, baroque office, which the squat man appeared far too inconspicuous to occupy. Chelyag remained behind the desk, which fit the office but not the man. No note-takers and therefore no records, Danilov realized.

Chelyag began speaking even before Danilov sat down, using a dossier that clearly contained the notes—possibly even the verbatim transcript—of the president's meeting with Henry Hartz. The recitation took the chief of staff a full fifteen minutes, and it was almost as long as that before Danilov understood why he was being told.

"Well?" Chelyag demanded, finally looking up.

"Nothing was held back, as far as the investigation is concerned," Danilov confirmed at once.

Chelyag allowed a rare smile. "That's good. They're being honest with us then?"

Danilov was surprised—and concerned—at the degree of American openness: It was more than he'd imagined from Cowley's account of his discussion with the secretary of state. "Quite obviously a lot of it—most of it—can't be made public."

"That point was made. And agreed," said the aide.

"Can I ask how many people were present at the meeting?"

There was a moment's studied examination from the other man. "You mean Russian?" Chelyag demanded pointedly.

"Yes."

"The president. Myself. A translator and a note-taker." The smile came again. "Nothing will leak."

"You should see this," said Danilov, offering a translation of the latest intercepted conversation. While the other man read, Danilov gazed around the office, curious why proletariat communism had found the trappings of tsardom so necessary. Because, he supposed, they had been hobnailed and dirty-fingered tsars themselves.

Chelyag's calm reaction was different from what Danilov expected. The chief of staff said, "Will you be able to prevent another attack here in Moscow? A totally honest answer!"

"Only if we learn of the target from another intercepted telephone call. And that would create a dilemma. To stop it—which we would have to—would alert them we *are* listening: know certainly who Naina Karpov is and that she's supplying the American terrorists. Who would without question or hesitation use their intrusion into American military headquarters when they realized it."

Chelyag nodded in acceptance, lips pursed, still calm. "In military campaigns—and these terrorists clearly believe they are involved in some sort of military campaign—it is very often necessary to make small sacrifices to achieve a larger objective. Particularly to deceive the enemy. . . . The British are supposed to have allowed an entire city to be bombed, many people to be killed, to prevent the Nazis knowing they had broken their most essential code during the Great Patriotic War."

Danilov was actually leaning forward in his chair, knowing this wasn't a lecture on military tactics or history.

The man tapped the record of the Hartz meeting. "I'm glad— the president will be glad—of this honesty. There is to be another session between the two of them. We will be just as honest: make it clear we understand all the difficulties but that no wedge can be forced between us, whatever new outrage occurs here. Immediately after their meeting the president will make a televised address to the nation, just as the American leader did."

What was it! Danilov sought desperately. Until he worked it out, he wouldn't know how to respond!

"The obvious complaint against Russia within the United States is that it was Russian weaponry used in the American attacks or attempted attacks. To reassure the American public, the president intends to announce that all military stockpiles throughout the country are to be placed under far more stringent and direct military control and supervision: no civilian involvement whatsoever. That strict and sole military supervision will, of course, apply particularly at Plants 35 and 43. To reinforce the commitment to that pledge, our chiefs of staff will appear with the president."

Danilov thought he saw a glimmer of light, almost too faint to recognize. Taking a risk, he said, "Will anyone else appear publicly with the president?"

"Appropriate minister," said Chelyag. He nodded as if approving Danilov's question.

"When's the television appearance to be?"

"Tomorrow," said the chief of staff. "You do understand the importance of my being fully briefed on every development, particularly over the next two or three days?"

"I think so," said Danilov, believing he did. The Duma impeachment debate would begin in two days. By which time the as-yet undeclared leaders—and military chiefs most affected by detente between Russia and America—would have been made publicly responsible for preventing the loss of any more Russian weaponry. Too much of which—apart from germ and biological warheads— Georgi Chelyag and the president already knew to be stolen and available for sale. On the pretext of preventing an American catastrophe, the president was going to imply to the American secretary of state that Moscow was prepared to sustain an atrocity to achieve the greater good of destroying a fanatical, international terrorist group. And in so doing, squaring the circle, to destroy the president's impeachment-seeking opposition.

"Then you'll also understand how important it was—and even more so is now—for you to continue to report only to me?" This time Chelyag's smile was much longer.

"I thought I had made clear to whom I was solely reporting," said Danilov.

"Precisely the reason I thought you might benefit from this meeting," said Chelyag. "But I don't think it's necessary for this conversation to go beyond this room. Or the two of us."

"No," agreed Danilov. Was the president's determination—desperation—to remain in office great enough for the White House to allow a germ warfare attack on Moscow? There was probably another cliché to describe his going from one impossible situation to another, but at that moment Danilov couldn't be bothered to search for it.

With no reason to return to Kirovskaya, apart from to sleep and change his clothes, Danilov had begun to spend his evenings with Cowley, and because of the time he drove directly from the White House to the hotel. He did so automatically, still trying to digest—but almost not wanting to—the conversation with Georgi Stepanovich Chelyag. There couldn't be any misunderstanding. So he was . . . was what? Corrupted wasn't the word. There had to be one far bigger, stronger, to describe the enormity of what he'd become inveigled in—*agreed* to become inveigled in. Or had he? Could he, if he knew there was a possibility of a warhead being exploded in Moscow, say nothing, do nothing? Would—could—the Americans? Probably, he answered himself, using the total cynicism to which he'd just been subjected. But that wasn't the question; it was an effort to avoid it. The question was what was he prepared to do—acquiesce to save himself or do nothing and knowingly let people die? Wasn't there a depravity—depravity a better word than corrupted, although still not right—in his even having to ask himself the question? What about the words he should be thinking, words like integrity and honesty and morality, words he'd personally paraded like the banners now being waved outside the embassy he'd soon be passing? Not a decision he had to make, not now, not immediately. Hypothetical, even. The unknown man in Chicago had said *maybe* there'd be something else in Moscow: that he needed to discuss it with people here. He'd wait, Danilov decided, recognizing the avoidance and despising himself for it. Wait and think. Not something that could be decided in minutes.

William Cowley was sitting at what had become his accustomed stool at the corner of the bar. He was alone. He drained his glass when he saw Danilov enter and had two more drinks waiting by the time the Russian reached him. Without any discussion they carried their glasses to a table out of hearing from the bar. Danilov told Cowley he knew about the second meeting between the secretary of state and the Russian president, waiting to be told that the Americans also knew of the planned television address. Instead Cowley said although the Chicago voice had been American, without any discernible foreign intonation, he'd asked that all the Chicago surveillance pictures be wired for comparison against the old Russian intelligence files. To Danilov's nodded acceptance, Cowley outlined the surveillance and photographic arrangements for that night. And then, frowning, he said, "You OK?"

"Sure. Why?"

"You're pretty quiet. How did your meeting go?"

Danilov hesitated. "Just passed on your intercept. He told me about the second meeting, like I said. Any idea what it's about?" How could he say this, behave like this!

"Hoped you might be able to tell me. It's at your side's suggestion, according to Hartz's people."

Danilov shook his head. "No. Sorry."

Cowley said, "Spoke to the director again. He's frightened the Chicago fuckup has skewed everything back home."

"Pamela in trouble?"

"He didn't seem very pleased. Says he's looking for the next break from here."

"Let's hope we don't keep him waiting," said Danilov, not knowing it would only be a matter of hours.

From his locked den Hollis carefully followed that evening's chosen, first-time stepping-stones through three consecutive online systems, not just to cut out any trace of his cracking—or of his being caught in a flytrap—but also to ensure the cost of that night's three- or four-hour surfing would be charged to someone else. Finally online himself—as the Quartermaster—Hollis began a regimented march through the war game sites and found the message on his third entry.

It said

THE GENERAL REQUESTS THE QUARTERMASTER'S REPORT

and was timed that day. The system was to wait a further three days before going to the newly designated telephone he hadn't used before. Hollis had expected more progress from Mark Whittier by now; perhaps it was time to lead the FBI auditor more positively.

Hollis surfed until he found what he wanted, the mapped and pictorially digitized re-creation of Paulus's street-by-street siege of Stalingrad. Hollis appointed himself to the Nazi side, attacking the Russians. How incredible it would have been to be there in person in 1942! But this would have to do.

It was the FBI's Moscow station chief, Barry Martlew, who made the initial identification of the immaculate, dark-blue 1962 Oldsmobile with upswept rear tail fins as it drew up to the rear of the Golden Hussar. And then recognized the driver as Yevgenni Leanov. In the momentary brightness of the opened door to the restaurant the photographer beside Martlew managed six shots of the former KGB linguist and his female companion.

"Got her perfectly," guaranteed the photographer.

"Like to hear her voice," said Martlew.

"Could be a long night if there's to be another call from Brooklyn," forecast the other man.

But it wasn't. The couple emerged after only three hours, actually stopping in the lighted doorway to talk to someone unseen behind, which gave the photographer the chance for four more shots. Leonov drove directly to Nikitskij Boulevard, where the woman waited pa-

tiently for him to put the Oldsmobile away in one of what appeared
to be at least three locked garages in a side alley before walking with
him, arm and arm, around the corner to an apartment block on
Pereulok Kalasnyj.

The garages were one hundred yards from Lev Ivanovich Baratov's Mercedes outlet. Which was more than a mile from Pereulok
Ucebyi, where two hours earlier the Cadillac in which Anatoli Sergeevich Lasin was setting out to collect a new, fifteen-year-old lover
exploded so violently when he turned on the ignition that the vehicle
was broken completely in half. The gas tank was full, and the re-
sulting fire totally destroyed Lasin's apartment and two others in
the same block. Three people died in the blaze.

31

The photographs were of Naina Karpov. After it was enhanced, one
of the departing shots showed the man to whom she was turning in
farewell to be Igor Ivanovich Baratov.

Five of the pictures were pinpoint sharp, and in three of them
she appeared to be looking directly at the camera, as if she were
posing. The transformation from the dowdy, distracted widow of
Pereulok Samokatnaja was so complete that Danilov thought that in
a casual, crowded situation he might not have even recognized her.
The neglected hair was coiffed perfectly around an oval, even beautiful face to show off the glittering earrings that, with the single-
strand choker, made a complete set that threw off enough light to
be genuine diamonds, which they probably were. There was a dia-
mondlike flare from the ring on her ring finger, too, but no wedding
band. The dress—maroon, according to Martlew—was close fitting
without being tight, cut bare-shouldered and in two of the pictures
exposing deep cleavage hidden by a covering stole of the same material. She was smiling—openly laughing in one frame—to show
sculpted, even teeth.

Yevgenni Leanov was just as immaculate—and smiling—in a single-breasted, Western-cut suit that Martlew remembered as dark blue. The surveillance photographs revealed a tactile attentiveness that had not registered with the two FBI watchers until the very end of the evening. In the arrival pictures Leanov had cupped Naina Karpov's arm to help her out of the Oldsmobile and had his hand familiarly in the small of her back as they'd gone in through the restaurant's rear door. Their hands had been touching in the first of the emerging photographs, and Leanov's was around her waist in the others.

It was not possible to see anything of Baratov, apart from his face, from the angle of the one print in which he'd been caught. He'd been smiling, like the rest of them.

Danilov was grateful the necessary responses to the identification—and the murder of Anatoli Lasin—had delayed his day's schedule until midday but he still felt crushed (the coming together of the rock against the hard place) by the hangover. It had been ridiculous—posturingly theatrical—to go on drinking as he had the previous night, as if integrity could be drowned in alcohol. He hadn't, in fact, become forgetfully drunk. At least the vomiting had stopped. He wished the remorse and the pain would.

Because of Henry Hartz's continued presence at the U.S. Embassy, they were again in Cowley's suite. The Golden Hussar photographs didn't occupy much space on the table around which they were sitting, even though they were enlarged as well as enhanced. The rest was taken up by official Russian prints of Anatoli Lasin's blown-apart car and fire-blackened shell of the Pereulok Ucebyi apartment block. Considerately, ever conscious of how Larissa died, Pavin had covered the murder scene pictures with those of the destroyed apartments.

"If it was a delayed wake for the sadly missed husband, they enjoyed themselves," said Cowley, disturbing the neatly piled prints of Naina Karpov. One of the American's early-morning checks had been to establish from the Manhattan eavesdropping that there had been no calls from Brooklyn to the restaurant the previous night.

"There as well as back at Leanov's apartment," said Danilov, working hard to disguise how he felt, surprised that Cowley was showing no discomfort whatsoever. Practice, he supposed. The ownership of the Pereulok Kalasnyj apartment was one of several things that Pavin had established during the morning. Another was that Leanov had divorced his wife four years earlier. A third was that the lock-up block listed on the same property register was owned by Lev Baratov's garage company.

"Why kill Lasin?" queried Pavin.

"Because he knew Nikov he was originally brought into headquarters, which might not have been the best idea," reflected Danilov, his headache so bad his words seemed to echo in his skull. "To keep her talking—to get as much for the voice comparison as we could—we told Naina Karpov we were going to reinterview everyone we'd already seen. Lasin was their weak link."

"The irony is that he didn't tell us anything," said Pavin.

"He would have if we'd threatened him with Lefortovo and a trumped-up charge over his handguns," said Danilov.

"Let's not forget, either, the example factor of the Nikov and Karpov killings," suggested Cowley.

"Or fail to take advantage of it ourselves!" said Danilov, with an awareness that pleased him. The band wasn't tightening around his head anymore, either.

"How?" Cowley frowned.

"We'll use our resident informer," decided Danilov. "Senior Colonel Ashot Ivanovich Mizin will work the two killings jointly. Tell him we're still going along with his turf war theory and that it's all part of the Osipov Brigade breakup. I want them to go on thinking they're safe, with the investigation under the control of their own man."

"We need to get to the Oldsmobile," said Cowley. "There might just be something for forensic. And there's an identification from the embassy guard."

Danilov's headache was definitely lifting. His stomach felt easier, too. "The Russian way," he said simply.

"Not admissible in an American court," refused Cowley, just as simply.

"In which court, under whose law, would an attack carried out from Russian soil—Ulitza Chaykovskovo—against what's technically American territory ever be heard?" demanded Danilov.

"You any idea how many guilty bastards walk free from American courts on points of law?"

"You any idea how many people will die from anthrax or sarin if these bastards beat us and get a warhead into America?"

"I think I've taken my eye off the ball a little here," Cowley abruptly apologized. "In Russia it's got to be the Russian way, hasn't it?"

The Russian president's ultimate coup was to make his worldwide televised address from the podium of the Duma that was preparing to impeach him. He asked permission to do so from an entrapped, unable-to-refuse parliament with the American secretary of state at his side at an apparently impromptu press conference after their second meeting. He even had Henry Hartz seated at the very edge of the dais so that in some shots the two men appeared together.

The towering, white-haired man actually began by sweeping his hand out toward Hartz to declare that the man's presence was physical, visible proof of the total commitment between their two countries to confront and defeat the fanatical terrorism that both were facing. So, too, was the fact that also in the chamber—there was another flowing hand movement to guide the cameras—were the military chiefs of all three armed services.

The announcement that all civilian participation in the safeguarding of all stockpiled Russian weaponry was being removed was accompanied by the raising high into the air of what the man declared to be a presidential decree he was lodging with the Duma. From that moment the security of every arsenal anywhere in the country was entirely in the hands of the military, who were trained for such a task and had the manpower to ensure it was properly and fully carried out. The camera-guiding gesture now was to the assembled ministers and their deputies—defense, foreign, and interior—with the insistence that although he had abolished civilian involvement at plant, installation, and stockpile level, appropriate civilian ministers should work with the military chiefs to ensure that never again would a single item of potentially harmful Russian war materiel fall into the wrong hands.

"Were that to happen—with the responsibility for preventing it so positively and clearly defined—the investigation to discover the culprits would be absolute, conducted by the special tribunals established by my decree today. Also set out in today's decree are the penalties I would expect to be imposed. I realize, of course, that the creation of law involving punishment is the function of the Duma and the upper house. I ask them to ratify those parts of my decree that require it."

Danilov and Cowley watched the address from the Savoy suite. Cowley said, "I don't know what the hell game that guy's playing, but I wouldn't like to be on the other side."

"Neither would I," Danilov said hopefully.

In the final moments of preparation, both Cowley and Danilov thought beyond the basic illegality of burglary to the fact that neither was trained—or had experience—for what they intended to do. Cowley had never attended a SWAT team intrusion. On the two occasions Danilov had used a *spetznaz* unit, the entry techniques and safeguards had been the responsibility of its commander. It was obviously among the worries of the subdued Paul Lambert, who very early in the briefing asked if they had a search warrant.

"The entry is upon my—Russian—authority," said Danilov. He didn't doubt he could have gotten approval from Georgi Chelyag, but it would have been given in the unrecorded circumstances of their conversation, so there'd been no point in asking. Danilov had excluded the protesting Yuri Pavin and the trusted but unaware group from Petrovka from any involvement, distancing them—and their careers—from himself if anything went wrong. Another unspoken awareness between Danilov and Cowley was that if it did go wrong, the danger wasn't so much from civilian arrest but from mobsters who imposed their own law with their own guns.

"No Russian backup?" persisted the leader of the forensic team.

"The embassy attack is an American-controlled investigation," said Danilov, uneasy with the threadbare logic. It was a relief that his hangover had gone.

"Which needs to be tightly controlled," broke in Cowley, just as uneasy. "I'm taking American responsibility for it being done this way."

With the early-afternoon departure of the American secretary of state and his entourage, it was easier for them to use one of the small conference rooms back at the embassy. A greatly enlarged section of the Nikitskij Boulevard street plan and the lock-up garage side alley was on a display board with a selection of that afternoon's photographs, also enlarged, alongside. Barry Martlew identified the garage in which he'd seen Leanov park the Oldsmobile and described how the up-and-over door had been secured at ground level by what appeared to be ordinary, snap-fastening padlocks.

"No obvious alarms anywhere," said the Moscow-based agent. "It's a cul-de-sac that bends where the garages are. Gives us some cover from the main road."

"How long did it take Leanov to close three padlocks?" demanded Cowley.

"A good fifteen minutes," said Martlew, understanding the question.

"So there are some precautions, and after New Rochelle that's our greatest concern," Cowley said to the two men whom Lambert had designated his entry specialists. "You lost friends in New Rochelle. After you're sure that everything's safe, I want you to go back to the beginning and start again. And if you have the slightest doubt, a bad feeling about anything, we walk away. OK?"

One man nodded. The other said, "OK."

Cowley looked back to include everyone else in the room. "Let's go play Watergate."

"Watergate fucked up," said someone.

The constant volume of roaring, speeding traffic in one of the busiest parts of the city—Ulitza Vozdvizenka, at one end of Nikitskij Boulevard—provided both the cover for the intrusion but also the risk of its being seen, despite the curve in the alley. Cowley had a rotating team cover the cul-de-sac from midafternoon, to ensure that the Oldsmobile remained inside its garage. Another group watched Yevgenni Leanov's apartment to see if the man emerged and appeared to be going to collect the car.

Upon their arrival Cowley reduced the alley surveillance—just one man, lingering close to its entrance as the last alert to the two entry men. The rest dispersed unobtrusively in the immediate vicinity, mostly along the more pedestrian-crowded Nikitskaya. Cowley kept in constant touch by throat mike, his hearing aid–style receiver in his undamaged ear.

"We've got a problem," alerted one of the FBI burglars. "The padlocks *are* wired: We can feel a lead. Guess the disarmament requires the approved key. Pick it and we ring the bells or whatever."

Shielded by Danilov and others feigning arm-waving conversation all around him, Cowley said, "Can you fix it?"

"Depends how much slack wire we can get."

"We can't leave any sign."

"Any alternative?" asked Danilov.

Lambert said, "There's some magic stuff, epoxy resin based, we can squirt into the lock to give us a key definition. It would take an hour to set sufficiently to withdraw it to cut a workable key. We're talking tomorrow. We wouldn't have to damage any outer casing if we could get enough slack for a wire bypass."

"Gotta clamp on the first," came a voice from the alley.

Cowley, Danilov, and Lambert turned around at Skarjatin, to walk back the way they'd come. Danilov said, "I don't understand the way it works."

Lambert said, "Each padlock is alarmed. Break or force one and whatever happens happens. If we can get a loop above each of the three padlocks we maintain the circuit, make the locks themselves obsolete. All we've got to do then is pick them. Each will have a different operating key, of course. It's quite simple."

"Sure," said Danilov. Three Americans in their group passed them without showing any sign of recognition, going in the opposite direction.

"Two neutralized," came the earpiece voice.

"What about you guys at Kalasnyj?" demanded Cowley, in apparent conversation with Danilov.

"Lights on in the apartment but the drapes are drawn," came the reply. "Maybe a quiet evening, six-pack and a ball game."

"No wise-assing: only what matters and what you're asked," ordered Cowley. Schnecker's brusque instruction against nervousness going into the UN building, Cowley remembered: a million years ago? Two million?

"Three immobilized," said the voice from the alley.

"Go back and start again," Cowley instructed at once.

"You sure they've got this much time?" demanded Lambert.

"Dead they've got all the time they could want. Eternity," said Cowley.

"Sneaky motherfuckers!" said the recognizable voice.

"What?" said Cowley.

"Secondary system, parallel to the guide rail for the up and over. Static wires, simple hook-and-eye connection on both sides. Door goes up but the wires don't, unless they're unclipped. Glad we had a second feel around."

"So am I," said Cowley.

"Thanks," said Lambert, to the other American.

"Whenever you're ready to join us," invited the burglar.

Their rehearsed arrival in the alley was intentionally straggled, to avoid attracting attention additionally risked by some of the forensic technicians' equipment. Further protective surveillance was reestablished along Nikitskij, on either side of the alley, with the existing man remaining in between at its entrance.

The up-and-over door was lifted a bare minimum to admit them, and no light was put on until everyone was inside. The sudden fluorescent glare momentarily blinded all of them. They recovered standing around the immaculately gleaming, dark-green vehicle as Lambert, assuming control, said, "We're not here to admire. Let's get it done."

The smoothly rehearsed movement of the forensic team was another uncomfortable reminder to Cowley of how Jefferson Jones's squad had automatically assumed their roles on the outskirts of New Rochelle. He physically turned away, conscious as he did so that Dimitri Danilov was already exploring the garage, at that moment at the very rear. Danilov pointed and said, "Steel door, steel framed. Locks top and bottom."

To one of the men who'd picked the outer locks Cowley said, "You spare a moment?"

The technician stood beside Danilov for several moments before saying, "Now, that's one hell of a door beyond which visitors aren't at all welcome."

"Try," urged Cowley.

It took an hour. The constant checks with the watchers outside in Nikitskij Boulevard and Pereulok Kalasnyj were virtually the only sounds from inside. The forensic scouring of the Oldsmobile ended with the entry technician still on his knees, the door frame alarm safely looped and one lock already picked. Scanning the door itself with a stethoscoped magnet, he found the tumbler device activated by the slightest uneven movement. He steadied it—attaching magnets at either end—and said, "I haven't seen anything like this outside a strongroom." The second lock took a further fifteen minutes. When he felt delicately inside the door that was open just enough for his fingers to get through, he found two separate, rigidly fixed alarm wires that would have triggered if the door had widened another half inch. It took another ten minutes to disconnect them, before the door was finally opened.

"Jesus!" exclaimed Cowley, when the light finally went on in the room beyond. It was not intended—certainly not used—as a garage. Stacked the entire length of the opposite wall were boxed mines and grenades, with other boxes marked to be grenades and timers and heavy-caliber ammunition. Near the door were four of the same A4-427 rockets and their launchers used in the U.S. Embassy attack. Unprompted, the forensic cameraman began to photograph everything. The rigid, inside door fixings were simple booby traps to separate wall-mounted antipersonnel mines. Another lead ran from the tumbler to disappear beneath the main stockpile itself.

Cowley said, "Jerk that door open and the entire block would disappear."

Lambert was bending over the mines, scraping off paint samples into a specimen envelope. Conscious of Cowley and Danilov behind him, he said, "The same as the Lincoln Memorial."

Abruptly, into their earpieces, a voice from Pereulok Kalasnyj said, "An Audi's just drawn up. It's Naina Karpov!"

"Out!" ordered Cowley. "Everybody out!"

He and Danilov remained with the entry specialists reattaching the traps and alarms to the inner door. As they got to the outer garage door, the Kalasnyj voice said, "The light's gone out in Leanov's apartment." Then, minutes later. "They're coming out. On their way to you."

"Shit!" said one of the technicians, failing to get the hook of the static alarm wire into its eye.

"Plenty of time," calmed Cowley. "No hurry."

"On to Vozdvizenka," came the voice in Cowley's ear.

"Got it!" said the technician. The three padlocks clicked home, one after the other.

"About to turn into your street," came the warning.

"We're out," Cowley assured him. "Anyone feel thirsty? I'm buying the celebration drinks."

Although it was much earlier in the day in Washington, Pamela Darnley said virtually the same thing to Barry Osnan when she emerged into the incident room from its side office.

"Celebrate what?" asked the man.

"Just had a call from Carl Ashton. The computer that brings *Challenger* back into Earth orbit had been misprogrammed. It would have gone out of trajectory just enough to burn on reentry."

"With two Russians on board."

In the Manhattan listening room the duty electronics officer called out, "Hey-up, guys! Arnie's just announced it's telephone time. Promised Mary Jo dinner with a special view."

"Make a change for her from his crotch," said agent in charge Harry Boreman.

There was a stir in the FBI office in Trenton, too. There the local bureau chief, John Meadowcraft, looked up from the surveillance pictures of Ivan Gavrilovich Guzov and Vyacheslav Fedorovich Kabanov and said to the photographer, "You're right. They're both using two different cell phones. Why two? Why not just one?" He decided against talking to Washington about it. An unwritten field office rule was never put a question to headquarters you didn't know the answer to.

"You know what we've done?" Reztsov demanded from his deputy, lifting the French champagne in invitation to a toast.

Averin lifted his glass expectantly and said, "What?"

"We've guaranteed our future. It's a good feeling."

"Very good," agreed the second Gorki homicide detective.

32

It was a feel-good (and for some, later, feel-bad) night of what turned out to be premature celebration, little sleep, some work, early-hour telephone calls, and a lot of political maneuvering. There were also, again later, some more overheard conversations and one that wasn't.

The most immediate result of the early-hour telephoning was the agreement by both White Houses that Dimitri Danilov be included in the sort of satellite link-up that had first been established for the American secretary of state when Hartz had been in Moscow. The Russian acceptance was reached while Danilov was still with Georgi Chelyag, whom he'd earlier alerted at home and who didn't bother to conceal his satisfaction at the embassy-developed photographs of the Nikitskij garage arsenal. The chief of staff absented himself for only fifteen minutes to get higher approval for Danilov's participation. With it came the politicking. Chelyag ordered Danilov to return immediately to brief the president before he made another call to Washington later in the day. Chelyag was going to bypass the Foreign Ministry to liaise directly with Henry Hartz.

Danilov had suggested that Cowley's celebration be in the security of the embassy mess rather than in the Savoy Hotel, and he'd strictly limited himself, determined against another hangover. Cowley hadn't—neither had most of the others—but showed no sign of suffering. Both Paul Lambert and Barry Martlew did, gray-faced and pouch-eyed.

"It's worth it, having something like this after so long," insisted the forensic team leader. After the party he'd had to supervise what could be done at the embassy—the development, enhancement, and wiring to Washington of the pictures—and what had to be packaged, with instructions, for Washington scientific tests.

The four of them made up the Moscow contingent. In Washington it was Frank Norton, Leonard Ross, and Pamela Darnley. Norton's opening to Moscow was: "You've done well there—damned well. We're getting a handle on things at last."

"There wasn't a warhead," Cowley cautioned at once. He, like Danilov, had begun to put the garage findings into perspective.

"We've got everything else," insisted Norton.

"Have we?" Danilov asked rhetorically, raising the uncertainty he'd already talked through with Chelyag. "We've no way of knowing that's their *only* stockpile—that this is even the weaponry they intend selling through Orlenko and Guzov."

"Whatever the intention, they're not getting this lot," said Norton. Addressing Danilov, he said, "You've got some official guidance on this?"

"It can be seized whenever it's decided, by our SWAT equivalent." Danilov looked sideways to Cowley.

"And of course we've got the garage under permanent surveillance. We won't lose it," said the American.

"You can't guarantee that: No one could," Ross objected at once. "It's too dangerous, leaving it there."

"We can't touch it," insisted Cowley, equally quickly, the euphoria all gone. "Finding it, like we have, still leaves us with as many problems as before, with the additional one that Dimitri's just pointed out."

An unformed idea, like a shadow in the dark, began nagging in Danilov's mind but refused to harden.

"We know what they intended to do with their Pentagon access," argued Norton. "It *was Challenger*, and we've got all the time in the world to correct it. We're safe back here."

"I'm not sure that we are," said Pamela, pleased that her success had been acknowledged without her having to prompt the reference. "Remember what the woman says on the Chicago intercept: "more surprises than they can ever guess." Surprise*s*. Plural, not singular.

I'm not convinced that we've got rid of the danger here by finding the *Challenger* interference. I've told Ashton to go on looking."

"You're surely not suggesting we do nothing about the Moscow cache!" Norton demanded incredulously.

"I'm reminding everyone that if we move too soon in Moscow—before we've got positive leads and identification here—we risk their triggering something we can't anticipate or stop," said Pamela. There was no hesitation, no deferring to rank or authority, and no one seemed to expect it.

"I agree," said Cowley.

"So do I. And it's the argument I've already put here, since we discovered what's in the garage," said Danilov. What was it that wouldn't come to him!

Pamela filled the silence from Washington. "Something might be moving. From what we overheard from Bay View Road, Orlenko made contact last night. The new number is the public phone at the River Café below the Brooklyn Bridge: the one with the view of the Manhattan skyline. We're putting a tap on it, of course. But the pattern is for him to speak to Moscow after hearing from whoever he talks to."

"It'll be about the money," remembered Cowley. "Any progress on that?"

"No," said Ross. "What did you get out of the Oldsmobile?"

"I'm hoping we'll get more from what we put *in*," said Lambert. "We wired it, two separate microphones, one inside the radio, one inside the pod on the turning indicator arm. We've lifted five different fingerprint sets: There's a match to the one print on the trigger guard of the launcher discarded after the embassy attack. We've got a lot of human hair and one cigarette butt from a filled ashtray on the front dash. We can pick up saliva from that for DNA—as well as from the hair—if we need a match. There's clothes fibers, too. There's some paint flakes from the trunk carpeting that could be from both the warhead and the missile that was fired at the embassy here. It's all already on its way back to the laboratory."

"I'm having the prints run through criminal records and against our ex–intelligence officer files," said Danilov. "We've already shown last night's photographs of the car to the embassy guard. He says it's definitely the one used in the attack."

"And you're telling me that we still can't move on it!" said the exasperated presidential aide. "I know the arguments, but we've really got to think this thing through. Do something!"

"From the photographs it looks to me as if there's more explosives than were put in the Lincoln Memorial," said Ross. "I know the reasoning for leaving it alone—have gone along with it until now—but I'm not so sure anymore. I don't see how we can."

The shadow in Danilov's mind became a positive thought, literally like a shaft of light. "We don't have to!" he announced.

The three men in the room turned to him, frowning. The same expression registered on the faces in Washington. "Naina Karpov and Yevgenni Leanov—and those we know about there, in America—aren't ballistics experts. They're stealing and selling. They won't know if the stuff is armed—operational—or not. We can get back in to where they're storing it—more easily than last night, because we know their security and booby traps now—and simply disarm everything. Remove firing mechanisms, sabotage the timers and detonators. The Watchmen would imagine its failure to be for the same reason as the UN missile: bad Russian manufacture. The last time they thought that, they came all the way from America to teach their suppliers a lesson."

There were slow, nodded smiles of understanding from inside the room and from Washington. Pamela said, "How do you make the warhead inoperative if they get it and we find it? After last time they'll check the detonating mechanism. That's what the newspapers and television said had failed."

The smiles went, but only briefly. Cowley said, "We won't have to try. We've got two empty warheads of our own, one from each source. We bring them back from Washington and simply swop."

"You haven't found the warhead," reminded Pamela.

"We'll go ahead with the switch with what's already there," declared Norton, making the decision that should have been Leonard Ross's.

"My people handle ballistics *after* their use," reminded Lambert.

"Why don't the Fort Detrick specialists come over? And bring the empty warheads just in case?" suggested Ross. "I want to be sure nothing can go off, no matter what's done with it if we've got to let it come here."

Danilov suspected that Georgi Chelyag used their second encounter as a planning rehearsal. The man seized the American sabotaging of the weaponry as a further distancing of Russian presidential responsibility. He insisted their agreement could be phrased as a favor to an America deeply embarrassed by the terrorists' Pentagon penetration.

"We'll have to be horrified at what could have been a space shuttle disaster involving our astronauts," said Chelyag, almost to himself.

"I *am!*" said Danilov, still uncomfortable with the other man's total political cynicism.

"And they still think there could be something more?" queried the chief of staff.

"Yes." They hadn't discussed it after the satellite closedown, but Danilov had been as conscious as Cowley of Pamela's aggressiveness.

"Maybe we should put all our early-warning systems on standby?"

"I thought there'd been an assurance that nothing is directed toward us?"

"There has. And according to you it was *Challenger*'s directional system that had been tampered with. What's to stop something being put back on course?"

"It would become public knowledge that we'd done it."

Chelyag smiled. "Of course it would. It's a presidential decision, and the president would be failing in his responsibilities to the Russian people if he didn't take the precaution, after what we've just learned. That can all be made clear in today's conversation with Washington, with the assurance that there will be no leak from this end that what was done to the space shuttle is the reason for our doing it. Which it won't, not even to the Duma as they prepare their censure vote. It might, of course, give them cause to pause and reflect, not having the slightest idea what's going on."

Danilov wondered how many situations there had ever been that Chelyag hadn't manipulated 180 degrees to his or a superior's advantage. Danilov suddenly decided the sewer life in which he lived and worked was preferable to what Chelyag inhabited and that he'd never again feel guilty at his own long-ago toe dip into what, by comparison, was perfumed corruption. He said, "I don't think there's anything else."

Chelyag said, "The investigation is producing far more here than it is in America, isn't it?"

"Because of American participation," insisted Danilov.

"That's a matter of interpretation," said Chelyag, smiling again.

"More names," announced a satisfied Yuri Pavin. "And we know which one fired the missile at the embassy.'

There were three names, all from the now-completed list of former intelligence personnel and all positively identified from fingerprints lifted from inside the Oldsmobile. One was a former *spetznaz*-seconded major. It was his print on the launcher trigger guard.

"He'd have had all the military training," Pavin pointed out.

"What about the Lasin murder?"

"Everything fed to Mizin, as ordered," responded the colonel formally. He smiled. "He said our thoughts were in line with what he was thinking."

"Let's hope"—started Danilov before his telephone rang.

"Leanov's picking up the Oldsmobile," announced Cowley.

The music went with the car, Billie Holiday in good voice, before the heroin took control. A tape, Cowley guessed. Leanov hummed along badly, obviously not knowing her tune rifts. There was no distortion on the tapes. The first bug was in the radio, not the speakers. From the frequent horn blasts, Nikitskij Boulevard was congested. Cowley looked up and nodded at Danilov's arrival. "He's alone. Got a voice like shit."

Danilov said, "We've got a name for who fired the bazooka: a *spetznaz* officer. Two other names, as well. Probably the attack group that Naina Karpov sneered at for needing transport."

"*Spetznaz* fits," said the American.

"A piece at a time," agreed Danilov.

"We got two cars behind but they're staying loose. Don't want to spook him."

The Billie Holiday tape was turned down in the middle of "Love for Sale," and Leanov stopped trying to sing along. Cowley strained forward at another faint noise and said, "Dialing out: the car didn't have a phone so it'll be a cell phone."

Lambert said, "Every digit's got a different tone. I can get a number from that."

"On my way," said Leanov. Then: "Good." A pause, for something from whoever he was talking. "We would have liked two." Another gap. "I didn't think the military was a problem?" A laugh. "Pay them the fucking money then; you're getting yours." The longest break yet. "I'm fifteen minutes away. . . . Stop worrying." There was the bleep of the phone going off.

At once the tape was turned up. The song was "Strange Fruit." Over a separate speaker an American voice said, "We're getting pushed apart by the traffic. You want us to close up, not to lose him?"

"Not if it risks his making you," said Cowley, into his handset. "We're hearing him loud and clear."

There was an interruption of the Billie Holiday tape while it reversed itself.

Cowley said, "Where'd you get the shooter's name?"

"Old KGB files. His unit was attached."

"Address?"

"*Spetznaz* barracks."

"Didn't expect it to be all easy."

"We're on the M10," reported one of the American pursuers.

"Which becomes the M11 and leads right up to Tushino," said Danilov.

"It's Plant 43," accepted Cowley.

"Turning off," came an American voice.

"Losing our traffic cover," came the second voice.

"Dropping back," said the first. Then: "We're almost at once in the boondocks: open as hell."

"Second car abort," ordered Cowley.

"There's a sign," said the observer from the first car. "Timiry-azev."

"It's all country. A huge park," identified Danilov.

"Only one car between us on the road," came the warning. "I think he's slowing."

"Abort," ordered Cowley, for the second time. "Let him go."

"Sorry," said the observer.

"Nobody's fault," said Cowley. "Don't try to pick up on the return journey."

Inside the car Leanov turned off the tape. There was a faintly discernible sound they couldn't recognize but the noise of the engine seemingly revved intermittently. Lambert said, "We're hearing rough ground. He's turned off, driving over bumps. Ruts."

The engine died, the click of a door opening, Leanov's voice shouting a greeting. Then the mumble of conversation they couldn't hear.

Martlew said, "Shit! They're outside the car."

Lambert said, "We can probably enhance what they're saying. Not here, though. Washington."

Two, maybe three doors slammed. There was the more solid sound of a trunk lid going down. A click, some more unheard talk, then a closer *whump*.

"Something's gone into the Oldsmobile trunk," said Cowley.

"So we know where it's going back to," said Danilov.

Words floated from the monitoring speaker like leaves in a wind: "Idiots . . . as much as . . . told you . . . no worry . . . dollars . . . soon . . ." The door opening, closer, the squash of Leanov sitting and for the first time the clear sound of his saying good-bye and a reply, in a man's voice.

Ella Fitzgerald sang all the way back to Moscow, ruined by Leanov's backing. The surveillance reported his arrival back at the garage. Leanov lowered the up-and-over door after him when he put the car away and didn't emerge for thirty minutes. He was carrying nothing when he did.

Cowley said, "Jimmy Schnecker and his guys arrive in three hours."

"What about the empty warheads?" asked Danilov.

"Diplomatic baggage, coming to the embassy separately."

Pamela Darnley read for the fourth time the official notification from the director of her second commendation, which had come with the equally formal confirmation of her appointment as permanent head of the antiterrorist unit. The satisfaction was a warm, comforting feeling.

"Congratulations," said Terry Osnan.

Pamela had told him not to boast, although there had been an element of that, but because the promotion wouldn't be circulated throughout the bureau until the end of the month, and he would have thought it odd if she'd kept it to herself until then. She was looking forward to telling Cowley. She realized abruptly that she would have liked to have done it personally rather than over a five-thousand-mile telephone link and was surprised at the awareness. "I had a lot of help, you at the top of the list," she said. She could afford to be magnanimous.

"I'd put Bill and Dimitri higher," said the man, who'd just listened with her to the Oldsmobile trip that had been relayed from Moscow. "It's happening fast there."

Which meant she had to work faster, Pamela accepted. Nothing of which she was in charge or controlled was going to end inconclusively, most certainly not that part of an investigation with which she was so personally identified. In two weeks' time everyone in the bureau would know she headed antiterrorism. Which would only be a start. Pamela wanted everyone else to know it, too. And they would when she emerged the principal witness in a prosecution in what would be one of the most sensational trials in American legal history.

It was, of course, too much to fantasize about breaking the tradition of the director of the Federal Bureau of Investigation always having to be male—they were invariably outside political appointments anyway—but she didn't see any reason in these days of sexual equality why the immediate deputy couldn't be female. Not something to discuss with anyone else.

Nor, by the same token, getting ahead of herself by thinking about it too much. Back to earth time. The River Café, at the base of the

Brooklyn Bridge, was the obvious new focus. The tap was already in place, but it wouldn't produce until Arseni Orlenko made another outing. And there was no way she could tighten the surveillance on Orlenko's two Russian landlords in New Jersey, whose existence seemed ordinary to the point of boredom. Would Carl Ashton and his sweepers be working with the same intensity after locating the *Challenger* tampering? Their success—or failure—would be *her* success or failure.

The new contact number was in a mall again, out on the Cohoes Road. As he drove Patrick Hollis wondered how the General obtained them. It wasn't important. Not a system he'd copy when his intended changes occurred. Not necessary, if you knew how to use a computer like he did. That's what his were going to be, a computer army. Enough of them available. Hundreds. Thousands. All out there on the war game sites, combat ready, awaiting recruitment.

Hollis managed to park conveniently close to the buildings, to avoid his having to walk too far. Didn't want to be breathless: might give the impression of nervousness. It had begun to rain, and he hunched deeper into his coat as he walked the last few yards, hands in his pockets, the pad and pens ready. Although he expected it, Hollis still jumped when the phone rang.

"Quartermaster?"

"Sir!" Hollis felt again the vague embarrassment when the accepted hacking terms were spoken aloud.

"You obeyed orders?" the rasping voice demanded at once.

"I'm here," said Hollis.

"That isn't the answer. What about account numbers?"

Hollis took a breath, preparing himself. "You've done it wrong. I told you not to take too much. The FBI has got teams in tracing you. It's not safe anymore."

Hollis felt warmed, close to being aroused, by the silence from the other end. At last the voice said, "What are they doing? How?"

"I don't know. All I know is that it's happening. I'm breaking contact."

"No! Wait! You've got a new assignment. Intelligence. You've got to find out."

This *was* orgasmic! He hadn't expect the concern—the panic—
like this. "It's too dangerous."

"You can do it! You have to do it! It's an order!"

"Just stop. Abort." He couldn't appear to capitulate too quickly.

"No! Everything goes ahead."

"Not like this," demanded Hollis. "I've got to have a way of
contacting you immediately. *Warning* you."

Silence again. Hollis could hear the man breathing heavily from
the other end. "You got something to write with?"

"Yes."

The website address was dictated slowly. "Read it back."

Hollis did so. Wonderful! A telephone number would have been
much more difficult. "Name?"

"You know my rank. Eleven o'clock every morning. I want to
talk about money now. The amount I want—"

Hollis didn't need to hear any more so he replaced the receiver.
Even better than wonderful! The stealing would go on, making it
all perfect.

He was the commanding officer now. It was a good feeling.

James Schnecker tapped the photographs back into their neat order,
offering them across the desk to Cowley. With him, from the United
Nations entry team, he'd brought Neil Hamish, Richard Pointdexter,
and Hank Burgess.

Schnecker said, "And you think you might have to let them run
to lead you back to America?"

"Yes," said Cowley. "Can you make everything safe?"

Schnecker shook his head. "Take three or four days to defuse
that much."

"What then?" demanded Danilov.

"The word you used," said the expert. "Sabotage."

"So that they couldn't be used for another attack," pressed Cowley.

"Guaranteed," promised Hamish. "We're the best in the business
to ensure that things don't go off."

"Not the way they're expected," added Pointdexter.

"If you lose them you'll want to find them again, won't you?" asked Schnecker.

"The whole point, if we let it all run, is to find who they're going to," said Cowley.

"We'll see that you do," promised Schnecker.

"Leanov's on the move," reported the man on the Nikitskij alley surveillance. "Naina's with him."

"Our cue?" suggested Schnecker.

"From the direction we're going, it looks like Pereulok Vorotnikovskij and the Golden Hussar," said the observer in the pursuit car.

"If it's for a telephone call from Brooklyn, it could be a busy night," said Barry Martlew.

It was.

33

It was Billie Holiday again but a different tape—*The Unforgettable Lady Day*—without either Leanov's accompaniment or a lot of conversation inside the car.

Leanov said, "How do you think they'll feel in America about the changes?"

"Important they know who's in control."

"We *do* need to meet the Americans instead of fucking around on telephones like this. It's ridiculous!"

"You got any problems with the idea?"

"You know I haven't."

"Gavri's the problem. He'll cheat again, if he gets the chance. Like he did the side deal with the intelligence agents' names."

"You want another example made?"

"Let's see how this goes. Decide afterward. Might prove something to the Americans as well as everyone else."

"We're here," announced the following surveillance car.

Only the two forensic experts who'd broken into the garage and knew the booby traps went with Schnecker's team and Cowley and Danilov. Barry Martlew remained at the embassy, as the pivotal liaison between the Manhattan eavesdropping, the observers outside the Golden Hussar, and Cowley.

They followed the same routine as before, only the two break-in specialists initially going into the alley. Pavin, included now, drove the lead car carrying the empty warhead and protective equipment—another trusted Petrovka detective at the wheel of the second—but was only halfway down Pereulok Merzijakovskij when the garage watcher radioed that the door was open. Danilov led Schnecker and his team in first.

By the time Cowley joined them, the forensic burglars had picked the locks of the linking door and were groping through the small opening to disconnect the final trip. Cowley immediately saw a rocket mounted with a double warhead that had not been there before. It was lying slightly apart from everything else, like a prize, which Cowley supposed it was. He said, "Now we know what Leanov drove out to Timiryazev to pick up!"

"And what we can do with it," agreed Schnecker. He did not, however, go immediately to the warhead but instead examined the wiring of the up-and-over door. He said, "Very simple, but very effective." "I'd say professionally rigged." He looked at Lambert. "Your guys did well to pick it up."

Hamish had already followed the door-activated detonating wires into the piled-up explosives. Without looking around he said, "Good job you didn't play around in here, though. There's a secondary trigger. It's all still live, ready to pop."

A visible stiffening went through everyone except Schnecker's group.

Lambert said disbelievingly, "I *did* play around with it: took paint samples and tried for fingerprints."

Hamish turned briefly to the forensic leader. "Then you'll never be as lucky again. Don't take any more chances because you haven't got any left."

"You want us out of the way?" asked one of Lambert's technicians.

"Won't save you being next door, if I get it wrong," said Hamish, his hands deeply inside the stacked mines, working by feel. "And if they've got a vibration detonator somewhere in here, you might even set it off by moving."

Total silence enveloped the room. Again Danilov became aware of breathing shallowly and knew others were, too. Everyone except the Fort Detrick team was frozen, where and how they stood. Schnecker wasn't. He crouched over the double warhead, probing between the missile and its launcher. Hamish himself breathed out, heavily, gently withdrawing his arm to flex his fingers before sliding them back in through a different opening. Without looking away from what he was doing, the man said, "I want a breath of tension on two."

Pointdexter knelt beside the second wire leading from the entry trap. He appeared to do little more than lift it from the floor.

Hamish said, "Bastards! Phony lead. No wonder they didn't think they had to have guards here." Then: "Hah! Got it!"

"What?" said Schnecker, without looking around from the warhead.

"Lead attached between the mines. Move the arrangement, bang. Safe now."

"What *about* vibration?"

"I don't think so."

Schnecker rose, stretching the cramp from his legs. To Cowley he said, "Let's switch the warhead. Get everyone out—one at a time, nice and slow—so we've got room to work."

"How long do you need?"

Schnecker looked back to the piled-up ordnance. "Don't like the Sneaky Pete stuff. So as long as it takes."

Martlew's voice crackled into Cowley's handset. "Just heard from New York: Arnie's told his loving wife to go for a walk because he's got a call to make. Our technical guys are fixing up a simultaneous feed, direct to us here, to warn when the conversation finishes with your restaurant: It'll give you a little more time if she leaves right away."

Cowley acknowledged and at once said into his radio, "You hear that, Golden Hussar?"

"Loud and clear," came a voice from the surveillance car.

"We'd get even more time if the Oldsmobile got a flat," said Cowley.

"Problem with old cars," agreed the observer.

"Let's get rid of the live warhead," Schnecker said busily.

When Burgess brought it in from the adjoining garage, Danilov saw the improvised container was a cello case. Everyone else realized it, too. Burgess said, "What can I tell you? It works."

"You think it'll pass?" Schnecker asked generally, pointing to the marks on the replacement device where Lambert's scientists had scraped off paint samples.

"There's no reason for them to think it's anything but an accidental mark," judged Cowley.

It was easier getting the empty warhead out than getting the loaded one into the case. The fit was perfect. Cowley used the handset again, to summon the circling car, and said to Danilov: "See you there." Hank Burgess was carrying the loaded warhead back to the embassy. Before they'd left it had been decided the American needed to be accompanied by a Russian speaker against any eventuality during the journey.

The lights in the first garage were doused for their exit. As they walked up the totally blackened alley, Danilov said, "What would happen if you dropped that thing?"

Burgess said, "Nothing. There's three inches of packing, so it wouldn't fracture. And it needs to be armed before it's fired. If it isn't, it doesn't detonate. Still a cockamamie design, though."

They got to the FBI offices at the embassy in time to hear Naina Karpov say, "Everything arranged?"

The duplicated relay from New York reduced the sound level and there was a hiss from the volume adjustment, but it was still recognizably Arseni Orlenko's voice. The Russian said, "He's very angry. Says he can only go to one and a half."

"Fuck him. He created his own problem trying to get things cheaper. The price stays."

"He said not to forget what happened last time."

"Is he buying or not?" the woman demanded impatiently.

"He wants to know how many warheads."

"One. Already available."

"So it's two million?"

"Have they got it?"

"He offered a million deposit. Rest on delivery."

Naina laughed. "Which he wouldn't pay, once he'd got it all."

"I expect not."

"I know not. That's why I set the price at the figure I did. When are you speaking again?"

"Tomorrow."

"So he's anxious?"

"I suppose so, yes.

"Tell him a million and a half deposit. That's all we'll get. If it's not the full million and a half, the deal's off."

Orlenko sniggered. "You've really thought it through, haven't you?"

"Totally. No money up front—full million and a half—no warhead, no nothing. His decision."

"What if he doesn't come back anymore?"

"We've made $1,500,000. He's lost a supplier. He say anything about another attack here?"

"Just argued about how much we wanted."

"Tell him we're not supplying anything here until we get paid in full, in America, for what we're sending. And that anything here's extra, which has also got to be paid for in advance, before it's supplied."

"It's not good dealing with him."

There was a pause from Moscow. "You're *frightened* of him!"

"Not personally. They've showed what they're prepared to do. What they *can* do."

"To amateurs. They come to Moscow again, they don't get dinner at the Metropole and whores. And he doesn't know you, does he?"

"He knows Gavri: where to find him."

"Which is Gavri's problem. You spoken to him?"

"You want me to?"

"Tell him Yevgenni Mechislavovich is coming over."

This time the silence was from the American end. "Yevgenni Mechislavovich taking over?"

"He's coming to see how things are running. Make things clear to Gavri."

"I see."

"I hope you do."

"You want to speak tomorrow?"

"Of course. Tell them everything's ready to be shipped."

"What about the arrangements for that?"

"Yevgenni Mechislavovich is bringing all the details. Tell Gavri that, too."

"Are changes being made?"

"Just do as I tell you. And call me tomorrow."

All but Schnecker's team were in the empty garage, but the ballistic experts needed extra light—trailing extension cords from the garage as well as using every outlet in the storeroom itself—and it grew uncomfortably hot, everyone sweating.

"We're not careful, they're going to smell there's been people here when they get back," warned Lambert.

"Forgot air freshener," said Schnecker. He and his team were in body armor, their faces streaming behind visors. Hamish was numbering each piece as it was handled.

From his embassy pivot Martlew reported the conclusion of the telephone call. Cowley said, "They've finished talking. How much longer?"

"Two hours," said Schnecker, without breaking away from what he was doing. "A little less, with luck."

It would have been practical for some to leave, but when Cowley thought about it, he realized that the only truly superfluous people there were Lambert and himself. He was the only one who spoke Russian, quite apart from it being unthinkable for the case officer to leave. He would have liked a drink. Not a lot. Just one. Later, he promised himself. Not another party, like last night, although there was as much reason. Maybe more. He'd see how it went. Schnecker and his guys had been damned good—professional—hitting the ground running like this. Right thing to do to offer them a thank you, although they'd probably be exhausted. Maybe, though, they'd be pumped up by adrenaline.

He was sure Pamela would be, ringing the bell like that with the space shuttle. Every reason to be. Would he ever get to know her better, beyond the environment of the J. Edgar Hoover building? A bizarre question in bizarre surroundings. Brought back to where he was, Cowley decided that Lambert had a valid point. The garage and storeroom stank of sweat and people.

Needing something to do, Cowley said, "Anything?" into his handset.

"Nothing" was like an echo from the embassy, the alley mouth, and the restaurant surveillance.

Then, almost at once, from the Golden Hussar watchers came the warning: "There's movement. They're on their way out."

"Let's wrap it up," Cowley called to the next room.

"Shit!" complained Pointdexter.

"They haven't seen the flat," reported the restaurant commentary. "Getting into the car . . . firing the engine . . . starts to . . . and there's the bump. He's out now, kicking the tire. Going back inside leaving Naina in the car . . . and here's big brother, Igor Baratov. Hope you guys are hauling ass back there. Both going inside again. . . . Wait a moment, here's a cab. . . . They're not bothering to change the tire."

"How's it going?" demanded Cowley; from the connecting door. Schnecker and Pointdexter were restacking the cache to Hamish's instructions, read out from his numbered chart.

Hamish said, "Almost done but we've got to reassemble the alarms."

"They won't have any reason to come here, if they're not in the Oldsmobile," Lambert, behind Cowley, pointed out. "Baratov might not get it fixed right away, either."

"We're not staying to find out," said Cowley.

"Cab's leaving," reported the observer. "You want us to follow or stay with the Oldsmobile? . . . Wait. . . . Some more guys are coming out of the restaurant. . . . The trunks open, they're going to change the tire."

"Stay with the car," ordered Cowley.

"Done!" declared Hamish. "Everyone out while I reconnect." He did so remarkably quickly and was panting when he got to the connecting door. To the forensic burglars he said, "You guys mind doing the rest? I'm fucked."

"Olds is off the jack," came the commentary. "And Baratov's getting in. Countdown time. Took twelve minutes to get here. And we're moving. Twelve. . . ."

The second lock clicked into place in the linking door. Schnecker and his team had stripped off their body armor and bagged it. Their coveralls beneath were sodden black by sweat. Crowded as they were at the entrance, waiting to emerge the moment the lights were extinguished, the smell was overwhelming.

"Eight . . . seven . . ." timed the following observer.

"Give it a minute left open," said Cowley, as the door lifted. "No one could miss the stink." To everyone except the two behind them he said, "Everyone else out of the alley."

"Five . . . four . . . here's luck. Lights against us."

"Close it," said Cowley.

The two men were rehearsed now, each working at opposing ends, securing the tripwire, then kneeling before the locks.

"Lights are green. . . ."

"Done," said one man, in the darkness.

The two pickup cars pulled up beyond the alley toward Vozdvizenka. Cowley got into the front of the vehicle already carrying Schnecker's team. As he did so the voice from the Oldsmobile pursuit car said, "Why isn't he coming the most direct way, for the alley turnoff?" Then: "Would you believe it! He's not coming back to the garage. He's going to his own garage, turning in there now. Sorry, guys. You needn't have left after all."

Cowley turned to the men in the back, but before he could speak Schnecker said, "No, we're not going back." He extended a tremoring hand. "We're bushed. There's five we haven't fixed. Next time it'll be easier."

Schnecker and his people declined the drink, and Cowley and the others only stayed for two—the second at Cowley's insistence—

before going back to the bureau's embassy offices. Waiting there for Lambert from his Washington laboratory was the tone-deciphered number Yevgenni Leanov had dialed from his mobile phone that morning.

Danilov said, "It's back on file at Petrovka, but from memory it looks like the direct line into the office of Vladimir Leonidovich Oskavinsky, the director of Plant 43."

"Why bother with the storeman when you can get your stuff from the boss?" said Cowley.

"And who exactly is the boss there?" demanded Danilov, after they had listened to the interception of the Brooklyn telephone call.

"Sounds like a question they're asking themselves," agreed Cowley.

"Leanov's personally carrying the shipping details with him," Danilov pointed out. "Cuts down our chances of overhearing them."

"Which we might have if he and Naina had used the Olds to get home tonight," said Cowley. "Maybe letting the tire down wasn't such a good idea after all."

"If there hadn't been the delay, we wouldn't have gotten out of the garage in time," reminded Danilov. "I think we need to think about the conversation in the car on their way *to* the restaurant."

"Which brings us back to who's in charge," agreed Cowley. "I'm reading it that Ivan Gavrilovich Guzov is the American boss and deals direct with the terrorists. But that Yevgenni Mechislavovich, his former KGB buddy, is on his way to take over. So if we join ourselves at the hip to Gavri, we could be led exactly where we want to go."

"That's how I see it," agreed Danilov. "I also think it's safe to assume there's only one cache. And that there don't appear to be any immediate plans to do anything else here in Moscow."

"The money dispute could be important," suggested Cowley. "If they haven't got enough and keep hitting the banks, we'll still have a chance of tracking them that way, too." He paused. "In fact, the intercept has thrown up a lot to be organized in America."

Pamela had instantly recognized that as she'd listened to the tape three hours earlier and was already making plans. So, too, was Patrick Hollis in the security of his locked den. He'd already cracked into the web address and confirmed it was a cybercafé. He was impatient for eleven o'clock the following morning to send a warning.

34

Pamela Darnley had concluded that Ivan Guzov headed the Russian arms smuggling organization in America before Cowley's Moscow message and was glad she had the previous night memoed the director on the urgency for an immediate tap on Guzov's and Kabanov's homes from the Trenton exchange. She'd also ordered the Trenton agent in charge, John Meadowcraft, to convene a 9:00 A.M. conference of every agent not specifically involved in that morning's surveillance on the Russians and was in Trenton by eight personally to address it. She took with her copies of Yevgenni Leanov's photograph, the man's KGB file, and transcripts as well as duplicates of all the telephone intercepts upon which Leanov featured. Also there by eight o'clock were the ten additional agents she'd drafted in overnight to supplement the surveillance teams.

From Meadowcraft's greeting Pamela guessed she'd been preceded by the gossip couriers and was glad of that, too. It saved a lot of time—and ensured that what she wanted done was done properly—for everyone already to know she stood up to piss like they did.

For the benefit of the ten newcomers, Pamela had Guzov's photograph mounted on the display board beside that of Yevgenni Leanov. She circulated the remainder of those she'd brought through the room for each individual team leader and promised the man's KGB file—as well as Guzov's—would be made available as soon as it was translated and duplicated. So would English translations of all the telephone conversations. In advance of their getting that, Pamela recounted the Moscow ordnance discovery—with the assurance that it was being made safe—but insisted that their Russian targets were their best chance of being led to the Watchmen terrorists. That, she said, would probably be in Chicago, where they'd had bad luck that wasn't going to be repeated.

"There will be no screw-ups," she said, pedantically spacing her words. "That's what I've come personally to tell you. You're going to live in their back pockets—Leanov's when he gets here—and they're not going to know that you're there. You're going to know—and tell me, when I ask—what they eat for breakfast, lunch, and dinner; the color of their underwear; and how many times they blink per second."

When Pamela said she expected Leonard Ross's personal pressure—the White House's, if necessary—to obtain the phone taps before noon, a black female agent near the front said, "Guzov uses a mobile phone a lot. Our surveillance pictures show two different handsets."

"We got the numbers? listening in?" Pamela demanded at once. The cell phone information hadn't been in any report from Trenton, for fuck's sake!

"Not yet," said Meadowcraft.

"Why not!"

"It wasn't thought necessary to have the homes as well as the office bugged until today," Meadowcraft pointed out defensively. He was a large, untidy man who reminded Pamela of Al Beckinsdale in age as well as stature. And now in attitude.

She said, "It's nine-thirty. I want us plugged in by noon, and I want the billing records for the last three months, to know the numbers he's called. I'd like those, at the Washington incident room, by this time tomorrow. Noon the latest. Don't screw around with any official obstruction or objection. Come straight on to Washington and it'll be resolved. Anything unclear?"

There were a lot of exchanged looks. The same black girl who'd mentioned the mobile phones said, "What about the other guy, Kabanov?"

"Just as tight and the same goes for mobiles, if we've got evidence of his using one," instructed Pamela. "Leanov's coming to make

changes—at least he thinks he is—and we might be able to manip-
ulate whatever they are if we get some idea what they might be.
There might even be a hit."

"Why don't we get inside their houses some way, wire the places
like we've done in Brooklyn?" asked one of the drafted-in agents.

"*Because* we wired Brooklyn," said Pamela. "We daren't risk
spooking them."

"What about state-line jurisdiction, courtesy to local forces?" queried Meadowcraft.

"Wherever they go, you go," insisted Pamela. "I'll do the telling,
if it's necessary. I don't want local shitkickers getting in the way."

"Chicago liaison?" asked the agent in charge.

"Direct, if speed's involved. Everything copied to me in Washington."

Pamela's arrival back in D.C., by 11:30, coincided with the Trenton judge's approval of the tap on the homes of Guzov and Kabanov.
Determined against another Chicago foul-up, she spent an hour on
the telephone to the bureau office there assuring herself there were
sufficient agents at the telephone exchange and in readiness in various parts of the city to respond when the number was picked up
from the impending call to Brooklyn's River Café. As soon as she'd
finished doing that, she repeated the process with Manhattan.

It was midafternoon before she reviewed everything with Terry
Osnan. The man said, "We shouldn't be overwhelmed like we were
last time. Orlenko being in the café, waiting, gives us the specific
time. His conversations average out at five minutes. The longest so
far has been ten, from the topless bar at Coney Island."

"The telephone engineers reckon they can run a trace in under
sixty seconds," said Pamela.

Osnan extended both hands, each index finger crossed over its
next digit. "This really could be it, couldn't it?"

"This really could be it," echoed Pamela. A bureau helicopter
was on standby, to take her to Chicago.

The impeachment debate in the Duma collapsed, televised for all to
see. There was a desperation about the communists' attack from the
outset, the speakers repeating themselves instead of coming to the

podium with the criticism apportioned between them. It didn't help them that the censure was predicated upon the economy and the unsuccessful reforms to reduce inflation and stabilize the ruble. The terrorist attack and apparent American intrusion into Russian law enforcement had too obviously been tacked on at the last minute, which made the debate as disjointed as its hurriedly rearranged planning.

By comparison, the Russian White House organized itself superbly. The presidential decree to put the country's early-warning system on standby was leaked overnight, forcing Washington to confirm that the precaution had been discussed and agreed during undisclosed president-to-president discussions. Both White Houses refused to give a reason for the move. By the time the Duma debate began, the speculation had settled on an attack of far greater proportions than that on the U.S. Embassy. It was seized on as fact by the president's parliamentary supporters. Their procession to the podium to talk of the man's strength and foresight, in defending the country and its people, swamped the stumbling criticism so much that the economic crisis appeared to be forgotten. Twenty-three communist votes were recorded against the censure motion.

Danilov watched most of it on his set at Petrovka, not hurrying to tell Georgi Chelyag of the ordnance sabotage he'd planned with equal cleverness. It still took three attempts—his first two calls not returned, despite promises—for Danilov to reach the chief of staff.

Chelyag said at once, "We won."

"I know."

"He's very pleased. Grateful. I'm to tell you. We're going to build on it."

"There's an update."

"I'm very busy. Can't meet. Tell me now."

Danilov did so, feeling a sink of apprehension. When he finished Chelyag said, "Good! It's going well. Keep in touch."

"I—" Danilov started but stopped, realizing he was talking into a dead phone.

It rang again, almost at once. Cowley said, "What the fuck's going on!"

Mary Jo had her usual martini, Orlenko his beer. They had their drinks on the outside deck, admiring the Manhattan skyline. It put them directly in view of the two bureau agents who'd arrived before them and got seats at the bar. The pursuit car from Bay View Avenue had already reported their arrival. There was a line permanently open from the exchange monitoring team to the FBI's Third Avenue Manhattan office and from there to the Washington incident room.

Orlenko brought his wife back into the restaurant ten minutes ahead of schedule and ordered her a second martini while she studied the menu. One of the agents followed Orlenko on his way to the telephone, continuing on to the men's room to warn the waiting listeners from his pocket-concealed microphone.

"A call's incoming," said the exchange listener.

"Tracing," confirmed the engineer at his elbow.

"Hello," said Orlenko.

"Got him!" anticipated Pamela, to Osnan.

It was the same recognizable voice—American—as before. "You tell Moscow what I said?"

"It's got to be a million and a half, all up front."

"Too much."

"Then it's off."

"I don't like threats."

"Neither do my people in Moscow."

"Gavri know?"

"He's being told by Moscow."

"I'll still talk to him."

There was fade on the line, the sound almost lost on one occasion. Pamela said, "Why's that happening?"

Osnan shook his head, not knowing.

The volume dipped again. Pamela only made out: ". . . when you are."

Pamela said, "They promised a trace by now."

Osnan didn't respond, leaning forward toward the speaker. There was a mumble from the exchange and then, much louder: "Shit!"

"What?" demanded Pamela, into her voice link with Manhattan. The reply was from the exchange, not the New York incident room: "It's a mobile phone. The bastard's driving—being driven, I guess—around Chicago. Chicago got a scanner ready?"

She hadn't made the provision, Pamela realized. Before she could repeat the question, Stephen Murray, the Chicago agent in charge, said, "We thought it would be a land line."

"Is there a scanner?" demanded Pamela.

"Afraid not."

"Do we have the mobile number?" It wouldn't appear her mistake, Pamela decided.

"Yes," said the New York monitor.

". . . usual way," Orlenko was saying. "And cash, of course."

"I'll talk to Gavri about that," said the fluctuating voice.

She'd still go to Chicago, Pamela decided. It wasn't a total disaster. By the time she got there they'd have the name from the cell phone records. She could personally supervise the surveillance; be there, too, when Ivan Gavrilovich Guzov arrived, which he'd have to if he were collecting the money. So, too, would Yevgenni Leanov.

The intercept totally faded. Orlenko said, "Hello! hello! I've lost you?"

". . . delivery . . . ?"

"I couldn't hear. Say again."

"What's the delivery?"

"Immediate. A week, upon payment."

"Tell them to ship it."

"I can tell them you have the money?"

"It'll be ready when the stuff gets here."

"When do we speak again?"

"We don't. I'll speak to Gavri."

"That's not how . . . hello? You there?" There was the click, of Orlenko hanging up.

Pamela said, "I'm still going."

Osnan nodded. "They're certainly falling out."

"Let's hope there's some way we can use it."

"Unfortunate about a scanner."

"Which Chicago will have to explain when I get there."

"It's a goddamned meet-the-people presidential parade, all the way around Nikitskij Boulevard and Leanov's place on Kalasnyj," protested Cowley. "Television and still cameras everywhere. I've withdrawn everyone on foot, to prevent their accidentally being photographed and recognized from the arrival pictures with the secretary. Trying to cover by car but it's too loose."

"I wasn't told," said Danilov. *We're going to build on it,* he remembered. "You want me to back up with people from here?"

"Even more risk of recognition by your guy on the payroll, isn't there?"

"The number Leanov called from the car is definitely Vladimir Oskavinky's line at Plant 43," identified Danilov.

"You're going to need extra jails," said Cowley. "The car hadn't been put back in the garage when I withdrew surveillance. I don't like not being there, actually on the ground."

"I'll get back to you," promised Danilov.

It was a full hour before he got a reply from Chelyag's direct line. The man said, "The footage will be useful after the arrests: show the president's personal involvement and awareness."

"How long?" said Danilov, impatient with the nothing-missed cynicism.

"Over any minute now."

"I'd like to have been told."

"It was not considered necessary," the other man dismissed, stiffly.

"Let's hope it wasn't," said Danilov.

When he called Cowley back, the American said, "The guys in the cars already told me. We're back in position. Jimmy and his guys are going in tonight to finish off."

Patrick Hollis timed his break five minutes after he watched Mark Whittier leave his desk. Before he followed, Hollis turned off his computer. The FBI accountant was already at a table when Hollis entered the cafeteria. So was Robert Standing, sharing with three girls on the far side of the room. One was Carole Parker. As Hollis got his coffee, he saw Standing lean forward and say something. All the girls looked in his direction. Two laughed.

Hollis approached the bureau agent with his customary hesitancy. Whittier smiled a greeting.

"How's it going?" Hollis said.

"Pretty good, I think."

"Arrests imminent?" He laughed, to make the question appear a joke.

"Who knows?" avoided Whittier.

"That sounds promising," said Hollis, not laughing this time. He saw Standing leave the cafeteria, putting his hand familiarly against the back of one girl as he held the door open for her.

"We've set a few traps," said the man.

"Can you do things like that on a computer?"

"If you know what you're doing," the accountant said condescendingly.

"So it shouldn't be long?"

"I hope not."

"Best of luck."

"Time I got back to see if I've had any," said Whittier.

Hollis detoured his return through the open-plan mortgage section to ensure Standing was at his desk. He was, but turned away from his terminal, talking animatedly into the telephone.

At his own desk Hollis logged on to his own terminal with Standing's computer pass code to dial the Chicago cybercafé. The e-mail message, addressed to the General, read:

DO NOT ADD ANY FURTHER TO THE WAR CHEST. ENEMY ALERTED.

Hollis didn't add a sender's name.

He saw Mark Whittier physically come forward toward his computer screen in the outer office. And smile.

Stephen Murray was waiting for Pamela Darnley in the security section of O'Hare Airport. She said at once, "Who's the owner of the cell phone!"

The Chicago bureau chief said, "A Frederick Porter. Runs a bar in Evanston and reported the phone stolen from his car yesterday.

Company hadn't got around to canceling the number yet."

"When in the name of Christ is something going to go according to plan!" Pamela demanded.

William Cowley and Dimitri Danilov were thinking roughly the same thing, looking through the just-opened door between the two lock-ups. The Oldsmobile's garage was empty. So was the adjoining one that had been used as a weapons and ammunition store.

It wasn't for some time afterward that they even began to suspect that they'd also lost Yevgenni Mechislavovich Leanov. And much later still before Danilov realized there might be some personal protection in the man's disappearance.

35

It was a time of continuing inquests without any conclusive verdicts. The first was, of course, immediate, and back at the American embassy. That night not even Cowley suggested a drink, although he wanted one. Several, in fact.

None of that day's motorized observers had seen any vehicle in the alley off Nikitskij Boulevard during the street watchers' two-hour absence, but each pointed out that the cul-de-sac curved, hiding the door to what had been the storage garage. Cowley's desperation was obvious in asking them to remember any specific van or truck in such a busy thoroughfare—quite apart from the extra crowds attracted by the president's walk. Schnecker showed how desperate a question it was by pointing out that only the trunks of two full-size cars were needed to transport everything. Until it was seen the following day with Igor Baratov at the wheel, a lot of hope was attached to the bugged Oldsmobile.

"So how dangerous are the five things that aren't fixed?" demanded Cowley.

Neil Hamish, the ballistics experts, spread his hands in an open gesture. "*Nothing's* been defused; it's the detonation and timing we've rigged. So technically it's all dangerous. The five untouched are two antitank mines made to shatter thick armor and three phosphorous incendiaries. If they're connected with any of the other stuff, we'll be OK. If all five were used separately and for one incident—and that's very unlikely—you've got a major explosion and an inferno at the target scene, not before. Explode them in a crowded environment, a shopping mall for instance, and you've got a catastrophe."

"I think it'll be judged that we've already got one," said Cowley.

Barry Martlew said, "For someone claiming to be on the side of the good guys, the president staged a hell of a diversion, didn't he?"

Danilov, who'd been waiting for the accusation, gave them Chelyag's explanation. Voicing everyone's exasperated disgust, Martlew said, "Jesus Henry Christ!"

"Let's consider the positives," Cowley insisted, briskly. "We've got a good lead on how the stuff will be shipped, and we've got the Chicago waterfront under wraps. We'll know from Customs in advance the arrival of any Cidicj line freighter. The cargo manifest has to be declared, so we'll even know if anything's specifically consigned to OverOcean Inc. I don't know how strong we are in Poland, but we could move some people up to Gdansk from the Warsaw embassy. We might have dropped the ball but I think we can pick it up again."

It was not until Igor Baratov returned the Oldsmobile to its garage the following day that they began seriously to suspect that Leanov was no longer in Moscow. Later that night they were sure. In between Danilov managed meeting with Georgi Chelyag.

"It had better be important!" greeted the presidential aide.

"Judge for yourself," said Danilov. His irritation ebbed at Chelyag's visible reaction to the weapons loss.

For once, although briefly, the chief of staff appeared lost for words, initially only saying: "Oh." Quickly he added, "*Definitely* while the president was there?"

Into Danilov's mind came Barry Martlew's remark and just as quickly the personal protection there might be in it. Maybe, he thought, he was no longer the discardable nobody who'd served his brief purpose. "Absolutely no doubt. The Americans are actually talking of it being a diversion."

"*What!*"

"If the surveillance had been in place, we wouldn't have lost anything."

"Washington been told that?"

"Yes," Danilov said, only slightly exaggerating. "If it leaks—not just now but any time in the future—it'll destroy most of what you achieved, won't it? It would be easy for the public to believe the president *was* involved, even. Reignite the whole censure debate."

From Chelyag's unblinking concentration Danilov wondered if he'd overemphasized the threat of his personal knowledge. Chelyag said, "What have you done?"

"Dismissed it as ludicrous; stressed the absolute, leader-to-leader cooperation. Problem is, the facts would hardly need manipulation, would they?"

"There could be further direct contact," suggested Petrov.

"To a suspicious mind, wouldn't the denial look like a confirmation?" How quickly Danilov had learned and adjusted to the way the chief of staff's mind worked.

"Will you be able to judge the way the American thinking is going?"

"I think so."

"I need to know; we can't be caught out."

"The greater danger would be for the leak to emanate from here."

"Yes?" encouraged the older man.

"Which can't happen." Danilov smiled. "I'm the only Russian who knows."

Chelyag didn't smile back. "That is very fortunate."

"Very," agreed Danilov.

The proof of Leanov's disappearance—agonizingly vague about the man, illuminating about others—emerged after Igor Baratov arrived in the bugged car to collected his sister from Pereulok Samokatnaja. Cowley and Danilov were already waiting in the embassy's bureau offices, alerted by the pursuit car from the garage. The conversation actually began with Naina Karpov asking about the Oldsmobile's flat, which Baratov said his garage had been unable to find. There was some conversation about educating their children—hers as well as his—abroad ("we can certainly afford the fees") before Baratov said, "Heard from Yevgenni?"

"I don't expect to."

"Long drive?"

"Worth it."

"He going to deal with Gavri?"

"He's going to see how he finds things."

"I think we should. It's undermining our position here."

"You heard from Petrovka?"

"A week ago. Osipov is definitely being dismissed as a turf war killing and Lasin's death as part of it. Ashot Yefimovich is handling it all. Insisting the brigade's disbanded."

The woman laughed. "You can't believe how easy it is to operate here, can you!"

Baratov laughed in return. "What about the presidential nonsense yesterday! There we were, right under the stupid bastard's nose, and none of them had a clue!"

The warning crackled from the following vehicle that the route didn't seem to be to the Golden Hussar.

Naina Karpov said, "Mizin's a good man. Needs looking after."

"I'm doing it," assured Baratov. "You and Yevgenni seem to be close?"

"I like him. It's good."

"Permanent?"

"It's an idea."

"How would it work? If we decided on a move, he'd have to replace Gavri in America, wouldn't he?"

"Too early to say. You want your kid educated abroad, what's wrong with America?"

"Nothing," said Baratov.

The restaurant was one of the latest on the current fashion list, out beyond the inner beltway. Called the New York Grill, it actually was run by an American. Cowley decided against his watchers going in to eat. For the first time in several days he and Danilov went to the Savoy bar to fill in the time. Over their third scotch Danilov

nodded toward the American's glass and said, "You seem to be enjoying it?"

"I always have."

"I know."

"That supposed to mean something?" Cowley demanded, defensively.

"Just talking." The Russian shrugged.

"You think it's a problem?" There was an edge to Cowley's voice
now.

"You know that better than me."

"It isn't."

"Good."

"Something been said?"

"No," said Danilov. He missed another two rounds and insisted
they skip a third to get back to the embassy for Naina Karpov's
return from the restaurant. They had to wait almost an hour, which
Cowley occupied drafting an account for Washington and speaking
directly to Terry Osnan. Nothing of significance was said during
Naina Karpov's homeward journey. Baratov played Billie Holiday
all the way back to Nikitskij after dropping his sister off. Cowley
said, "We need to keep this up much longer, I'll buy them a new
fucking tape."

Pamela Darnley's first full day in Chicago, which had only just
ended, had been one of inquests and frustrations, too, only lifted at
its very end by the news of Robert Standing's Albany arrest and
learning that she'd been right about another illegal entry through
the Pentagon. Her concern at hearing from Terry Osnan that Cowley and Danilov had lost the arms shipment and the man seemingly
on his way from Moscow went beyond the professional. Secure now
in her own permanent appointment, she was worried about Cowley,
well aware the scapegoat vacancy was available if there were many
more mistakes or failures.

Protected herself—wishing there was something she could do to
help Cowley—she insisted that Steven Murray write an official, case
file explanation for the failure to provide a scanner and ordered six
top-of-the-range devices from bureau headquarters, both analog and

digital, against the contact being made to Bay View Avenue the same way again.

She'd seized the Albany identification of the computer café, Cyber Shack on Halsted Street, as a major, potentially case-solving breakthrough, particularly when she saw how much concealment there was among the milling students from the Illinois University campus less than a block away. She carried with her Patrick Hollis's anonymous first cable and the second he'd sent that morning, again using Robert Standing's computer ID and also addressed to the General. It read:

WAR CHESTS ARE LOCKED.

It was 12:32 P.M. and crowded inside and out when Pamela arrived, with Stephen Murray and a five-man backup, with a SWAT team on standby. They'd already established that the café was owned by brothers Herbie and Jason Montgomery, both former computer science students at the university who had no criminal convictions, no civil court orders against them, no posted debts, and permanent addresses in the city. Pamela said, "This is letterbox rental: We go straight in and identify ourselves?"

It was Pamela's first encounter with nerds. Herbie Montgomery wore thick-lensed John Lennon glasses and looked like a bright-eyed nesting bird peering from inside a tangled hedge of hair that merged with an unclipped beard spread to his chest like a bib. His brother was clean shaven, without glasses, and had the soap-faced pallor of someone who never strayed from the sunless vastness of cyberspace. Both wore bib-and-suspender overalls and work boots. Their back office was a snake's nest of cables, coils, wires, and blank-eyed terminals.

When Pamela showed the two men copies of the two messages, Herbie said, "Hey! Guy didn't take anything that wasn't his."

"Let's go from the beginning," said Murray.

"One cool cracker," obliged Jason. "Came in last Wednesday, said he wanted to rent page space. Called himself the General, like all hackers and crackers do. Paid fifty dollars up front. Expected him back from time to time: That's the usual way, not on the web themselves so they use our home page and our terminals. But this guy collects his own mail from outside. Cracked in, downloaded, and was away.

"But like I said," took up Herbie, "he paid. He's still in credit."

"OK," said Pamela. "So let's go back again. Proper name?"

Herbie smiled sympathetically. "Cyber gypsies don't use real names. Surfing you can be who you like, go where you like. Nobody knows you've been or gone 'less you want them to. This guy wanted to be the General so that's who he was."

"How'd he pay?" asked Murray, anticipating the answer.

"Cash. Fifty-dollar bill."

"Where is it now?"

The brother looked at the local bureau chief in astonishment. "How do we know! It was four days ago! Might have banked it, used it in change, spent it. Could be anywhere."

"You ever see him before?" persisted Pamela, all expectation gone.

Herbie shook his head. Jason said, "Nope."

"Describe him."

Both men thought. Herbie said, "Big guy. Obviously kept himself in shape: no gut. About forty-five. Stood tall, like an army type." He buried his hand into his bird's-nest hair. "Had that sort of haircut, too. You know, right up to the top of his head."

"And a tattoo," reminded Jason.

"What of?" demanded Murray.

"Eagle. The American eagle, on his left arm."

"How could you see it?" asked Murray.

"He was wearing a short-sleeved sport shirt, with jeans. New. And combat boots. Like the others."

"What others?" demanded Pamela.

"There were three other guys in the jeep outside—a modern one, not an army type, but the doors were open and he sat with his foot up against the dash, so I saw his boots," said Jason.

"What color was the vehicle?"

"Maroon," said the brothers, in unison.

"I tell you what I want you guys to do," said Pamela. "I want you to come down to the bureau offices with us and take all the time in the world to work with an artist on an e-fit of the General and the others, if you can remember enough about them. And we'll look through every make of jeep there's ever been until you recognize the one they had."

"What the hell's this guy done!" demanded Herbie.

"Caused a lot of trouble," she said.

On their way back out to the car, Murray said, "It's good."

"Not good enough," Pamela said.

When she got back to the office, there were call-back messages from the director and Terry Osnan.

Osnan said, "The navy has a navigation satellite in geostationary orbit over the Pacific. It had been put out by two degrees. Would have put everything off course."

The director said, "I'm not sure how many more commendations I can award. Looks to me like you might be heading for a presidential medal."

What about a deputy directorship? wondered Pamela.

Robert Standing had been led away from the building in handcuffs, with virtually every window occupied by watching bank staff. Hollis was sure Standing had been crying; certainly two or three girls inside had been weeping. Carole Parker had been one of them.

36

The most intense inquest was obviously long distance, from Washington. Leonard Ross insisted on a written, detailed account to which Cowley had to add two further responses to the director's subsequent queries. In addition there were repeated, tense-voiced telephone conversations. Ross actually echoed Barry Martlew's diversion cynicism, which Cowley answered by quoting Igor Baratov's intercepted ridicule of clearing the lock-up garage under the Russian president's nose. The protection-seeking Danilov had already decided to keep the recorded ridicule—the entire tape and its contents—from Georgi Chelyag.

From the "long drive" remark on the recording, they guessed the man had left Moscow by road, most likely with the arms shipment. Nevertheless, they checked passenger lists of Aeroflot's U.S. flights and of all the American carriers for the preceding two days. They found no record of Yevgenni Meckislavovich Leanov leaving Moscow by air.

"Viktor Nikov had two passports," reminded Danilov. "The KGB printed genuine documents. Leanov's farewell present from the Lubyanka could have been as many as he wanted."

Cowley spent a long time on the telephone to the FBI office at the Warsaw embassy—which had already received independent priority instructions in the director's name from Washington—and wired all the available photographs, including Leanov's from his KGB dossier. The Polish-based agent in charge apologized for not having any useful contacts within the Gdansk port.

"And we can't risk approaching Cidicj direct, can we?"

"No," agreed Cowley.

"You've no idea what sort of vehicle—or vehicles—will be delivering the stuff? Just that it'll most likely be Russian registration but that's not definite?"

Cowley squeezed his eyes shut in exasperation. "I don't need reminding!"

"Don't hold your breath that we'll get anything," said the other man.

Pamela Darnley was still in Chicago when Osnan relayed the request for Customs authorities there to post an "instant advise" watch for incoming Cidicj freighters. When she spoke to the Washington incident room, Osnan said, "We're also circulating Leanov's photograph with a detain order to all airports, harbors, and border crossings."

"What's the atmosphere like?"

"Deeply unhappy. You coming back?"

"Albany first, to hear all that Robert Standing has to say." The case-closing breakthrough might only have been delayed, not lost. The three-D digitized computer drawing of the General looked good—like an identifiable living person—and the physical description was far better than most she'd known, with the bonus of the eagle tattoo. And the Montgomery brothers were positive about the maroon Toyota Land Cruiser. All she had to do was break Standing; in the euphoria the heat would be taken off Cowley. Her sudden desire to do that—help him however she could—surprised her. Then she thought: Why not? They were level-grade colleagues now, no longer with a superior-to-subordinate barrier. And it would be her choice, just like in a singles' bar.

Pamela went cautiously into the interview at Albany police headquarters, warned by Anne Stovey ("thanks for the commendation") of her initial arrest interrogation.

"He won't shift," said the local FBI agent.

"He been Mirandaed?" queried Pamela. It didn't matter how many people she had to teach to suck eggs, she didn't intend getting screwed by a legal technicality like failure to advise the man of his legal rights.

"Read out, in full, in front of his lawyer—the top guy here in Albany—to whom he was granted immediate access before being asked a single question," confirmed Anne. "Everything recorded on tape."

Pamela looked up from the transcript of the first interrogation. "He got a mental problem?"

"Those are his answers," said the other woman.

"Let's try again," said Pamela.

Robert Standing was unshaven and unshowered, the underarms of his shirt sweat-rimed, and he was red-eyed. There was a smell. In total contrast, the lawyer beside him was immaculate in pinstripes, with a mustache and goatee in a miasma of after-shave and cologne. He insisted on a formal exchange of cards, identifying himself as Albert Lang, which she already knew. Pamela had to search through her purse for a card to return.

He looked pointedly at the recording apparatus, waiting for it to be turned it on. As soon as Anne Stovey did so, the man said, "My client has cooperated fully with your investigation. Having done so, he has the right to refuse this second interview, but I have advised him to continue to cooperate. I want to place on record, at this juncture, that it is my client's intention to sue the Federal Bureau of Investigation for harassment and illegal arrest."

"Thank you. Your cooperation and future intentions have been noted," said Pamela. Textbook testosterone, she decided. Not difficult to understand how Anne Stovey had been steam-rollered. It would be interesting how long the pomposity would last under different questioning by someone from out of town. Pamela slid a print-out of the General's e-fit across the table toward Standing and said, "Who is this man?"

Standing studied it for several moments. "I have never seen or met anyone like him before." His voice was strong but he was moving one hand over the other, as if he were washing them.

"For the benefit of the tape, I would like this image identified," intruded Lang.

"The General," said Pamela, still talking to Standing. "The man—the pseudonym—to whom you sent two messages at the Cyber Shack on Halsted Street, Chicago. I'd like you to tell me his real name."

"I do not know anyone who calls himself the General. Or of the Cyber Shack on Halsted Street or anywhere else in Chicago," replied the man. "I have never been to the city."

"I am showing the suspect an electrically generated depiction of an American eagle," said Pamela, doing so. "Who do you know who has this type of tattoo within a scroll?"

"I don't know anyone. Or what you're talking about."

"I consider this questioning technique irregular," said the lawyer.

"A protest that can be made in open court to test admissibility," dismissed Pamela. To Standing she said, "What's a Land Cruiser?"

"This is preposterous!" said Lang.

"Sir, your objections do not concern points of law, they are intentionally diverting interferences which I am objecting to, on record, for later consideration by the court." She went to Standing, who had begun to sweat again. "Will you answer, Mr. Standing?"

"A car?" The man frowned.

"Who do you know who owns a maroon Toyota Land Cruiser?" To the tape she said, "I am showing the suspect a dealer's photograph of such a vehicle."

"No one."

Copies of the Cyber Shack messages were added to the exhibit pile, identified by Pamela as she offered them. She said, "What do those mean?"

Standing again took several minutes. "I don't have the slightest idea."

Pamela pushed over another piece of evidence, conscious that the lawyer's interruptions had stopped. "Is this your personal computer log-on that identifies you, by name, to your bank's computer system?"

"Yes," confirmed Standing.

"Both messages I have just shown you were sent to the Cyber Shack in Chicago from *your* branch on *your* computer log-on."

"Not by me."

Another sheet of paper went across the table. "Do you recognize this photocopy to be that of your current bank statement?"

"Yes, but I don't know anything about the deposits you're talking about."

"What deposits are those, Mr. Standing?"

"The ones she asked me about before, that come to $3,400," said Standing, nodding toward the silent Anne Stovey. He was sweating more heavily now, soaking his shirt anew.

"That amount, in total, was stolen from client accounts in branches of your bank in Schenectady, Rochester, and Rome, and your computer ID has been traced to those illegal withdrawals," Pamela set out. "How do you explain that?"

"Somebody else must have done it."

"No one else has—or should have—access to your personal computer identification, should they?"

Sweat was leaking from the man now. "No."

"Have you shared or given your personal ID to an unauthorized person?" Her warmth was frustration.

"No."

"Then how was it used to withdraw these amounts of money and send messages to Chicago?"

"*I don't know!*" erupted the man, so unexpectedly that both women and the lawyer jumped. Standing began to cry. He let his nose run, uncaringly. "I'm sorry. I don't know what's happening. I haven't done any of this. Any of anything. I'm being framed."

"Why? By whom?" demanded Pamela. She wished he'd wipe his nose.

"I don't know!"

"Is there anything you *do* know, Mr. Standing?"

"No!" said the man, answering the ridicule genuinely as he at last wiped his eyes and nose. "Please believe me!"

"Your problem is that I don't." She tapped the bank statement and computer ID. "That's prima facie evidence of grand larceny."

"My client is prepared to undertake a polygraph test," said Lang. There was very little pomposity now.

"That's a trial defense prerogative," accepted Pamela.

"I meant now, at this stage of the investigation."

"Mr. Lang, my investigations concern the attack upon the United Nations building, the massacre of FBI personnel at New Rochelle, the bombing and attempted bombing of the Washington Monument and the Lincoln Memorial, and several other matters. I intend charging your client today with grand larceny, pending further investigation, and the government will oppose in the strongest terms any bail application."

The bearded lawyer sat regarding her open-mouthed, wordless, able only to shake his head.

Robert Standing fainted.

"Clever ploy. Never had it happen before," said Pamela. At her suggestion they'd gone directly across the street from the police headquarters and sat with coffee and Danish between them.

"The doctor said it was genuine," reminded Anne.

"Shit scared of medical malpractice," dismissed Pamela. "Safer to put him in the hospital for observation."

"Delays the formal charge though."

"He's still in official custody. I'll speak to Washington. I don't want him copping any medical plea."

"You going to go along with the polygraph?"

"Washington's decision, but I don't see why not. If he sweats while he's on the lie detector like he did today, he'll send the needle off the paper." Her anger at being tricked was going, but only very gradually.

"You think he's guilty?"

Pamela regarded the other woman disbelievingly over the rim of her coffee cup. "Do I *think* he's guilty! Come on!"

"Why make stupid mistakes now?" questioned the local agent. "If he's our man, he's been doing it for years and could have gone on doing it except for a bookkeeper named Clarence Snelling who literally counted his pennies. And who we still might not have caught on even if the amounts went into dollars. Why, suddenly, does Standing start stealing so obviously and leaving ID traces all over the place—send crazy, war-type messages—and dump over three grand in his own account, in his own bank, where everybody knew there was an FBI audit going on?"

"That's what I'm going to have him tell me when he gets over the phony stress attack," promised Pamela. The case-closing break had only been postponed, and not for long. The collapse *had* been phony, when he'd known he was going over the edge: worked once but it wouldn't work again. Next time she was going to make sure he went over the edge and broke into a lot of little pieces.

It was William Cowley's idea to return to America, which in the normal circumstances of a normal investigation he wouldn't have cleared first with the director. He did in these abnormal circumstances, left in no doubt that Leonard Ross held him to some degree responsible for lifting the street surveillance on the Nikitskij cul-de-sac. He made the approach a request to let some of the team he'd taken with him remain in Moscow, with Barry Martlew as supervisor.

"There's a lot happening here," agreed Ross. "But you sure there's nothing else to do in Moscow?"

"Nothing that Martlew can't handle. Or the Warsaw station."

"Give it a couple of days," insisted the director. Ominously he added, "I want your personal assurance we're covered on all bases. Pamela seems to have things in hand here."

"I'd like to come with you," said Danilov, meaning it, when Cowley told him.

"I'd like it, too, but there'll need to be a lot of coordination between both places," reminded Cowley.

"Let's hope we get it right." At once Danilov said, "That didn't come out as it was meant to. It wasn't a criticism of you. It was the right decision: I'm sorry."

Cowley smiled, ruefully. "Get up off your knees. I know it wasn't a crack."

"You going to be all right?" Danilov asked seriously.

"It'll blow over. You know the saying."

"The buck stops here," provided Danilov.

"Or where it's most convenient," qualified the American.

Danilov was suddenly caught by the thought that the aphorism of a long-ago American president was probably more appropriate for him than for Cowley. Chelyag was now initiating the approaches, but with the passage of days what had seemed as protective knowledge didn't appear as strong as he'd first thought. And the political embarrassment it would cause ended when the case did. Danilov acknowledged that ironically his future would be best safeguarded by the case not, in fact, being solved at all.

"I liked the other car!" protested Elizabeth Hollis. "Everyone drives Fords like this."

"I told you," said Hollis. "It was an economy decision that I return it. There'll be a policy change soon. We'll get another one just like it." Hollis didn't like being reminded of the one extravagance that might have made people curious.

"You've heard that news already on the other channel," complained the cantankerous woman, jabbing an arthritically twisted finger toward the radio.

"I wanted to check something, make sure I didn't mishear," said Hollis. There should surely have been a public FBI announcement by now? He didn't understand it.

He'd specifically timed their arrival at the mall the General had designated and was walking his mother by the telephone on their way to J. C. Penney when the public telephone rang. He continued on by without pausing, looking back only when the ringing stopped. A boy of about eighteen in jeans and a back-to-front ball cap was shaking his head. He was still shaking it when he put the phone down and walked away.

The announcement Hollis was anxious to hear concerned Robert Standing, but as they'd arrested him, the FBI must have a lead from the Cyber Shack to the General. Who, wondered Hollis, would the General turn out to be?

37

Robert Standing was charged with larceny, despite passing a polygraph test that went beyond the bank stealing to include every attack the Watchmen had committed or attempted. The man did not break down or cry, although he did perspire heavily during his second encounter with Pamela Darnley. After that the New York State district attorney, who'd appointed himself prosecutor, demanded further corroborating evidence of Watchmen association before permitting a third attempt to obtain an admission linking Standing to the terrorists.

With the agreement of both a subdued Albert Lang and his client, bail was discussed in camera before a judge. The term "national security" was repeatedly invoked by the New York state lawyer. He'd been in frequent contact with the Justice Department in Washington and was aware of the political platform an eventual trial would provide. Bail was not sought after the judge indicated it would be set at millions. The publicity-attracting sum would jeopardize the unbiased fairness of any jury.

Throughout the legal maneuverings Pamela Darnley seethed at what she considered the second lost breakthrough opportunity. She briefly considered moving Terry Osnan as Albany agent in charge to head up the continuing investigation there until deciding the man's total command and knowledge of the Washington incident room would be weakened. Instead she put Anne Stovey in charge of three drafted-in agents with the instructions to find out more about Robert Standing than he knew about himself.

To herself privately and to Anne Stovey very openly Pamela vowed to find another Watchmen tie-in to justify a third confrontation with the bank official. It was Anne Stovey who suggested tracing any association Standing or his family might have with any branch of the military. Allowing Anne the credit—and the chance to tell her official supervisor of her own supervisory promotion—Pamela let Anne ask Osnan to initiate the Pentagon check, taking over the telephone only to ensure that the Chicago e-fit image and the full, detailed description of the General was being run through all military records, past and present, and even extended to the navy, despite the rank.

It was during the call that she learned of William Cowley's impending return to Washington. She said, "Atmosphere any better there?"

"No," Osnan said shortly. "Got something to run by you when you get back."

"Why not now?"

"Not the time or the place," refused the man. "It's personal."

Pamela spent the return flight mentally examining the past few days, searching for oversights. She had forgotten Osnan's remark when she entered the J. Edgar Hoover building to find another setback awaiting her.

"Problem," announced John Meadowcraft when she returned his call. "Both Guzov and Kabanov *are* using two different cell phones. But there's only one issued in each name. They must have the other under other names."

"How's that affect us scanning in?" queried Pamela.

"They don't use it to talk," declared the man.

"I don't understand."

"Each number on a cell phone pad also represents three letters of the alphabet and can be used to send text messages: no conversation."

"Which we can't break into?"

"The experts say it would be difficult, even if we had the number. We've only caught them using text on a few occasions, always in the parking lot of their realtor building. I sent a gal in looking for apartments. She saw Kabanov and Guzov both hammering away separately. They've only got one floor of a twenty-story building. So many phones it sounds like a bird aviary scanned from outside."

"There must be something!"

"I spent the morning with virtually every electronics expert we've got."

"Bank statements!" she demanded. "They have to pay!"

"Sure they do," agreed the Trenton bureau head. "But not off any statement we've accessed, private or company. It's either cash—and we haven't followed either to any cell phone office or outlet—or a check in the name in which they hold the phones. And we don't have that name, so we're back where we started."

"Shit!" Pamela said vehemently.

"So much I can't see through it," accepted Meadowcraft. "You or anyone else have a way around, I'd like to hear it."

"I'll run it by technical."

"I already have," reminded the man.

Too much was going wrong: confusingly, frustratingly wrong! "I'll talk around," she said, aware of the hollow echo of empty words.

It was only when she was setting the latest difficulty out to Osnan, for him to take up with any bureau division he thought might have a suggestion, that Pamela remembered his remark on the telephone in Albany.

"What's personal?" she asked.

"How well do you know Bill? Socially, I mean?"

"Hardly at all. We only met on this case. A dinner, a few drinks is all." The man wouldn't have understood the nursing overnight.

Osnan hesitated. "Would you say he had a drinking problem?"

"No," Pamela said at once. "Why?"

"A few rumors going around since the technical guys got back."

"Who?" she demanded.

"Rumors don't have names attached."

"Being given as the cause for lifting the surveillance?"

"Inevitably."

"Find the source. This isn't the time for a story like that."

"That's why I told you. And why I thought you ought to know."

There wasn't any relaxation in Moscow. Cowley convened a conference of those he was leaving behind with Danilov present, making it clear the Russian unofficially shared control with Martlew and should know everything that went on, but there was the impression of slowing down. The round-the-clock watch was maintained on the Oldsmobile's garage, but Baratov didn't take his sister out again. There was no advance warning from the Manhattan listeners of telephone contact between Brooklyn's Bay View Avenue and the restaurant on Moscow's Pereulok Vorotnikovskij. The Warsaw agent in charge called several times, apologizing on each occasion for not being able to locate any Polish freighter shipments to America. They hadn't located the name Yevgenni Mechislavovich Leanov on the passenger list of any Aeroflight or America-bound airline, but it was possible for people to travel on tickets in a name different from that on their passports. Georgi Chelyag's concern at the president being associated with the ordnance loss revived when Danilov told him of Cowley's return to America. Danilov exacerbated it by suggesting the American was going back for an inquiry into the disappearance, which didn't actually amount to a lie.

Danilov even found time to go to Larissa's grave in the Novodevichy Cemetery and was shocked by its neglect. The few flowers that hadn't been stolen for other graves were atrophied, the vase on its side. They were dead leaves everywhere, and the headstone was covered in birds' shit from a now-abandoned nest in the overhanging tree. It took him a long time to clean everything up and arrange the fresh flowers he'd brought. Afterwards he went to the other side of the cemetery, where Olga was buried. The headstone and surroundings were scrubbed clean; there wasn't any leaf or tree debris, and the flowers were fresh. Igor, he guessed. One of the photographs he'd given the man had been mounted in a mourning frame and fixed to the base of the headstone. Danilov was surprised how attractive—beautiful—his wife looked. On each of the concluding evenings Danilov and Cowley drank, Cowley increasingly too much.

Until the very last night, that was. Things had, in fact, started to happen much earlier in the day. Danilov had only been in his office for an hour when the call came from Chelyag, asking if he had an available television. When Danilov told the chief of staff that he had, Chelyag said, "Watch the parliamentary coverage. I'll see you at three."

The reshuffle had the approval of the president, declared the prime minister. The reforms the White House had initiated needed fresh impetus from a revitalized government. And those reforms were being extended beyond the economy. The U.S. Embassy attack and the ongoing investigation had focused attention on Russian law enforcement and exposed a totally unacceptable level of corruption. The minister ultimately responsible had to bear the burden of that fault. Nikolai Gregorovich Belik was therefore being replaced. In the new democratic system of Russia the role of the Federal Security Service had changed, taking on more of a law enforcement role. Therefore it was as culpable for a level of criminality all too often described in the West as being out of control. It was an accusation that could not be allowed to continue. For that reason Viktor Kedrov was also being moved. The use of a Russian chemical and biological warhead in a fortunately failed attack upon the United Nations and of other Russian devices in further outrages had greatly embarrassed and humiliated the country as well as initially placing some strain upon relationships between Russia and the United States of America. As the Duma already knew, some steps had been taken to rectify clear lack of military supervision. Defense Minister General Sergei Gromov, who should have prevented that failure, was being retired.

"You chose correctly," said the president's chief of staff later.

"Unfortunate there was a need to choose," said Danilov.

"The president supports people who are loyal to him."

Danilov recognized they feared a parliamentary fight back. A battle in which he could still be the equivalent of a germ warfare missile fired against the White House. A mistake to ease the tension on the ratchet wheel. "I do not know the new interior minister."

"An advocate of reforms and the new Russia."

"Whom I should brief?"

Chelyag's face hardened and Danilov was glad: He wanted the man fully to accept he'd not only deciphered the code but was able to communicate in it, just like a foreign language.

Chelyag said, "The crisis committee no longer exists because so many who formed it no longer exist in any position of authority. It is not being reestablished. You will continue to report only to me. The arrangement is understood by the new minister. Everything is now understood by everybody."

A mistake to believe he was a better exponent of the newly learned art, Danilov recognized. "I'm sure it is."

"How sure are you of this all concluding as it has to conclude, Dimitri Ivanovich?" demanded Chelyag, tightening his own ratchet wheel.

"The Russian end of the conspiracy here will be destroyed," declared Danilov. "There's still uncertainty—and a Russian element— in America."

"We don't want anything involving Russia ending inconclusively," said the other man. "Don't forget that, will you, Dimitri Ivanovich?"

That night Baratov did collect his sister in the Oldsmobile, and again they ate in the American-themed restaurant. Their conversation was inconsequential except for two minutes on the recording tape.

Baratov: It must have been good, talking to him again?

Naina: He said he went straight through—that it was the easiest route imaginable.

Baratov: What about the stuff?

Naina: Waved over at Grodno without being stopped. Halfway there by now.

Baratov: What about Gavri?

Naina: Hasn't made contact yet.

Baratov: I spoke to Svetlana about moving to America. She likes the idea.

Naina: The more I think about it, the more I think
   Gavri needs to go.

Cowley looked around the embassy listening room and said,
"Yevgenni Leanov got past U.S. immigration. He's in America,
waiting for enough materiel to arrive to cause a major catastrophe."
" 'Already halfway there,' " echoed Martlew. "And he's probably
going to kill another Russian."
"Hell of a busy guy," said Cowley.

Exasperated by the military's insistence that it would take at least a
month to run a three services' personnel comparison against the
Chicago e-fit and the manufacturers' equally frustrating estimate to
collate the distribution and purchase of maroon Land Cruisers
throughout Illinois, Pamela seized the Oldsmobile intercept as the
breath of air to blow her out of the doldrums.
   Acknowledging the near impossibility of a search without a
name—if indeed Leanov hadn't traveled under his own—she used
Frank Norton's White House muscle to have immigration check
every Russian passport arrival at every U.S. port or airport, East
and West Coast, and to run checks for American residency addresses
on the visa forms. There was renewed frustration at further insistence that such a search could take weeks despite the narrow timeframe since Leanov's disappearance from Moscow.
   "You want to tell the president it's going to take that long or
shall I?" Pamela asked the deputy director of Immigration, guessing
the director himself had ducked her call.
   Observing local territory protocol, she had Stephen Murray pass
to Chicago Customs the information that the arms cargo ship was
already in the Atlantic. In minutes Terry Osnan's master index identified Peter Samuels as the Customs director who'd attended the
first Washington emergency meeting. Unlike the head of Immigration, Samuels personally and at once took her call.
   "We've got planes as well as ships," said the man. "If it's somewhere in the Atlantic, we'll find it."
   "We don't want them to realize we're looking."
   There was a pained silence. "It's something we've done before."

And they did it again, in just six hours. Pamela immediately called Leonard Ross. She said, "We've located the shipment. But we wouldn't have been able to without Bill Cowley."

"I still can't believe it," said Patrick Hollis. There were six people around the cafeteria table, including Carole Parker. They were all so occupied with Robert Standing that they hadn't rejected Hollis when he'd joined them.

"I don't know," said Carole. "There was always something about him not just quite right."

"There must be a lot involved for there not even to have been a bail application," suggested a teller.

"You spent a lot of time with the FBI guy," said another, to Hollis. "You get any idea how much?"

"No," said Hollis, enjoying being asked for an opinion. "But I got the impression it was fairly substantial."

"So he'll go to jail?"

"I would think so," said Hollis. "Poor guy."

"Why ever feel sorry for him?" demanded Carole.

38

The aerial surveillance docking estimate of five days was confirmed by the Cidicj *Star*'s cargo manifest filed with Chicago Customs. It gave the fifteenth as the arrival date and listed three containers of tractor and engine parts for OverOcean portside collection. With so much time to prepare, William Cowley had the uneasy impression that he was returning to a vacuum, an impression heightened by all the necessary planning already under way. Worryingly, Leonard Ross's diary was too full to see him on his first day back.

Terry Osnan had installed a large map of the eastern seaboard of the United States, extending up to include the east coast of Canada and the St. Lawrence Seaway entrance to the Great Lakes. On it he marked the progress of the Cidicj *Star*—appropriately designated by a red stick pin—constantly updating from Coast Guard aerial reports. Pamela had organized three SWAT teams and fixed at twenty the number of extra agents needed in Chicago to maintain the necessary surveillance on the containers once they were unloaded, to lead them to the terrorist group and the General for whom the military hadn't offered any identification. Neither had the General made any further approach to the now totally FBI firewalled Cyber Shack.

Although the contact between Washington and Moscow had been absolute, Cowley and Pamela reviewed every development in his absence. Pamela began to regret the meeting halfway through, because it came out like a litany of her achievements, which she hadn't intended. She thought Cowley looked drained—worse, he looked distracted.

She was even more discomfited when, at the end, he said, "Quite a success story! Congratulations!"

"You already said that, from Moscow," Pamela reminded him curtly. "I got a couple of lucky breaks and you had a bad one. From which we've recovered. We're still in good shape." Her ex-husband had drunk too much—it was as much that as her career determination that wrecked the marriage—but she couldn't recognize any of the signs in Cowley, although there was perhaps the vaguest hand tremor.

"Can't think of anything you haven't already got in hand," he said. There was something like condescension in Pamela surrendering the desk chair to him. The irritation came at once. That was self-pity—or something like it—and went way beyond any remorse he needed to feel. Unless, perhaps, the uncertainty wasn't remorse at losing the cargo—which she'd pointed out they'd found again—but something else. Back on base now. Time to get a grip on himself.

"What about going there ourselves?" Pamela said.

Cowley considered the question. "Chicago's going to be the focus. Nowhere else we need to be."

"Together."

Cowley wasn't sure if it was a question or a statement. "There'll have to be split-second coordination between us and Dimitri in Moscow. I can do that as easily from Chicago as from here; better, even, actually being on the spot."

"I think we should be together," stated Pamela.

"So do I."

"How's Dimitri taking the death of his wife?"

Cowley had forgotten Pamela had known. "OK."

"What was it?"

"Routine operation that went wrong," avoided Cowley. "Don't know the details."

"Your hair doesn't look as if it's sliding off the side of your head anymore. How have you been?" She couldn't talk about what she wanted to in official surroundings like this. When—how—could she talk about it?

"OK," he said, leaning sideways to his briefcase. "I brought you a present." It was a joke *matroyshka* set; the one-on-top-of-the-other doll representing Boris Yeltsin had a red nose and a glass of vodka in its hand.

Pamela smiled her thanks and said, "I haven't been anywhere to justify bringing back a gift. I could buy you dinner if you're not one of those old-fashioned guys who thinks a man always has to pay." Was this how it was done in singles' bars? Not that the intention was sex. She wanted a different setting for a quite different sort of intimacy, and this was the best she could think of.

Cowley appeared as surprised as Pamela was at herself. He said, "That would be a nice welcome home."

They went to Georgetown again. It was Cowley's suggestion to stop for a drink at the Four Seasons, and Pamela chose a martini to his scotch. She changed to mineral water at Nathans and because that meant a half bottle Cowley fit in a second whiskey while she finished it. After walking aimlessly along M Street, they decided on the restaurant in which they'd eaten with Danilov. Again they were early enough not to need a reservations. Cowley had another scotch while they considered the menu and chose a French beaujolais to go with the meal.

Pamela said; "I've forgotten who's to be the host."

"So had I. Sorry. Want me to cancel the wine?"

"Shouldn't you?" she asked, taking the opening.

He was caught by her seriousness. "Have I missed part of the plot here?"

"I hope not."

"Why don't you sketch it out for me?"

Pamela did, in seconds, knowing nothing beyond what Osnan had told her the day she returned from Albany. Anticipating the question, she said, "I tried to get a name but couldn't."

"I drink," Cowley declared flatly.

"I've noticed."

"But it doesn't—will never—screw up how I work a case. Booze had nothing to do with my lifting the street surveillance in Moscow."

"I accept that. But I'm not the person you've got to convince if these stories build."

"How can I stop them? The stories, I mean?"

Pamela shook her head. "I don't know. It was important that you knew they were circulating."

"I appreciate it."

"*Were* there any problems in Moscow?"

She couldn't have heard of the previous occasion with the hooker. Only Danilov knew that. She was talking about *now*. "There were a couple of sessions: a celebration when we found the arms cache. Other people drank more than I did."

"I just wanted you to be warned," Pamela said. She supposed there had never been a right time but decided that her moment had been wrong. Until at least halfway through the meal Cowley toyed with just one glass of wine before deciding—and declaring—that it was a stupid reaction and began sharing it properly with her. It was an improvement and each relaxed a little, but what she'd said hung between them. Finally he said, "Was that what this was all about? Warning me?"

"Partly, I guess."

"What's the other part?"

Pamela shrugged, bemused by her difficulty. "Maybe an apology."

"For what?"

"Being such a tight-ass before."

"Got you what you wanted."

"So let's make another part a celebration," she said. "For you as well as me. I *did* get some breaks. You prevented the Lincoln Memorial catastrophe. If we're scoring points, we're about even."

Cowley finished the bottle between their two glasses. "So here's to us."

"I'll drink to that," said Pamela.

Once more he was caught by her seriousness. "Is there another part we haven't covered yet?"

"I'm not sure. I think there could be." Wasn't that the way of single bars, always up front, in your face?

"So how we going to cover it?"

"My taking control ends with my buying the meal."

Cowley was very nervous, frightened at first that he was going to fail, which made him even more nervous. He tried to cover his difficulty with foreplay, which she seemed to enjoy and matched him, stroke for stroke, tongue for tongue, hand for hand, and it began to happen. They joined hurriedly and came hurriedly together, but he didn't need to stop. Their second orgasm took longer but was again together, Pamela bucking and crying out and then arcing under him.

It was a long time before they spoke. Cowley said, "You were right. If we'd tried that the last time you stayed over, it would have killed me."

"You believe me when I tell you I had no idea this was going to happen?"

"Easily. I had no idea it was going to happen, either. Sorry?"

"No. You?"

"No."

"We don't need to analyze anything, do we?"

"No," he agreed again.

There was another long silence before he said, "I can handle it, you know. Booze."

"I'm here now. We can handle it together."

Dimitri Danilov had the same time during which to organize the simultaneously coordinated swoop the moment the Americans were led to the terrorist group but was confronted with the difficulty of Petrovka security, particularly now that Ashot Mizin had been positively identified as the eyes and ears of the other intended targets. He considered and rejected going to Gorki, not wanting prematurely to confront Reztsov and Averin. He continued using the U.S. Embassy facilities to produce enlarged, identifying photographs he personally distributed to the commanders of the three *spetznaz* units selected for the seizure operation upon the personal authority of Georgi Chelyag. Danilov spent most of one day with the three men, all colonels, a lot of it convincing them that such a level of cooperation really did exist between Moscow and Washington.

Yuri Pavin reached the end of an inquiry that had begun while Danilov had still been in America, folding back layer upon layer of company concealment finally to discover that the ownership of the Golden Hussar was joint between Naina Karpov and Igor Baratov. Naina also turned out to share ownership of both of Baratov's garages.

The watch was maintained on the Oldsmobile's garage, but during the one outing there was nothing of any significance in the overheard conversation between brother and sister, apart from Baratov wondering what the terrorists planned to hit, to Naina's dismissal that she didn't know. Intriguingly she added, "We'll probably find out soon."

It was during another cleaning visit to Larissa's grave that Danilov began reflecting on the militia corruption that her husband had so epitomized and how his determination to eradicate it at least from Petrovka had been overwhelmed by her death.

He summoned Pavin as soon as he got back to militia headquarters and said, "How many detectives on your suspect list?"

"Six," replied his deputy. "Seven including Mizin."

"Who'll tell us everything we want to know to save his neck," judged Danilov. "And I want it all. Every name, every brigade or organization. We'll put Mizin in court as a prosecution witness against those he knows about and in turn use what they know to get the others. I'll clear the whole damned place out." It would be sensational, Danilov recognized. But at that precise moment he was in a strong enough position to initiate such a purge. Which wasn't entirely the altruism of an honest policeman. Quite a long way from it, in fact. He was following the cynically discovered—and practiced—rules of survival. There were few more effective ways of bringing himself to the attention of the newly installed interior minister as well as publicly demonstrating the declared aim of the president.

Pavin regarded him curiously. "It's a hell of an undertaking."

"So's what we're doing now."

"It'll just be the two of us."

"That's enough," decided Danilov. If Yevgenni Kosov hadn't been in the pocket of a mob, Larissa would still be alive.

William Cowley's meeting with the director wasn't the inquest he had expected, although he was glad of Pamela's warning. It was Cowley himself who raised the shipment loss, to Ross's dismissal that it had been found again. And the man listened, without comment, to what had been arranged for the Cidicj *Star*'s arrival.

It was toward the end of the encounter that Ross said, "How you feeling yourself?"

"Fine, sir," said Cowley, to the jangle of alarm bells.

"You've been working at a hell of a pace after being caught up in that explosion. Maybe too hard."

"I really am quite all right."

"Did you ever have a follow-up check?"

"No."

"Maybe after it's all over."

"Maybe after everything's all over."

"About as subtle as an avalanche," Cowley told Pamela as soon as he got back to the incident room.

"Sure you're not overreacting?"

"Positive."

"You're back now, under his and everybody else's nose. All we've got to do is prove them wrong."

Cowley liked the "we've." "That's all."

They flew together to Illinois for a conference with the Chicago police commissioner and his division chiefs. They encountered no resentment from a force clearly more than content for the responsibility to be anyone else's but theirs. In the office of the local Customs chief there was virtually an identical map of the eastern seaboard showing the progress of the Cidicj *Star* as the one Terry Osnan was maintaining in Washington.

It was when the man was taking them through the unloading and dockside collection procedures that the opportunity became obvious to Cowley.

"A six P.M. arrival?" he pressed.

"Approximately," confirmed the man. "It won't be earlier. Add an hour, maybe."

"Unloaded immediately?"

"That's what I said."

"But held in a bonded warehouse until clearance the following morning? No dockside clearance or collection *after* six?"

"That's right."

"You've got search specialists?"

"Rummage officers." The man frowned.

"Could they breach a container and reseal it without OverOcean being able to tell?"

The man smiled, understanding the conversation. "No problem at all."

Cowley turned to Pamela, smiling as well. "We can fix what we weren't able to in Moscow."

The police commissioner hosted that night's dinner in a private dining room of Le Perroquet, on East Walton Street. Cowley wished Pamela had been next to him, although acknowledging the social need for them to separate. Besides the police division chiefs, Stephen Harding, the local bureau head, the Customs chief and his four most senior officers, and the commanders of the SWAT teams were invited. Cowley had one scotch for an aperitif and one glass of wine with the meal. He'd forgotten the publicity of his televised entry into the United Nations tower and the brief recorded appearances in Moscow, that concentrated the attention on him. Twice he caught Pamela smiling tolerantly toward him.

They'd booked separate rooms for propriety but ensured they were adjoining and used his. He wasn't nervous anymore, and he hadn't thought it could be any better than it had been the first time but it was. Afterward, in mock rebuke, Pamela said, "That wasn't just great, it was reassuring. Guys are supposed to hit on me, not you."

"If anyone had tried, I'd have torn their heads off."

"Bit soon for jealousy, isn't it?" She was still surprised at how fast everything had happened between them and how good she felt about it.

"You've got a lot to learn about me." He waited for her to remark about his near abstinence but she didn't. "I hadn't expected to be able to get into the container. We're safe now."

"I've been thinking about their Pentagon access."

"You got both of them."

"That's what I'm nervous about: that there might be a third but that the sweeps might start getting relaxed."

"Talk to Carl Ashton."

"We've got a couple of days and we're going back to Washington anyway. Think I might just go over the river and satisfy myself no one's laying back."

"If you think you should," he accepted.

"I know we're looking good but we've got a hell of a lot of loose ends," she pointed out. "We still don't know by whom or from where the Pentagon entry is being made. We've run a blank on the General. We know there's a Russian mafia man loose somewhere in America, and two others aren't doing a thing wrong in New Jersey, and there's a legal bar up against us sweating Robert Standing like he should be sweated. I don't think we had much cause for all those toasts tonight."

"I don't need the reminder," said Cowley. Which wasn't true. With the speed with which everything seemed to be coming together in Chicago, he had put the other unresolved things to one side. Brought together, as Pamela had just brought them together, the mountain suddenly seemed much higher and steeper.

They were back in Washington by midday. Pamela remained only long enough for them to lunch together, leaving Cowley to brief Ross on the Chicago preparations and ask James Schnecker to complete the sabotage that he and his group had started, even though germ or biological weapons weren't involved any longer.

Pamela had to drive around the Lincoln Memorial to get to the Arlington Bridge. As she did she added to her depressing list of things they still didn't have their total unawareness of the Watchmen's next target. There was a slight reassurance in telling herself that the net around it was going to be so tight they weren't ever going to get the chance *to* use it.

Pamela had intentionally not notified anyone of her visit. Carl Ashton arrived flushed and frowning at the gatehouse to authorize her admission.

"Why didn't you call?" he demanded.

"Driving back from the airport," said Pamela. "Decided to drop in on my way into D.C. A bad time?"

"No, of course not."

"How's it going?"

"Scoring two out of two should win us the big doll on the back row." Ashton smiled.

They *were* relaxing, Pamela decided at once. "You need three—four maybe—to get that sort of prize."

Ashton stopped smiling. He stood back for her to enter his office ahead of him, and as he followed her into the room he said, "We're keeping at it."

She shook her head against the offer of tea or coffee and said, "Give me the overview."

It sounded impressive. According to Ashton, they'd swept and confirmed clean all terminals at the four topmost levels of Pentagon security and changed all access codes. Checks on all satellite positional and operational programs would be completed by the week's end. All silo and missile arming systems had been totally reprogrammed. The sweeping of the National Security Agency and NASA had been completed and every system recoded.

"So what's left?" asked Pamela.

"Seaborne missiles, automatic submarine guidance systems, and the undersea tracking systems: We're liaising with the navy at Annapolis. And some AWAK reconnaissance systems are outstanding."

"It seems—" Pamela began but then stopped at the sound of the door opening behind her. She turned as Bella Atkins started into the room.

The woman stopped and said, "I'm sorry . . . I didn't know—" Then: "Hi! You got something on Roanne?"

Pamela later congratulated herself on the smoothness with which she picked up her supposed role as D.C. homicide, not bureau. She rose, offering her hand to give herself a few seconds, and said, "That's our problem, getting anything at all. That's why I've come back. Running things by Carl again to see if there's something we've missed."

"Is there?"

"Doesn't seem to be."

"So what's it look like?"

"As it looked from the start: burglar with a rape opportunity who took it."

"Poor kid." She looked at Ashton. "Funny thing, I was coming to talk about Roanne's replacement, but it'll hold. I'll come back. Nice to see you again," she said to Pamela from the door.

"And you."

"I was about to say that you do seem to be on top of it," resumed Pamela. "We're making progress elsewhere. But not enough. It's from here—or from one of the linked agencies—that the spectacular will come. It's all our heads, Carl. We don't want to lose any innocent ones."

"I know. And I'll remind everyone I think needs reminding."

Pamela drove easily back toward Washington, deciding it hadn't been a wasted journey. Ashton—and maybe too many others—*had* relaxed, sure they'd found everything. There was even a satisfied glibness about the security man's recitation of all the precautions that had been taken. Pamela wished . . . It was as far as her reflection got. Her mind blocked abruptly, and she actually experienced a physical sensation, a tingling numbness that lasted almost all the way back to downtown Washington and the J. Edgar Hoover building.

She'd alerted Cowley and Osnan from the car, and both men were waiting for her. So were a team from the bureau's Technical Division, who had already set up the recording apparatus in the office beside the incident room. They all backed out to give Pamela room when she dialed and was connected immediately to the extension she asked for. Pamela talked looking out of the small room, toward the forensic technicians. After little more than two minutes, one of the men began making throat-cutting gestures, indicating they had enough.

"How long?" demanded Pamela, the moment she replaced the telephone.

"Not long," assured the technician leader. "Quite a simple electronic comparison."

"How sure are you?" Cowley asked Pamela.

"Eighty-five, ninety percent. *Now!* Why the hell did it take me all this time!"

The technician returned to the incident room just short of one hour. He said, "Absolutely no doubt. A classic voiceprint, the peaks and troughs fitting perfectly over each other."

Pamela looked at Cowley. "So Bella Atkins is the Pentagon mole?"

"And the first voiceprint comes from her conversation to Chicago with someone who's more than likely the General."

39

What everyone else regarded as yet another coup Pamela Darnley considered a failure. Why hadn't she pursued her belief that she recognized the voice beyond the one comparison against the New Rochelle telephone call? Her anger at herself fueled the urgency as well as her need personally to organize the concentrated investigation.

The entire Washington, D.C., field office—which operates separately from the J. Edgar Hoover building—was assigned to Bella

Atkins. To it Pamela added from Roanoke the four agents still working the Roanne Harding murder. Pamela summoned Carl Ashton from the Pentagon with the widowed Bella's personnel file and warned the stunned man that every check he and his sweepers had been so confident of having completed, not just throughout the Pentagon but in all the other associated agencies, had to be repeated.

"She's got Grade V clearance, so she'll know that some codes at least have been changed. She'll have been literally following in your footsteps all the way."

"So she'll know we think Roanne wasn't the mole, that we're still looking," said Cowley, sitting in on the meeting.

"Not necessarily," said Ashton. "It's routine to change codes."

"Make *Challenger* and the satellite navigational system your first rechecks," insisted Pamela. "She'd go back to her sabotage—do it again—if she suspected we were looking."

"It's almost too fast to keep up," protested the Pentagon computer specialist.

"Don't let it be!" Pamela urged worriedly. "We'll do all we can outside. But inside—which is where it matters—you've got to reverse what's been happening. You've got to follow in Bella Atkins's footsteps now. Whenever, however, she accesses a computer, you've got to be right behind her. You think you can do that?"

"Technically, yes."

"What about practically?"

"I hope so," said Ashton.

"She got a cell phone?" demanded Pamela, conscious of the continuing Trenton problem.

"Not Pentagon issued. She might have a private one; most people have."

"We're searching under her own name through all the providers," picked up Cowley. "But if there's a way you can find out without her knowing, we need it."

There was a routine familiarity in attaching an exchange monitor on Bella Atkins's telephone, which was as much as they could do overnight. From the surveillance already in place they knew that she was in her York Avenue apartment. The judge had also approved a search warrant, enabling them legally to enter the following day to install listening devices while she was at the Pentagon. And by the time she got to work that day a listening device would have been attached to her office extension.

"We forgotten anything?" demanded Pamela. It was past nine, dinner abandoned.

"I don't think so," said Cowley.

"You know what we've got?" Pamela said rhetorically. "We've got another loose end."

There were more about to unravel.

It was the predictability that began the problems, which compounded themselves as the day continued. Ivan Gavrilovich Guzov and Vyacheslav Fedorovich Kabanov left their executive homes at the same time as they did every morning, and the discreet FBI surveillance slotted into place as it had done every morning since it had been imposed. Dutifully both observers reported that the two Russians were on their way, which was logged by the duty officer in the Trenton office. No one bothered anymore with tired airwave jokes or traffic complaints.

Kabanov lived closer to their office than the other Russian, so the first alert came from his followers, the sudden announcement that he wasn't going in the expected direction, almost immediately followed by the similar realization from those behind Guzov.

"The station!" decided the first observer. "There's the Amtrak commuter service to New York."

The quickly summoned John Meadowcraft decided to wait until he reached the office before ringing any headquarter bells. By the time he got there both Russians were aboard a Metroliner due at Manhattan's Penn Station at 10:15, which gave the New York office forty-five minutes to get into position. Meadowcraft told the protesting Harry Boreman it didn't matter that the New York office didn't have a full team available on such short notice. The two Trenton observers were three tables away in the approaching Metroliner club car, watching the serious-faced Russians drink Bloody Marys. Both were on their third.

Boreman himself was one of the four New York agents waiting

when the train pulled in. All instantly identified Kabanov and Guzov from their photographs, without needing the additional marker of the two closely following Trenton officers. Boreman fell into step with one of the men as soon as the Russians passed, saying as unobstrusively as possible that he needed them as reserve backup but until that need arose for them to remain in the waiting surveillance vehicles so they wouldn't be recognized from the train.

The Russians had to line up for a cab, so all six agents were distributed in three bureau vehicles by the time the Russians were moving. Boreman, in the lead vehicle, gave the commentary on the open line to the bureau's Third Avenue office, from which it was simultaneously relayed to the Washington incident room on what had grown into a sophisticated electronics system manned by specialist officers.

When the arrival in the New York office of other agents was reported back to Boreman, Pamela said, "They weren't ready! Why the hell weren't they ready!"

No one answered her.

"Crossing Seventh," Boreman was saying. "South now, downtown on Broadway, turning . . . we're turning on to Twenty-third."

"Heliport!" Cowley guessed at once.

As he spoke, Boreman said, "Could be a helicopter to the airports. Call our own helo, start moving from the office by road. I want agents on their way, direct to La Guardia and Kennedy."

"They'll never get there in time!" Pamela moaned, exasperated. "Won't get anywhere in time."

"There'll have to be a helicopter flight plan," said Cowley.

"To LaGuardia or Kennedy," insisted Pamela. "Buy an internal flight anywhere within the United States for cash and you don't show up on a passenger list or a credit card slip. They get to an airport, we've lost them. And we can't risk airport police. Immigration doesn't come into it. Fuck! Fuck! Fuck!"

"Not the heliport," came Boreman's voice. "They've gone over FDR. . . . it's looking good, going into Waterside apartments. We're stopping short—" There was the sound of angry horn blasts and the muttered driver's voice "Go suck pussy." Then Boreman said: "Shit!" There was a momentary pause. "They're going into the marina alongside the apartments. Got guys going on foot over the road bridge. . . . Let me talk on the phone. . . ." There was the muffled sound of a separate conversation. Then: "There was a cruiser waiting. One guy as far as they could see. Backing out. They're trying for a name . . . I want a boat. . . . Get on to Customs for something unmarked. And a helicopter. I still want a helicopter. There's enough in the air to cover us. We'll pick them up."

"I wouldn't like to bet," Pamela said dully.

Pamela would have lost, if she had. It took more than thirty minutes to get a Customs helicopter to the 23rd Street pad and longer—just under an hour—for a launch to reach them. The cruiser's name wasn't logged at the marina, because it only pulled alongside to pick up passengers, and no one remembered it by chance or could guess how many people were on board, apart from the two men who joined. The unmarked Customs launch and helicopter checked a total of twenty boats in a three-hour period. Neither Guzov or Kabanov was on any of them.

"Lost us without trying!" Pamela said incredulously. "The biggest, most concentrated investigation in the history of the Federal Bureau of Investigation and two of the main targets just walk away!" She snapped her fingers. "Poof! Just like that."

"We couldn't have been ready, no matter how early the warning," argued Cowley. "There's no way we would have anticipated a boat."

"It could have been the guy—the General, even—who fired the first missile," said Pamela.

"Yes," agreed Cowley.

"You think they could be casing the U.N. tower—planning a second hit?"

"If they are, there doesn't have to be a public warning, any panic," Cowley pointed out. "Their missile's empty. But they're not going to get the chance to fire it, are they?"

"You feel sure about that after today?"

"Yeah," said Cowley. "I feel sure enough about that."

"I wish I did," admitted Pamela.

"You won't have to wait long," Cowley pointed out. They were flying to Chicago that night for the following day's arrival of the Cidicj *Star*.

"You think we can both afford to go now that we've lost them?"

"Chicago is where it's going to happen," said Cowley. "It's where we've *got* to be."

The search of Bella Atkins's treble-locked apartment just slightly lifted the depression beyond installing the listening devices, although the limited findings initially created more questions than they answered.

The place was almost too immaculate. Nothing had been left uncleared or unwashed in the kitchen—even the trash bin liner was clean—and all the pots and pans were meticulously in order, according to size, and every knife, fork, and spoon in its allotted part of the silverware tray. The label on every can in the pantry faced outward, instantly readable.

One of the dusting technicians said to no one in particular, "I'm going to be lucky to lift any prints at all from a place as polished and buffed as this."

"Make sure you clean up well after yourself," warned Paul Lambert. "Her alarm system is the cleanliness and neatness."

There wasn't the slightest disorder in the bedroom. Her clothes were hung in color coordinates, matching shoes laid beneath each outfit, and in bureau drawers sweaters and shirts and underwear each had its own drawer, in which items were crisply folded. The impression in the living room was of furniture being arranged to measurement, the easy chairs precisely the same distance from the sofa, each chair spaced the same around the table in the dining alcove. Books were shelved according to height and author; from the complete works of Elmore Leonard, she appeared a crime thriller fan. The video library was all wildlife or Discovery Channel programs. There were no messages on the answering machine and the recording tape was blank.

The most obvious discovery were the photographs. There were a lot of a smiling, younger Bella with men in army uniforms, jungle greens and camouflage and dress. There were several of her very young, a child, with an older dress-uniformed master sergeant who could have been her father and then with three men in the same age range as herself. None was annotated with names or descriptions, but one of the men had an American eagle tattoo on his left arm. The searchers' equipment included cameras and each print was copied.

There was a sofa bed in the second bedroom but otherwise it had been turned into a study, although surprisingly there was no computer. Neither were there any personal papers or correspondence, apart from bank statements into which the only income appeared to be Bella Atkins's monthly Pentagon salary. Outgoing was limited to regular utility payments cross-referenced to supply company statements neatly clipped together in a bureau drawer. There wasn't any billing record of a personal cell phone.

"Not as polished and buffed as I feared," said the fingerprint specialist, hunched over the opened-up sofa bed. "Got a nice set that don't appear to be Bella's off this metal strut."

"And there's an interesting divide in the clothes closet," said another of the team, emerging from the bedroom. "Most of the stuff is size fourteen, Bella's size. But four outfits are size ten. There's two pairs of shoes smaller than Bella's, too. And in the underwear drawer there are three smaller bras than Bella seems to need."

"According to the lease, she's the sole tenant," said Lambert.

"Then she's got a smaller friend," said the bedroom searcher.

"Wonder how difficult it's going to be to find out who she is?" said Lambert.

It wasn't, in fact, difficult at all. The fingerprints on the sofa bed were those of Roanne Harding. Her dress and shoe size matched what few items were found in the murdered girl's Lexington Place apartment.

"And we've pulled up the photographs to get the units," Lambert told Cowley and Pamela. "It looks like one was in the Rangers and the other two were Special Forces. And the old guy with Bella when she was a kid: He's Special Forces, too. Got a Medal of Honor and a Bronze Star among all that stuff on his chest."

"These guys had jungle training for sure," remembered Cowley, aloud.

"What Jefferson Jones told you up in New Rochelle, just before the explosion," said Pamela, matching the recall. "Let's see how fast the military can move their asses when they get everything on a plate."

"Time we moved ours," reminded Cowley. To Osnan he said, "I'll speak to Dimitri from the Chicago office. Anything I need to know, reach me there."

Osnan did, within fifteen minutes of their arrival, while Cowley was on the telephone to Dimitri Danilov.

"What?" demanded Cowley, passing the Moscow connection to Pamela.

"Vyacheslav Kabanov got off the train from New York thirty minutes ago. Picked up his car and drove home like all the other commuters."

"What about Guzov?"

"Didn't show. Car's still in the station lot."

"He'll be on his way here to Chicago for the Cidicj *Star*'s arrival," predicted Cowley. "It's going to be OK."

40

The Cidicj *Star* had been allocated a berth beneath the main Customs building. A conference room directly overlooking the harbor was transformed into yet another incident room.

The freighter had been under continuous Customs air, sea, and radar surveillance from the moment, just before midnight, it passed through the Straits of Mackinac from Lake Huron into Lake Michigan and began to sail the final gauntlet between the states of Michigan and Wisconsin. Its estimated docking time remained the same, and its hourly progress was marked on a familiar map. Additional telephones, computer terminals, and a wide-screen television had been installed. Operating staff stood around with not enough to do.

Everyone assembled too soon, before midday, crowding the room unnecessarily. Cowley was reminded of the early need of people in high places to be seen to be involved. He was briefly concerned that Peter Samuels, who arrived from Washington before nine, might expect to take personal command until the Customs chief asked to be briefed and made it clear it remained a Bureau operations. The Chicago police commissioner, included as a Washington-instructed courtesy, arrived with his deputy and seemed surprised that at least a deputy FBI director wasn't present.

James Schnecker and his team also flew in by midmorning, but with a reason. Both Cowley and Pamela went with them to the warehouse in which the OverOcean containers were to be bonded, again specially chosen because it could be entered through a series of corridors from dock authority administration buildings unseen by any OverOcean watcher on the dockside.

Schnecker immediately said, "Couldn't ask for anything better, after how we worked in Moscow."

"You won't have any trouble identifying what's outstanding?" queried Pamela.

"Just a question of finding it," assured Neil Hamish.

"We'll even have time to go over everything we've already done," suggested Schnecker. "We're looking good."

Cowley thought so, too, when he made his first contact of the day with Washington to be told there'd been no interference with the reprogramed *Challenger* or the navigational satellite. There'd been no telephone calls, incoming or outgoing, the previous night or that morning from Bella Atkins's apartment. There'd been obvious cleaning sounds—almost a full fifteen minutes of vacuuming—the previous night. She'd hummed a lot, although not a recognizable tune. And laughed aloud at *Friends*.

"What's Ashton say about watching her in the Pentagon?" asked Cowley.

"There's an instant trace on her computer ID: comes up directly on Ashton's monitor," said Terry Osnan. "They've actually got one of those phony antistatic bands on her terminal lead as a backup."

"Office phone?"

"Five calls so far this morning. All work related."

"What do we know about her?"

"Still waiting to hear."

"I'd like a preliminary biog early afternoon."

Leonard Ross called thirty minutes later. When he heard Samuels and the police chief were already there, he spoke individually to both. When Cowley went back on the line, the director said, "Any jurisdictional problems?"

"None," said Cowley.

"It's our case."

"Everyone's accepting that."

"Unfortunate about Guzov."

"I'm expecting him to turn up here."

"I'm expecting you to wrap this whole thing up. It's time."

There was California wine and hard booze for the buffet lunch set out in an adjoining room. Cowley drank mineral water, as Pamela did. Pamela ate a piece of fruit. Cowley didn't bother with anything. The police commissioner wanted to know how quickly they expected to make arrests and the timing of their being publicly disclosed. To the man's second and obvious disappointment of the day, Cowley made a lot of the difficulties of coordinating split-second seizures in America and Russia and of the disastrous consequences of premature publicity. It was even possible, after the international significance of the investigation, that the president himself might decide to make the announcement.

Cowley was about to call Washington when Terry Osnan came on to the line. "We've learned an awful lot about Bella."

Hers was a family steeped in a military tradition stretching back to World War II, although Atkins was her married name. The family was Barrymore. The tradition had been established by her grandfather, who had been a major and served in Patton's Third Army general staff all the way through to Berlin. The son—Bella's father—had been a career soldier who'd served in Korea, remained there as part of the military administration in the south after the cease-fire, and been on his second tour in Vietnam when he'd been killed at Da Nang in the first Tet offensive.

Bella was the youngest of four children, the others all boys and all career soldiers like their father. George, the next in line to Bella and the Ranger in the York Avenue photographs, had died in Operation Desert Storm. So had Bella's husband, a lieutenant in a tank unit. Her other two Special Forces brothers, Peter and Jake, had also fought in the Gulf. The operations they'd been involved in were classified, but an application was being made to get the security embargo lifted. Peter Barrymore was the one with the eagle tattoo.

Both had been invited to leave the service, to avoid the war hero publicity of a court-martial, after their membership in the John Birch Society had emerged when they'd been discovered trying to recruit within their own and other units for what had been described as an unacceptable right-wing offshoot. There was also an untraced, substantial loss of military equipment. Both had left the army with the rank of major. Peter Barrymore's last known address was North Rush Street, Chicago, which Osnan had already told the Chicago office, direct. He'd also personally given Al Beckinsdale the army discharge address of Jake Barrymore on Reynolds Avenue, in the Point Breeze district of Pittsburgh.

Osnan said, "The army finally shifted their butts."

Cowley saw Pamela talking animatedly on another telephone. The attention of everyone in the room was on both of them. To Osnan he said, "Bella's voiceprint—and maybe the connection with the Roanne Harding murder—is reasonable suspicion for warrants."

"Already being applied for."

"Chicago and Pittsburgh know?"

"Told both myself," said Osnan.

"Get hold of Anne Stovey in Albany. I reckon this is new information sufficient to get at Robert Standing again."

"Will do."

"Better warn Trenton. And tell Manhattan to get more people closer to Orlenko in Brooklyn. No one's to move until I say so, but when I do say so there's only got to be one sound from the trap snapping shut."

"Moscow?"

"I'll talk direct."

Pamela was already walking toward him when Cowley put down

the phone. She said, "Steve Murray called to say he was going to North Rush Street himself. Filled me in quickly. So I spoke to Pittsburgh. Beckinsdale's going himself there, too."

"Just a stakeout!" Cowley qualified hurriedly.

"That's all," assured the woman. "A look-see, then back to us. You organized Standing?"

"Yes."

She grinned at him. "We work as well out of bed as we do in it."

"Keep your mind on the job," he said, but still smiled. For the first time he thought they really had a reason *to* smile.

Danilov expected a telephone call to be sufficient, but Georgi Chelyag insisted on seeing him.

"It's not just the arrests that have got to be simultaneous," said the chief of staff. "The president doesn't want to follow any American announcement. He wants to make it and he wants it to be at precisely the same time—unarguable proof that it really has been a totally joint and coordinated investigation." The man paused. "It's as important to you as it is to us that it's seen to be so."

"I haven't discussed that sort of detail with Cowley," admitted Danilov. "I'm not even sure he knows the official thinking about public communiqués; he's not in Washington."

"The alternative is for us to time our statement with the arrests here," declared Chelyag.

"That's *not* an alternative," rejected Danilov. "The arrests are to be coordinated but *un*announced, to ensure we get everyone. It won't be simultaneous; logically it can't be. If we go public too soon, we could ruin everything in America." He hesitated, seeing how to strengthen the objection. "It wouldn't achieve what you want if America publicly complained we *wrecked* the cooperation *and* the investigation, would it?"

"That argument applies equally here."

"Isn't it one you should be making politically? That's what we're talking: politics, not criminal investigation."

The presidential advisor managed a bleak smile. "It is being made.

But I want you to press it, as hard as you can, at your working level. It would be understandable for America to want to take all the credit."

As you are straining to do, thought Danilov. "There's going to be a lot more conversation tonight. I'll talk it through as much as I can."

"Could it all be over by tonight?" asked Chelyag.

"It's possible," said Danilov.

In Chicago the approaching Cidicj *Star* was being pointed out to Cowley and Pamela on a radar screen.

They saw it as a ship, although indistinctly, through binoculars from the top of the Customs tower, a black smudge at first, gradually forming into a recognizable vessel. Cowley had imagined everything would be in the holds but when it was clearly in view he saw a lot of containers were strapped on the deck, making the freighter appear top heavy.

They were back in the converted conference room, with its closer view of the dockside, for the arrival of the shipping agents. The two from OverOcean were identified by the two FBI agents who followed them from the importer's office. Neither was Ivan Guzov or Yevgenni Leanov.

Pamela said, "This is clerks' stuff. They don't need to show until tomorrow."

It took a long time to reach the OverOcean shipment. It wasn't part of the deck cargo, which had to be cleared before the holds could be opened, and it wasn't in the first of those. It was seven-fifteen, although still light, before the containers were finally swung clear, already identified by a Customs officer inside the ship. Forklifts driven by bureau men materialized and were loaded. Other agents dressed as stevedores and dock workers watched the two importers briefly inspect the shipping documents. One agent was close enough to hear the arrangements made to collect from the bonded warehouse by eleven the following morning. Neither the OverOcean clerks showed particular interest in either of the containers, apart from ensuring their storage.

It was another hour before they ventured into the warehouse.

They used the rear corridor entrance. Schnecker implacably refused the police chief's protests ("It's live and dangerous and I'm responsible for everyone's safety") and limited those present at the container opening to just the two Customs officers who were going to do it without detection in addition to Cowley.

Schnecker also insisted on hand testing the heat of the steam gun intended to sweat off the container seals and ensured that no electrical drill would be used. He also made the two men wear face shields and body armor.

To Cowley's unasked question the bearded team leader said, "We didn't have time in Moscow. Here we work by the book." He handed Cowley his protection. "It's the biggest we've got."

They all waited until the last-minute warning from the rummage team that the first container was about to be opened before putting on the protective gear.

Neil Hamish said, "If it's the right one, we'll be upstairs partying in an hour."

It wasn't. Each compartment inside the container held genuine American-manufactured engine parts for overhaul and reconditioning. The Customs experts were already working on the second container with their steam-hissing gun before Schnecker's team completed their fruitless search.

"If at first you don't succeed," said Hamish, turning to the other container. He didn't finish.

"They're not in here, either," declared Schnecker, who was directly in front of the crate.

The only noise was the shuffling forward of the encumbered Cowley. "They must be!"

Schnecker stood back for Cowley to see fully inside. The container was packed exactly like the first. Cowley said, "It's hidden under all the other stuff! Has to be!"

It took another hour to search each interior compartment before he accepted it wasn't. As he reentered the upstairs conference room, Pamela said, "Neither Peter nor Jake Barrymore has been seen in the area in which they live for the past four days. Each drove away packed as if he was going on a trip."

The OverOcean container had been offloaded in Toronto during a three-hour, 1:00 A.M. to 4:00 A.M. stop five days earlier and collected later that same day. The delivery note was signed in the name of Ivan Guzov. All the official documents were in perfect order. Canadian Customs had released the shipment—again described as engine parts—without examination.

It took Cowley only a few minutes and one telephone call to the Toronto harbor authorities to establish all that. Pamela, on another telephone, took longer trying—but failing—to trace the container's entry into America through any of the Lake Ontario ports or across the Welland Canal and Niagara River land routes.

Throughout the recriminations and attempted avoidances swirled around the room, Samuels insisted he'd ordered liaison with the Canadian authorities to prevent just such a thing happening but the Chicago office chief claimed no knowledge—or written proof—of any such instruction. On the telephone from Washington Leonard Ross said, "I didn't think it was possible for anything more to go wrong."

Cowley said, "Neither did I."

"What leads we got left?"

"Brooklyn, Trenton, and Bella Atkins."

"And you're going to tell me we can't bring any of them in?"

"Yes."

"No," refused the director. "I want everyone we've still got a trace on picked up—carefully orchestrated seizures. Lose just one more and the bureau loses you."

41

Bella Atkins called in sick at 8:45 the following morning, two hours after Cowley and Pamela got back to the J. Edgar Hoover Building. They'd driven directly from the airport to coordinate the scheduled 9:00 A.M. seizures and stood listening to Bella's croaked explanation that she had the flu.

Leonard Ross answered his home phone on the second ring. Cowley said, "Just give me a few more hours! See what she's going to do!"

"What if she *is* sick? We know what they are going to do and we haven't got any way of stopping it."

"We might find out if we wait a little longer."

"And we might not, and by waiting a little longer we give the bastards time to commit more mass murder."

"Midday," pleaded Cowley. "There's got to be a reason for her staying at home, and whatever it is we'll hear it. If there's nothing by noon we'll round them up. Just three hours is all."

"You haven't forgotten what I told you last night?"

"No, sir."

"I meant it."

"Yes, sir."

"Noon," agreed Ross.

Cowley replaced the receiver to see—and hear—Pamela replaying Bella's call to the Pentagon. Pamela said, "She's trying to *sound* sick. It's the sort of voice she used for the New Rochelle call."

"And sixteen guys died," reminded Terry Osnan, immediately wishing he hadn't from the look on Cowley's face. "Sorry."

Cowley shook his head against the apology. "We've got a postponement."

"Flu would keep her off for more than a day," Pamela pointed out.

Cowley said, "Let's get people out to Reagan and Dulles. And to Union Station if it's a train, not a plane."

"Including females," said Pamela. "If she goes into a washroom, we need to go with her."

"I'll wake Schnecker; maybe we'll need his input," said Cowley. The Fort Detrick team had returned from Chicago on the same Bureau plane and gone straight to the Marriott where Dimitri Danilov had stayed.

"We've got Bella under a microscope. If this is prearranged, why didn't we hear the conversation?" queried Pamela. She was probably under the same threat from the director as Cowley, and she was damned if she was going to lose everything. They—she—had to second-guess everything.

"They've had the shipment for six days; we've only had Bella for two days," reminded Osnan. "They've had plenty of time."

"If she's going anywhere she's not going far," estimated Cowley. "In those six days they could have driven that stuff anywhere in America. And if it was Midwest or West, they'd have offloaded it in Chicago. It's East Coast." To Osnan he said, "Go sit on that telephone monitor."

As Osnan moved into the incident room, Pamela said, "You all right?"

"What's that mean?" Cowley regretted the stiff scotches he'd had in front of her after the Chicago debacle, although everyone had gone to the improvised Customs bar—including Pamela—and he hadn't by any means had too much.

"It means are you all right."

Now Cowley regretted the defensive sharpness. "I'm impatient and I'm nervous: He's given us three hours. If there's nothing by then, we move."

Pamela shrugged. "What the hell can we do in three hours, even if there is some contact! You know what you've done! You've made yourself the scapegoat for anything that goes wrong."

Cowley recognized she was probably right. So he'd hammered yet more nails into his own coffin. But there were so many already it hardly mattered anymore. "If we get a lead we can get another extension. I want the Watchmen as well as the rest."

He personally called the FBI chiefs in Trenton and Manhattan, explaining the delay. In New York Harry Boreman said there'd been no movement from Bay View Avenue, but it was early for them. Everyone was in place, ready to go.

"We've got them boxed," he guaranteed.

In New Jersey John Meadowcraft said they hadn't heard any movement from inside the Kabanov home, either. Usually the Russian was up by now. Kabanov's car was in the driveway. Guzov's was still in the station parking lot. From Albany Anne Stovey said the state attorney was still objecting to any requisitioning of Robert

Standing. The bureau lawyer was considering an application to a judge in chambers.

It was nine-twenty when Cowley finished all the calls. He told Pamela, "I think you're right. There wasn't any point in my arguing the postponement."

"Don't wait then," she urged at once, seeing escape for both of them. "Whatever happens after the arrests won't be your fault. You'll be following Ross's instructions."

Terry Osnan began waving exaggeratedly from the incident room. As they hurried into it he said, "Bella's got a caller. So has Orlenko, in person! Brooklyn surveillance has positively IDed him as Yevgenni Mechislavovich Leanov!"

"We're sure where everybody is?" demanded Georgi Chelyag.

"Absolutely," said Danilov.

"And the *spetznaz* are in place?"

"They have been for two hours."

"Briefed?"

"Fully."

"No risk of a leak?"

"My deputy is personally going to arrest Mizin—had already summoned him for a conference, about the murder he's supposed to be investigating."

"Were you surprised at the American openness?"

"No," said Danilov. "I always expected it to be this way." Cowley had sounded crushed when they'd talked the previous night from Chicago. With every reason. There wasn't any germ or bacteriological danger, but the explosives could still cause a catastrophe.

"There's no way the Americans can turn the loss of the shipment into a Russian mistake?"

"No," agreed Danilov. It was the third time the chief of staff had asked the same question.

"You think there's any likelihood of Ivan Guzov trying to get back here? If we got him we'd be clearing up American's mistakes, wouldn't we?"

"If the terrorists have got the weapons, Guzov's got the money.

Some of it at least. It wouldn't make sense his trying to get back here after the publicity there's going to be."

"I want to hear the moment we make the last arrest. The announcement will be in the president's name, with another televised address to follow."

As the recognizable voice of Bella Atkins's caller echoed into the totally silent Washington incident room Pamela said, "It just might work."

Cowley said, "Fuck! I didn't tell Dimitri!"

The man said, "Ready?"

Bella said, "And waiting. How'd it all go?"

"Looks like there's changes. A new Russian."

"What about Gavri?"

"Disposed of. Seems he cheated with the money. Tried to cut Moscow out for a new supplier."

"That going to be a problem?"

"Theirs, not ours. Our problem is that son of a bitch of a bank guy. Won't respond."

"What can we do?"

"Hit the banks he gave us access to a second time."

"Where's Jake?"

"With me. And the missile."

"So we're hearing Peter. Peter's the General," breathed Pamela. She looked sideways at Cowley's return.

Cowley said, "I can't reach Dimitri. He's going by the old time."

Before Pamela could respond Osnan declared, "He's using a cell phone. We're getting a scan intermittently. So they're moving, like they did in Chicago."

"But somewhere in D.C.!" seized Cowley. "Surely we couldn't pick it up outside the district!"

"Affirmative," confirmed Osnan.

"Get guys out to the obvious places. The monuments and memorials again. White House. Emphasize the maroon Land Cruiser."

"What are you going to do about Dimitri?" asked Pamela.

"Nothing I can do."

"It going to go off this time?" Bella was saying.

There was a muffled exchange away from the mouthpiece and the sound of laughing. Peter Barrymore said, "The detonator pins are intact. Jake says something that big, a monkey could hit it. He's going to get a window, like before."

"We going to be OK?"

There was another laugh. "Of course I checked. Wind's southwest. Property's going to be as cheap as hell in Crystal City and Arlington by tonight."

"Where are you?"

"In traffic, on the bridge. You leave now, it should work out fine."

"I'll be waiting."

The line went dead.

"Windows!" seized Cowley. "Not a monument."

"The White House!" said Pamela. "It's going to be the White House!"

"From around Lafayette Square, with the wind behind them," said Osnan.

"Switch from the monuments. Concentrate on the White House. Bring in the SWAT teams. Use Bella as a marker. . . ." There was a general movement throughout the room, and Cowley turned to see Leonard Ross entering.

The director said, "I overheard enough. We need to evacuate?"

"The missile's empty," reminded Cowley.

"What about the explosives?"

"We're not hearing anything about those," admitted Cowley.

Ross found James Schnecker. "The stuff's still got explosives in it, right?"

The bearded expert moved forward. "It's the timers, detonators, and the fuses we've fixed. It can't be rigged and left."

"What happens if they don't try until they get to the target? Nothing sophisticated like the Lincoln Memorial: just a crazy car bomb?"

"It'll go at the first attempted connection. That was all we could do in Moscow, anticipate their trying to assemble a lot in advance, like they did for the memorial."

"We get the president out," decided Ross, hurrying from the room.

"Bella's moving, on foot," came the voice of an observer. "Walking nice and easy down York. We're by the Civic Center."

"It's a straight line to Lafayette," said Pamela.

"Everything's in place around the White House: virtually sealed," reported Osnan. "She's going directly to us. Everyone's watching for a maroon Land Cruiser."

"They could get at least half the explosives in a vehicle that big," estimated Schnecker. "But there's got to be more than just two of them."

"She's changed direction!" the observer said urgently. "Made a left on Massachusetts . . . now she's hailing a cab, going toward Union . . ."

"Surely it's not a train," said Cowley. He looked toward Osnan. "We still got people there?"

"Withdrew them to the White House," the other man replied.

"Get them back," said Cowley. He was sweating but dry-throated.

"Windows," Pamela said quietly. "The Capitol's got windows. Hundreds of them. And it's as easy to reach down Massachusetts as the railroad terminal. And a far more dramatic target."

"She's getting out at North Capitol . . ." said Osnan, maintaining the commentary. ". . . going away from Union Station . . . Jesus! She's taken a park bench on Louisiana . . . sitting there, waiting."

"Let's go!" said Cowley. "Keep the White House covered. Move one SWAT team up to Union forecourt. . . . Tell our guys with her not to approach. We want the brothers. . . . Talk to me in the car before moving, even if they arrive." Both Schnecker and Pamela moved with him. Cowley paused momentarily, then continued on with both of them following.

Orlenko: You should have called.

Leanov: I wanted to surprise you.

Orlenko: You have.

Leanov: I surprised Gavri, too.

Orlenko: Where is he?

Leanov: In a wood, with a bullet through the mouth for not telling the truth.

Orlenko: Yevgenni, I want to say—

Leanov: You haven't told the truth either, have you, Arseni?

Orlenko: Gavri said—

Leanov: That we could be cut out in Moscow? I know. He told me he was sorry about that. And he was, in the end. Are you sorry, Arseni?

Orlenko: Yevgenni, I want to explain.

Leanov: You don't have to, Arseni. I know all about it now from Gavri. You're superfluous now, just like Gavri.

The crash of intrusion thundered onto the tape and a megaphoned voice echoed: "Down! FBI! Down on the floor! Down!"

Cowley drove. Pennsylvania Avenue was arrowlike ahead of them, rising up the hill to the domed seat of government.

Pamela said, "Anyone see anything that looks like a maroon Land Cruiser?"

"Too far to see," dismissed Cowley.

"The missile will misfire, but if they're Special Forces they'll have a lot more besides," said Schnecker.

"We're armed," said Pamela.

"Body armor?"

"No."

"What about the guys who followed her?"

"I doubt it."

"We're going after guys trained for any reversal. There'll be a lot of casualties. Wait for the SWAT team," urged Schnecker.

The traffic was slow moving. Cowley beat his hands against the wheel in frustration.

Pamela said, "Capitol security should be warned."

"They'd try to intervene, *become* casualties," rejected Cowley.

"That's wrong, Bill! That's not a decision you can make."

"They'd fuck it up."

"You going to take the responsibility for that?"

"I'm not asking you to—not endangering your career."

"That wasn't what I meant, and it was a cheap shot!"

Cowley hammered the wheel again. "Any sign of a Land Cruiser? Of anything?"

"Negative," Osnan crackled into the car. "Manhattan has got Orlenko and Leanov. Where are you?"

"Third," reported Pamela.

"SWAT team is behind you," said Osnan. "They say to wait."

"I'll tell the Barrymores that," said Cowley.

They finally came to a complete halt.

"Shit!" said Cowley. He pulled out, then made a tight left across the horn-protesting traffic line, forcing his way through the downward flow to go up 2nd Street and out on to Louisiana. As he did so Pamela ducked out of sight behind the dashboard.

Osnan said, "Our guys have made a maroon Toyota Land Cruiser moving down from Union Station!"

"Got it!" responded Cowley.

The vehicle was already parked, two men in fatigues walking away across Taft Park. They were close together, with what had to be the missile between them, draped in a tan tarp with a makeshift rope handle. Without any recognition between them Bella Atkins was walking parallel with the road, easing herself into the driver's seat of the Land Cruiser.

Cowley dragged on an FBI armband and spoke into Pamela's cell phone. "Everyone identified. Go in to my command. NOW!"

Cowley emerged bent, running, Colt .45 muzzle upward with the safety still on. He was aware of the two agents from the pursuit vehicle seemingly a long way to his left. He was almost at the Land Cruiser before Bella turned. Immediately she slammed her hand flat on the horn. Her two brothers turned.

Cowley shouted, "Put it down! Go down! Down! FBI!"

He knew they wouldn't have heard over the sound of the horn. It stopped abruptly as the woman fumbled beside her. He wasn't aware of Pamela until she appeared beside him, her gun outstretched in both hands. She fired, intentionally sideways, blowing out the rear passenger window. That momentarily halted Bella, who was still swinging a MAC 10 machine pistol across when Pamela jammed her gun into the side of the woman's head so hard the skin broke.

"LET IT GO! YOU DON'T LET IT GO, BELLA, I'LL BLOW YOUR FUCKING HEAD OFF! NOW!"

Just as loudly Cowley shouted again for the two men to drop the missile. They did, but not to obey. Their movements were practically choreographed, in perfect unison. One discarded the tarpaulin while the other smoothly took up the missile and its launcher and came up with it into a kneeling launch position. The first snatched another MAC 10 from inside their improvised carrying case as one of the FBI men who had followed Bella yelled something Cowley didn't hear. The man with the pistol responded to the sound, scything the weapon crossways on automatic, virtually cutting both running agents in half. He continued the sweep toward the Land Cruiser.

"Down!" screamed Cowley.

He felt himself hit, from his left, and couldn't stop himself falling. He landed on his side, his head protruding beyond the front wheel. A woman was screaming, but it wasn't Pamela's voice. Cowley had a perfect view of the two men in the middle of the park, as one of them had a head-and-shoulders view of him and began to aim the rapid fire weapon. Cowley tried to get his own gun up from under him but knew he wouldn't be in time. Something was heavy, unmoving, beneath his feet, stopping him from crawling back. He tried to lever himself up, to get behind the vehicle, but then there was a blinding eruption of yellow fire and he saw the flame-out of the missile launch engulf the intended protective shield and then the man's head behind it. There must have been a scream, because the second man turned in time to see what Cowley and Pamela were seeing, the brief unreal moment when a man remained totally upright but completely without a head before toppling backward.

From somewhere farther along the cruiser, Schnecker said, "We switched the heat shield. Put highly flammable plastic in its place."

Cowley was up, using the hood of the car to steady his gun arm. As the man swung the pistol back toward them, Cowley fired, missed, and hit the second time, spinning the man back on top of the corpse. The wounded man rolled as he fell, keeping hold of the gun. Cowley stopped running toward him, firing and hitting again.

The man was still trying to move when Cowley reached him,

kicking the MAC 10 away from the scrabbling hand. Cowley said, "You make a move for anything you might be carrying and I promise to God I'll kill you. Your war's over, asshole. You lost."

They told Bella Atkins the same thing, several times, in their urgency to find the rest of the arms shipment. The second of Cowley's two shots had punctured Peter Barrymore's right lung, and he couldn't be interviewed.

They interviewed her only after she had been read her Miranda rights and every other legal requirement had been complied with. When she rejected an attorney, Cowley ensured every utterance was recorded. Bella Atkins responded to the machine but not in the way they wanted, providing an indication of how she and her brother were later to use their trial, as a platform for the entire spectrum of far right bigotry. Her only sneering admission was that Roanne Harding had been totally duped, a sacrifice to mock her Black Power commitment.

In their desperation, Cowley and Pamela several times suspended the interview for legal guidance from the attorney general herself. They even suggested—and were refused—a plea bargain in return for being told the whereabouts of the explosives.

It was during the breaks that they learned of Harry Boreman's initiative in Manhattan, ordering the SWAT team entry into Bay View Avenue when it became obvious that Yevgenni Leanov intended to kill Arseni Orlenko. And of the Russian president's pronouncement, without the supposed prior consultation with Washington, of the roundup of everyone involved in Moscow and Gorki.

It was the media that answered the question Bella Atkins was refusing and by what was quickly labeled another miracle without the potential carnage. There were program-interrupting news bulletins on local radio and television stations within fifteen minutes of the Taft Park shootout and the harmless landing of the empty warhead in the Capitol parking lot. The only two maimed survivors of the eight-strong former Delta Force bombers said much later the attack was to avenge the capture of their leader—whom both respectfully referred to as the General—that they'd started to rig the explosives in a Maryland forest shack. They wanted to prepare to blow up the control tower and as much of the terminal buildings at Dulles Airport as possible. Two of the terrorists who died were engulfed in phosphorous fire from one incendiary device that James Schnecker and his team hadn't managed to booby trap in Moscow.

It was from the late-night news coverage that Patrick Hollis finally discovered the identity of the General. His mother, who was watching with him, said, "Can you imagine the evilness of such people?"

"No, I can't," said Hollis.

42

The trials would take months, lawyers picking their slow and profitable way through the maze of international law, but the evidence emerged comparatively quickly through the almost immediate collapse of some of the arrested men.

Determined on maximum revenge against the man who'd intended to kill him, Arseni Orlenko set out in minute detail the snake-pit double-crossing of the Russian arms smugglers. It had been Ivan Gavrilovich Guzov who'd plundered KGB files to discover the weaponry-seeking Watchmen. And Yevgenni Mechislavovich Leanov, his former KGB colleague, who'd said he could supply them for a 50 percent cut, through the Osipov Brigade. Viktor Nikov, Orlenko's Gorki friend, had only wanted a 20 percent share. It had been Leanov who'd rid himself of a business rival by killing Nikov and his mistress's husband by murdering Valeri Karpov—having sexually blackmailed Plant 43's homosexual director into being their new supplier—and spread the story that it had been an American hit. Leanov also had had Mikhail Osipov blown up to clear the way for Naina Karpov's takeover of the Osipov Brigade. His only regret, insisted Orlenko, was not being able to tell them the whereabouts of Guzov's body, for a murder charge to be brought in America.

There was no way Danilov could have anticipated the extent—criminal as well as political—of Ashot Mizin's babbled confession. He had, insisted the senior investigator, been promised personally by former Interior Minister Nikolai Belik that he would head the Organized Crime Bureau if he sabotaged Danilov's investigation. In Gorki, Colonel Oleg Reztsov had been assured promotion to militia commissioner. While Danilov was in Gorki, with arrest warrants against Reztsov and Major Gennardi Averin for complicity in the murder of Aleksai Zotin and the Plant 43 employee who'd supposedly hanged himself, Nikolai Belik shot himself.

"You really did make the wise choice, didn't you?" said Georgi Chelyak on Danilov's return to Moscow with the two Gorki detectives in custody.

Cowley flew to Moscow for conferences three times with an American legal team, and Danilov returned twice to Washington for the same purpose. Pamela was obviously living with Cowley at his Arlington apartment in which Danilov ate several times. They didn't explain and he didn't ask. On each occasion he drank more than the American.

The first of the trials in either country was scheduled to be that of Robert Standing in the New York state capital of Albany.

"Legally it's the simplest," said Cowley. "There are no overseas complications with any of the charges. And we've got Peter Barrymore's provable voiceprint on tape talking about the financing. A conviction against Standing—even if he persists in these denials—will be evidence against the leader of the Watchmen."

Patrick Hollis decided not to wait for the trial. On the Saturday afternoon he took his mother with him to choose the new, replacement Jaguar and let her decide the color should be blue.

That night, while she prepared supper, he went into the den and roamed the server sites. He was in no hurry, and wanted to avoid one that Peter Barrymore might have used. When he was ready he hesitated, savoring the moment, before writing:

A GENERAL SEEKS RECRUITS FOR AN UNFOUGHT WAR AGAINST CAPITALISM. FINANCIAL ABILITY IS ESSENTIAL.

He'd monitor every account he provided for his troops. Anyone disobeying orders by stealing more than a penny would be instantly court-martialed. The sentence would be exclusion from the elite force he intended.